BEAUTEOUS MAXIMUS

Volume One

The Climate of Truth

D. MICHAEL BERTISH

Beauteous Maximus: Volume One, The Climate of Truth

© 2021 by D. Michael Bertish

All rights reserved. Published and distributed in the United States by Empowered Whole Being Press. No part of this book may be used or reproduced in any manner whatsoever without the written permission of the author or the publisher, except in the case of brief quotations embodied in critical articles and reviews.

Written as a trilogy, "Beauteous Maximus" is inspired by true events. "The Climate of Truth" is the first volume of the trilogy.

Based on hundreds of the author's personal interactions during the COVID-19 pandemic, the characters' stories are woven through the geo-political landscape of the time.

The characters presented are fictionalized and are not intended to depict actual people.

Library of Congress Cataloging-in-Publication Data

Author: Bertish, D. Michael

Title: *Beauteous Maximus: Volume One, The Climate of Truth*

ISBN: # 9780578373034 (Paperback)

ISBN: # 9780578373041 (eBook)

1. FICTION World Literature / American / 21st Century   2. FICTION / LGBT / General FICTION / LGBTQ+ / General   3. FICTION / Visionary & Metaphysical

Cover Photo & Author Photo Credit: Barry Blanding

Empowered Whole Being Press
www.EmpoweredWholeBeingPress.com

Acknowledgements

Special Thanks to those who helped the author
find his voice for this book, listed alphabetically:

Catherine Black, Barry Blanding, Carrie Jo Hoelzel, Joyce Lackie, Margaret McDonald, Deborah Menenberg, Jamie Mathieu, Lynn Nadal, June Petersen, Helen Radcliff, Glenna Scheidt, Sarah Sharp, David Stubbs, Francesca Thoman, Sue Vanlaanen, and Emily Wishman

For My Beloved

Irma

Foreword

"Fiction is the lie through which we tell the truth."
-- Albert Camus

    The era of the COVID-19 pandemic was unquestionably defined by the sharpened divisions between political, social, and existential ideologies. Those divisions were not only heavily saturated and deeply controversial, but they were also poignantly clarified. Those who were firmly set in their beliefs remained steadfastly unchanged and vehemently opposed to the very existence of ideas that differed from their own. That was the bold nature and the breathtaking power of human choice at the time of the pandemic. Human choice then filtered the mainstream definitions of "right" and "wrong" through the lens of personal experience rather than through the unity of vision. The perceptions, ethics, morals, wisdom, and mores of human experience were then crafted directly from the events that happened to the individual rather than the collective conscience, and by the conclusions made about the source of those experiences. That is how the definitions of "right" and "wrong" came to be so fiercely prolific at the time, and how humanity learned the crippling consequences of its own misdirection, confusion, and hidden agendas.

    In 1947, Camus published *"The Plague,"* a novel that became a best-seller during the globally imposed lockdowns at the outset of the COVID-19 pandemic. Camus portrayed an outbreak of the bubonic plague in a French Algerian city and chronicled how the people were slow to realize the threat, even downplaying it at first. They then fought with each other about how to respond to and treat the disease with quarantines, plague wards, martial law, religion, and a new vaccine that was in short supply. The story revealed how widespread disease precipitated the complete unravelling of society, including the eruption of violence induced by madness and the despair of isolation. The parallels between Camus' novel and the real-world events of the COVID-19 pandemic were undeniable. The plague finally abated in Camus' story and the inhabitants of the city slowly began to reintegrate with civilization, but only after witnessing the horde of death and the rush of psychological torment. Yet there was salvation in hope for the future.

Camus' prophetic vision became so popular and relevant to the world in 2020 that the publisher could barely print enough copies to keep up with the demand. The main character of *"The Plague,"* a modest doctor who treated the infected throngs simply as a required service to humanity, came away from the experience with a profound realization:

"There are more things to admire in men than to despise."

Perhaps that same philosophy allowed many of us to unite behind the most common purpose of our time, to survive the deadliest pandemic of the 21st century. Perhaps we learned that survival is not achieved through selfish motivations, but through the will of the human spirit that is sustained by the resilience and generosity of courage, honesty, and compassion.

Written as a trilogy, "Beauteous Maximus" is inspired by true events. "The Climate of Truth" is the first volume of the trilogy, representing the path of Truth we navigate when public opinion is firmly aligned with delusion and denial. Climate not only reflects our physical and environmental world, but also the psychological, philosophical, and spiritual mindset. Based on hundreds of the author's personal interactions during the COVID-19 pandemic, the characters' stories are woven through the geo-political landscape of the time.

The characters presented are fictionalized and are not intended to depict actual people.

Chapters

Prologue	1
Wildfire	7
Synchronicity	38
Judgement	105
Main Street	135
Eyes	154
Flowers	194
Patriots	244
Identity	287
Anniversary	338
About the Author	370

Prologue

 "COVID" was a word that we heard every single day. There was no way to avoid it. It was the absolute star of the show with top billing in our culture, politics and our various faiths. It commanded our daily thoughts and conversations. The virus appeared to be omnipotent and unstoppable, which made it seem supernatural. For many, that made COVID an angry god to be feared because we could not control it, understand it or outflank it.

 Viruses are microscopic spores that can only survive by replicating inside a living host. Technically, viruses are not even classified as living organisms because they don't have metabolic components. It was baffling to contemplate how something so minuscule that wasn't even alive and that didn't have the capacity to think could overpower and outsmart the entire planet. However, a virus has genetic mechanisms that can adapt to human nature and existing environmental conditions in order to modify itself for more efficient replication. As it reproduces, a virus alters its own behavior and physiology, often becoming more lethal and contagious in future derivations. And yet, as was said by one of my clients who was an architect for hospitals, "COVID is very easy to kill." The irony of her statement was earthshattering.

 I imagined COVID as a paradoxical prehistoric beast that took the form of a T-Rex, with a giant head and wildly snapping jaws that held multiple rows of huge, razor-sharp teeth. The fantastical COVID

Prologue

T-Rex vanquished our lives as we trembled in the darkest recesses of Stone Age caves in my dreamworld. Intellectually, I was aware that dinosaurs predated humans by 68 million years, and they never hunted Paleolithic tribes. But emotionally, I couldn't help but visualize the COVID T-Rex gnawing and devouring the unfortunate throngs of human flesh as if we were all fast-food hamburgers served up by *McDonald's* restaurants; that corporation stopped keeping count in 1994 when their red marquis with the golden arches read *"Over 99 Billion Served."* The world sick map that monitored the millions of COVID infections and deaths made me think of our disposable society; we tossed the remnants of forgotten lives into the trashcan of history as if they were spent ketchup packets.

Philosophically, I compared survival in the COVID age to praying for mercy so that my village would not be sacked and burned to the ground by an invader like Genghis Khan. Though he was a fierce and bloody emperor who could not be deposed, Genghis Kahn was also one of the greatest unifiers in human history. Similarly, COVID conquered all the peoples of the Earth and brought us to submission. But the virus was also a great equalizer that smashed through all race and class distinctions with perfect impunity.

Creatively, the design of the COVID spore resembled a cloved orange, the kind that could be hung from a decorative ribbon as an ornament to fill a room with the scent of holiday spice. Classified as a coronavirus that caused severe pneumonia, COVID mutilated the lungs and was known to ravage and destroy various other organs and systems of the body, often with long-term effects. The term "coronavirus" referred to its shape; it was among the largest of single-strand RNA virus spores with red club-shaped spikes that protruded from its orbed surface in a way that resembled the aura of the sun. The common cold is also a coronavirus.

The solar corona, derived from the ancient Greek word for "crown," is a searing mass of plasma energy that explodes millions of miles into space with temperatures that far exceed the sun's surface. This solar energy controls the ebb and flow of all life on Earth, an analogy that succinctly described the way COVID ordered all our lives. Humanity had no choice but to be humbled by the relentless invading army of microscopic, aerosolized particulates.

When first analyzed, COVID-19 was dubbed a "novel" virus because, to our knowledge, the exact species had never been

The Climate of Truth

encountered before. The word "novel," as well as the "-19" extension, lasted about a month before it was discarded by popular culture. From then on, the virus was colloquially known as "COVID." The moniker "COVID" was chosen for this book because the abbreviation was singularly used by the general public in everyday conversation.

The *World Health Organization* first assigned a temporary name for the virus, "2019-nCoV," based on the year it was discovered. It was later renamed "Severe Acute Respiratory Syndrome Coronavirus 2," or "SARS-CoV-2," by the *International Committee on Taxonomy of Viruses.* It was also known as "Human Coronavirus 2019," or "HCoV-19." The acronym "COVID-19" (derived from "Coronavirus Disease 2019") was the formal name chosen by the *World Health Organization* to avoid stigmatizing the origins of the virus with specific populations, geography, or animals as the root cause of the pandemic.

SARS-1 was the first pandemic and the first known coronavirus outbreak of the 21st century, having occurred in 2002-2004. It spread to at least 8000 people and to nearly every continent before it was effectively contained. More than 700 people died, and SARS-1 was estimated to have cost between $30 and $50 billion to the global economy. SARS-1 was a mere hiccup compared to what happened to us with its successor, the COVID pandemic that began in 2019. Humanity failed to contain COVID as it ravaged the entire world.

History is written by the survivors. As a survivor of the COVID pandemic, I wrote this book as a contribution to the historical record for those in the future to better understand what happened to us during this terrible time. This work is also a study in how we handled the unprecedented pressures we faced, both as nations and as individuals. Included herein are examples of how the perfect storm of coinciding factors completely overwhelmed all our systems of civilization and infiltrated every aspect of human existence.

I committed to recording this tribute because societal memory is often very short, sometimes merely generational. I was astonished to discover that children who sat in my styling chair had no idea that terrorists flew planes into the twin towers of the *World Trade Center* in New York City, the Pentagon, and planned to destroy the nation's Capitol Building on September 11, 2001, a mere 20 years prior to the COVID pandemic. And because my own family members refused to speak about the atrocities they witnessed firsthand during the Holocaust, I also knew how the silence of those who were

Prologue

traumatized in catastrophic events tended to magnify the suffering they endured by failing to educate future generations.

When COVID took over our lives, I realized that what I was hearing from my clients needed to be honored and remembered for history. In my experience, people were being far more authentic than ever before, and my little hair salon became a microcosm of what was happening all around the globe. COVID was the single most important thing that ruled and defined every one of us at the time. It was the one thing that brought us together, and it was also the one thing that ripped us apart. I believed the COVID pandemic was the most historically significant event in hundreds of years. It changed absolutely everything about the way we lived.

I often wondered how it came to pass that people widely embraced the idea that a hairstylist's job included regular and frequent counseling and therapeutic services. During my 30-year career, countless clients told me that "hairstylists are like bartenders – it's part of your job to listen to everyone's problems." My clients expected me to bear witness to all forms of their personal traumas, whether or not I agreed to participate. In so doing, I understood the *Wisdom* found in retelling the many stories of our collective COVID journey; it was the pathway to healing for us all.

In the early 1990's, my cosmetology educators instilled the fundamental lesson that there were three things a stylist should never discuss with clients: sex, religion and politics. I never could have dreamt that clients would make it virtually impossible for me to follow that professional advice as we fought to survive. All social boundaries and rules of engagement were cast aside in the COVID age. I only hope this work captured the true essence of our struggles, the same way I was moved when reading the first-hand accounts written by those who were caught up in The Civil War, World Wars I and II, and Vietnam.

In August 2020, six months into the COVID pandemic, a dear friend sent me an internet link to a *YouTube* video, entitled "*Cycles of Time*" with Gregg Braden. The video was originally posted in January 2017, three years before the COVID pandemic began. Mr. Braden, an acclaimed author, scientist, and international educator, had been honored as one of the top 100 of "the world's most spiritually influential people" for each of the preceding 11 years. In his video, Braden explained that science had recognized three distinct,

The Climate of Truth

measurable cycles of global changes in time, any one of which could singularly turn the world upside down: 1) the cycle of climate change, 2) the cycle of economic change, 3) the cycle of human conflict. According to Braden, these three powerful cycles repeated at regular, predictable intervals in time. Furthermore, Braden pointed out that the year 2020 marked the peak of a rare, massive convergence of all three of those powerful cycles. This meant the convergence brought an unprecedented amount of chaos with it. Science correlated the rise and fall of the greatest conflicts in human history with the regular and repeated peaks and valleys of the noted cycles of change throughout time.

There is also a direct correlation between the three noted *"Cycles of Time"* and the magnetic energies of the Sun, the Earth and the human form. Science has proven that the human heart has a magnetic field 5000 times stronger than the human brain, and the magnetic energies of the human body are directly impacted by the celestial bodies in our corner of the galaxy. The convergence of the three great *"Cycles of Time"* with the magnetic energies within and around us resulted in the complete melding of Earth's various cultures, religions, governments, economic platforms and ideologies. In essence, the convergence was the intentional blending of all conscious awareness in the human continuum. The phenomena gave us the greatest opportunity to achieve a higher level of *Wisdom* that could allow us to usher in universal *Peace*, as long as humanity did not succumb to the impetus of conflict that arises with the fear of change and mass annihilation. It was the supreme test of our time. Braden observed that nature tends to push humanity through extreme conditions in order to encourage and facilitate evolution.

I began writing this book during the first COVID lockdown in March 2020, long before I knew anything of Braden's work. Final edits on this first volume were finished before the outcome of the pandemic was fully known at month's end of December 2021. At that time, health officials stated that because the virus spread so thoroughly throughout the world, humanity could be dealing with the impacts of COVID in perpetuity. From the time my business was allowed to reopen after lockdown in June 2020, until the end of December 2021, I completed 3260 salon services. I was blessed to be able to work masked face to masked face with all those clients without experiencing any symptoms of COVID disease. Leaders in the US promised that we would not be placed into lockdown again.

Prologue

But the virus had mutated to forms that were far deadlier and more contagious, and it appeared that survival might require further isolation to slow the spread of disease. To me, COVID was telling us all to take a very long "time out" because we needed to better understand our own souls and relate more positively with each other in a time of violent disharmony. Some called the COVID pandemic "the age of fear."

    I spent my life observing the common patterns of exchange between humans and the Divine all around them. I discovered how the events portrayed in this book lent themselves so easily to Braden's analysis of the universal mechanics of our earthly existence. Therefore, in keeping with Braden's example of the three *"Cycles of Time,"* this work is written in three corresponding volumes: 1) The Climate of Truth, 2) the Economy of Truth, and 3) The Spirit of Truth.

Wildfire

 Because the virus was a severe airborne pneumonia that spread quickly indoors, we had to reduce the time we spent breathing together in an enclosed space. Indoor capacity was slashed to a fraction of what businesses usually accommodated. Capacity restrictions eviscerated the cash flow of the vast majority of businesses, and that caused many of them to fail. But I was fortunate because public health mandates did not greatly hamper the flow of clients to my one-man hair salon, *Blow Your Top*. In fact, as if I had planned for emergency procedures years in advance, the layout of my shop lent itself perfectly to the COVID safety protocols. I did not have to install room dividers or plexiglass shields like so many other establishments did to curtail the spread of highly contagious, aerosolized virus droplets. Nor did I have to alter my general operations very much because my open-room salon was designed with social distancing greater than six feet already in place. However, it was impossible for stylists to be socially distanced from their clients to prevent contagion as we trimmed their sideburns and bangs. I spent many a haircut staring down the gap of a client's protective face mask toward their nostrils, wondering what might escape in the hot breath that whooshed out from the thin veil of fabric that was our primary defense against a deadly disease. I often had to ask my clients to hoist their masks back up over the bridge of their nose because they had fallen and exposed their nasal passages where the virus was known to lurk. I tried not to focus on the fact that I was risking my life every time a client sat in my styling chair. I wasn't always successful in keeping my fears in check.

When businesses first reopened after lockdown, we didn't fully understand how the virus was transmitted. Science couldn't provide instant information as the public expected and demanded. The novel coronavirus had never been seen before. It had to be studied. It took time for scientists to gather the data and discover how this new plague behaved. Early in the pandemic, shop owners went so far as to lay out all the cash from their tills and attack it with spray bottles of disinfectant. Boxes of materials purchased from supply warehouses were also drenched with virucide just in case some unknown infected person had wiped COVID spores all over the containers. Workers stripped off all their work clothes (including their shoes) before they entered their own homes in order to prevent tracking the disease into their living space. I never chose to adopt those behaviors.

Safety protocols called for leaving doors and windows ajar (even in cold temperatures) to allow fresh air to circulate indoors and to diminish a potential virus cloud. I purchased expensive HEPA air filters that zapped lingering virus spores with ultraviolet light and ionization. One filter machine sat right next to the styling chair, hissing and humming like an alien spacecraft as it sucked up whatever might have escaped from the lungs of asymptomatic clients.

Three months into the pandemic, back in May 2020, two stylists who worked at a shop in Missouri were found to have been infected with COVID when that state first tried to reopen after lockdown. President Trump relentlessly pushed the Governors to reopen before it was safe to do so. "Our country wasn't meant to be shut down," Trump insisted. "This country is poised for an epic comeback. Just watch. It's already happening."

The infected hairstylists in Missouri made the national news. A public panic ensued. Between them, the two infected stylists had worked on 140 clients before their disease was discovered, and both worked with several other stylists in the same building. Because everyone at that particular salon wore masks at the outset, no one else caught the virus from the infected stylists in that case. No one. Despite the demonstrated proof that the simplest safety measure worked to protect everyone, we stylists had to endure relentless harangues from those who found mask wearing to be an audacious infringement upon their personal freedoms.

The Climate of Truth

Several of my more aggressive clients tried to push their way into my shop without wearing a mask. "What are you afraid of, Mike!" they sneered.

"I'm not afraid of anything," I answered while placing my hands on their collar bones to block their attempt to enter the premises prematurely. "There's another client sitting over there that I have to protect. So, if you want a haircut, it's no surprise you have to wear a mask. Those are the rules."

The aggressive clients would spend their haircut time glaring at me, breathing heavily, looking for reasons to gripe about their discomfort. "You should try wearing a mask for 12 hours every day while using a hot blow dryer," I said. That comment usually helped to quell the disturbance. Even though it saved countless lives, the ubiquitous COVID mask, made of layers of folded fabric or paper fiber that came in any color or pattern imaginable, became one of the most heavily politicized and contentious accoutrements of the pandemic.

An elder couple from Chicago, married for 59 years, had been isolated for months. They avoided holiday gatherings and did not travel. They were diligent in their adherence to safety protocols. The elder couple's daughter worked in a hair salon and agreed to give her mother a much-needed in-home haircut for the first time in many months. "Well, why don't I just come by and cut your hair, so you don't have to come into the salon?" the stylist said to her mother. Everyone wore a mask for the duration of the visit. The daughter tested negative for the virus immediately before the haircut and all care was taken to avoid infection. Just to be safe, the daughter quarantined four days after her negative test. They sat beside an open window during the haircut. In fact, all the windows in the apartment were open to ensure air circulation. They did not hug or touch. The visit was only 40 minutes. The daughter developed COVID symptoms the following day. Her mother was hospitalized on Thanksgiving Day. The elderly couple were both dead two days before Christmas, only ten days apart. The entire family contracted the virus. The daughter felt responsible for killing both of her parents. This case made me very nervous for my future.

Wildfire

  I swept up the remnants of hair that surrounded the hydraulic base of the styling chair from the prior haircut and began the process to disinfect my shop as required in between each client. I always started the disinfection process on the restroom sink so that I didn't leave a trail of hair clippings across the white porcelain there. I sprayed hospital grade virucide to kill any COVID spores that might have been skulking about. I found that four paper towels wadded together was sufficient for wiping down the restroom sink, the shampoo sink and chair, the styling chair, the glass overlay on the antique desktop that served as my workstation, the rolling tool caddy, the credit card machine, the surface of the front desk, the window sill and garbage can lids, and all the doorknobs and light switches that clients might have touched. The smell of the virucide was so strong that it made me wheeze. I never failed to disinfect my workspace for every client throughout the pandemic, even though countless people berated me for sticking to public health and safety standards. They called my efforts "pure theatre," even though the disinfection protocols I used were directed by the *Washington State Department of Health*. I felt vindicated when I learned that health officials in large cities and in airports used COVID-sniffing dogs in public spaces to detect live virus spores on surfaces that an infected person had touched. Those dogs could also detect people who were infected.

  I used two fresh paper towels to wipe all the surfaces of the client toilet because science showed that virus spores could linger there. A hospital architect I knew fully approved a decorative sign that sat on the back of the toilet that read, "*Pandemic Safety – Please Close the Toilet Lid Before You Flush.*"

  "I commend your efforts to be on top of COVID research!" the lady architect said. Regardless, most clients who used the toilet either failed to read the sign or chose to ignore it. I never scolded anyone about leaving the toilet lid up, but I always climbed the 14 stairs to my apartment on the upper floor of the house to use my own private restroom.

  The COVID cleaning ritual caused me to plow through a jumbo 12-pack of paper towels every four to five days, and a bottle of virucide every other day. It was expensive to stay in business, but I was committed to doing everything in my power to protect myself and my clients from the plague. Many vulnerable people came to my one-man shop because I was so careful. I had the place completely

The Climate of Truth

locked up so no one could wander in and breathe on us without warning. It was a relief for me to have total control over who had access to my building. I wouldn't allow entry to those who refused to follow the safety rules, not even my best friends. I lost quite a few clients who refused to wear a mask for the duration of a hair appointment.

When I first opened shop in the front parlor of the old Victorian house, it made my life a lot simpler. A mixed-use commercial/residential building made good business sense because it cut down on expenses. But when the pandemic happened, I worried that anyone among hundreds of clients could potentially carry the virus right into my inner sanctum. I tried not to notice that the odds were not in my favor for escaping infection.

I bought my 116-year-old Victorian house in December of 2012, when those with nihilist tendencies believed the terminus of the ancient Mayan calendar corresponded with the end of the world. I suppose that's why I was able to buy my house at a bargain price during a supposed apocalyptic Christmas. Eight years later in 2020, a lot of people thought we were living through *Armageddon* with the COVID pandemic, yet my house had increased in value by more than 2 ½ times. I suppose that meant COVID was very lucrative for the real estate market. Housing prices set record highs and half of all houses on the US market at the time were sold above the asking price, even $100,000 above in my region. Housing prices jumped to the highest levels in more than 30 years, driven by pandemic buyers who fled city apartments to the suburbs. COVID was the harbinger of a steep inflationary cycle that would only make life much harder for the disadvantaged working poor and the middle class. The ultra-rich became even wealthier during the pandemic, some becoming the first trillionaires in history. But according to Gregg Braden's video, "*Cycles of Time*," the rise of crippling inflation in global markets was predictably right on schedule.

One of my favorite clients happened to be a doctor. She was certain I had obsessive compulsive disorder because I knew the exact number of stairs in my Victorian house.

Wildfire

"Do you count the stairs every time you climb them?" she asked, amused. I could tell she was grinning at me underneath her pastel pink mask. She wriggled her eyebrows at me as she spoke.

I was busy clippering the back of her head to maintain her ultra-short haircut. "I have a commute of only 14 steps. I count my steps because I can't see my feet when I'm carrying Irma up and down those steep antique stairs every day," I said, defensively. "That way, I won't trip and fall and hurt my Corgi girl. I always say, 'One-two-ready-go, one-two-ready-go,' as my feet touch every step. Because I do that without fail, I never fall. It's a perfectly normal thing to do when you can't see your own toes, and it doesn't mean I have OCD!"

"Do you count the stairs when you are not carrying Irma?" the Doctor asked with sparkling eyes.

Her follow-up question nearly paralyzed me. "I don't have OCD just because I count the stairs!" I said, defiantly.

My doctor friend smiled wryly beneath her pink mask again. I could tell by the way the elastic around her ears moved as she wrinkled the bridge of her nose. "Go ahead and keep telling yourself that," she said with a chuckle.

"Irma's long body doesn't fit on those weird stairs," I objected as I brushed hair clippings from the Doctor's forehead with a towel. "She throws her back out trying to climb them, and that makes her scream in pain. Any 'dogfather' would carry his wee lass up and down those stairs and count every step to make sure he doesn't trip. It's not Irma's fault she's built like an articulated bus that doesn't fit."

"Uh-huh," the doctor hummed. She wore a lot of pastel pink because it complimented her short-cropped, silvery white hair and her alabaster complexion. She insisted on having her hair cut extremely short every two to three weeks because it gave her the creeps to have her bristle grow out and touch her ears. She openly admitted to being obsessive compulsive herself, especially when it came to her hair, and to bottles of styling product that were out of perfect alignment on my display shelves. She made sure to correct any misaligned product bottles at every one of her appointments.

"A PhD with OCD is a really great combination!" the doctor said with a laugh, though it didn't seem like she was joking. "If more doctors had OCD, fewer people would die of COVID," she said, nodding her head in affirmation.

The Climate of Truth

She had the clout to make such claims, given that she was a head honcho at the *Veteran's Administration* who testified before Congress. She oversaw more than 367,000 full-time medical staff at nearly 1,300 medical facilities across the country. She was also personally responsible for installing COVID wards at VA campuses and for designing the protocols for treatment and containment of COVID patients. Oddly, the lady Doctor's husband was one who avoided taking any COVID vaccine because he was afraid it would make him sick or befuddle his brain. The Doctor asked me to try my hand at convincing her husband to get with the vaccination program, but his resistance was impenetrable. It was unsettling to know that one of the leading national experts in COVID safety couldn't get her own pandemic household in order, even with her vulnerable 85-year-old mother in residence. The doctor, her husband, and her mother were all regular clients of mine. All of them flew around the country frequently for work or to visit friends and family. Any of the three could easily have brought COVID into my home, but I didn't have the heart to banish them from my shop. I accepted the risk, even though I had to remind each of them to hoist their masks back up over their noses whenever they told me about their travels.

"I'm a Doctor," the lady Doctor told me repeatedly. "I would never do anything that would put you at risk, Mike." Despite her proclamations, she did put me at risk every time I saw her or anyone in her family. COVID was all about personal choices.

My attention was drawn to the picture window at the front of the shop as an ambulance sped by with its siren blaring. Emergency vehicles raced past my window all day, every day. They were probably hauling COVID patients to the overcrowded hospitals. Cars pulled over to get out of the way, often coming onto the sidewalk in front of my house, practically into my front yard. I installed several tons of large boulders across the perimeter of the front garden to protect my property from off-road mishaps. There were a few instances when acutely depressed COVID lockdown drunks got behind the wheel of a car and sailed right into the living rooms of neighboring properties, and sometimes into telephone poles along the boulevard. Flying hubcaps that spun in the middle of the road like toy tops at 2:00am was a rather poignant COVID sound effect.

Wildfire

  A song on the stereo caught my ear as I wiped down my workstations with virucide. I was in the habit of focusing on the lyrics of songs because they had the uncanny tendency to align with what was happening around me at the time. The stereo played Michael Murphy's somber ballad from my youth, *"Wildfire,"* recorded in 1975. The lyrics were a story told by a homesteader about a young woman who died in a blizzard while searching for her runaway pony named *"Wildfire."* The homesteader also found himself trapped by a deadly winter storm. He believed that a hoot owl perched outside his window was a sign that the spirit of the young woman who died in the blizzard was calling to him. The homesteader hoped to join the young woman in the afterlife, where together they could ride *"Wildfire"* for eternity and leave the troubled world behind. With COVID everywhere, I could certainly relate to the urge to permanently escape the misery of the world. I sang along with the stereo as I disinfected the shop for my last client of the day.

> *"On Wildfire we're gonna ride*
> *We're gonna leave sodbustin' behind*
> *Get these hard times right on out of our minds*
> *Riding Wildfire"*

  On Labor Day weekend of 2020, a powerful typhoon centered near the Philippines ushered wild weather to the American west. Torrential tailwinds from the storm shoved a polar vortex deep into Colorado, causing the 101-degree record heat there to drop into the low 30s in mere hours, suddenly dumping a foot of snow. The same typhoon's brutal lightning barrages unleashed white-hot plasma explosions up and down the west coast that sparked the worst wildfires ever seen in our region. Heavy winds churned up by the typhoon fanned the flames, and vast swaths of the countryside erupted in towers of fire for weeks. Hundreds of people died and thousands of homes were destroyed. Many lost their businesses and their livestock. Whole towns were burnt to the ground, wiped from the map. Millions of people were evacuated and millions of acres were lost. At one point, fifteen states were all ablaze. The worst of the fires were in California, Oregon and Washington. Through it all, the alien sun hung eerily in the sky like a giant maraschino cherry, an illusion caused by sunlight that filtered through the microparticles of

The Climate of Truth

ash that were carried aloft by the wildfire smoke. The sky itself was an otherworldly Martian orange.

Trump claimed that had we liberals of the western "blue" states simply raked the forests like he told us to, we would have avoided all the wildfire devastation with ease as they did in Finland. But most of the west coast fires exploded on federally owned lands, and we didn't see Trump out there with his rake. Instead, he attempted to withhold emergency federal funding to fight the fires. I suppose he wanted to watch us burn in the west, because our assured destruction would both amuse him and strengthen his ability to be reelected as a "red state," Republican President. It sounded so very tribal.

The wildfires pushed everyone even further to the edge of sanity during the pandemic. We breathed the charred debris of disaster as the smoke filtered into our homes and clung like a poisonous fog that hovered about four feet off the floor. It was shocking to know that wildfire smoke could drift into our living spaces like the angel of death, even with all the doors and windows firmly locked and sealed shut. It made us wonder if the virus could float into our homes in the same way. Within months, we learned there was a link between air pollution and increased susceptibility to COVID. When heavy wildfire smoke settled over a city, there was a sudden surge of nearly 18% in new COVID cases. Scientists discovered that COVID spores could attach themselves to wildfire particulates (about $1/30^{th}$ the diameter of a human hair) and hitch a ride directly into the smallest air sacs of human lungs. COVID spores were also found in municipal water supplies and in sewage.

I prayed for and welcomed any indication of precipitation to help quench the fire-scorched countryside. I prayed for no more fire tornados.

Health officials begged for us all to forgo Thanksgiving gatherings. Families and friends were known to be the primary vectors of viral transmission. We were urged to remain isolated in our own "pods" (familiar contacts) and to meet our relatives only in video conferences or telephone calls. But it was nearly impossible to get 350 million people to hunker down indefinitely in order to protect the greater good of our country. Health officials explained that the public's noncompliance with safety mandates was a symptom of

Wildfire

"COVID fatigue." People justified their resistance to public health mandates with the familiar refrain, "I'm so <u>done</u> with COVID!" But that pervasive sentiment didn't change anything. In my mind, COVID, the wildfires, and Trump were synonymous; all three were all-consuming and all three were far from being done with us.

The rest of the world thought America has lost its mind as millions of our fellow citizens prepared to fly for the holidays. Despite the dire warnings from health officials, advertisements bombarded the masses with images of crowded holiday tables adorned with heaps of colorful and festive food. Jolly holiday guests were pictured without wearing masks, the primary protection known to us at the time. Airlines that were facing financial ruin offered ultra-cheap fares to entice travelers out of their lockdown prisons. There were even "flights to nowhere" that allowed people to go airborne without a destination, only to return home at the end of the flight. These misinformed messages overpowered the basics of science and common sense and lured people to travel, which spread the disease even faster. It was absurd to make people believe they had a real choice between promoting the economy, celebrating the holidays, and survival. I, for one, never traveled during the pandemic. I never ate inside a restaurant, even when everything reopened fully. I never removed my mask in public. I never visited with any of my friends, and the only social contact I had was with those who sat in my styling chair five days a week – and that was more than enough togetherness for me.

The surge of infection from Halloween 2020 parties had already caused spikes of COVID cases across the country. Hospitalizations and death rates were shattering all daily records, with three million people infected in a fortnight. America had the majority of infections and deaths worldwide, and that would remain true throughout the pandemic. To the dismay of exhausted doctors and nurses, many COVID patients lying on hospital gurneys still denied that COVID was real, even with their dying gasps. Thanksgiving travel and family gatherings escalated the plague to a point that nearly crashed the entire healthcare system. The same thing happened during the Spanish Flu pandemic of 1918 – 1920, and too little had changed in human behavior over the 100 years that followed.

In good conscience, I couldn't risk the lives of my clients just to have a traditional turkey dinner with other people on Thanksgiving. So, I planned for a holiday to be spent in isolation.

The Climate of Truth

The churlish President urged his followers to resist the mask, and they believed him blindly. Trump said, "I think wearing a face mask as I greet presidents, prime ministers, dictators, kings, queens, I don't know. Somehow, I don't see it for myself." No one in Trump's cabinet wore masks. Neither did his family, or many of the Republicans in Congress.

The mask complainers didn't stop to think that one ceases to enjoy personal freedoms once they are dead. Those who swore masks were stupid didn't consider that refusing to wear one was a thunderous declaration that my health as a stylist was non-essential to their interests. To the complainers (notably, the majority of Trump's followers), I was a lowly sap and a lackey who was ruled by the 'establishment.' Many devoted Republicans literally believed the 'establishment' was comprised of a secret cabal of liberal, Satan-worshipping pedophiles who drank blood and ate the flesh of dead babies. To them, COVID was nothing more than a giant conspiracy hatched by the Democratic Party, which made no sense because COVID was a global phenomenon that had nothing to do with political agendas. It stung even more to discover that several of my anti-mask clients worked as doctors and nurses on the front lines with COVID patients.

Eisla was the last client of the day. She was waiting for me in the parking lot. I had already called her on her cellphone to tell her that I would be out to get her as soon as I finished disinfecting all the surfaces in the shop for her. COVID safety regulations set by the *Washington State Department of Health* for hair salons required clients to wait for their appointments outdoors. On the security camera monitor that sat on the front desk, I could see Eisla sitting in the driver's seat of her car. She stared blankly out the windshield toward the busy boulevard that ran past the front of my building.

Eisla left her engine running so she could have heat while she waited in the parking lot. This caused clouds of vapor from the tailpipes of her car to float toward my security cameras. The exhaust transformed the digital view of the driveway into what looked like the foggy airport scene at the end of "*Casablanca*," where Humphrey Bogart uttered the famous words "Here's looking at you, kid," to the teary-eyed Ingrid Bergman. The sharp contrast of black against white

Wildfire

in film noir was heavy on my mind. It reminded me of the boiling racial tensions that coincided with the global COVID nightmare, an example of a peak in the concurrent cycle of human conflict.

The rain on that particular Friday was a welcomed comfort. It was already getting autumn-dark with a crisp, wet chill in the November air. I loved the early evenings when daylight savings time finally ended, when the world seemed to return to a more natural order. October and November were my favorite months because the scorching heat of summer was finally subdued by the consistent soft gray of the Pacific Northwest skies. I moved to Washington State more than 30 years prior to avoid blizzards and excessive heatwaves, and to bask in the temperate calm. But the region had been plagued by severe drought conditions several years in a row. I began to worry about the impending heat in March of each year. There were months of unseasonably dry, high-pressure days that built domes of excessive heat across the continent. The evergreen forests turned into cracked kindling, further weakened by invasions of pine beetles that chewed through the heartwoods, and relentless boreal fungi that devoured the tree canopies. The natural world was showing us how we had pushed the web of life to come undone.

At least the November weather allowed me to rejoice with the aerial ballet of fallen leaves, and the glistening raindrops that glittered like diamonds on the driveway. The leaves left strange brown smudges all over the cement, probably residue from the wildfire ash. The air was chilled just enough that night to see a faint wisp of my breath as I headed out to the parking lot to escort Eisla into the building. I unlocked the white, wrought iron gate off my back patio, through which I could see her sitting in the driver's seat of her car. She was deep in thought and didn't notice my presence. She held her *Bible*, though she wasn't reading it. She looked to be caught in a trance. After 30 years of haircuts, I noticed that the strangest things usually happened at the end of my workday, when all I wanted to do was sit and put my aching feet up. Add the stress of everyone's COVID anxiety to the mix, and it was a supreme challenge for me to remain optimistic, humane, or even kind.

I escorted my clients into the building through the back gate, not the front door of the shop, so access could be safely and completely controlled. I approached Eisla's car and waved my hand to get her attention, but she did not respond. I called her name. She was startled by my voice, but quickly recovered with a flutter of her eyelids and a

The Climate of Truth

shake of her head. She donned her pale blue surgical mask, the one she kept in her glove compartment to use during her pandemic haircuts. There were a few old snips of hair still stuck to the front of her mask from her last visit to my shop.

"How are you?" Eisla asked me with an inflection that indicated a forced smile was hidden behind her disposable mask.

"I'm well, thank you," was my stock response. I repeated that same response to that same question several times every day, even if it wasn't true. The exchange, though polite and expected, was the enactment of a social obligation designed to help others cope while under duress. The white, wrought iron gate provided the illusion that I could fend off the virus from the outside world with a turn of the lock and key. But I knew better than to be fooled by those kinds of imaginings.

Eisla walked past me through the gate, ducking under the wet leaves that clung weakly to a dwarf tree in the corner of the patio. The tree was quickly heading into winter hibernation, and a pile of large, yellowed leaves littered the patio paver stones at the trunk's base. Eisla wore a long, knitted, cowl-necked scarf that wrapped around her neck. She had no coat. Having proudly lost 35 unwanted pounds with a strict diet the year before, she was back to wearing loose, shapeless, black pants because her legs and thighs were hugely swollen from painful fluid retention. She'd regained all her lost weight, and then some. The skin on her forehead was flush with red, blistered acne. She said it was because of allergies, but as a licensed esthetician, I was sure there was more to it.

Eisla was a grandmother several times over. The most recent addition to her family was born a few months prior. She was proud that her daughter was on track to adopt an orphaned infant, the product of a drug-addict birth mother. Eisla's daughter was looking to adopt while still nursing her own baby boy, all while wrangling three other younglings in addition.

Eisla worked for many years as a victim's rights advocate for city government. She left that job when she (along with several other women) experienced sexual harassment in various city government offices. The pervasive negativity at the workplace made her bitter and physically ill, but she didn't have the stomach to fight the system. She never wore makeup, so her ruddy complexion glowed even brighter when her blood pressure shot up every time she thought about the

Wildfire

social injustice of it all. The city claimed it investigated the various allegations of sexual harassment, but nothing came of it. Nothing ever did. I can't remember if Eisla resigned, or if she was unceremoniously fired without cause by some arrogant city lawyer. Either way, she was relieved to be gone from the politics of a place long ruled by the dysfunction of dirty men in cheap trousers.

Eisla traded that disappointing city job for one as a *Transportation Security Agent* at the local international airport, only to discover the federal workplace was just as nasty as city hall. She worked to profile travelers and cornered the ones who might be terrorists. She searched carry-ons for explosive devices. She performed pat downs on hundreds of unwilling passengers every day in search of narcotics and weapons. She worked tirelessly during the graveyard shift while her hawkish supervisors threatened to punish her with criminal charges for reasons unknown. It was demoralizing work. Anyone with an intellect and an ounce of self-esteem hoped to transfer out of the TSA as quickly as possible. And that was precisely what Eisla did. She was laterally hired into a far more tranquil position at the *Veteran's Administration*, where hordes of former TSA agents commonly went to decompress from their mutually shared airport traumas. Eisla endured all the abuses at work just to earn a federal pension and a lifetime supply of health insurance in retirement.

Eisla explained that her faith and *Bible* study gave her the strength to live through her trials, and that God got her out of the TSA before COVID could finish her off. She was absolutely certain of it. During haircuts past, she told me that, according to scripture, we were going to see some very strange things happen in our lifetimes. Eisla believed it was unavoidable, that it was preordained. She spent many years contemplating the *Book of Revelation* and fully accepted what she thought was the inevitable end of the world. It was supposedly already underway.

Eisla was influenced by the media mogul and televangelist, Pat Robertson, who founded the *Christian Broadcasting Network* and sought to be the Republican nominee for President in 1988. Robertson prophesied in October 2020 that Trump would be reelected, and then the Earth would be destroyed by a giant asteroid a few years later. Supposedly, God delivered that news to Pat Robertson on his television show, "*The 700 Club*." Robertson didn't explain how he bet on the wrong racehorse in the 2020 election. I guess we were still waiting to see how the alleged asteroid disaster would turn out.

The Climate of Truth

    To Eisla, the wildfires and COVID were clear portents of the "end times." Just like the "Y2K" scare was the supposed calling card of the expected apocalypse in the year 2000, when people feared that airplanes would fall out of the sky because their onboard computers would suffer aneurysms at the exact second of the turn of the 21st century. Several people took swan dives off high-rise buildings twelve years later on December 21, 2012, because of the end of the Mayan calendar. They must have forgotten that time is endless; when one age ends, a new one always begins.

    I wondered how Eisla could look into the eyes of her grandchildren and believe in such terrible things as the end of the world, for doing so would surely rob them all of a future. For whatever reason, she couldn't allow herself to believe differently. Though sweet natured, she resigned herself to fully embrace her interpretation of ancient terrors. I'm sure she looked out her front window every morning to see if she could spot the Four Horsemen of the Apocalypse galloping down the street in front of her home. To her, the *Great Tribulation* had ensued. Next, the Columbia River would surely turn to blood and a plague of frogs would fall from the sky. Though she could never admit it, the juxtaposition of her kindness with her religious cynicism was an intellectual conflict that she couldn't reconcile. The opposing forces in her mind pushed her even closer to self-destruction.

    I held the infrared digital thermometer to Eisla's forehead without touching her skin. Everyone who came to my shop was scanned for a fever in the first year of the pandemic. Because her usual temperature was well below average, I joked that Eisla must have been part lizard.

    Standing on the patio in the November dark, I asked her the required screening questions by memory: "Have you had any symptoms of COVID over the past two weeks?...Have you ever had COVID at all?...Have you traveled outside the metro area?...Have you received any travelers or visitors, including friends or family?...Have you been exposed to anyone suspected of having COVID?...Have you had a recent COVID test?"

Wildfire

Mechanically, she answered, "No…no…no…no…no," looking past me to the dwarf tree in the corner of the patio. I understood many people were lying to me when answering those COVID safety questions, because they would not allow a mere virus to inconvenience them and get in the way of a haircut. The "honor" system that drove social order in the past had been entirely thrown out. Eisla, however, was not a liar.

I asked her the newest safety question separately: "Have you spent time indoors while unmasked in front of people you don't live with?"

"Is that a fig tree?" she asked blankly, looking at the dwarf tree over my shoulder. Her lips quivered, and her chin trembled. The tree must have held a deeper symbolic meaning for her.

Michelangelo portrayed the races of Adam and Eve on the vaulted ceiling of the Sistine Chapel; both of the characters looked fearless beneath the canopy of the sacred fig tree at the center of the *Garden of Eden*. The artist also painted a serpent's tail coiled up the trunk of the fig tree, it's head and torso in a female human form – a symbol of the Goddess as the *Serpent of Wisdom*, also known as the *Kundalini* to the mystics of the Far East. The *Serpent of Wisdom* is the electromagnetic energy of consciousness housed within the human body that traverses the spinal column (the trunk of the tree) and flows upward toward the brain stem and both hemispheres of the brain (the branches and leaves of the tree). Michelangelo depicted the *Serpent of Wisdom* as providing a handful of figs to Eve's outstretched hand. Figs symbolize universal knowledge, awareness of self, unity with the Divine, and the abundance of *Truth* – all benefits of *Wisdom* in action.

There was nothing seductive or inherently evil in Eve's acceptance of those figs, yet her receipt of the *Wisdom of Truth* was commonly portrayed as the moment humanity fell from grace into eternal sin and damnation. Throughout history, strong women were often disparaged in this fashion to subjugate them. But Michelangelo's frescoes on the vaulted ceiling did away with that disillusion. Instead, the artist celebrated the soul's longing for liberation from injustice and oppression, particularly from the arbitrary control perpetuated by the church. Michelangelo's symbolism expounded the philosophy of Renaissance Humanism, the more liberal belief that humanity could learn from, speak to, and cohabitate directly with the Divine without the intervention of priests or rulers to "save" or "protect" them. In other words, enlightenment came from within oneself, not from some outside source. Partaking of the fruit of the *Wisdom of Truth* was, in essence, the celebration of Adam and Eve's coming of age. It was their rite of passage, their bar/bat mitzvah. The expulsion of Adam and Eve from the *Garden of Eden* could be interpreted as the inherited burden of independence in free thinking -- having to care for and nourish oneself rather than expecting someone else to do it for them. The expulsion could have been nature's expression of "tough love" used to boost humanity's will to thrive.

But those were not the same kind of esoteric thoughts that Eisla had about the fig tree on the patio that November evening. Something was wrong with her. I could feel it. She wouldn't look me in the eye, which was unlike her.

"How strange that I never noticed that fig tree before," Eisla said with a far-off look. "I've walked right past it and never truly saw it for what it was."

I saw my fig tree as something that gave me incredibly tasty, sweet fruits to revive me in the hottest days of summer. But that's not what Eisla was referring to either.

"*'For Judah and Israel lived in safety, from Dan even to Beersheba, every man under his own grapevine and under his own fig tree, all the days of Solomon.' First Kings, Chapter 4, verse 25*," she said as if in a daze.

Confused by her reverie, I opted to repeat the last COVID safety question. "Eisla, have you spent time indoors while unmasked in front of anyone you don't live with?"

"No," she said as she started to cry.

"Are you ok, honey?" I said, worried for her.

She took a shallow breath. "I just got some terrible news," she said very softly. "I should have known, because it is Friday the 13th, after all. Friday the 13th is always an unlucky day."

She searched my face for a reaction, and I gazed at her warmly as a friend. "What is it?" I asked. "You can tell me if you want."

Her jaw began to shake, and her face grew red, visible even in the soft darkness of the patio. "I was just diagnosed with multiple myeloma…It's really bad," she said. Several crystalline tears rained down her cheek and disappeared behind her surgical mask. The tears looked like lemon drops, colored golden yellow from the floodlamps that lit the driveway behind us. She turned her face away from me, embarrassed.

I reached up and touched her shoulder, though I was careful to remain at arm's length. "It's OK, Eisla. Just be yourself. You are safe here."

"I'm sorry," she demurred, still quivering.

"What's myeloma?" I asked, having never heard the term.

"A cancer of the blood. A cousin of leukemia…You know how I hate oncologists. I called for the results, and the nurse said, 'oh no, multiple myeloma, that's a very painful one.' Yeah. That's just great to hear it like that! Just bam! There it is! Dump it on me without a care in the world! It was just plain cruel."

Other people's sorrow often colored my days. I felt like a helpless tourist, forced to observe the long journey of their misery. Sometimes their trauma clouded my brain. "At least it's not like bone cancer," I said, hoping to offer a glimmer of optimism. "Bone cancer is god-awful. I knew someone once who had it. They were always crying from the pain."

Eisla grimaced with the shock of my ignorance. "Myeloma attacks the bone marrow. Your bones can just snap like a twig," she said bluntly. "At least that's what it says on the internet."

"Oh God. I am so sorry!" I said the worst possible thing at the worst possible time. I'd just hurt someone without meaning to. It was the curse of empathy, trying to show that I cared. I was even more horrified to know about the gut-wrenching pain Eisla would soon have to endure. I grew instantly nauseous.

"**It is what it is**," she said quietly as she hung her head and sobbed.

I couldn't help but remember when Trump used those very words during a televised interview the prior summer, when he decided not to organize a sustained national response to the COVID pandemic. He avoided his sworn duty to protect Americans from all enemies, foreign and domestic. He ignored the fact that more than a quarter-million Americans had already died from COVID and that his lack of action left all 50 states to fend for themselves individually, forcing them all to compete for scarce medical supplies. Eisla told me

The Climate of Truth

that she knew Trump was chosen by God to be President, and she believed the 2020 election was stolen from him.

Trump, who falsely claimed the virus was completely under control, was asked to clarify his position when 1000 Americans were dying every day.

"They are dying, that's true," Trump said, smugly, "**It is what it is**. But that doesn't mean we aren't doing everything we can. It's under control as much as you can control it. This is a horrible plague."

When asked how he thought 1000 daily deaths was the best the US could expect in controlling the outbreak, Trump said, "First of all, we have done a great job. We've gotten the Governors everything they needed. They didn't do their (jobs) — many of them didn't, and some of them did. Someday, we'll sit down, we'll talk about the successful ones, the good ones. We had good and bad."

"**It is what it is**," Trump said again with a shrug. He was far more dedicated to holding his rallies during his campaign for reelection than he was in saving lives.

Eisla's head bobbed up and down fitfully as she cried into her cowl-necked scarf. I could hear her gasp for air. I noticed how terribly thin and fragile her short silver hair had become. Hair is built from and nourished by the blood supply. When a blood disorder happens, the human body declares hair to be expendable -- just like people who thought masks were stupid and cast them aside. The ailing body diverts the blood supply away from the scalp to protect the internal organs. This process starves the hair follicles until they shed. Eisla's condition had advanced to the point that her scalp was noticeably shiny and pale, her sparse hair like a thin veil of fuzz spread across the lint trap of a clothes dryer.

I desperately wanted to reach out and hug Eisla as she sobbed. Inherent compassion demanded it of me. But I couldn't do it. COVID protocols wouldn't allow me. Getting too close, touching, breathing the same air was prohibited. Hugging could kill you. It was a terrible sinking feeling that I was depriving her of the simple comfort of consolation. I knew that cancer patients were far more likely to die of COVID. I reached out and placed my hand on her neck instead and squeezed gently. She needed more from me, but she sighed and stepped back, knowing she had to keep her social distance to lower the risk of inhaling aerosolized virus droplets that might escape from the confines of our masks. It seemed like one of the most helpless moments in both of our lives.

The year before I could reach out and hug her when she cried on my shoulder having been diagnosed with breast cancer. I had to console so many women the same way as I cut their hair. I held Eisla for a very long time then as she sobbed into my neck. We talked openly about her double mastectomy, and I hugged her again when she suddenly whipped out a knitted false boob from her bra, one she crafted with red, white and blue circular stripes of yarn. We both laughed and cried at the same time as she made me touch the falsie. It was incredibly intimate. She refused chemotherapy after her mastectomy. She said she didn't want poison in her body and the sickness that came with it. She preferred to take vitamins and keep to a strict diet instead.

"I am so sorry to hear this news," was all I could say about the myeloma. What can anyone say that is truly meaningful when you hear such a thing? How does one avoid sounding trite, condescending or pitiful?

"**It is what it is**," she repeated.

Irma, my Corgi, was seated on the landing by the patio door, watching us. She usually barked at clients to welcome them, but this time she knew to remain quiet for Eisla's sake.

After a few moments of silence, Eisla shouted in a rapid switch to excitement, "Oh! I have a picture!" She retrieved her cellphone to show me a photo of a friend of hers with a short, cropped haircut and snow-white hair. "What do you think? It's cute, right?"

"Very," I said immediately, attempting to determine if she had enough hair left to make it happen.

"Can I have this cut?" she asked, searching my eyes for permission. "Let's at least try. That's all I ask."

"Absolutely," I said, gesturing for her to ascend the stairs to my shop. It was the strangest haircut consultation I could remember, standing in the dark, wearing masks on the patio, with cancer, COVID and wildfires all looming as if they were hunting us. After nearly three months, southern California was still ablaze, and I swore I could smell the smoke from more than a thousand miles away.

The Climate of Truth

Irma met us inside the patio door. She looked up at Eisla and smiled widely, showing the pink polka-dots on her gums and her pristinely white teeth. People were always impressed by Irma's bright smile, especially when she wiggled her little bunny-bump of a tail, and tap danced with her toenails on the floorboards. As a sign of affection, Irma placed her paw on top of Eisla's foot and looked up at her masked face.

"Hello there, Miss Irma. It's very good to see you again," Eisla said.

With her responsibilities as the shop's director of entertainment satisfied in the moment, Irma curled up for a nap in her doggie bed, a stuffed brown thing I called her "couch potato."

I instructed Eisla, "Please put your stuff down on the left side of the desk, take off your scarf and hang it on the coatrack, and head to the restroom to wash your hands with soap and water for twenty seconds." All were safety protocols for COVID control.

As I shampooed Eisla, wads of her silver hair filled the drain cap of the sink. She couldn't afford any more thinning. I gently patted her hair dry with a towel to prevent friction from yanking more hair from her scalp. Many questions swirled in my head as I began her haircut, but I didn't want to pummel her with mental noise.

I gathered myself to ask the most obvious and the most difficult question: "What stage is your cancer?"

"They won't tell me," Eisla explained. "Because I refused chemotherapy again."

My heart sank for her, but I tried not to let it show on my face. I avoided looking directly at her eyes.

She continued, "You know how I hate those oncologists. They say 'You _will_ do this! You _will_ do that! _We_ tell you the way it's gonna be and that's the end of it!' Well, I'm not going to live my life that way! I watched my friend go through a year of this torment and pain, only to die three months later. Quality of life is important to me. And they really put me through the ringer with the breast cancer! I can't go through that again." She bit her lip and stared at herself in the antique mahogany wall mirror that hung in front of my styling chair.

Wildfire

"Did the breast cancer cause the myeloma?" I asked carefully.

"It's a totally different thing. Not at all connected," she quipped.

At that moment, I was holding a snip of her frail silver hair in my fingertips. She had attempted to grow her hair longer to cover the thinning spots, but it didn't work. It made her look even more sickly, like *"Gollum"* in *"Lord of the Rings."* People don't often want to accept reality when it comes to their hair, but Eisla came to an understanding on her own. She knew the combover look wouldn't serve her. As I cut her hair, the clippings floated to the floor like gossamer, fine as dust. She eyed her reflection in the mirror. The color of paint on the shop walls, "Peach Smoothie," was chosen specifically because it made all skin and hair types look better when gazing at oneself in a mirror, even when the observer was wan with illness.

"My hair looks so much better!" she said with amazement, as if some life-altering miracle had occurred with her haircut.

I tried even harder to smile with my eyes because the mask covered my mouth. The impulse was strong to hug her again, but I stopped myself. She caught me thinking about her.

"Statistics give me two to twelve years," she said straight up, answering my question before I asked it. "My legs are all swollen like this because my kidneys are failing. I don't want dialysis either. Can't go there! I'll just take my vitamins. I'm losing motor function in my hands because of the neuropathy, so I'm thinking this short haircut will be easier for me to handle. Thank you, thank you!"

"I am glad I can help," I said looking into her eyes. "Is a little hairspray, OK?" We looked at each other deeply for a few seconds, frozen in time. I knew I would not be able to cut her hair for very much longer into the future.

"Sure," she said. "Just a little hairspray will be good."

I hot-ironed, combed and fluffed her hair as best as I could to fill the sparse patches and then gave her a few bursts of finishing spray as I maneuvered the style with my fingers.

"Will you pray with me?" she asked, abruptly.

"I'm sorry – what?" I replied, surprised.

"Here, hold my hands and pray with me," she insisted, grabbing my hands even though I was holding a comb and scissors. "Right

The Climate of Truth

now! We don't have much time! Pray with me to ask Jesus to come into your life, to be your Lord and Savior!" She looked at me with deep expectation.

Instantly I knew I had to be careful not to crush her spirit with my words. "It's me, Eisla. I'll be alright," I said.

"Please!" she pleaded. "I don't want to go knowing things are not settled with you. I want you to be safe. It's important to me!"

"I'll think about it," I said, softly, patting her hands.

"OK," she said, somewhat satisfied. "At least I tried."

"Yes, thank you. It means so much to me that you care," I said, quietly. She watched me put the finishing touches to her hair.

"My husband and I found this amazing new light therapy machine," she said, staring at herself in the mirror again.

I stood in front of the same wall mirror for twelve hours a day, and rarely looked at myself. I only looked at the way the hair draped around a client's face.

Eisla spoke as if in a daze again. "They have a $5000 unit, and a $6000 unit. We opted for the $5000 one. The light therapy machine was devised by a doctor in the 1930s to treat all kinds of cancers, and there is a specific program in the machine for my kind of cancer. That doctor successfully treated myeloma, and there are no side effects at all. There's all kinds of literature about it, and I've been doing my research. So, we are going to try it out and see what happens. We ordered the machine already. With COVID, things are really slow being manufactured and delivered, so hopefully we will get it soon…before it's too late."

I never heard of the doctor Eisla mentioned, nor his machine, nor the claim of successful avantgarde treatment for terminal cancer. Neither had most anyone else.

"I feel good about using the machine," she said with a sigh. "So much better than chemo, don't you think?" She asked the question with what was left of her balding, raised eyebrows.

"Do you have to be naked to use the machine, like in a tanning booth?" I asked.

"Not at all. Just sit in front of it. It goes right through your clothes, as long as there aren't a lot of thick layers like a heavy

Wildfire

sweater or a coat. I go to my naturopath's office three times a week. She doesn't charge me a dime. I should be doing it twice a day, every day, so I can't wait until I get my own unit. I always feel much better right after I use it. Hopefully I can ride it out another two years until I can retire. I would like to live long enough to use the healthcare plan I paid into the system for so long!"

She looked right at me through her reflection in the mirror to assess my reaction. It was not my place draw doubt upon her choices. It was not my place to explain to her that all her planning for retirement was functionally obsolete. I was simply there to listen and nod with affirmation and understanding. It was the hardest, cruelest part of my job, to bear witness to the disintegration of a life, and to already miss someone while they were still alive. It frightened me. All I could do to manage the fear was to promise myself to keep living through kindness.

❖

Eisla and her husband had been using the COVID lockdown time to remodel their kitchen. Her husband lovingly stripped all the paint off the old cabinets and restored them with a gorgeous new stain. Being handy, he found a lovely antique pantry door that he refinished and installed, and they hung some framed drawings of vegetables and spices on the kitchen walls. They had plans to change the recessed lighting and swap out the countertops. Eisla's eyes were distant as she contemplated her remodel.

The words to the song that played on the stereo caught my attention. It was the 1974 hit by Terry Jacks, *"Seasons in the Sun."* The popular tune was written about one of the songwriter's best friends who had leukemia and was given just six months to live. The songwriter's friend died in only four months.

"Goodbye my friend, it's hard to die
When all the birds are singing in the sky
Now that the spring is in the air
Pretty girls are everywhere
Think of me and I'll be there"

The Climate of Truth

I couldn't help but hear Eisla's thoughts as she wondered if she would live long enough to enjoy her new kitchen, or if her husband would choose to remain in the house after her passing. She wondered who would cook for him since he wasn't talented in that department. She wondered about the hospitals becoming overwhelmed with COVID patients, and if, when the time came, she would be able to receive palliative care so her husband wouldn't have to watch her die. She considered taking a bunch of pills to make it happen faster. The thought embarrassed her. She considered exposing herself to COVID on purpose to get her life over with. Then she shook her head to clear her mind.

"Well, none of us get out of this life alive, do we?" she said with a chuckle. "But I gotta do it on my own terms, not how some jerk oncologist dictates it to me. Enough about me," she said quickly, "How are <u>you</u> doing, Mike?"

It was a particularly awkward transition, since her appointment had come to its close. Over the past several months, I had absolved myself to answer that particular question briefly and concisely. "I'm doing as good as can be expected under the circumstances," I said.

Eisla changed the subject again by telling me she had a small round brush, like the one I had just used on her. Even with the neuropathy caused by her cancer, she determined she probably had enough strength left in her hands to blow dry and style at home. She said she was grateful for my hairstyling talents. Optimistically, she made two additional haircut appointments, the customary six weeks apart. Because she told me she had probably been suffering with undiagnosed myeloma for years already, I wondered what I should say since it might be the very last time we would see each other.

Irma always knew a client's appointment was finished when I used hairspray, or when the styling cape was unsnapped from around the client's neck. She usually barked to usher the clients out the door. This time, however, she approached Eisla quietly, stood very close to her, and gently licked her hand; it was a very rare thing for Irma to do.

"Aw, Irma Lu! Thank you for giving Eisla kisses when she needed some lovin'," I said.

Eisla, gently stroked the top of Irma's head.

Wildfire

"Remember not to touch Irma's ears," I warned. "I don't know why, but she always screams when someone touches her ears. I'm the only one allowed to do that kind of thing."

"Yes, I remember," Eisla said softly. "You are such a pretty girl, Irma. I hope one day to be as pretty as you."

I walked Eisla out to the white, wrought iron gate, unlocked it with the key from my pocket, and opened it for her. "Be good! Behave yourself," I said after her.

She turned and pulled the surgical mask off her face as she stood at least ten socially distanced feet away. It was the first time I could see her whole expression, a huge, bright toothy smile in the crisp night air.

"Behave myself! That's no fun!" she laughed. "Have yourself a happy Thanksgiving, Mike!"

I shut the gate and relocked it and watched her back her car out and drive away. I couldn't help but think I was shutting the gate on her life.

❖

I climbed the stairs to the shop and stood staring at the weak wisps of Eisla's silver hair sprinkled about the base of the styling chair. I considered those tiny little shreds of protein to be all that was left of Eisla in my life. I swept it all up and threw it in the trashcan to mix with all the other genetic material in there. It seemed fitting because, as we'd been told by health officials throughout the pandemic, "We're all in this together."

It was weird to contemplate Eisla's words for me to have a "happy Thanksgiving." I felt thoroughly violated by the idea of Thanksgiving. I didn't know what to be thankful for, save for the fact that I had been successful in avoiding infection to that point. I knew I would be spending the holiday alone with Irma. I planned not to shower because Irma wouldn't care. I planned to wear my sweats all day. I wondered if I would summon the energy to decorate for Christmas as I usually did with Irma every year. But the idea of having to sanitize my collection of ornaments because of floating COVID spores made my stomach churn.

The Climate of Truth

It felt like I only had the strength to celebrate Thanksgiving by staring at the television. Some of my favorite fall shows were finally on, but only a few episodes. COVID interrupted everything in production. During the first episode, the characters all wore masks. For the second, they wore masks a short time, but spent the rest of the time pulling them off so we could see their mouths move; there was no social distancing involved. If there was a third episode, it was marked by the absence of masks altogether, followed by some exciting teaser that new episodes would magically appear sometime in the new year. We all felt cheated. The news was full of reports about well-known performing artists who died from COVID.

My chest stiffened. I held my breath. I checked my appointment book as my heart pounded. I saw that Eisla's next haircut was scheduled for Christmas Eve. It seemed ominous.

My gaze shifted to four framed portraits that I created from watercolor pencil. They hung high on the wall near the ceiling on one side of the shop. The "Fab Four," I called them, portraits of John Adams, Benjamin Franklin, Thomas Jefferson, and George Washington, forever my heroes. They were depicted as revolutionaries, before they held their highest office in the newly minted United States. I preferred to contemplate the greatness of those four noble statesmen rather than pondering the Four Horsemen of the Apocalypse, as conjured by some of Trump's Evangelical supporters who wrongly identified America as a Christian nation. I knew America was founded on the principle of religious freedom for one and all and supposed freedom from persecution in that belief. Leaders in Trump's inner circle, including members of his cabinet, told Trump that he was chosen to lead the United States in the same way God chose kings to lead Israel in the *Old Testament*. Trump publicly referred to himself as "The Chosen One," while shifting his gaze to the heavens. His most ardent supporters compared his political opponents, or those who disagreed with his views, to "demonic forces." They also praised Trump for supporting things that "people of faith really care about."

Fundamentalists claimed they had to obey elected leaders because God intentionally put them in positions of power. The US Attorney General, Jeff Sessions, cited *Romans: 13* to justify Trump's policy to separate illegal immigrant parents from their children and put them in cages at the southern US border. The White House press secretary tried to quiet the swelling controversy by claiming Trump's immigration policy was akin to upholding biblical law.

> *"Let everyone be subject to the governing authorities, for there is no authority except that which God has established. The authorities that exist have been established by God. Consequently, whoever rebels against the authority is rebelling against what God has instituted, and those who do so will bring judgment on themselves.*
> *For rulers hold no terror for those who do right, but for those who do wrong." -- Romans 13: 1-3*

However, Trump's followers refused to embrace the notion that God chose a Democrat for President in the 2020 election. Rather than honor the result of that election, Trump and his supporters pursued various attempts to overturn the vote of the people. I told myself that I would never again be able to use the word "trump" in a sentence.

The first American President, George Washington, left office because he believed in term limits, not the indefinite rule of kings or dictators. In his farewell address, George Washington warned against the rise of "cunning, ambitious, and unprincipled men [who] will be enabled to subvert the power of the people and to usurp for themselves the reins of government, destroying afterwards the very engines which have lifted them to unjust dominion." The Commander-in-Chief of the American Revolution spoke against partisan politics that are "sharpened by the spirit of revenge" as the sign of "a more formal and permanent despotism" brought about by the "absolute power of an individual" who works "to the purposes of his own elevation, on the ruins of public liberty." This despot would foment "riot and insurrection" and open the door to "foreign influence and corruption." It was as though America's first President read a crystal ball in 1797 to foretell the very things that the 45th President would do to retain his hold on power.

❖

It was the early morning hours of Friday the 13th, in October of 1307, when the Knights Templar of Europe were suddenly rounded up by the King of France. They were put in cages, like the way the

The Climate of Truth

Trump administration caged illegal immigrants at the US border. The doomed Templars, armored warriors for the Pope, were gruesomely tortured. Their feet were slathered in butter and roasted in cooking fires to compel their false confessions of "depravity." Their arms were bound and stretched behind their backs to yank them out of socket. Falsely accused of witchery and sodomy, many of the warrior monks were burned at the stake, drawn and quartered, and condemned as heretics. The shock of their torturous ruin still resonated every time Friday the 13th appeared on the calendar, up to three times in any given year. Several of my clients refused to have a hair appointment on a Friday the 13th.

The fate of the Templars came to mind as I watched a riotous mob of thousands of Trump supporters storm the Capitol Building in Washington DC on January 6, 2021, in a brutal attempt to overturn the Presidential election. Instead of firing their sidearms at the angry mob, the Capitol Police, like the Templars of old, suffered beatings by the hands of their own countrymen, simply for honoring their sworn duty to defend their oath of office.

The Templars, having invented the international banking system, had become too powerful for the monarchy to tolerate. The King of France annihilated more than 600 of the Knights to avoid repaying vast sums of money he borrowed from them to settle his personal debts. Crimes against humanity are often committed in the name of religion and money, often in that order.

Trump told his 74 million supporters they could overturn the election if they donated to his reelection campaign. That resulted in the Trump campaign earning at least $495 million in the two weeks that preceded the 2020 election. Most of those funds were transferred to a new political organization created by Trump, called the *"Save America PAC,"* a type of slush fund with few restrictions on how the money could be spent. Losing an election proved to be extremely lucrative for Trump.

❖

I was relieved when Eisla texted me to cancel her appointment on Christmas Eve. I wasn't sure I could handle seeing what the cancer had done to her body. Five weeks after that, I received yet another

Wildfire

text from her: *"Per COVID rule number 2, I will need to reschedule my next appointment. I hope you are well."*

I replied, *"OK, Eisla. Will cancel your upcoming appointment. Please call me to reschedule as it is very difficult for me to do it going back and forth by text. You had to cancel for the same reason in December. Please know that I won't be able to see you unless you can follow the COVID safety protocols and avoid being indoors with others who are not part of your household, while unmasked. Thanks. (Emoji: red heart.)"*

Eisla wrote back: *"I understand, Mike, and I won't lie to you. I hold a Bible study at my home for five women, all unmasked. I'll call you when Bible study is over. Stay healthy my friend!"*

The idea that the quality of my life was directly impacted by everyone else's choices and beliefs, good or bad, made me shiver with panic.

The following month, February 2021, a year into the pandemic, I was sitting at my desk in the upstairs office while working on the computer. My desk sat in front of a western facing window, outside of which were two giant Trees of Heaven. City arborists referred to them as invasive "Weeds of Heaven," but I admired those trees and found comfort in their afternoon shade. I could watch the gray city squirrels perform aerial acrobatics in the branches and enjoy the songs of birds perched there. Looking out the window at the leaves rustling in the trees, I began to think of Eisla. Then I caught a glimpse of something I had never seen before -- a Western Screech-Owl sat aloft a branch right outside the window. Clients of mine who lived in the more rural areas of the county had seen owls in their yards, but I had never heard of one being seen in the downtown core of the city. The Screech-Owl swiveled its head as if to look right at me with enormous yellow eyes. The color and pattern of its feathers made it appear to blend into the tree bark and it was nearly invisible. It made a quiet sound, a trill of "cr-roo-ooo-ooo-ooo-ooo," which maintained a constant pitch but sped up at the end. In that moment, I remembered Michael Murphy's somber ballad from my youth, *"Wildfire,"* when the hoot of an owl represented the spirit call of a woman who died.

The Climate of Truth

"There's been a hoot-owl howling
By my window now
For six nights in a row
She's coming for me, I know
And on Wildfire we're both gonna go
…We'll be riding Wildfire"

After listening to the owl outside my window, I was compelled to dial Eisla's cellphone number. With my heart pounding, I heard a recorded message: "Hello. You've reached Eisla's phone. I'm Eisla's husband, Joe. This message is to let you know that Eisla has gone to sit with God in Heaven, and although we all miss her very, very much, we are so happy that she is in a much better place. Thank goodness the COVID took her swiftly from us before the cancer did. I hope you will understand that I only have the strength to say these few short words. Thank you for calling."

Synchronicity

When I first opened the salon in the old Victorian house on the boulevard, a lady client who traveled to Nepal and Tibet surprised me with a ceramic picture frame. She offered no explanation for the gift other than she knew I must have it. I gave her only one haircut and never saw her again. Though I can't remember the lady's name, I often sat to stare at the ceramic picture frame she gave me, wondering why our paths had crossed.

The frame sat on the end table in my living room. It was decorated with two sculpted twigs from a tree, one on top, the other at the bottom. A single leaf protruded from each twig, both facing opposite directions. The design reminded me of the ancient symbol of balance and harmony, the yin-yang, the male and female energies. At the center of this eight-inch square picture frame was a two-inch piece of clear glass, behind which the lady inserted a typed quote on white paper:

> *"I am open to the guidance of synchronicity, and I do not let expectations hinder my path.*
>
> *-- The 14th Dalai Lama"*

The Climate of Truth

The psychologist Carl Jung coined the term "synchronicity" in a 1930 lecture about the concepts of Chinese religion and philosophy. Synchronicity is defined as "the simultaneous occurrence of events which appear significantly related but have no discernible causal connection." Synchronicities are considered to be incidents of spiritual significance that tend to focus our attention on the possibilities of the Divine. According to Jung, what appear to be random coincidences are, instead, interpreted as the intentional confluence of events that activate an individual's intuition and self-awareness. Synchronicities are woven throughout our cultural experiences, to draw our attention to patterns that provide us with insights to the deeper meaning of the events that happen in and around our lives. To me, it seemed that COVID was the mother of all synchronicities, sewing us all together in the tapestry of our collective humanity.

In contemplating these phenomena, it is important to consider that synchronicities are independent of chronology, because (in universal terms) linear time is illusory. Without this distinction, the contemplation of synchronicities solely in the confines of chronological order can result in what some frustrated minds might refer to as "temporal whiplash." Attempting to define synchronicities according to linear time is, in reality, the application of expectation – the very thing the Dalai Lama inferred was a hindrance to the quest for self fulfilment.

❖

The earliest known documented COVID case was traced back to a 55-year-old in Hubei Province, China, on November 17, 2019. By the time a doctor in the city of Wuhan first reported the outbreak of a novel coronavirus to Chinese officials on December 27, there had been more than 180 infections recorded. Doctors were not aware that all of those cases were COVID related until they later reviewed individual medical charts.

On January 7, 2020, Chinese authorities publicly reported the novel virus to be in the "coronavirus family," and specifically detailed that it "spreads via airborne droplets."

A 35-year-old man had travelled to visit his family in Wuhan. He then returned to Seattle on January 15 but landed in an urgent care clinic four days later with symptoms of severe pneumonia. He would

Synchronicity

become the first documented COVID case in the US, located just three hours north of my home.

Trump's first Senate impeachment trial began the following day on January 16. Two days later, on January 18, Trump received his first COVID threat assessment briefing. That same day, despite knowing for more than two weeks that coronavirus was loose in the community, the city of Wuhan held a *Guinness World Record* food festival, where more than 40,000 households sat down at long rows of tables all at once to share nearly 14,000 homemade dishes. That food festival was among the first COVID super-spreader events of the new year.

One day later, on January 19, several gamblers were infected at an illicit mah-jongg parlor at the *Huanan Seafood Market* in Wuhan. The secret gambling den was found in an unventilated, smoke-filled room hidden atop a public toilet, accessible only by a climbing a ladder. The virus spread from the gambling den to the seafood market below, where 27 COVID cases were initially traced.

On January 21, two COVID patients were released from a hospital in Spokane, more than 275 miles east of Seattle. COVID was spreading in Washington State.

By January 22, COVID was reported in several major cities in China, and in Hong Kong, Taiwan, Thailand, South Korea and Japan. The virus spread mostly though international air travel. That same day, Trump made his first public comments about the virus, declaring that he was not at all concerned about a pandemic.

"It's one person coming in from China," Trump deflected, referring to the 35-year-old who was the first documented case in the US. "We have it under control. It's going to be just fine."

The very next day, on January 23, Wuhan, a city of 11 million people, was forced into a militarized lockdown. The world was fixated on the images of the shuttered seafood market and all the live animals sold there as exotic cuisine. The public was led to believe that the market was "ground zero" of the outbreak. However, it was reported in *"The Lancet"* medical journal on January 24 that some of the earliest confirmed COVID cases in China had no direct link to the seafood market.

On January 27, Trump was warned that a pandemic could cost his reelection. In a top-secret national security briefing on January 28, Trump was informed that COVID could become as prevalent as the

The Climate of Truth

Spanish Flu of 1918, which killed at least 675,000 Americans and 50 million people worldwide. He was also told that half of all who were infected in China were asymptomatic, meaning people were spreading the virus but did not even know it.

Trump was advised on January 29 that COVID could claim half a million American lives and that a pandemic could cost $6,000,000,000,000 in economic damages, projections that proved to be more than accurate. Trump dismissed these figures as being alarmist. There were only about a dozen confirmed cases in the US at the time, but the virus was not being actively tracked or investigated.

The *World Health Organization* declared COVID to be a global health emergency on January 30, with 200 deaths and 9800 cases reported. It was only the sixth time such a public health emergency had ever been declared. On the same day, "*Time*" magazine reported the Chinese findings that COVID spread through airborne transmission.

On January 31, Trump announced travel restrictions from China. Two days later he boasted that his team had "pretty much shut it [COVID] down coming in from China" during a Super Bowl interview on *Fox News* on February 2. The Trump administration formally acknowledged COVID as a public health emergency the day after the Super Bowl on February 3.

During his *State of the Union* address on February 4, Trump acknowledged the COVID threat very briefly. His only words on the subject were: "Protecting Americans' health also means fighting infectious diseases. We are coordinating with the Chinese government and working closely together on the coronavirus outbreak in China. My administration will take all necessary steps to safeguard our citizens from this threat."

On February 5, Trump was acquitted by the Senate at his first impeachment trial. In his rambling, hour-long post-impeachment speech, Trump declared, "if we didn't win (acquittal), the stock market would have crashed." He did not mention anything about COVID. That same day, senators urged Trump to take the virus more seriously and to appropriate emergency funding for testing and procurement of medical supplies, but the administration ignored the request.

❖

Synchronicity

Karen's haircut was on February 6. In her mid-seventies, Karen wore tight jeans that had been pressed with a seam down the shin, polished loafers with tassels, and a push-up bra under a tight, pullover angora sweater that made her petite frame look exceptionally perky. Her sweater matched the intense periwinkle blue of her eyes. She had a golden eagle brooch pinned to the left side of her sweater, over her heart. For a woman her age, she was very proud to have preserved her hourglass figure. She had a thick, undulating mass of salt and pepper hair that looked like a chimney whisk by the time she needed her regular haircut. She had the kind of hair that would dull my scissors, and her snipped follicles made my skin itch for the rest of the day. If cut incorrectly, her hair could flare out like the barbs of a poisonous puffer fish.

Karen had the annoying habit of speaking in an indecipherable, squeaky whisper, making it impossible to converse without leaning in and placing my ear very close to her mouth. No matter how many times I asked her to speak up, she persisted with her tiny, breathy voice. Her habit of communicating this way came across as a passive-aggressive ploy to force people to pay closer attention to her. Tired of straining my ears, I continued Karen's haircut but shifted the conversation to another woman, Laurel, who sat across the room with color processing in her hair. I often worked on two clients at once that way, but COVID would later change that.

Laurel was scanning the pages of a magazine, holding her eyeglasses to her nose to avoid hair color from getting on her frames. "Did you see those poor Chinese people on the news being hauled off by men in hazmat suits? Kicking and screaming in their face masks, being dragged around by their ankles. It's barbaric!" She fanned herself nervously with the magazine. "The news used a different word." She snapped her fingers rapid-fire, trying to remember. "They said it was…it was…oh yeah! They called it 'draconian'! I hate it when there's a word on the tip of my tongue, but I can't quite reach it…I wonder if they are going to force us all to wear draconian masks here too. I don't think I could handle having my face closed in like that."

"I'd think people would want to wear masks to save lives," I said. "Doctors have been doing it for at least a hundred years. It can't be all that bad. All the Asian countries are used to it. They automatically put a mask on whenever there's something like bird flu. Or swine flu, or H1-N1. Wearing a mask is really no big deal."

The Climate of Truth

"I don't know why anyone would even want to visit China, let alone live there," Laurel replied. "It's a filthy place. All those coal plants. I think they use human waste as fertilizer in the rice paddies. And if that's not bad enough, they eat dogs…Sorry Irma."

Irma cocked her head sideways at the mention of her name.

Laurel continued, "Gives new meaning to the phrase 'how much is that doggy in the window?'…Did you see the other creepy-crawly critters they buy over there from that weird market? Can you believe they eat bats, and monkeys, snakes, beavers, porcupines – how the heck do you eat a porcupine? Baby crocodiles and God knows what else. To think the virus might have come from one of those weird animals, because Chinese people snack on things they shouldn't. So disturbing!"

I kept my visual focus on the burly hair around Karen's ears and used thinning shears to lessen the bulk. "The reports coming out of Wuhan are that nobody's allowed out of their homes," I said. "They have armed guards and flying drones to keep watch, making sure people don't step two feet out of their front doors. It sounds horrible, but maybe it will save a lot of lives and keep the virus from spreading. You gotta do what you gotta do. They are going around with these big stainless-steel canisters that look like fire extinguishers, spraying disinfectant all over the place -- the sidewalks, the roads, doors and windows. They wear hazmat suits while they spray, with the gas masks and all. I'm not sure our country is taking the virus seriously like they do in China."

"Government goons go door to door over there," Laurel sniped. "They zap everybody's temperature, and if anybody even looks a little bit off, they haul their little Chinese butts right outta there. Maybe never to be seen again. As if they just disappeared and got tossed into a pit or something. There's no such thing as human rights in China!"

"It can't be that blatant. Not with whole world watching," I said.

"I saw it with my own eyes!" Laurel shouted, her voice cracking. "Communists are ruthless."

"It's not like Atilla the Hun is running around anymore, Laurel! Come on! The Chinese will do whatever is necessary to put a stop to this. They have to, politically. They've got the winter Olympics in Beijing next year…The Chinese are just different than we are, that's all. We are the entitled, spoiled brats of the world."

Synchronicity

Laurel cleared her throat. "The Chinese are not on the up and up. They won't let investigators in to look around. They tried to silence the doctors who were speaking out to warn the world about the killer virus. And now that whistleblower doctor is very sick with the plague. He might die."

"Maybe the government was trying to prevent mass panic. Did you think of that? Can you imagine more than a billion Chinese people running around in full freak-out mode? That would make everything so much worse," I said. "Sounds like the Chinese government is trying for damage control to prevent hysteria. I bet the US would do the same."

"Why are you defending them?" Laurel asked, pointedly.

"I'm not defending anybody. I'm just trying to make sense of it. I'm looking for the facts. It's not about blame. There's no us versus them. We're all human," I said.

"Nah! It's all about control and saving face over there," Laurel said. "It's a cultural thing. The Chinese can't tolerate being shamed. They're embarrassed. And that makes them tight-lipped and stingy with details. But I tell ya, they are definitely at fault, and they've got a big old can of shame-ass coming their way. They deserve it. That's the point. They tried to cover it up. We may never know the whole truth. And now we have their damned virus over here. Thank you, China!"

"It's not their virus. They didn't ask for it. It just showed up over there," I said.

"That remains to be seen," Laurel replied with a smirk.

"Yeah, well the Spanish Flu didn't come from Spain. It started at an army camp in Kansas. But you didn't hear about anybody pointing fingers at 'G.I. Joe' did you?" I said.

"I don't know. I'm not a history geek like you," Laurel said as she shrugged her shoulders. "I have no idea what happened with the Spanish Flu."

"A new disease can't be cured in the blink of an eye," I said. "People have to be patient, that's all I'm saying. Patience is hard when you're afraid. China had no idea what they were dealing with at first. It took a minute for them to figure out that it wasn't just a regular flu. Nobody's ever seen this virus before."

The Climate of Truth

Laurel looked at me over the rim of her glasses. "I suppose that's possible," she sighed. "You know what they say, 'paranoia will destroy ya.'"

"I tell ya, the Chinese are handling things much better than what's going on in North Korea," I said. "Word is, from people I know -- if you get the virus in North Korea, they just take you out to the back forty and shoot you in the head. They don't bother with testing. Right out of *'Game of Thrones,'* don't you think?"

"That's crazy. How can you know that!" Laurel said, aghast.

"People I know work with the South Korean government, international educators," I said. "Word gets around."

"Damn!" Laurel said, sounding despondent. "I may never be able to eat Korean barbeque ever again…People in China were literally running for their lives trying to escape, but they got caught by the lockdown police. It's so *'Big Brother.'* They can't drive anywhere. The streets are empty. They shut down all the public transportation. They have to get permission to go buy groceries, like a lottery or something. Nothing else is open except for the pharmacies. It's like a bad horror movie."

"People are usually packed onto the trains like sardines over there, armpit to armpit. It sounds like a smart thing, that they closed it all down to prevent the virus from spreading. Hopefully it will all pass in a few weeks, right? I think that's what they were saying. Maybe a few months at most," I said, attempting to sound positive.

"I just hope we don't end up with armed guards at our doors too. I'll lose my shit. You don't want to see me get all claustrophobic. It isn't pretty!" Laurel said.

Karen surprised the room by guffawing quite loudly and slapping her thigh.

"What's so funny, Karen?" I asked, confused by her outburst.

"Yes, well I'm celebrating!" she said in her breathiest voice. Her piercing blue eyes contacted mine for the first time that day.

"OK…I give up. What are you celebrating?" I asked.

"I'm celebrating President Trump's acquittal!" she squeaked, thrusting her fist in the air.

"Oh!" I said, startled.

Synchronicity

There was a deep, penetrating silence. All eyes were on Karen. In all the years that I knew her, she never once mentioned her political beliefs. There was never an indication that she was a Trump devotee. All she ever talked about was the weather.

"Huh," Laurel said with a twitch.

"That fake impeachment trial was the biggest witch-hunt in history. I'm so proud of my man, Donald-J! You can't mess with him. He's unbeatable! He's a superhero!" Karen said, jutting her chin.

Laurel stared at Karen in disbelief. The tension in the room was palpable. No one spoke for a moment. No one moved. I found myself holding my scissors and comb in mid-air, not sure what to do next.

The lapse in conversation brought my attention to an old song by *Paul Revere & The Raiders* playing on the stereo, a song called *"Indian Reservation."*

> *"They took the whole Cherokee nation*
> *Put us on this reservation*
> *Took away our ways of life*
> *The tomahawk and the bow and knife*
> *Took away our native tongue*
> *And taught their English to our young"*

The hair on my arms stood straight up when I heard those lyrics. First, I never liked that song. It made me uncomfortable. It was a song about the oppression of ethnic minorities. Being a gay man myself, I didn't want to be reminded that I was often on the receiving end of oppression. For decades, I had a visceral reaction to the song every time I heard it and would always change the channel. What's more, I never added that song to my *Pandora* playlist. In fact, I gave it the "thumbs down" button, so it should have been stricken from my playlist, never to be heard again. But there it was playing on the stereo in my shop, loud and unnerving, as the tension mounted in the room with Karen and Laurel. I didn't know how at the time, but I had the feeling the song was trying to tell me something. For the first time in more than 40 years, I let the song play, uninterrupted. I listened to the lyrics as I proceeded with my hair cutting.

I weighed my next words carefully, aware that I was walking a tightrope as a businessman. "Personally, I can't stand Trump," I said

The Climate of Truth

to Karen, politely. "So, it's probably best that we don't talk about him any further. I wouldn't want to say anything that might offend you. OK, Karen?"

Karen did not respond but looked at me while remaining quite still. She finally nodded her head slowly in affirmation.

"We are all adults here, and we can just agree to move on respectfully, right?" I said, looking at Karen. But she didn't say a word.

"Good idea," Laurel interjected. "As was said by the divine Michelle Obama, 'when they go low, we go high.'"

"Maybe you should just calm down and put a sock in it!" Karen fired back, whipping her head sideways to glare at Laurel. The tone of her voice was hostile and aggressive, quite unlike her usual breathy, whispered voice.

"Pardon me?" Laurel said, raising her hand to her chest defensively.

"You sound like a flibbertigibbet!" Karen insisted. "What a load of baloney! 'When they go low, we go high!' The truth is not low. The truth is the truth, and that's all there is to it! And sometimes the truth hurts. Everybody knows the Obamas were Muslim carpetbaggers. That one time, they stopped to have split pea soup at a restaurant, and Obama, he wouldn't eat the chunks of ham in the soup. Everybody knows Muslims don't eat pork. So there it is. The cold, hard truth. How's <u>that</u> for going high!"

"It just shows that you're a bigot," Laurel said under her breath.

"I kind of figured you to be the tree-hugging snowflake type," Karen said with a flair of her nostrils.

"This is not a drill, lady!" Laurel said, fluttering her eyes in exasperation. "It's not about some random, meaningless opinion about split pea soup! There's a virus coming for us. The sky is <u>really</u> falling this time! And *'Henny Penny'* is probably dead!"

"Come on ladies," I said, attempting to deescalate. "Valentine's day is just around the corner, and *'Punxsutawney Phil'* just predicted an early spring this year because it was snowing, and he didn't see his shadow. So, before you know it, spring will be here. I heard somebody say that the warmer weather might keep the virus from getting too bad. Let's hope for the best."

Synchronicity

"But prepare for the obvious worst," Laurel groaned.

"We need to keep our heads in an emergency," I said.

Resentment registered on Laurel's face, but to her credit, she did not escalate to shouting. "Bill Gates saw the virus coming," she said defiantly. "But certain leaders wouldn't listen to him. Certain <u>arrogant</u> billionaire types with orange skin and a really bad haircut," she said, looking down her nose at Karen. "You'd think someone with all that money could afford a better haircut, but who am I to judge? Anyway, here we are – doomsday! Bill Gates literally predicted this would happen at a world symposium last October! I saw the video! They had a *PowerPoint* presentation and everything!" Laurel sounded increasingly offended. "They flat out predicted that air travel would spread this shit all over the globe in mere hours. And look what happened only three months later. Trouble in paradise! How prophetic!"

"Oh please," Karen scoffed. "President Trump said he has everything under control. He banned the airplanes from China already, so we'd be safe. He doesn't mess around and color everything with feel-good malarky. He's not going to tell you what you want to hear. He's going to say it exactly like it is, unfiltered. That's why it's so refreshing!" Karen said, chuckling to herself. "Obviously, you've been brainwashed by the liberal media. You suck it up with a straw, all the hype-hype-hype goes right into your frightened little 'sheeple' brain. Calm down already. It's just a flu. Thirty thousand people die of the flu in our country every year. So go get a flu shot and you'll be fine. Besides, I hear that Bill Gates may have let this virus loose to scare everyone half to death so he could make more billions selling us a vaccine. You watch. The truth will come out. President Trump will see to it. Bill Gates and the super-Jew, George Soros – they're trying to take over the world."

There was another uncomfortable silence in the room. "*Indian Reservation*" played on:

> "*But maybe someday when they learn*
> *Cherokee nation will return, will return*"

Laurel looked at Karen over the top of her eyelids. "Where do you get your news?"

The Climate of Truth

"The only place that says it like it really is," Karen said with a nod of her head for emphasis. "*Fox News*."

"Pegged that one," Laurel said, turning her chair to face the opposite direction, away from Karen. "I hate when I'm right about people!"

I could tell Laurel was enraged by the quick snapping sound she made as she flipped the pages of the magazine she was holding.

I filled the void, trying to hold Karen's bobbing head still in order to finish her haircut amidst the commotion. "This one kid I saw was all excited because he needed a haircut and a back wax for a hot date he had in Seattle. With some young thing he met on *OK Cupid*. He wasn't going to let a silly little virus in Seattle get in the way of his nookie. He's not worried at all. So, he drove up there, right into the middle of all this, just for a weekend of sex. How dumb can you be? And then he's gonna drive all the way back down here on I-5, and maybe bring the virus with him. That's how it happens, you know, the spread. It's just a matter of time…How do you get millions of people to behave themselves and do the right thing? Are your bangs an OK length, Karen?" I asked, catching her cold gaze in the mirror.

Karen whispered something unintelligible under her breath. I stared at her for a moment until she nodded her head in approval. I applied some anti-frizz cream to soften Karen's hair in preparation for the blow-dry, followed by a soft, flake-free gel.

I attempted to reengage with Laurel but had to talk loudly over the force of the blow dryer. "Did you see they built two brand-new, fully operational, state-of-the-art hospitals in only ten days over in China just to deal with this virus! Simply amazing! Who does that? We should hire them over here to build hospitals for us!"

It was clear Laurel wouldn't converse any further with Karen around.

Karen waved her hand to get my attention. "We don't need those gooks and chinks over here!"

"Jeeze Karen, can you tone it down a little?" I said.

"Everything they make in China falls apart in a week. I say buy American and put Hop-Sing out of business!"

I did my best to diplomatically redirect. "At least the Chinese are uber-efficient!" I said. "I don't think we could build two hospitals in

Synchronicity

ten days over here. Heck, it'd take us six years just to get blueprints and building permits."

I finished drying Karen's hair in silence as both women stewed.

Irma had been watching me, waiting expectantly for the moment I unsnapped the cutting cape from around Karen's neck. She came running over to bark, then grabbed a stuffed animal from her toybox that sat next to my desk. It was the giant purple spider with long legs, her latest favorite that one of her devoted fans had given her for Halloween. My clients showered Irma with toys, and I never had to buy her any. She shook the very devil out of the purple spider, and the long legs slapped her in the face. Irma growled and yipped, then threw the spider across the room. That made both ladies laugh. Yes, Irma was a true professional who knew exactly how to command and change the energy of a room. I often wondered who was really inside that dog suit.

The moisturizer Karen used that morning made the hair clippings stick to her face like glue. I spent extra time wiping her skin with a towel. She grew annoyed and pushed my hand aside.

"There you are, my dear. How do you like your haircut?" I asked her.

Karen looked at herself in the mirror and smiled just with the corners of her mouth. "Wonderful as usual. You certainly have the magic touch."

"That's why they call me 'Magic Mike,'" I said with a flourish and a curtsey.

"Indeed," Karen said as she quickly handed me cash.

"But I draw the line at leather pants," I teased. "You don't want to see this body in leather pants with all that body oil like Mathew McConaughey! Especially not those assless chaps. Eeewwww!"

"OK then," Karen said, sounding disinterested.

"Let's see," I mused, looking at my schedule. "You have your next appointment already booked in six weeks. Do you want to add your second one out?"

"Certainly," Karen said. "Thank you very much."

I filled out her appointment card, and she left through the front door, shutting it quietly behind her. The front door was still in use at that time.

The Climate of Truth

"Bye Karen. Drive safely!" I called out to her, but she did not respond.

As soon as Karen left, Laurel let loose. "It's because of people like <u>her</u> that we are stuck with the orange maggot in the White House! I can't even stand to be in the same room with people like her! Don't ever have me in here again while she's here. Or I will have to go someplace else to get my hair done!"

"Simmer down, Sparky," I coaxed.

"Don't patronize me when I'm angry!"

"Why let anyone get under your skin like that?" I said with a shrug.

"I wanted to slap her! That shitty little grin of hers!" Laurel said flicking her foot.

"She's just a little old lady with pressed jeans and a very tight sweater."

"Oh, she's more than just a little old lady," Laurel said in a sinister voice. "That was Satan's spawn you had in here. Less talking, more slapping -- that's the only answer."

"She just sounds like she's lost, that's all. She's all bark and no bite, right Irma Lu?"

Irma cocked her head sideways and swiveled her radar ears in my direction.

"You're too nice to ass-wipes," Laurel said with a sneer. "That's why they take advantage of you."

❖

At 2:00am that night, the business phone rang and yanked me out of a peaceful dream. Once awakened, I couldn't get back to sleep unless I first went downstairs to check the answering machine. That's my nature. It couldn't be good news at that hour. I had to press my ear against the speaker of the answering machine because I could barely hear Karen's soft, squeaky voice.

"Cancel all of my remaining appointments," she said. "I have already located a new hairdresser. I will never set foot in your shop again." The phone clicked and a loud dial tone sounded off.

Synchronicity

My stomach flipped. My mind immediately went into overdrive. Anger welled up within me, and I felt my face grow hot and itchy. My immediate reaction was that I should return Karen's call in the middle of the night and leave her a snarky message in return, because I didn't want her to have the last passive-aggressive word. Anger got the better of me because I didn't see it coming. It wasn't my finest moment at 2:00am.

Mysteriously, while my blood came to a full boil, the sage words of Abraham Lincoln filtered into my head as if he whispered them into my ear himself: "You can never please all of the people all of the time." I felt my fury deflate like a red balloon. Thank goodness Abraham Lincoln's wisdom had reclaimed me. I decided a non-combative response to Karen was necessary to ensure my personal integrity. After sleeping very little that night, I waited until a respectable time the following day to leave Karen a voicemail. I knew she wouldn't pick up the phone when I called.

"Hi Karen, I have cancelled all of your appointments as you requested, no problem. This was rather surprising, given that you were just here and said you were happy with my work. It would be helpful if you would be so kind as to let me know what brought you to this decision. I wish you well and thank you for the many years we've had together. Thank you for your time."

I never expected Karen to return my call, and she didn't. The way I saw it, I handed her negativity back to her and left it in her lap where it belonged. I felt much better having done that. I thought about Karen's message on my answering machine for months afterward. I heard the song about the Cherokee people in my head every time I thought of her. That blasted song was the last thing I thought about as I fell asleep, and the first thing I remembered when my alarm clock rang in the morning. It was maddening. That is how I entered the COVID lockdown phase.

❖

When the state finally allowed salons to reopen after lockdown three months later, I described the Karen incident to Felicia, another one of my elderly clients who happened to know Karen personally. Hair salons are the navel of the universe, and stylists always know somebody who knows somebody. Three months later, Karen still had a grip on my psyche.

The Climate of Truth

Felicia looked at me with sadness in her eyes behind her yellow fabric mask decorated with carrots. "Well, that's true-blue Karen," Felicia said with a heavy sigh. "Years ago, she accused me of stealing her boyfriend. It never happened. I would never do such a thing. But Karen had it in her head that I was a Jezebel, and nothing would ever change her stubborn mind. We used to go dancing together all the time, and it was really fun. Until this jealous side of her came out. Then all the fun stopped, and we never spoke again. Now she lives alone, and her own children have nothing to do with her. Because she's always angry. Something always sets her off. And it never makes any sense. That should tell you everything you need to know about Karen."

"Is this painful for you to talk about?" I asked, putting my hand on Felicia's shoulder.

"It hurts a lot. I'd rather not," Felicia said, her eyes watering over the splash of carrots on her mask. The largest carrot was positioned perfectly down the center of her nose, making her look a bit like a snowlady.

"I won't mention it to you again, sweet pea," I said.

"Trump is a great destroyer, isn't he?" Felicia looked deeply into my eyes and said, "He brings out the worst in people."

A few weeks after this conversation, Felicia failed to show up for her scheduled perm appointment. She had never done that before in all the many years I knew her. Concerned for her wellbeing, I left several voicemails asking after her but never heard from her again. I wondered if she had a stroke because she had swollen legs that caused her to limp with a cane.

I thought of my Karen when the *"Central Park Karen"* of Manhattan (Amy Cooper) appeared on national news because she yelled at an innocent Black man, "I'm going to tell them [the police] there's an African American man threatening my life." The Black man, a birdwatcher enjoying the park, simply asked her to put her dog on a leash as required by law. It was a very reasonable request, but it sent the White woman into a tirade. The *"Central Park Karen"* was criminally charged in May 2020 for falsely reporting the incident to the police, something that angry White folk tended to do quite frequently when they got miffed at Blacks. The criminal charge was dropped after she completed mandatory education and therapy classes on racial equity as required by the Manhattan District

Synchronicity

Attorney. The day after a video of the incident went viral on social media, the *"Central Park Karen"* was fired from her job because her employer "did not tolerate racism of any kind." One year later, the *"Central Park Karen"* filed suit in US District Court against her former employer for wrongful termination, denying her actions were racially motivated. Suing for defamation of character, she sought compensation for lost wages, emotional duress, and punitive damages. Her former employer dismissed the allegations of wrongful termination as "baseless." It would be logical to posit that any reasonable, law-abiding person would have determined the *"Central Park Karen's"* actions were indeed racially motivated simply by watching the video of her abhorrent behavior in full public view.

The term "Karen" arose as a pejorative cultural meme that referred to the behavior of incorrigible White women who demeaned others to defend their own beliefs of superiority. A staff writer for the *"Atlantic"* magazine who analyzed that cultural phenomenon referred to Trump as the *"Karen in Chief."*

It was very strange to know that I had been "Karened" by a real-life Karen. A quick search on the internet told me that even *Fox News* covered the story about the *"Central Park Karen."* So, if it was on *Fox News*, it was quite possible that my Karen saw it. Whether or not the lightbulb went off in her head that she embodied a cultural meme was a whole other matter.

"Cancel Culture" is described as a practice of boycotting products, services, individuals or groups because of a difference of beliefs. Karen used *"Cancel Culture"* against me personally. Trump often complained about being a victim of *"Cancel Culture,"* referring to it as a purely leftist weapon. Yet he wielded the practice himself in vengeful ways. He called for the firing of professional football players when they knelt during the *National Anthem* as a form of protest against racism. He denounced a multitude of reporters and news organizations, calling them "the Enemy of the American people," and targeted specific media figures he wanted to be fired. He called for boycotts of specific retail chains like *Macy's* and *Goodyear*, because they opposed his views. And Trump publicly fired a plethora of officials within his own administration who disagreed with him. The firings were often without warning, officially enacted through the posting of a sarcastic tweet on *Twitter*. The public firings included: Secretary of State, Attorney General, FBI Director, Chiefs of Staff, Communications Director, Director of Cybersecurity, US Attorneys, Secretary of Homeland Security, National Security Councilmembers

The Climate of Truth

and Advisors, Ambassadors, and the Secretary of Defense. Numerous other officials in the administration resigned their positions to protest Trump's behavior, further defining Trump's tenure as volatile, chaotic, and unstable. Never had an administration conducted the nation's business through official posts on social media.

❖

Herman Cain, a Black businessman and former Republican candidate for President, served on the Trump campaign's Black Advisory Board, and was the chairman for an action group called *"Black Voices for Trump."* In his weekly podcasts, Cain encouraged the wearing of masks to protect against COVID. He also advocated for the use of social distancing, as well as the wiping and cleaning of surfaces, handles and knobs. However, during Trump Campaign events, he argued that "the virus was not as deadly as mainstream media made it out to be." Cain pointedly refused to wear a mask while campaigning for Trump at his *"Keep America Great"* rally in Tulsa, Oklahoma on June 20, 2020. Nine days later, Cain was hospitalized with COVID, after having been infected at the Tulsa rally. After 29 days in the hospital, including being intubated, he died from COVID. Noting Cain's death, Trump said, "Unfortunately, he passed away from a thing called the China virus."

Herman Cain's *Twitter* feed was set to automatically post tweets from certain syndicated sources. After his death, as if he were tweeting from the grave, his *Twitter* account continued to post articles that disputed the severity of the COVID pandemic. This bizarre twist of fate resulted in headlines such as *"Herman Cain Tweets Coronavirus Not That Deadly – Despite Having Died From It."* Ironically, Cain was infected on the 99th anniversary of one of the worst racial massacres in American history. The massacre took place in the racially segregated part of Tulsa known as Greenwood, or "Black Wall Street," the most affluent Black community in America at the time, mere blocks from where the Trump Campaign rally was held.

In the early summer of 1921, a White mob of thousands dropped bombs from airplanes on the Black community of Greenwood and burned 35 city blocks full of black-owned homes, businesses, churches, schools, a library and a hospital. An estimated 300 Black people were murdered, many of them shot with machine guns. Nearly all the remaining Black residents were arrested and placed in

Synchronicity

confinement centers. Thousands of Blacks were left homeless. The massacre ensued because of a false accusation that a young Black shoeshine man raped a White teenage girl. That same false accusation was used to justify mass lynchings of Black people throughout American history.

❖

Nadine was a referral from another long-time client of mine. It was usually a bad sign when a new client complained about a former stylist. I proceeded with caution, knowing full well that things could go awry. Nadine was concerned that she had developed an allergic reaction to hair color because her former stylist used some new concoction that caused her to break out in hives.

"She put some cheap crap on my head and then all hell broke loose on my face! How could she do that to me! We were friends for a very long time!" Nadine fumed. "You saw the photos. I looked like I was tarred and feathered!"

I explained that allergic reactions were uncommon with my top-quality brand of color, and I suggested a patch test just to make sure. Nadine sat in the passenger seat of her car with three feisty, yapping Papillons in her lap. Her husband, the driver, remained silent. They were both masked in their car in my driveway.

"This is the first time we've been out of the house in weeks!" Nadine said through the passenger window. "I just didn't feel safe going to my old salon where there were so many people. I appreciate your being so careful with me."

I reached in through the window to pet each dog, and then applied a dab of test color behind Nadine's right ear in the soft spot of her neck. I instructed her to leave the dab in place for the evening, and then report back to me in 24 hours to determine if there was any kind of inflammation or swelling. As predicted, Nadine failed to contact me with the results, so I called her to inquire. She had no adverse reaction, and she was excited to book a cut and color appointment with me.

"My other stylist just ruined my hair, don't you think?" Nadine asked me over the phone.

"If you think it's too dark, we can adjust the base color up with highlights. Would you like me to do that?" I replied.

The Climate of Truth

"I don't know what to do," she whined.

"I need to know your preference so I can book the right amount of time," I said. "Highlighting takes longer, that's all."

"Well sure, that makes sense. Let's do what you said. What could it hurt?" Nadine said.

I flinched. "What could it hurt" had proven to be a dire warning at various times in my life.

On the day of her appointment, Nadine proved to be quite chatty, as if we'd known each other for decades. The stereo was playing a funky song from 1969 with a psychedelic beat. Admittedly, it was weird to associate a pro-Jesus rock-gospel song with a Jewish hippie named Norman Greenbaum, but he wrote a hit for the ages, *"Spirit in the Sky:"*

> *"Prepare yourself you know it's a must*
> *Gotta have a friend in Jesus*
> *So you know that when you die*
> *He's gonna recommend you*
> *To the spirit in the sky"*

"I was on *Facebook* today," Nadine said, starting right in. "My husband and I have a page together. Fewer people pick fights with you when you have a *Facebook* page as a couple. But I have to say, I think we are about ready to cancel our page and get out of there. There are a lot of people who have this picture of Trump standing next to Jesus, and Jesus has his arms around Trump to protect him. And you wonder where Trump got the idea to tell people he was 'The Chosen One.' These people are ready to go to war over the idea of Jesus hugging Trump."

"It's the American Jihad," I said. "How is it any different than what happens with extremists in the Middle East?"

Nadine looked at me blankly. "I was with my other stylist for 21 years," she said, sounding confused. "Tell me honestly, do you think this last color job she did was any good?"

Experience told me that I had to proceed with caution. "Well, you've told me that you weren't satisfied with the color as it was, and that's why you called me. It doesn't help for me to rehash someone

Synchronicity

else's work. We all have different ideas. So, it's best to focus on how to change things up to help make you feel better. You said the color looks too dark because your silver halo pops out really quickly. You instructed me to introduce highlights to lessen the contrast as your roots grow out. This will give you a fresh start. It's a more complex multiple color service known as color correction. It takes more time and skill, which is why I had to consult with you in advance."

Nadine looked at me intensely over the top of her mask. "I hope it doesn't ruin my hair and make everything worse."

Part of me wondered if I should have backed out of the service then, but I said, "Nothing you have asked me to do is going to damage your hair. I would not do that to you."

"I hope you're right," she said under her breath. When I began my work to insert corrective highlights over the old color she despised, she continued with her awkward vein of conversation. "I've been friends with Betty for 30 years. She doesn't tell just <u>anybody</u> about you, you know, Mike."

"Is that so?" I said. Betty was one of my long-term clients whom I considered a friend.

"It took months for me to coax your name out of Betty. She's very guarded, you know. She wants to keep you all to herself," Nadine said. "It's true! She's very protective of you."

"Betty and I go way back. I've known her a long time, and I'm very fond of her and her granddaughter," I said. "It's fun to watch Audrey grow up. It happens so fast."

"That's nice," Nadine said, sounding rather bored.

"Betty and I respect each other," I said. "She wouldn't refer someone to me like her obnoxious neighbor," I said.

"I know just who you mean!" Nadine said with slow nod of her head. "That woman came over to Betty's house uninvited with a plate of Christmas cookies and wanted to barge right in. But Betty said, 'You can't come in my house – there's a pandemic, and you're not wearing a mask!' The nosey neighbor lady said 'I don't need to wear no flipping mask! My husband and I already had the COVID! And we didn't have any symptoms!' That nosey woman grabbed for the screen door, but Betty pulled it shut and locked it. Forgive me for saying it, but the bitch is only ten years younger than Betty, and she said to Betty, 'You old, retired people are a drain on the system. You

The Climate of Truth

should just get COVID and die to make more room for the rest of us!'"

I kept a straight face with my eyes on my foiling work, deciding it best to remain silent.

Nadine continued, "And Betty said, 'I have to be careful to protect my granddaughter.' And do you know what that nasty woman said? She said, 'You should just die and leave Audrey to me and my husband! We will take care of her when you die. We're the '*Silent Majority*,' and we're coming for you!'…Can you believe that! I swear, that's the same mentality that attacked the Capitol…Betty threw that plate of Christmas cookies from that horrible woman right in the garbage…You know, the FBI is asking for tips about anyone known to have gone to Washington, DC on January 6th. My daughter knows a family that went, and they even took both of their children."

"Did she report it?" I asked.

"Yes, she did. She said she didn't know if they went into the Capitol Building, but they were definitely in the crowd. That's what it's come down to, everyone having to report people they see on *Facebook*. Sons reporting their own fathers. Wives reporting their own husbands…I tell you, social media is a curse. Just a bunch of freaks and narcissists having at it.

"I don't have any social media accounts for that reason," I said.

"But the big tech companies are banning Trump left and right. They're cutting off his ability to make money. Corporations are calling him to task better than Congress ever has. The tech companies should start banning all the Congress people who lie and don't do their jobs but spend their time posting hateful things on *Facebook* and *Twitter*! If they can't raise money on social media, they can't campaign. That's hitting them where it really hurts -- in the wallet! I should call and report Betty's nosey neighbor to the FBI. Even if she wasn't in Washington, DC, it would serve her right!"

Nadine tried to make eye contact with me, but I kept my eyes focused on her hair and my color brush.

"I'm certain that the mess we're in right now is all backlash for electing a Black man as President," she mused, referring to President Obama. "When I was a little girl, I got pneumonia and had to stay home from school for several weeks. When I was finally able to go back to school, I found that my desk was pushed up against another

Synchronicity

little girl's desk. She was the new girl...and she was Black. The rest of the class was moved far away to the other side of the room, but my desk was right there with the little Black girl. It was all so strange and different...We became friends anyway, me and the little Black girl. I was only nine, so I didn't know people were different because of their skin. But it was Arkansas after all...There was a 17-year-old Black boy that was lynched in a tree because they said he raped a White girl. As it turned out, the girl was impregnated by her own father. Incest, you know...The KKK was everywhere back then. When we found out that the baby was born totally White and they lynched that Black boy for no reason, that was when my granddaddy got rid of his white cape and hood...Then one day, I was walking home with that little Black girl. For the life of me, I can't remember her name...We came up to my grandparent's house, and the dogs started to bark terribly. They just went nuts. My grandma -- she was always very sweet to me -- she said to the little Black girl, 'You need to go on home now! The dogs don't understand your smell because you're not like us! You've got all the dogs upset!' I didn't understand. 'What do you mean, Grandma? Not like us?' I asked her. 'Never you mind, just never you mind little miss Nadine!'...I lived through the assassinations of JFK, RFK, and Martin Luther King. It was really bad back then with all the race riots in the 60s. But what we've got going on today – this is so much worse! The leader of our country tells people that it's OK to hate and to be violent. I am afraid of what is happening in our country...But here in your shop, Mike, I feel very safe."

Nadine left that day after telling me that her she loved her new color-blended hair and that she felt much better. She made several additional appointments as well. About a week later, I got a greeting card from her in the mail. It read:

"Dear Mike. I want to thank you for making me feel safe at your shop. I truly appreciate all the steps you take to protect everyone from the virus. Your shop is very beautiful, and you have done wonderous things with it. You should be very proud of what you have accomplished. That being said, I need to cancel all of my future appointments with you. I've decided to go back to my stylist of 21 years who agreed to work on me at her home. So, I don't have to go to a salon after all. Thank you for everything. All my best, Nadine."

To be honest, I was relieved. But I didn't expect to receive a troubling text from Nadine's long-time friend, and my client of ten years, Betty. The text arrived shortly after Nadine cancelled her future appointments.

The Climate of Truth

Betty wrote: *"Mike, just received information from the doctors that we have had COVID, and I'm still having some side effects of it. Audrey is also. She has what is called COVID toes. They thought Audrey was having circulation problems. After testing last Wednesday, they found out, and because I was having stomach problems and other things, they confirmed it too. We had no idea that we had gotten it, so as of right now, I'm going to cancel all my appointments. Thank you."*

I responded immediately: *"Betty, thank you for letting me know. I hope you both feel better soon. Please know that it is not necessary to cancel all your appointments. You should be symptom free in time for your next cut and color, as it is four weeks out. I've seen all kinds of people who have recovered already. Don't be so hard on yourself. There's no need to be punitive. I will honor your decision but wanted to give you this insight first. Please get back to me when you feel up to it. Hang in there, kiddo." Signed with a red heart, "Mike."*

Afterwards, I called two other clients, a married couple who were also Betty's friends. They often babysat for Audrey, and they all spent a great deal of time together. I needed to speak with Rochelle and her husband to reschedule their upcoming haircuts under the circumstances.

"Hi Rochelle," I said over the phone. "I just heard from Betty that she and Audrey both have COVID. So, I need to push your appointment out for the 14-day quarantine period because of your exposure. Have you talked to Betty?"

There was an uncomfortable silence. "I'm sitting here with her right now," Rochelle said, sounding quite strange and perplexed.

"Oh! Well…I guess I should say for you to be careful, and maybe say hello to Betty for me," I said. I made the adjustments to the schedule and hung up the phone, thoroughly confused as to why Rochelle would choose to be in the company of at least two people who apparently had full-blown COVID symptoms. One would conclude that Rochelle was either incredibly careless or stupid, or that Betty had lied about having COVID in the first place.

After nearly a week, I hadn't heard back from my text to Betty. I left her an additional voicemail, asking how she was feeling.

Uncharacteristically, Betty texted a response a few days later. *"Hi Mike, It's Betty. I'm doing OK. Pretty darned tired all the time. So, I'm just doing what I can do. They're not sure how long it will last. And Audrey's feet will take a long time to heal. Thank you for asking."*

Synchronicity

I responded promptly to Betty's text: "(*Emoji: Red heart.*) *Miss you! FYI, I still have your appointments on my schedule. Will take you off if you insist. But my hope is that you will both be up and around by the end of the month. Rest up, cute stuff! May your healing progress with grace and ease.*"

Three days later, Betty texted again: "*Mike, there's just no easy way of saying this, but I have decided with all this time, resting and thinking, I am going to go to someone else who can cut my hair in short spikes that I want. I want to thank you for everything.*"

Betty's words were like a thunderbolt to my chest. In ten years, she had never indicated any dissatisfaction with her hair, and she always left my shop happy with her spikey style and punky pink streaks across the front. I struggled with what to do next and decided that I needed to sign off with integrity. I wrote, "*Betty, it's sad to find out this way that you were so disappointed with me and my work. I had no idea. It feels like there is more to it, but out of respect, I will take my leave. I am sorry if I have offended you or anyone else while trying to navigate these difficult times. I wish you and Audrey well, and hope you recover with blessings. I will miss you both.*"

I never heard from Betty again and didn't learn what triggered the conflict. I did not broach the subject with Rochelle or her husband who both remained in my client roster. None of it made any sense to me, other than the fact that everything happened immediately after my strange encounter with Nadine. I had been subjected to the maddening sting of "*Cancel Culture*" yet again.

I spent the next several months wondering what to do with all the assorted gifts Betty and Audrey had given me over the years; several Christmas ornaments, potholders, trivets, and coffee cups, many of them handmade. Part of me wanted to include a snarky note in a box used to return all the items to Betty in the mail. But it wasn't like me to do such a thing. More likely, the harm would linger because I would hold onto those gifts but never use them. I was never any good at getting over relationships gone bad for no apparent reason, but that seemed to be a common thing in the age of COVID.

❖

The true motive for the racial massacre committed in 1921 in Tulsa was jealousy. White people were unsettled by the immense success of the Greenwood community that included professional

The Climate of Truth

offices for Black doctors, lawyers and dentists. The segregated district had developed great wealth, all of which was spent within the confines of the district. Greenwood had its own movie theatres and nightclubs, salons and barber shops, restaurants and grocery stores, clothing and jewelry stores, hotels and pool halls, luxury shops, and homes with grand pianos. All of this was destroyed in coordination with city government, and these acts were hidden from history and ignored by the greater community of Tulsa for decades. It wasn't until 2021 that victims of the massacre were found to have been buried in mass graves.

The Tulsa massacre is remembered annually on "Juneteenth," June 19 (also known as Emancipation Day), the date Abraham Lincoln ordered all slaves to be freed. There was a decades-long movement to have Juneteenth recognized as a federal holiday, especially because the tragic events in Tulsa were purposefully excluded from textbooks. On June 17, 2021, President Biden signed legislation enacting the Juneteenth National Independence Day, a federal holiday commemorating the end of slavery in the US. Sadly, Tulsa was not the only place where such a massacre took place. The US held the dubious distinction of being home to an extremely long and sordid list of historical massacres against many thousands of people of color, many of them perpetrated in order to prevent minorities from participating in elections.

Trump's "*Keep America Great*" rally in Tulsa was his first reelection campaign event since the COVID pandemic began. Businesses and residents sued to stop the rally, arguing that it would be an "imminent and deadly risk to the community" that violated federal disease prevention guidelines specific to the COVID pandemic. The Oklahoma Supreme Court denied the injunction despite warnings from health officials that the rally would become a super-spreader event.

The rally was originally scheduled on Juneteenth until public outcry forced the event to be rescheduled to the following day. Trump complained that "nobody had ever heard of Juneteenth" before the controversy erupted around his rally. The week before, Trump claimed that "almost one million" people requested tickets to his rally. The Tulsa Fire Department estimated the rally crowd to be 6,200 in an auditorium that sat 19,000. The poor turnout infuriated Trump, and he accused protesters of scaring off his supporters. Tulsa officials feared that Trump's "*Keep America Great*" rally would turn violent, so the National Guard and police in riot gear were deployed.

Synchronicity

Protesters played music outside the Tulsa arena while carrying signs that opposed police brutality and supported racial justice. They marched with an orange banner that read *"Impeach Trump."* They were protesting the pandemic that disproportionately infected and killed more people of color, police officers who disproportionately killed more Black people, and the Trump administration's refusal to acknowledge institutional racism in America.

While protesters were peacefully chanting *"Black Lives Matter,"* Trump supporters shouted, *"All Lives Matter."*

A Black protester countered, "All lives can't matter until *'Black Lives Matter!'* Why don't you understand?"

A Trump supporter hollered back, "So do White people! So does White skin!"

The *"Black Lives Matter"* movement arose the month before when a White police officer in Minneapolis knelt on the neck of an unarmed Black man for more than nine minutes, causing him to suffocate and die face down in the street. George Floyd's murder, seen as a public lynching, was captured by a horrified onlooker's cellphone. The video was witnessed by millions of people around the world and was the catalyst for violent protests across the US. Several buildings, including police precincts, were burned. Businesses were vandalized and looted. The protests went on for months.

Nearly 100 years after the Tulsa massacre, Trump began his *"Keep American Great"* rally speech in Tulsa with a clarion call to his devotees: "I stand before you today to declare the *'Silent Majority'* is stronger than ever before!" The term *"Silent Majority"* had been used by President Nixon in his attempt to quash the Civil Rights Movement and the protests against the Vietnam War in the 1968 Presidential election. Nixon's shout out to the White, middle-class workers at the time, referring to them as the *"Silent Majority"* who found the dramatic and sometimes violent protests distasteful, got him elected in one of the closest races in American history.

Copying the playbook from Nixon's campaign, Trump's invocation of the *"Silent Majority"* in Tulsa was a "divide and conquer" strategy to polarize Americans into two distinct groups: one, conservatives who worshipped him; the other, all those outside the arena who disagreed with him, those he labelled in his rally speech as "very bad people," "thugs," "left wing radicals" and "violent extremists." Aligning himself with the party of

The Climate of Truth

Abraham Lincoln and the party of law and order, Trump vowed to the rally crowd: "We are going to stop the radical left. We're going to build a future of safety and opportunity for Americans of every race, color, religion and creed." Apparently, safety and opportunity were not going to be offered in an equitable manner to the people outside the arena who opposed Trump's views.

Trump's rally goers were not required to wear a mask or social distance inside the arena, where he referred to COVID as the "Chinese virus." Five days before the rally, Trump tweeted that testing for COVID "makes us look bad." During the rally, he announced that he asked his "people" to "slow the [COVID] testing down, please." At subsequent press conferences, he insisted that "When you test, you create cases." That statement was blatantly false. Increased testing proved the rate of infectious disease to be increasing exponentially with unchecked community spread. The number of COVID cases tripled in Oklahoma in the four weeks that followed Trump's "*Keep America Great*" rally. Eight of his campaign staffers were infected. This was the cultural backdrop against which Herman Cain, a prominent Black businessman, lost his life. Sadly, it was all preventable.

❖

I was never trained to work on African American hair, which required a unique formulary of chemicals, products, and services. I found it interesting that Black women spent a fortune having wefts of Remi hair, human hair extensions from Europe, India or Asia, attached to their own natural hair. The Remi hair was sewn or glued onto their own hair in order to achieve a longer, smoother style that looked more like the hair of White people. Hair extensions were the anti-afro.

In my 30-year career as a hairstylist, I remember serving only three Black people. The first went to jail for writing a bad check. Her defense was, "I just had to get my hair done." She walked out of the shop with a boatload of product after spending three hours in my chair. The second Black person had me straighten her hair with a flatiron. She spent the entire time laughing at me as I struggled to get a comb through her hair. I was successful, but the encounter was unsettling. The third person was in for a lady's haircut, and I only saw her once. I couldn't tell if she was happy with my work.

Synchronicity

I received calls, maybe once a year, from a Black person who moved to the area. Lacking confidence in helping them, I referred them to the only shop in town that catered to ethnic hair. If the wrong products were used on a Black person's hair, it could cause it to burn or snap right off. I regret to admit that my hands never touched the head of a Black man. Equally as significant, it seemed that Black people generally did not want me to touch their hair. As the pandemic progressed, I began to see Black people walk on the sidewalk in front of my shop. The community was clearly diversifying. In the 30 years prior, I rarely saw a person of color in my part of town.

Some of my clients aggressively complained about the racial protests that gained momentum with the advent of COVID; they weren't keen on having to contemplate the suffering of others who weren't like them. As if I was one of the instigators of her displeasure, Carla stared at me one foggy morning with large brown eyes affixed beneath brows raised in contempt. She asked a pointed question from the styling chair in a tone of accusation that was intended to bait me: "What do you think of the whole '*Black Lives Matter*' thing, and all the violence?"

I imagined that her jaws separated to expose her gritted teeth beneath her mask. I could see that she clenched the muscles in her neck. Carla was exceptionally growly that day because George Floyd's murder happened in Minneapolis, the town where she was born and raised.

Carla was growing her wiry, silver hair longer, past the shoulders for the first time in decades. Her goal was to be able to pull it into a banana clip. The longer her hair got, the more it looked like a haystack on a rock. But she was happy with it, so that's all that mattered. In the wintertime, Carla wore a red, plaid hat with ear flaps that made her look like "*Elmer Fudd*" when he was out hunting for "*Bugs Bunny*." She purchased a lifetime supply of plastic elastic cozies that fit over her ears to protect them from getting wet during the shampoo. I never knew another soul to wear ear cozies at the shampoo bowl. Prior to Carla, I didn't even know ear cozies existed. I never saw her wear makeup or dress clothes. Vanity wasn't anywhere on her radar.

Carla was overly fond of fancy chickens. I told her they were ugly and looked prehistoric, but she gushed over them, calling them "gorgeous and friendly." She adored old-fashioned farm tractors and

The Climate of Truth

sought images of them for her Christmas cards. She called tractors "romantic," especially when the pictures of them were coated with glitter to emulate the crystals of snow. She spent months writing lyrics for Christmas carols, practicing them religiously so that she could record seasonal ditties on her answering machine. We shared our mutual appreciation for theatre and musicals, and often sang songs together as I cut her hair. She loved to polka and played the drums and guitar as only a misplaced Lutheran Minnesotan could do -- with great restraint. I told her that I always wanted to be the guy in the orchestra who played the triangle and the cowbell.

I gave Carla a few red dahlia tubers from my garden; she planted them in pots, and then sent progress photos to me as they grew. She lovingly referred to the dahlias as her children, "Crimson" and "Clover." She loved to send me copies of silly, innocent jokes of the "Scandahoovian" variety, often using "Crimson" and "Clover" as character names.

Her cat was named "Mr. Hissyfit." But over the 12 years that I knew her, never once did Carla ever mention the name of her husband. I asked several times and received nothing more than scornful stares. She clearly despised the man, and barely tolerated living under the same roof with him. From what I could tell, they rarely spoke or ate meals together. After many years, Carla finally explained that it was financially impossible to risk separation, and she resigned herself to stay like a hoarder in a house packed with stuff from floor to ceiling.

I thought about my answer to Carla's question regarding the racial protests. "I suppose you have something witty to say, like it's supposed to be 'All Lives Matter.'"

"I like the way you think!" she said sarcastically.

"That's not what I think, really. I'm just trying to figure out the reason for your question."

"Enquiring minds want to know these things," she said, goading me further. She looked at me wide-eyed, expecting a response. "And don't tell me to *Google* it!" she demanded.

"I understand why people of color are angry. I've taken the time to contemplate it. Have you?"

My question startled Carla. "Well, you know me, I'm just a simpleton," she said.

Synchronicity

"When real police reform happens…"

She interrupted, "Oh, so you support 'defunding the police!'"

"Of course not. I didn't say that. Neither does the Biden administration."

"I see," she said, dismissively.

I continued. "It will be interesting to see what happens with the *George Floyd Anti-Lynching Bill*, if the brutal act of lynching finally becomes recognized as a federal hate crime. I can't believe that only one White senator blocked that bill, a bill that had wide bipartisan support. And he did so while attempting to school Black senators on what it meant to be lynched – as if Black people didn't already know. It was more than cruel that one Senator blocked that bill on the very day of George Floyd's funeral. So yeah, I understand why the protesters are angry. It's because there aren't enough White people who are angry about all the racist, yes, even supremacist cops who have been allowed to slaughter Black people without being held accountable. When you see real police reform get the bad cops out of the system, you might see the protesters stop. What a shame that justice is not yet being served. What a waste to everyone's life."

"What about all the violence at the protests! Do you agree with that?" Carla stared at me, bug-eyed. The look on her face meant that she demanded yet another explanation.

I took a moment to collect myself before I spoke. "If you want to talk about violence, let's discuss the full spectrum in the name of fairness," I said. I focused on my scissors as I snipped away her split ends. "How about a mob of thousands of angry White people, some of them taking baseball bats and hockey sticks to the faces of Black Capitol Police officers on January 6th, shouting 'get out of the way, nigger-nigger-nigger!' Fifteen times nigger! So, they could overthrow a free and fair election. What do <u>you</u> think of that example of violence?"

Carla was silent for a moment as she studied my eyes. "I didn't know you had such impassioned opinions."

"Please don't reduce my review of the facts to mere bluster. You can leave that sort of thing to Trump who called into *Fox News* again, saying that the insurrectionists were a 'zero threat', and they were 'hugging and kissing the police' because they had 'great relationships.' Nothing about the bashing in of people's brains with

The Climate of Truth

flag poles and fire extinguishers and gassing police with chemical spray. Nothing about the 140 injured law enforcement officers, or the five people who died, or the nearly 200 officers and soldiers who were infected by COVID that day."

"How can you possibly remember numbers and details like that?" Carla said, sounding suspicious.

"How can you not?" I said, shifting my gaze to look her right in the eyes. "How can you not be outraged by what happened?"

Carla did not answer but stared at me through her reflection in the mirror.

"I'm not interested in defending opinions these days," I said. "I'm only interested in the truth."

Carla remained somber for the remainder of her appointment. It looked like she was busy thinking behind her mask. I lathered in some anti-frizz cream, and styling lotion to soften her curly hair, and gently scrunch-dried her coif with a diffuser. She was pleased with the result, and we parted cordially, though Carla was noticeably subdued.

The following day, Carla sent me a text that read: *"Kind wishes for a 'Happy 1ˢᵗ Week of Spring"! (Emojis: Blue butterfly, chick popping out of egg, red tulip, white bunny, yellow daisy, green frog, pink rosette, bunny face front, smiley face.)"*

❖

With record-breaking COVID cases surging in the vast majority of all US states in the summer of 2020, and while health officials plead with Americans to stay away from crowded Fourth of July celebrations, Trump enticed another crowd of thousands to attend his blistering speech and a fireworks display at Mount Rushmore on July 3. There was also a military flyover by the *Blue Angles* that left contrails in red, white and blue.

Kimberly Guilfoyle, a top adviser for the Trump Campaign and Donald Trump Junior's girlfriend, was diagnosed with COVID at the Mount Rushmore event after attending a "packed maskless" fundraising party hosted by a billionaire in Bridgehampton. Guilfoyle's diagnosis sent wealthy campaign donors running in all directions to get tested as she was whisked away to Washington, DC

Synchronicity

on Air Force One. The Governor of South Dakota had direct contact with Guilfoyle but tested negative. The Governor argued that the Mount Rushmore event would not lead to new outbreaks of the virus, saying that her state "[hadn't] even come close to reaching the capacity of the amount of people that we can take care of [in COVID wards]." The Governor also disputed medical studies that determined face masks to be effective at preventing the airborne transmission of COVID.

The following month, August of 2020, the Governor of South Dakota also permitted the *Sturgis Motorcycle Rally* to he held with 450,000 in attendance. What happened at Sturgis made the giant Chinese buffet with the 40,000 people in Wuhan at the start of the pandemic look like child's play in comparison. Masks were not required in Sturgis and social distancing was impossible with the crowd packed into the tiny town. At least 600 COVID cases were officially traced to Sturgis in 2020, including outbreaks that resulted in other states. Using cellphone data from the region at the time of the event, a model from the *San Diego State University Center for Health Economics and Policy Studies* projected that up to 260,000 COVID cases could be tied to the motorcycle rally nationwide. Though the Governor criticized the study, calling it "fiction," cellphone data was later used by various states to track population movements in order to determine the timing of COVID surges. The cellphone data was also used to implement phased reopening plans after lockdowns. Patterns of human behavior were being recorded en masse.

The *Sturgis Motorcycle Rally* returned even bigger in August of 2021, even though the more lethal and highly contagious Delta variant was surging throughout the country at the time. 700,000 bikers crowded into bars, tattoo parlors, and rock concerts without masks and without a requirement to be vaccinated. It was a boom for tourism that added $800 million to South Dakota's coffers. T-shirts were sold at the event that read: *"Screw COVID. I went to Sturgis."* The official theme of the rally was *"Spreading Our Wings,"* but health officials worried that a lot more would be spread than that.

A husband and wife went to the Sturgis rally in August of 2021. They owned a "mom and pop" business near my shop. As loud and proud Trump supporters, the married pair were rabidly opposed to COVID vaccines. They also refused to wear masks, both at the Sturgis rally and at their workplace. Both contracted COVID in Sturgis, but they did not mention it to the rest of their staff for three days. They managed to infect all their employees, even those who were already

The Climate of Truth

vaccinated. Their administrative assistant was one of my clients. The result of this married pair's actions was an additional 47 infections among friends, family, and staff. The office was closed for two weeks for decontamination. All staff had to be paid for sick leave. The husband was hospitalized and suffered serious long-term neurological side effects for many months. When they were both well enough to return to the office, the husband had a pronounced limp and could barely stand up. Neither of them apologized for causing all those infections, and they continued their habit of refusing to wear masks. My client, their administrative assistant, did not tell me she had been infected until she was already sitting in my styling chair; there she loudly proclaimed she wouldn't touch anything in my shop, and she spent the rest of her appointment clutching her hands to her chest.

At least 50 people within Trump's inner circle (including himself and his immediate family members, White House administration and staff, campaign staff and advisers, the Vice President's staff and advisers, and White House residence staff) were infected with COVID in 2020. Agents in white hazmat suits with gas masks sprayed chemical disinfectant throughout the White House on multiple occasions, costing the taxpayers millions of dollars. Additionally, at least 130 secret service agents contracted COVID on Trump's campaign trail, as well as 123 frontline workers at the Capitol complex, and other military officials at the Pentagon. In direct contradiction of federal public safety guidelines, various high-profile attendees at several crowded White House parties and official ceremonies were infected with COVID. There was no contact tracing or disease tracking performed after those events.

❖

Approximately 200 protesters representing several Indigenous tribes blocked the access road to Mount Rushmore hours before Trump's speech on July 3. Tribal members, ranging from seniors to ten-year-olds, many of them women, were wearing masks to protect themselves from COVID. They carried signs that read *"You Are On Stolen Land," "Dismantle White Supremacy," "Respect Mother Earth,"* and *"Honor the Treaties."* They chanted and prayed to protect their sacred lands in the Black Hills surrounding Mount Rushmore. They smudged their people as well as the police with smoke from burning sage and danced with eagle feathers and headdresses to protest

Synchronicity

Trump's alleged opposition to Native American and minority interests. They called upon the strength of their ancestors to make their voices heard.

The protest was staged to oppose Trump, whom they called the "Great White Father," who "came onto the most sacred lands that belonged to Indigenous people without so much as a courtesy call." The tribes objected to Trump's mass gathering at Mount Rushmore without his concern for public health in the pandemic. Other Eurasian diseases like smallpox, cholera, and the Spanish Flu decimated Native American tribes. Like Blacks and Latinos, Native Americans were hit harder by COVID. The Indigenous protesters said they had to fight for their survival because White people didn't even recognize they existed. They claimed Indigenous voices were ignored for hundreds of years. Therefore, the tribes chose to place their bodies in harm's way in protest because they felt it was the only way for them to be heard.

In a move negotiated in advance with the county Sheriff, the tribes blocked the access road to Mount Rushmore with disabled vans for three hours. The blockade led to conflict with Trump supporters who were furious over being stalled from reaching their destination. A woman among the Trump supporters yelled at the protesters, "Go back to where you came from!" even though the protesters were standing on their own native land. A White man carrying a *"Trump 2020"* flag referred to the Native Americans as *"Antifa* people" who were "damn near ruining this country." There were no *"Antifa"* affiliates present. The Trump supporters chanted "USA!" and "Four More Years!" and complained that the issues raised by the Indigenous protesters all predated Trump. Referring to the Native Americans, a White man wearing a stars and stripes bandana across his bald head said he was "going to go over and kick some ass," and "They'll learn their lesson."

The Pennington County Sheriff, South Dakota Air and Army National Guard, National Park Service, South Dakota Highway Patrol and Rapid City Police Department deployed in riot gear with shields and gas masks to disband the unarmed Native Americans. A phalanx of officers used riot shields to force the protesters back, and the protesters tried to hold their blockade by pushing back against the advance. Close-range shells were fired at their feet, and they were pepper sprayed as Trump flew directly over the scene of conflict on Air Force One. All hand-to-hand conflict paused for a brief moment as everyone watched the fly-over at low altitude.

The Climate of Truth

The protesters were then given 30 minutes to disperse, or they would be arrested. Several chose to stay, and at least 20 individuals were arrested, including one child. Nick Tilsen, the organizer of the protest, was previously awarded a fellowship with the Rockefeller and Bush Foundations. His Jewish grandfather was a prominent civil rights attorney. Tilsen, a citizen of the Oglala Lakota Nation, was arrested and charged with three felonies and two misdemeanors, including second degree robbery and assault of a National Guard for seizing a riot shield that was shoved at him. He was also charged with unlawful assembly, impeding a highway, and disorderly conduct. He faced 17 years in prison for those offences, charges that were opposed by the *Human Rights Council* of the *United Nations*.

Referring to Mount Rushmore as a symbol of oppression and imperialism, Nilsen described the protest as a means "to continue on with a culture of resistance and a culture of responsibility that we have as Indigenous people, to protect our land, our community, and future generations."

Trump's speech held at the outdoor amphitheater at Mount Rushmore later that evening further inflamed the culture war. With the usual sideways cock of his head, Trump railed to the crowd that consisted almost entirely of thousands of unmasked White people: "I am here as your President to proclaim before the country and before the world, this monument will never be desecrated, these heroes will never be defamed, their legacy will never ever be destroyed, their achievements will never be forgotten, and Mount Rushmore will stand forever as an eternal tribute to our forefathers and to our freedom." Trump referred to the protesters as "far left fascists" and "angry mobs" who were "openly attacking the legacies of every person on Mount Rushmore." Trump said the goal of the protesters was to "end America."

Prior to the July 3rd event, White House aides contacted the Governor of South Dakota to discuss plans to add Trump's face to Mount Rushmore beside the likenesses of Presidents George Washington, Thomas Jefferson, Abraham Lincoln and Theodore Roosevelt. A model of the monument, with Trump's face added, was presented to Trump directly by the lady Governor.

Trump used the colossal granite sculpture of the four White Presidents who were carved into the face of Black Elk Peak as the backdrop for his speech to exploit social divisions. He quoted the *Declaration of Independence* by repeating that "All men are created

Synchronicity

equal." He then referred to liberals as "evil people," and went on to say that "one of their [referring to liberals] political weapons was *'Cancel Culture'* – driving people from their jobs, shaming dissenters and demanding total submission from anyone who disagrees. This is the very definition of totalitarianism, and it is completely alien to our culture and our values, and it has absolutely no place in the United States." No one cheering at Trump's rally on July 3rd seemed overly concerned or even aware that peaceful protesters were subjected to Trump's spoken definition of totalitarianism on the road to Mount Rushmore that very day. Trump's Mount Rushmore rally concluded with aerial fireworks that spelled *"Trump 2020"* in flashes of red, white and blue, despite tribal concerns that a pyrotechnic display could spark a wildfire like the one that occurred in the area just the week before. Soon after the event, Mount Rushmore would be closed when three wildfires erupted in winds reaching more than 70mph, causing mass evacuations in the region.

❖

I was foiling Brandy's hair with two shades of blonde while we talked about the state of our country. Recently retired, Brandy fretted about her hair feeling half as thick as it used to be. She vacillated between growing it out and cutting it off, and she had taken to just letting it air dry to enhance its natural wave. She used a small plastic clip to fasten her side bangs out of her eyes during the pesky grow-out phase. Rather than using ear cozies like Carla, Brandy asked for cotton to keep water from getting in her ears.

"I don't want to die of COVID," Brandy said, peeking out at me from beneath a row of foils. "But when I do die, I want to go gracefully...Do you want to be buried or cremated?"

The sudden question about death jarred me. "Cremated," I said. "It's better for the environment."

"I only want to live another 20 years," she said. "That's it...I feel so sorry for my grandchildren, to know what they are going to live through in the future. I don't understand the hate for all the races."

"It's based in fear," I said. "White people, for example, are afraid of losing control of everything."

The Climate of Truth

"Without the races, there wouldn't be all that wonderful food, or that amazing music. Life would be so boring. So vanilla, without spice," she said.

"People who hate are afraid of those who are different from them," I said. "They are afraid of what they don't understand. The answer to that kind of fear is simply to offer kindness."

"I think the answer is mixing the races so there is no more pure White. And if there is any pure White left, there won't be enough of them with all their money to have any power!" It was strange to hear a blonde White woman with piercing blue eyes speak in those terms.

"You may be on to something," I said cautiously. "Because the White population is quickly becoming outnumbered in our country, and that scares the crap out of certain people. It won't be too long before Whites are no longer the majority in this great melting pot experiment. That's why they are working so hard to suppress the minority vote. They are trying to hold onto power, but it's drifting away from them."

National census data at the time showed that the White majority population had declined for the first time in US history. The White population was expected to lose its majority status by 2045, with Black, Asian, and Latino populations expanding at rapid rates. This news made a lot of White people very nervous.

"I don't get the whole *'Cancel Culture'* thing," Brandy said, shaking her head.

"People are feeling the sting of discrimination when they get 'cancelled.' Some White people dish out *'Cancel Culture'* in droves, but they can't take it very well themselves. They whine and complain about it. Where do you think the most COVID cases are in the world?"

Without a moment's hesitation, Brandy said, "China."

"Nope. It's true that COVID originated in China, but China was not the epicenter of the pandemic. The most cases are in Europe and the US, where White people currently hold the majority of the population. We've got almost 30 million cases of COVID here in the US. China has just over 100,000. That's an eye opener. China contained it. We didn't. We let it rip."

"That can't be. China isn't giving the right numbers," Brandy objected.

Synchronicity

"I have friends who live in Beijing," I said. "Teachers at the International School. They flew back to China to start school again six months ago. While we are still dealing with schools being closed because of horrible spikes in cases, heading into yet another surge because of obstinance and stupidity. My friends have been teaching in Beijing classrooms, full time, for the last six months with no issues whatsoever. There isn't any COVID in Beijing. Millions of Chinese people travel, eat in restaurants, go to work and school. They are still careful and wear masks, but it's nothing like it is here."

"I had no idea," Brandy said with an air of sadness.

I continued, "What most people don't know is that the strain of the virus that first wiped-out Europe and the US came from northern Italy. But you don't see Americans boycotting pizza and pasta and beating up old Italian guys named Guido. You see them beating and murdering Asians because they blame them for the virus. The most horrible part is that countries that are predominately White are seeing Black, Brown, and Native American people who are getting sick and dying two to three times more than White people. What does that tell you?"

"That they don't have the same standard of living," Brandy said.

"People of color don't get the same opportunities that White people do. They generally don't eat as well, earn the same wages, get the same health insurance, receive the same level of treatment. They don't get the same access to the vaccines."

"I heard a lot of Black people are really afraid to take the vaccine," Brandy said.

"There's that too. People of color assume medicine comes solely from Whites who can't be trusted. It's a conditioned response based in fear. The US government experimented on Blacks for 40 years to study syphilis. Blacks were told they were getting free health care from the government, but no treatment was ever given. Black people died from untreated syphilis. Black people were purposely infected. Children were born infected. All of it studied in secret. It's considered one of the most unethical, immoral experiments ever performed in our country. Those crimes were stopped by a whistleblower who went to the press in 1972, after spending years trying to stop the study through government contacts. Because of that Tuskegee experiment, Blacks are suspicious of treatments provided by the government."

The Climate of Truth

"And people wonder why there is a *'Black Lives Matter'* movement," Brandy said, looking shellshocked.

"COVID shows us that minorities are seen by conservatives as the untouchables in our society," I said. "Minorities are the ones who pick your fruit and cotton, clean your house and wait on you hand and foot. They do all the things that privileged White people don't want to do…Maybe there is a lot of bad karma stacked up for perpetuating that kind of system. Maybe dealing with COVID is the price we all pay for atonement, and we all have to 'take our pepper' as one of my evil aunts used to say. Maybe COVID will do what has yet to be done, level the playing field by shining light on racial injustice."

We paused in silence. I stopped foiling Brandy's hair for a moment.

"I still don't get the whole *'Cancel Culture'* thing," Brandy said. "What's so terrible about the name *'Jeep Grand Cherokee?'*"

I froze. I held my breath. The refrain from the song that haunted me filled my head like it was being played through a megaphone.

"Cherokee people, Cherokee tribe
So proud to live, so proud to die!"

"Are you OK, Mike? Did I upset you?"

I collected myself. "You've never done anything to upset me. It's just that I've been knee-deep in research on that very topic. And here you go asking a question about the very thing I've been obsessed with. It boggles my brain sometimes, how the universe works." I resumed the color application, dipping my brush in a formula designed to tone grey hair with silvery ash blonde.

"Ah. So, my question about the *Jeep Grand Cherokee* inspired you." Brandy's blue, almond shaped eyes slanted upwards, and her complexion turned red, indicating that she smiled widely with amusement under her mask. "Can you explain it to me, Mike?"

"If you were a Native American, you would understand without question. If you had the experience of being part of a tribe that had been maligned and brutalized by White people for centuries, who then turn around to capitalize on your identity, you would want to

Synchronicity

reclaim it. You would fight to restore your own sense of personal power and independence. That is why Native Americans are offended by sports teams with Indian mascots. It's understandable if you humble yourself and think about it without judgement. White people scoff when they are called out as usurpers. They don't care to be inconvenienced by change."

"I didn't realize," Brandy said, looking bereft.

"How is it any different than Trump threatening to sue the Republican Party to keep them from using his name to raise money? That happened."

Brandy gasped. "Now I get it," she said. "I didn't before. I always get an education coming here."

"Native Americans view Mount Rushmore as a racist symbol that commemorates White European invaders who stole their sacred land."

"Why is that?" Brandy said, looking confused.

"It's not something you will ever see in the brochures provided by the National Parks Service. Under two treaties with the federal government -- not one, two treaties, dating back to 1868 -- Native Americans literally own The Black Hills of South Dakota, including Mount Rushmore. Then in the 1870s, prospectors discovered gold there, and the government invaded the Black Hills to force the Indians off their own land. This led to Crazy Horse and Sitting Bull defeating General Custer at the Battle of Little Bighorn. The saga ended when more than 400 US troops descended on an Indian encampment at Wounded Knee in South Dakota. The soldiers used machine guns to mow down 300 unarmed Indian men, women and children. The soldiers threw the bodies in a mass grave, mutilating some of the corpses to take trophies -- women's breasts, ears, and scalps. Twenty of the soldiers who participated in that massacre were awarded the Congressional Medal of Honor. So, you can imagine with a history like that, Native Americans are incensed about having to witness a Trump campaign rally at Mount Rushmore in the middle of a pandemic."

"I had no idea," Brandy said, plaintively.

"In 1980, the Supreme Court decided that the federal government did in fact steal tribal lands. The court said it was the worst case of dishonorable dealings ever found in our country's history, and the

The Climate of Truth

Sioux Nation was awarded something like $106 million, including interest. But the tribe turned the money down. They wanted their land back instead, including Mount Rushmore. Millions of acres."

"All this time I thought it was just a monument to our heroes, as patriotic as baseball, hot dogs and apple pie."

"Did you know Mount Rushmore was funded by the KKK?" I asked.

"What! No!" Brandy shrieked.

"And the artist who created it, Gutzon Borglum, went to *Klan* rallies and was on *Klan* committees. One of his good friends was the Grand Wizard, or Dragon, whatever he called himself, of Indiana. He called the *Klan* 'a fine lot of fellows' and said they were capable of getting a President elected."

"Oh my God! I get it, I get it!" Brandy hollered.

"I guess that means you're 'woke,'" I said.

"What's that?" Brandy replied, squinting her eyes.

"It's the latest buzzword. Republicans make fun of it, but it's an actual word in the dictionary that means you are up-to-date on racism, discrimination, and social justice."

"I guess I'm moving up in the world!" Brandy said, laughing. "'Woke' -- it sounds like I'm 'born again' or something, doesn't it?"

"Sort of."

Brandy looked up at me in the mirror as I finished wrapping a quadrant on the back of her head. "You're one of very few people I allow into my personal space with COVID going on," she said. "You, my doctor, and my dental hygienist. That's it…I was in the dental chair this week, with my mouth hanging open, and the hygienist's fingers in my mouth, so I was a captive audience. She's really a nice person, a good person, and I really like her a lot. But she starts in on me. She tells me how much she loves Trump because of his policies. I was so uncomfortable. She was right in my face, talking in my ear."

"Why didn't you tell her to stop?"

"Because I felt like I needed to hear so I could understand her better," Brandy said.

"Did you feel obligated to listen?"

Synchronicity

"Listening to her made me angry, but I didn't tell her," Brandy said, furrowing her brows. "She was talking to me so gently, with a soft, kind voice. It was weird. She was telling me all about how America was founded as a White Christian nation."

"We were founded with freedom of all religion," I said.

"My hygienist goes to this seminar in Colorado every year. It's invitation only, so you know there is a lot of money behind it. The guy who runs it, he's in his eighties and he writes a lot of books. He's an Evangelical with a focus on family values. It's very political. Anyway, she said this year's speakers were Sarah Palin and Ted Cruz. And I thought to myself, 'uh oh!'"

I laughed and patted Brandy on the back. "Remember when you told me that you would have to find another hairstylist if I supported Trump? So, you've changed."

Brandy suddenly looked sheepish. "I owe you an apology for that, Mike. I should never have said such a thing."

"We're cool. No worries, honey."

"I couldn't stand listening to the dental hygienist," Brandy said. "But I like her as a person. It's as if we're all in a paradigm shift. But right now, we are all in a deep valley, and there's no bridge to the other side. I don't know what to do."

"You are building the bridge through understanding," I said. "With anything less than kindness, the bridge collapses."

"But the more the hygienist talked, the angrier I got."

"Did she notice?" I asked.

"I think she did. But that didn't stop her. She kept right on going, and that made everything feel worse!" Brandy squeezed her eyes shut for a moment.

I touched Brandy's cheek softly so she would open her eyes and look at me. "This I know…A python is gentle at first when it wraps around your neck. It tickles your ear with its tongue so it can gauge your body temperature. It waits until it feels the very last heartbeat in your neck as it slowly strangles you, and then it swallows you whole."

Brandy grabbed her mask with both hands and laughed uproariously. Her face turned bright red. "I get it! I get it!"

The Climate of Truth

"I'm sure some people would take exception to the analogy, the whole thing about Adam and Eve and the serpent in the *Garden of Eden* and whatnot. But I'm not saying that a python is good or evil. A snake has to eat, just like everyone else. That's all. It's the natural order of things. A python overcomes its prey in this way. So, the moral of the story is…if you want to survive, it's probably best to avoid being mesmerized and strangled by a python."

"That is so funny Mike! That makes so much sense!" Brandy squealed with delight.

"I've been reading medical journals about the conservative brain," I said. "Yes, it's a measurable thing. Conservative brains are wired to think in a particular way. Just like gay people have a certain part of their brain that lights up to control physical attraction to the same sex. Conservative people are more active in the brain's fear center. So maybe this paradigm shift you describe is all about people learning how to communicate with others who can't help but think differently. People fear change. Then we get into flight or fight syndrome, and that doesn't leave room for discussion."

Brandy thought for a moment. "I adore my son. He lives in Texas with his wife. They sure are different down there."

"Understatement."

"But he says to me on the phone the other day, 'I love you Mom. I miss you so much. We haven't seen you in over a year. We want to come up for a visit, but we're not going to wear a mask. And we've decided that we aren't going to get vaccinated.' I asked him why. And he said he didn't trust the vaccine, and everything was a violation of his personal liberties."

"So, his world view dominates yours and he controls the decisions between you?"

"No," Brandy said quickly, eyeing me intensely. "I didn't argue. I just told him we would have to revisit the idea about his coming to see us."

"To me, it sounds like he doesn't respect your boundaries. And you don't accept his choices. So, there is an impasse. COVID uncovers these conflicts."

"My husband and I don't even go to restaurants for goodness sake," she said, throwing her hands in the air.

Synchronicity

"Neither do I. Haven't been out to eat for a year and a half."

"We never leave the house!" Brandy shouted in exasperation. "Why would we hunker down all this time, follow the rules and precautions, and then toss it all out the window when we seem to be so close to the end of the nightmare? It would all be for nothing. I don't want to die, no matter how much I miss my son!"

"Sounds like you've made a decision," I said.

"Maybe…We should be doing everything we can to stop this pandemic. There's no other choice to make when you think about it…But my son tells me not to let COVID rule my life. It's breaking my heart."

"He got those words right from Trump. Stubborn people, like some of the far-right Republican Governors, are lifting all the mask mandates and opening everything up 100% while all the variants are spiking. We're all going to be drug through more surges because of that mindset. I think we might be living like this for quite some time to come," I said. "Just because you're vaccinated, doesn't mean you can't still become infected and spread the virus to others. Maybe you just won't feel the symptoms as much. But vaccinated people still die."

"I agree," Brandy said. "I hear the health officials say it. That's why I ask my son why he expects everyone else to 'carry his water' because he refused to get vaccinated…And I have to say, it makes me so mad that all this money is being spent to fly to Mars with COVID going on. We should be using that money to clean and heal our own planet instead. It's so disturbing. Why go to Mars in the middle of COVID? It's bizarre."

"Think about it," I said. "It took six months for a group of physicists and engineers to work as a team, all of them wearing masks, to successfully land a rover on Mars. What a miracle! But in that same timeframe, Congress couldn't cooperate to pass a COVID relief package because they politicized the virus…The answer to the Mars question is simple. The Earth is going to run out of natural resources. We will have no choice but to become galactic citizens, like the United Federation of Planets on '*Star Trek*.' We are going to have to venture out into the universe for humanity to survive. To do that, we can't be countries and tribes. We have to be humans. Trump's '*America First*' motto will make us all extinct if it is allowed to continue."

The Climate of Truth

Brandy placed her hand on my arm. "I always enjoy coming to see you for my dose of enlightenment."

Two months after this conversation, Brandy called to tell me that she wanted to cut her hair quite short. This surprised me because she had spent the better part of a year growing her hair longer so she could pull it back. When I pressed for more details, she confided that she had just been diagnosed with breast cancer. I asked her if she told her son. She replied, "Yes, I told him…Even <u>that</u> didn't convince him to be vaccinated. With all the cancer treatment, I won't be able to be around anyone who isn't vaccinated, so I guess I won't be able to see my son or his family for a long, long time."

❖

In speech after speech throughout his reelection campaign, Trump referred to COVID as the "China Virus." Without evidence, he declared that COVID was leaked from the *Virology Institute* in Wuhan, a facility that just happened to be located around the corner from the infamous seafood market. However, through genetic sequencing, a team of international research scientists resolved that it was not possible for COVID to have been generated in a lab. Science figured COVID to be a naturally occurring pathogen, but the actual source had yet to be identified. Regardless of those developments, conspiracy theories continued to flourish that professed COVID to be a Chinese bioweapon. It was a stubborn narrative born of Sinophobia, magnified by Trump's rhetoric. Never had misinformation been so prevalent in the public square.

Research showed that many species studied in labs were susceptible to COVID: hamsters, macaques, ferrets, chimpanzees, fruit bats and cats. Outside the lab, various animals were known to have been infected with COVID, probably through human contact: domestic cats and dogs, sheep, farmed mink, and lions, tigers, snow leopards, gorillas, and hippos at zoos. Another conspiracy theory claimed the source of COVID to be various exotic animals that were illegally sold at the Wuhan market, such as the Malayan pangolin, known to carry other strains of coronavirus. However, genetic sequencing determined the pangolin strains were far different.

The Chinese government provided COVID's genetic profile to the world. This allowed several effective vaccines to be bioengineered. The first COVID vaccine approved by the US was

Synchronicity

created by *Pfizer* in only one weekend in January 2020, while the Senate was embroiled in Trump's first impeachment trial.

On February 7, the day after Karen 'cancelled' me as her stylist, Trump was recorded in a telephone interview by veteran reporter, Bob Woodward. Woodward was surprised that Trump wanted to talk about COVID instead of the impeachment trial.

"It goes through the air," Trump said, wistfully. "That's always tougher than the touch. You don't have to touch things. Right? But the air, you just breathe the air and that's how it's passed. And so that's a very tricky one. That's a very delicate one. It's also more deadly than even your strenuous flus." He told Woodward that he knew COVID could be five times more deadly than the seasonal flu.

Following the Woodward interview, Trump spent the next several weeks blatantly lying to the American public, telling us that COVID was no worse than the seasonal flu. Toward the end of February, Trump announced that the "China Virus," or the "Kung Flu" would just "disappear" with the warmer spring weather. A true test of our time in the COVID age was our ability to discern and separate fact from fiction, a measure of cultural competency.

During a subsequent interview with Woodward on March 19, 2020, Trump admitted, "I always wanted to play it [COVID] down. I still like playing it down, because I don't want to create a panic."

Documented reports of attacks against Asian Americans during the first year of the COVID pandemic escalated to 3800 incidents. The actual number of Anti-Asian attacks was severely under-reported. Asians described being publicly heckled with the chant "Virus!" Asians were harassed, boycotted, beaten and murdered.

On March 11, 2021, President Biden gave his first primetime address to mark the one-year anniversary of the declaration of the COVID pandemic. In that speech, he referred to "vicious hate crimes against Asian Americans who have been attacked, harassed, blamed, and scapegoated," and how "they are forced to live in fear for their lives, just walking down streets in America. It's wrong, it's un-American, and it must stop."

On March 16, 2021, a lone gunman shot and killed eight people at three separate Asian spas around Atlanta, Georgia. Six of the victims were Asian women. Police quickly apprehended the assailant through a GPS tracker on his vehicle. That same night, Trump called in to *Fox*

The Climate of Truth

News and referred to COVID as the "China Virus" during a primetime interview, paying no mind to the murders in Atlanta.

A former classmate described the 21-year-old Atlanta gunman: "He was sorta nerdy and didn't seem violent from what I remember. He was a hunter and his father was a youth minister or pastor. He was big into religion." On one of the shooter's social media accounts, he posted: *"Pizza, guns, drums, music, family, and God. This pretty much sums up my life. It's a pretty good life."* It bothered me to see the words "God" and "guns" used in the same sentence. It implied the intent to take up arms to overthrow the government in the name of religion. In my view, that was never a good thing. The same phrase was used by Trump at his campaign rallies, where at least 30,000 of his cheering fans were infected with COVID and some 700 died because they refused to wear a mask. His supporters wore T-shirts emblazoned with the phrase in red, white and blue, *"God, Guns, & Trump."*

❖

The Battle of Atlanta during the Civil War crescendoed with field artillery positioned high upon hilltops that overlooked the glorious city of the South; Howitzers, Napoleons and Parrots fired thousands of exploding shells and solid cannon shots. Union Army General William Tecumseh Sherman said he had no choice but to fire upon his own people. He called it "the devil's own day." General Sherman ordered the destruction of homes, businesses and railway depots to cut off Atlanta's supply of food and weapons. The Union Army counted a loss of 31,627 lives in that conflict. The Confederate count was 34,979 killed, wounded, crippled or captured. General Sherman was branded a "barbarian" by the newspapers. A man whose flesh had been ripped apart by bullets several times in battle, Sherman was overwhelmed with the sadness by what he was compelled to do in Atlanta. He could barely stand or even speak. He asked to be relieved of his command. He was then labelled "insane."

However, Sherman's victory at Atlanta propelled Abraham Lincoln's reelection by a great margin. Lincoln was then able to steer the country back to the cause of national unity. Without the Battle of Atlanta, American Democracy could have dispersed like the whiff of sulfurous smoke at the end of a spent wooden match. History showed that it took a crisis to shock the body politic to change.

Synchronicity

President Biden and Vice President Harris dropped their executive agendas and flew immediately to Atlanta after the Asian spa shootings to console the community and speak with Asian community leaders. Those who attended were touched by the sincerity and thoughtfulness of both leaders. They said it helped tremendously to be heard.

The hair stood up on my arms and I got the chills when I heard the televised press conference regarding the mass shooting at the Asian spas in Georgia. The incident took place in, of all places, **Cherokee** County. The song that had been haunting me for months instantly flooded into my mind again:

> *"Cherokee people, Cherokee tribe*
> *So proud to live, so proud to die"*

Captain Jay Baker, the public information officer for the Cherokee County Sheriff's Office, was asked by reporters if the mass shooting was classified as a targeted hate crime against Asians. Captain Baker's response was shocking. He claimed there was no indication that the shooting was intended as a hate crime. Instead, Captain Baker offered, "He [the gunman] was pretty much fed up and had been kind of at the end of his rope. Yesterday was really a bad day for him, and this is what he did."

The Captain's comments seemed to imply that it was understandable for a frustrated young White man to take out his "bad day" on unsuspecting Asians. The public was outraged. It was later disclosed that the gunman had been treated for sex addiction at an Evangelical facility. The following morning, it was reported that in April 2020, at the height of the first wave of the pandemic, Captain Jay Baker, who posted photos of himself on *Facebook* in uniform with his badge and name tag visible, also posted a photo of a T-shirt. The phrase on the T-shirt read: "*COVID-19 imported virus from Chy-na.*" Captain Baker posted a caption underneath the image, "*Love my shirt,*" and "*Get yours while they last.*"

Once those details were reported, Baker's *Facebook* page was immediately deleted. When he was asked to explain his noted social media posts, his only response was "no comment." The Asian community worried that they would continue to be targeted, including by members of law enforcement in the ongoing culture

The Climate of Truth

war. It was a well-founded fear. Tragically, there were 20 mass shooting events across America over the two weeks that followed the Atlanta spa shootings.

In 1863, the state of California passed a law that declared Asians could not testify in court against Whites. This meant that Asians had no protection under the law, and they could be abused without recourse. Whites resented the growing population of Chinese immigrants, and discrimination was rapidly increasing. In October of 1871, the city of Los Angeles had a total population just over 5,700. A mob of 500 Whites and Hispanics overtook Chinatown, and attacked, robbed and murdered members of the Chinese community that consisted of only 172 residents. The attack served as revenge for the deaths of a Hispanic policeman and a White passer-by, both of whom were caught in the crossfire between two rival Chinese gangs. The gangs were fighting over ownership of a Chinese prostitute – women were scarce at the time in the wild west. The conflict was internal to the Chinese community, but rumors spread throughout the city that claimed the Chinese were "killing Whites wholesale."

What followed was described as the worst mass lynching in American history; 19 Chinese were killed, 15 of them lynched by the vengeful mob after they had already been shot to death. Only eight men in the mob of Whites and Hispanics were convicted of manslaughter, but the convictions were all overturned on appeal. Only one of the murdered Chinese had anything to do with the gang violence that sparked the massacre.

❖

While the country's flags were still at half-staff because of the mass shootings at three Asian spas in Atlanta, less than a week later another lone gunman shot and killed 10 people at a grocery store in Boulder, Colorado. The shooter, identified as a 21-year-old Syrian Muslim, emigrated with his family and lived most of his life in the US. He was armed with a *Ruger* AR-556 pistol modified with an arm brace, a 9mm handgun, and tactical gear. The shooter passed a background check to purchase the *Ruger* days before the mass shooting.

The sale of the weapon used in the attack was approved by the *Colorado Bureau of Investigation,* even though the gunman was known to the FBI as a violent offender. In 2018, the gunman was charged and

Synchronicity

plead guilty to a misdemeanor count of third-degree assault on a high school classmate. Having been harassed and bullied for his ethnicity and religion for weeks, the Syrian teenager rose from his desk and punched another male student several times in the head in front of the entire class.

The Boulder gunman was described by family members as temperamental, anti-social, and paranoid, and was thought to be suffering from mental illness. Yet the gunman's family and people who knew him claimed surprise when events unfolded at the supermarket. The mass shooting happened only ten days after a judge blocked a ban on assault rifles that had been passed by the City of Boulder in 2018. The shooting took place across the street from the home of one of my clients who traveled back and forth to Washington State to visit a friend. I colored her hair for her on those occasions. When I asked how she was doing after the mass shooting, she simply said, "I will never be able to buy groceries there again."

Citing Captain Jay Baker's bizarre, dismissive comments about the shooter's motive in Atlanta six days earlier, writer Emily Julia DiCaro tweeted: *"Extremely tired of people's lives depending on whether a white man with an AR-15 is having a good day or not."*

In response to DiCaro's tweet, Hemal Jhaveri, a "race and inclusion" editor for *"USA Today,"* posted a comment following the mass shooting in Boulder: *"It's always an angry white man. Always."*

Ms. Jhaveri, a woman of East Indian descent who experienced racism in the workplace, was not surprised that her tweet about the shooter in Boulder erupted in controversy on social media. Her tweet was ridiculed for being "inaccurate" when police released the information that the shooter was a Syrian Muslim, <u>not</u> a White man. Jhaveri apologized publicly and deleted the offending tweet. She was then harassed, received death threats, and was fired from her job. Right-wing media took to mocking the disgraced "race and inclusion" editor as a racist. Jhaveri claimed that White staff members at *"USA Today"* were also reprimanded for controversial statements, but none of them were terminated from their positions because of it.

Jhaveri and DiCaro brought up a very valid point. More than half of all the mass shootings that occurred since 1982 were perpetrated by White males. And more than half of the shooters showed prior signs of mental health issues. The controversy over Jhaveri's tweet erupted because an East Indian woman mischaracterized a Syrian Muslim as an "angry White man," when the shooter's mugshot showed him to be pale complected. Jhaveri's most outspoken critics included prominent White men in far-right media who did not address the lengthy history of violent mass murder at the hands of White males.

Regarding her very public firing, Jhaveri wrote: "*Like many places, USA TODAY values 'equality and inclusion,' but only as long as it knows its rightful place, which is subservient to white authority."*

❖

I knew Roy for 25 years. He came for a haircut two or three times a year if it killed him. Each time I saw him, I imagined him in a toga from the time of ancient Rome, presiding over the Senate. He had a Socratic face. His profile sported a prominent aquiline nose, high cheekbones, and a protruding brow etched with furrowed lines that showed his tendency of habitual incredulity. As long as I'd known him, he had silver-white hair and a matching bushy beard adorned with a wax-tipped handlebar mustache. No matter how many times he groomed his beard with a comb that he carried in his back pocket, his face always looked like it was being attacked by a tumbleweed. Flakes of dead skin and crumbs from yesterday's lunch would fall to the floor whenever he took that comb to his beard. Thankfully, he never asked me to trim it. His warped plastic comb never once touched the wild hair on his head. His forehead, shiny as a polished agate, reached to the middle of his skull.

Roy worked most of his career at a drugstore photo department. For years on end, he operated the film processing equipment, a job that led him to become an amateur photography enthusiast. He punched a timeclock and donned a smock every day for decades to develop countless rolls of film. His retirement coincided with the advance of digital photography, when he, like *Kodachrome*, became irrelevant.

Roy did not care a whit about his appearance. That did not seem to bother his wife, who was a younger mail-order bride from the Philippines, and who later became a research biologist. Due to COVID, she was a permanent home-based worker, a trend that transformed a vast swath of the American workforce. According to Roy, the two of them didn't mind leading very boring lives because of COVID, though he worried about the decline in his wife's health. The increase in her Essential Tremor Disorder made it impossible for her

Synchronicity

to hold a computer mouse or slice anything with a knife. She would soon have to go on disability.

By the time I saw Roy in the styling chair in March of 2021, great tufts of fur had sprouted out of his ears and climbed up the back of his collar. His body hair was tangled in the leather cord around his neck that held a bear claw pendant inlaid with turquoise. His ultra-pale and liver-spotted complexion contrasted with the antique pair of black, horn-rimmed glasses that loudly announced his rank as a serial nerd. His socks, if he wore them, often didn't match. Sometimes he wore a straw cowboy hat and black cowboy boots that looked entirely foreign on his body. He often wore a dingy T-shirt that said something sarcastic, like *"I'm with stupid,"* or *"Kinky as an Artichoke."* One of his favorite T-shirts showed the image of a neon-colored screw inserted within the opening of the letter "U."

Roy walked gingerly due to a persistent case of gout that caused the seams of his overly snug clothes to visibly strain against the flex of his body. Because of the constant pain, he walked with the persistence of a circus elephant that had its ankles cruelly shackled in chains, often swaying to and frow when standing in place to shift the weight from his aching toes.

A few years back, he arrived without his signature beard for the first time in decades. Jokingly, I commented that without a beard he looked a bit like *"Barney Rubble"* from *"The Flintstones,"* with two-toned skin separating his mouth, upper lip and chin from the rest of his face. Having been on the receiving end of his diabolical insults and tasteless jokes for the 25 years that I knew him, I thought poking fun at his beardless face was well within the spirit of our relationship. But for some reason, that particular day left him humorless. He didn't say a word about it, or even flinch from my joke. He just looked straight ahead into the mirror, poker faced. He left the shop in silence and disappeared for two years. Not knowing what happened to him, I placed his client profile card in the inactive file. Two years later, Roy called out of the blue to make an appointment for a haircut.

"Where have you been!" I asked, surprised to hear his voice. "It's been forever! Is everything OK at home?"

He sidestepped my questions. When he arrived for his appointment, he was unusually gloomy and unwilling to make eye contact. Experience taught me to be gentle with such behavior. Halfway through his haircut, Roy finally looked at me. With his glasses removed, his eyes were more soft-focused.

The Climate of Truth

"You told me I looked like '*Barney Rubble*,'" he said in a plaintive voice.

"What?" I asked, confused.

"You heard me," he said angrily, turning his gaze toward the mirror.

"After all the years you've teased me from here to the moon and back, you quit coming here because you couldn't take an innocent joke? Then why did you come back here?"

"I don't know…Because my wife's hands were getting so bad she couldn't hold the scissors. I was afraid she was going to cut my ear off instead of my hair," he said, sadly.

"I'm sorry to hear your troubles, Roy…But I'm always happy to see your face."

Roy looked up at me to assess whether he should continue to speak. He was a man suddenly weakened by secrets. "When I was a kid," he began quietly, "I went to a barber. The guy put his hand under the haircut cape and fondled me." Roy's eyes welled up, and his face turned to pewter. "So it's always difficult for me to get a haircut because the whole time I'm sitting in the chair, I'm thinking about that nasty barber."

I put my hand on Roy's shoulder to reassure him. "What a horrible thing to carry around all these years. Thank you for trusting me enough to tell me about it. I am so very sorry that you were treated that way, that you suffered. It should never have happened. But you are safe here…Have I ever said or done anything to trigger your memory of it?"

"No. Never," Roy said, looking at his feet. "That horrible man's face is always right in front of me when I get a haircut, that's all."

"Roy, no matter what happens from here, I want you to know, from me to you, that what happened to you all those years ago does not define you. It does not make you who you are today. Sometimes just saying it out loud helps to heal the wound."

After that poignant conversation, Roy resumed his regular, infrequent haircuts along with his usual tasteless jokes. During the pandemic, he became increasingly outspoken about his political views; we hadn't discussed politics in the 25 years before. I

Synchronicity

remembered Roy was originally from Colorado, and I saw him just a few days after the mass shooting in Boulder.

When he sat in the shampoo chair, I asked him to unbutton his collar so that I could turn it under and place a protective towel around his neck. Doing so, he then pulled the open collar flirtatiously, wriggling his eyebrows at me as he revealed an abundance of grey chest hair.

I ignored the display and said, "Please take this safety towel and place it over your eyes and nose as you recline into the sink. This is to protect you from backsplash and from my breath as I stand over you during the shampoo."

When we got back to the styling chair, Roy became noticeably agitated as he began to speak about events in the national news. "I'm sick to death of people politicizing guns to suit their own agendas," he fumed.

I was shaving mounds of white fuzz off Roy's neck and shoulders with clippers. "How does a man with mental health issues, a man known to the FBI with a history of violence, pass a background check to purchase assault weapons?" I said.

"That's a very good question, Mike. It just goes to show you that background checks and bans on assault weapons will not work. Because it's people who kill people. Guns don't kill people."

I saw that overused excuse from gun enthusiasts as an insult. "Don't tell me guns aren't made with the intent to kill people. Guns kill when someone aims and pulls the trigger, as intended by the manufacturer and by the person holding the gun. In my opinion, if you want to play with weapons of war, go join the army."

"The government needs to go after the bad guys, the evil doers! Not us average folk who are just trying to defend ourselves as is our right to do," Roy said gruffly, adjusting his mask.

"Why do 'average folk' need bazookas to defend themselves?" I asked. "You don't need an assault rifle to hunt elk either. Half the members of the *NRA* are hunters who want reasonable gun control measures in place." My clipper hovered around Roy's sideburns, and I held the elastic of his mask out of the way to edge his cut. He squirmed a bit, and his mask shifted below his nose. I asked him to pull his mask back up several times.

The Climate of Truth

"The FBI is at fault for what happened in Boulder! They dropped the ball!" Roy complained.

"The FBI has its hands full with all kinds of domestic trouble percolating in our country. I don't think it's possible to stop all these people from wanton murder. It's an epidemic in the middle of a pandemic. What are there, 450 million guns in our country?"

Roy laughed. "That number is way too low. The FBI knew the guy in Boulder was a terrorist with '*ISIS*' sympathies," Roy insisted.

"Where did you hear that?" I asked.

"He put stuff on *Facebook*."

"On *Facebook* he called Trump a '*dick*' who refused to help refugees," I said. "And that Trump won the election because of racism."

"That's a load of crap," Roy said.

"The shooter was also a homophobe because of his religion," I continued. "He wrote stuff like '*God created Adam and Eve not Adam and Steve,*' and some other nasty anti-gay slurs. He posted comments about the mass shooting at the mosques in New Zealand, done by White supremacists, and about the attack at the club in Paris. So maybe he thought about shooting up a grocery store as payback for what happened to Muslims at prayer. I don't know. No one knows yet. He complained about being stalked and hacked by racist Islamophobes. I didn't see that he had ties to '*ISIS,*' and investigators haven't identified a motive. He's the right age to develop paranoid schizophrenia, and he seems to exhibit those symptoms and behaviors. I think a judge ordered a 90-day psych evaluation."

Roy glared at me. "I'm here to tell you, if I'm parked in the lot, waiting for my wife at the grocery store, and somebody comes at me out there, you can be certain that I will take care of the matter. I will act first and be questioned after the fact. My wife is Asian. If anyone comes at my wife in the grocery store, I can guarantee you that the perpetrator will have to be buried. I will never be a victim. I will not allow my wife to be a victim. It's a common-sense approach shared by many millions of people."

I took a step back from the styling chair, holding my scissors and comb. "I don't want to debate with you, Roy. All I know is that people shouldn't be murdered going to buy groceries. Our children shouldn't be shot at public schools, but they are, over and over.

Synchronicity

People shouldn't be shot at churches, mosques or synagogues, or shopping malls, period. It's gone on and on, incident to incident, and nothing has changed. It has to stop. It seems to me the only way to stop it is to control who has guns, and what kind of guns."

"I agree with you, Mike! Absolutely! Kids shouldn't be shot at school, and people shouldn't be mowed down at church or at the grocery store. But taking away all the guns won't solve anything."

"Nobody's taking all the guns away. We're talking assault weapons," I said.

"They took all the guns away in the UK, and now all they've got is a serious knife problem. Everybody being stabbed to death by a lunatic every time you turn around." Roy's chest was heaving.

"The minority view, those who want every gun under the sun, are controlling every aspect of this issue. How? By ignoring each and every mass shooting that comes along. As usual."

"What weapon is most used to kill people in this country?" Roy asked.

"I have no idea."

"Handguns. Not assault weapons," he said, definitively.

I took a moment to center myself and went back to work with my scissors on the crown of Roy's head. "The majority of people in this country don't want assault weapons in the hands of dangerous people. More than 80% of the 190-million gun owners in this country want common-sense gun control laws. Those who don't want guns in their lives can't get away from them. There's something wrong with that scenario. Too few have controlled the narrative for too long, completely ignoring the obvious. Over many years, the government has instituted all kinds of safety regulations with the goal of zero tolerance for the auto industry. As a result, cars have become much safer. We wear seat belts and have sensors that detect blind spots and automatically slam on the brakes if we get too close to the car in front of us. The cars of the future will all come equipped with breathalyzers so drunks can't drive. It makes no sense that we continue to be murdered in mass shootings and nothing changes to address that simple fact. It's plain stupid…And as I said already, Roy, I don't want to debate with you. So please, let's stop."

"I don't want to debate with you either," Roy said, attempting to sound considerate. "Out of respect for our friendship, I won't go any

The Climate of Truth

further." The word "friendship" was a strange choice, given that we had no contact beyond scissors and combs, and our conversations had always focused previously on aimless banter for the sake of entertainment. "But I would love to take you out for a cup of coffee sometime," Roy continued, "so that I can straighten you out. You can't see it right now, but you're coming down on the wrong side of things. It's only a matter of education. You'll see."

Roy opened his wallet to pay cash for his haircut. He pulled out a fake *"Trump 2020"* bill and handed it to me with a wide-toothed grin. The image of Trump's smug face was accompanied by a hand gesture of the flying middle finger, accompanied by the phrase *"Impeach This!"* printed across the top of the bill.

"No thanks," I said, recoiling reflexively.

"You sure? It's collectible." Roy was gauging my response to determine the degree of my political bent.

"By law, no living person is supposed to be on US currency," I said with a chuckle.

"Not into funny money, eh?" Roy laughed.

"The Andrew Jackson along with the Abraham Lincoln in your wallet will do just fine, thank you. Unless you prefer credit or debit?"

"Will you have to disinfect the greenbacks because of COVID, or because they touched Trump's twenty-dollar bill?" Roy's eyes sparkled and he wriggled his eyebrows like a clown.

"Cash isn't a vector of concern for me in the pandemic," I said. "I've been handling legal tender for months without incident."

"Well, all right, compadre. You charge a hard bargain," Roy said, reaching for the acceptable greenbacks.

At his next appointment a few months later, Roy arrived wearing a black T-shirt that read *"Support the Second Amendment and Pass the Ammo!"* Images of giant bullets (adorned with stars and stripes) that looked like rocket ships stretched from his navel to his chin. He waited for me to notice and traced the path my eyes took as I read the words scrawled across the top of his chest. I could tell he had a wide smile beneath his mask, and his eyes sparkled with glee. I didn't say a word about his T-shirt or gun rights.

❖

Synchronicity

The sun finally came out after several days of rain. It was a very pleasant day in the middle of March 2021, a full year after COVID first closed my business for three months. Stella arrived for her cut and color. I'd known her for a few years. She worked as a corporate executive.

The flowering plums were in full bloom with their cascades of pink petals and nubile purple foliage. In celebration of spring, Stella was wearing wedged, open-toed sandals to show off her French pedicure, sparkling white capri pants, and a loose, frilly, floral blouse in a pastel shade of aquamarine. She was the first person of the year to wear a springtime ensemble to the shop. That seemed significant to me for some reason. She was svelte and petite, with a light bronze complexion splashed with freckles, and beautiful hazel eyes. Her energy that afternoon defied her diminutive size and made her appear much bigger than life. She was reserved and usually shy, but willing to force herself to engage in conversation with me. It was as if she finally allowed herself to be open.

Following safety protocols, Stella headed straight to the restroom to wash her hands as all my clients were accustomed to do when they first arrived. As she scrubbed up, she let me know that she had just taken the "one and done," the single dose *Johnson & Johnson* vaccine. She knew somebody who knew somebody who could get her into a grocery store pharmacy in the northern part of the county. The *Johnson & Johnson* vaccine was hard to come by because its manufacture had not yet been ramped up. Stella explained that the side effects of that vaccine tended to hit women harder than men, and she took to her bed for a day with a terrible migraine, chills, fever, and body aches. The migraine left her unable to watch television or read, so she lay on her bed and tuned into a music station until the side effects subsided after ten hours.

I was a bit downhearted after her explanation because I was after the "one and done" vaccine for myself – it was the only shot that my doctor said I could use to avoid an anaphylactic response. The *Pfizer* and *Moderna* vaccines both used petroleum-based preservatives that accounted for more than ten times the normal occurrence of allergic reactions. Because I had a long history of severe, life-threatening allergic reactions myself, my doctor told me to avoid *Pfizer* and *Moderna*, but he approved *Johnson & Johnson* for me. Everything I read about *Johnson & Johnson* said that less than a few hundredths of a percent of the population reacted adversely to that formulation, and it manifested in only a very slight fever. The idea of going through full

The Climate of Truth

flu like symptoms like Stella described made me nervous. My immune system was always on overdrive, and if there was going to be a bad reaction, chances were that it was going to happen to me. Regardless, I knew I needed to get vaccinated to keep from dying of COVID.

I told Stella that I couldn't find the *Johnson & Johnson* to get dosed. Health officials told the public just to take whatever vaccine they could get, but I couldn't go that route. Furthermore, I couldn't call any participating pharmacy to request *Johnson & Johnson*. Everything had to be done online, and scheduling websites wouldn't allow a patient to specify a brand name. The state database showed that *Johnson & Johnson* could not be found in my county, even though I knew some places were stocked with it. The whole scheduling apparatus was not user friendly, and I was not willing to get vaccinated blindly.

"My daughter-in-law works at the *Albertson's* pharmacy. I'll see her tomorrow. I'll ask her if she can hook you up!" Stella said as she dried her hands. Her positive vibe soothed away my agitation.

The stereo was playing Michael Jackson's *"Thriller."* It was incredibly strange to hear the lyrics to that song in the context of COVID symptoms:

> *"And though you fight to stay alive*
> *Your body starts to shiver*
> *For no mere mortal can resist*
> *The evil of the thriller"*

"When I was a kid," Stella said as she sat in the styling chair, "I would binge-watch *MTV* and just zone out on music videos. '*Thriller*' was such a big deal with all the dancing zombies in that 20-minute video. That was considered the coolest of the cool. That's why I like your playlist, Mike. It takes me back in time when things were simpler, and it helps me forget, even for just a little while, all the terrible things going on in the world. It's a comfort to me in here. Thank you for that."

I separated Stella's hair into sections, and began applying color in reverse, starting at the nape of her neck. She preferred the shadow-box effect with a warm, dark golden blonde on the lower sections at

Synchronicity

the back of her head, and a pale, light golden blonde on the top and sides. When combined with a long-layered cut, the darker color would peek out from the bottom of the style. As I applied her hair color, the conversation shifted quickly to the two mass shootings that had rocked the nation, less than a week apart.

"Clearly the gentleman in Colorado was suffering from mental illness, and no one did anything about it," she said. The word "gentleman" was a curious choice to describe the Syrian Muslim who murdered ten people.

"They saw him playing with guns just a few days before the massacre," I said. "But the family didn't report it to anybody. They didn't intervene."

"People can't continue to look the other way," Stella said. "There has to be accountability."

"He seems to have the signs of being a paranoid schizophrenic," I said. "I know several families who are dealing with young men with this disorder. It's impossible to control them. They don't sleep. They're high on drugs. They get mad and punch holes in the walls. They can't hold a job. They're in and out of jail. It's a never-ending cycle. They refuse to take their meds, and they spin out of control. It breaks everyone in the family down with despair. Sounds like something similar with this guy in Boulder…I'm sure it will be just a matter of time before we see anti-Muslim hate crimes because this shooter's a Muslim."

"People are not willing to believe that one mentally ill man killed all those people for no good reason. I don't think he was a jihadist." Stella's comment surprised me because she described herself as a staunch conservative.

I took her up on her offer of open-mindedness. "Just like people are unwilling to believe that only one mentally ill man shot and killed JFK. They would prefer to conjure conspiracy theories for decades rather than accept the prospect that a misfit took out one of the most powerful people in the world," I said.

"Makes me wonder who put the man in Georgia up to shooting Asians," Stella said. He had to have been influenced by someone nefarious."

"Well, with respect," I said, "all last year Trump kept saying 'China Virus' and 'Kung Flu.'"

The Climate of Truth

"Yes, he did. I remember that very clearly," Stella said.

"People ate it up. And then they made T-shirts with those disgraceful words."

"Our country is broken when we see the signs of trouble and we do nothing to stop it," she said, sounding dejected. She quickly shook off the troubling thought. "But I am hopeful. It is my nature to be optimistic. Now that I am vaccinated, I think things will be looking up toward some form of 'new normal.'"

"You're an exotic beauty," I said, looking at her in the wall mirror. "What is your ethnicity?"

Without a moment's hesitation, Stella said, "My great grandfather was married to a Cherokee princess."

"Wow! I'm in the presence of royalty!" I said. The word Cherokee was not one that I heard often during any other year in my life. But it was prominent in the year that COVID came. The haunting song flooded back to my mind:

"Cherokee people
Cherokee tribe
So proud to live
So proud to die"

I continued the topic of ancestry with Stella. "On both sides of my family I'm 99.9 percent from a 200 square mile region in Eastern Europe -- just east of Hungary, south of Poland, and west of Ukraine. It was known as the 'Settlement of the Pale.' It doesn't exist as a region anymore. It was wiped out in World War II. So, the families of both of my parents were from the same place for many hundreds of years, but they never knew each other. My parents met on a blind date in Detroit after both sides of the family immigrated to the US. My father proposed on the second date. My mother accepted, not because she even liked my father, but because she hated both of her parents and wanted out of the house…I'm one one-hundredth of a percent Mongolian too, so I am a wee tiny bit Asian."

Stella laughed. "I'm just a fraction Cherokee, really. But it gives me a sense of pride to know that my great grandmother was a

Synchronicity

Cherokee princess. I'm a mutt. Scottish, Norwegian, and German to boot. My great grandfather was a six-foot-ten, full-blooded German."

"How in the world was he able to snag a Cherokee princess for his wife? How would the tribe allow that? I wonder what they looked like standing next to each other, with him being such a giant. And if you were her size, you know, you'd look like a '*Hobbit*' in comparison."

"I don't really know how they came to be married," Stella said. "But I do know they were very much in love. I guess you had to be tough in those days to have a mixed-race marriage. It probably turned a lot of heads…or worse. But who was going to argue with a six-foot-ten German dude who looked like he could eat you for lunch?"

"Are you registered with the tribe? You must have tribal rights," I said.

"Yes, I have the right to register," she said, "but I haven't done so. My father asked all of us kids not to apply. He didn't do it either. He said the government had never abused him, and that tribal monies should go to those who really need it, those who have suffered all the wrongs. My family hasn't suffered."

The conversation shifted to the origins of COVID.

"I believe the virus was created in a lab," Stella insisted. "Even so, I don't think it was let loose on purpose. It probably got out of containment when they were working with the bats. Regardless, I don't think we should be blaming China for the pandemic. That won't get us any closer to the finish line, and we are so close. We need to focus on doing everything we can, but we will probably be stuck with COVID for at least another year."

It was peculiar to hear Stella's comments because Dr. Redfield, the former head of the CDC in the Trump administration, had just been interviewed on *CNN* and offered the same opinion, almost verbatim. It surprised me that Stella, a staunch conservative, would take a peek at what she might consider alternative news.

Without factual evidence to back up his claim, Dr. Redfield offered a controversial opinion that the COVID pandemic began even earlier, in September or October of 2019. He theorized that the source of the outbreak was a lab-grown version of the virus that probably infected a lab worker at the *Virology Institute* in Wuhan. Dr. Redfield claimed that a few lab workers were infected with what appeared to be coronavirus symptoms at that time, and that the lab workers inadvertently spread the virus into the community. It was highly irregular for the former head of the CDC to cast doubt on documented scientific evidence that opposed conspiracy theories.

The *World Health Organization* quickly released a statement that declared Dr. Redfield's "lab leak" theory to be "extremely unlikely." In the interview, Dr. Redfield went on to say that he had the right to his own opinions, knowing full well that others would strongly disagree with him. He justified his beliefs, noting his lengthy career as a virologist who was familiar with the lab practices used to make viruses "better and better"(more potent and lethal) in order to create effective vaccines.

"When trying to grow virus in a lab, we coax it to grow so we can experiment on it and figure it out," Dr. Redfield said. He opined that it was nearly impossible for a coronavirus to jump from a zoonotic source to the human population and then turn into a world pandemic as quickly as COVID did. Dr. Redfield's comments seemed sinister, as if they were intended to magnify tensions with China. He didn't consider that the virus could have been looming in the countryside for an undetermined time, mutating and becoming increasingly efficient. He didn't cite the fact that there were literally thousands upon thousands of mutations of COVID that had been identified over the course of the first year of the pandemic, some of them far more lethal and contagious than the original strain.

At least it was clear that Dr. Redfield influenced Trump to shout, "China Virus" and "Kung Flu." In the end, Dr. Redfield said science would figure out the source of the COVID outbreak.

I explained to Stella that, according to an international team of geneticists (comprised of 17 Chinese scientists and an additional 17 international scientists, all working under the supervision of the *United Nations* and in collaboration with the Chinese government on site in China) had proven that COVID was not developed in a lab and that it was a naturally occurring pathogen. I told Stella that coronaviruses were commonly known to begin as bird flu, and that the whistleblower, Dr. Gao in Wuhan, said that a lot of cases had no connection to the wet market.

"But we were all led to believe it came from bats from that wet market!" Stella objected, sounding annoyed.

Synchronicity

"We were led to believe a lot of things. It was misinformation disguised as facts."

"Ugh!" Stella said, crossing her arms defiantly.

"Things were propagandized to polarize our country and make us all fight with each other. Because 'divide and conquer' makes us a weaker nation. It destabilizes us. And yes, the Russians and the Iranians were hitting us with propaganda during the election to make us all distrust each other, magnifying the divisions. China thought about messing with the election too, but they chose not to. This information comes from our own intelligence operatives. It's quite possible that misinformation about COVID has been fed to us by the Russians through social media. But did you ever think in a million years that your own government leaders would pursue propaganda campaign to attack Congress in a vicious attempt to overthrow an election?"

"No, it never occurred to me. But it's a betrayal that my great grandmother, the Cherokee princess, would understand." Stella looked up at me with clarity in her eyes.

"The geneticists haven't yet found the exact source, but they know it didn't come from the wet market in Wuhan, or the virology lab," I said.

"Blaming the Chinese for the virus isn't helping to solve the problem," Stella insisted. "Blaming anybody doesn't change anything. Wearing a mask and getting vaccinated will."

"Now we're up against the brick wall of deniers, all the bazillions of people who will refuse to take the vaccine because they only see it as a threat to their personal freedom," I said.

"The virus happened. Get on with it!" Stella replied. "It doesn't matter where it came from. Everyone needs to do their part. That's the only way out. Being part of the whole. Being part of the solution instead of being part of the problem."

A direct descendant of a Cherokee princess was sitting in my styling chair, ruminating. Our talk seemed to help us both find peace within the crisis.

The Climate of Truth

*"But maybe someday when they learn
Cherokee nation will return, will return"*

Just days after this conversation with Stella, officials at the US State Department confirmed that that both the Russians and Chinese were spreading disinformation through the internet to undermine public confidence in the COVID vaccines used in America. The propaganda campaign continued for at least the following six months and contributed to the steep decline in the number of Americans who took their jabs. The disinformation campaign spread false information that the Biden administration was forcing the American public to take vaccines that were ineffective and unsafe at precisely the same time that the more infectious Delta variant was surging in 90% of all US counties. Case counts and death rates soared to some of the highest levels of the pandemic. Hospital operations were overwhelmed in America and faced complete collapse. Patients were turned away because of a lack of hospital beds. Parents were told that their COVID-infected children would have to wait for another infected child to die before a hospital bed would become available.

Meanwhile, the Chinese and the Russians joined forces to hold joint military exercises as a show of force against the US military. I worried that the Chinese would invade Taiwan, and the Russians would invade Ukraine simultaneously to expand their goals of global domination. According to US Intelligence, Moscow's foreign policy was focused on exacerbating tensions in Western nations, and some of the most blatant disinformation was targeted at far-right American audiences. The disinformation specifically targeted the culture wars regarding the COVID vaccines and the use of mask mandates. This resulted in violent outbursts at schoolboard meetings across the country where officials were attempting to implement mask mandates to protect children who were not yet able to be vaccinated and who were succumbing in massive numbers to the Delta variant.

❖

Jessica Estrada, a freelance writer and contributor to "*Well + Good,*" a publication dedicated to wholistic lifestyles for women, wrote an article specifically about synchronicities. I did not go looking for her article – it appeared randomly on my cellphone newsfeed as I was putting the finishing touches on this chapter. Ms.

Synchronicity

Estrada wrote, "*…spiritual synchronicities can also show up as a song on the radio that reminds you of something or someone or has lyrics that are a clear message to something you've been debating.*"

On the eve of my "one and done" inoculation, I held the ceramic picture frame in my hand that was given to me by a client I saw only once when I first opened my shop in the old Victorian house on the boulevard nine years before. The eight-inch fame was decorated with sculpted twigs, one on top, the other at the bottom, each with a single green leaf protruding. To me, the twigs formed the ancient symbol of balance, the Chinese yin-yang. A typed quote was inserted behind a two-inch square of glass at the center of the ceramic frame:

> "*I am open to the guidance of synchronicity, and I do not let expectations hinder my path.*
> *-- The 14th Dalai Lama*"

Judgement

~❖~

  I listened to streaming music for twelve hours a day in the shop and never grew tired of my favorite songs, especially soft rock classics. To me, the familiarity of music brought comfort in a time of heavy pandemic stress. My nerves couldn't handle a void of silence while I worked on my clients. I preferred a subscription to *Pandora,* where I could stream unlimited selections without the jarring interruption of hyperbolic news or supersonic commercials. Music played a large part in the soothing atmosphere of my shop, *Blow Your Top.* Music also served as an anchor for the memories of the pandemic era. Clients often commented on how much they loved my playlist that took years to perfect. They told me my choice in music helped make the shop feel very "Zen" and peaceful.

  Music increases the release of endorphins in the brain, aiding the listener to feel more hopeful and to better cope with pain. Music can be as addictive as narcotics. Increased levels of dopamine in the brain (that are triggered by listening to music) provide the same pleasure-reward sensations as when eating chocolate or having an orgasm. When a favorite or familiar song is heard, the resulting dopamine boost can stimulate higher bonds of trust and generosity, empathy, kindness and cooperation, all things that are vital to human survival. When a song came on the stereo that did not appeal to me, I felt an electric jolt shoot up my spine, forcing me to rush to the computer to give the selection a very quick "thumbs down" vote of no confidence.

Judgement

My ability to work was disrupted if the vibe of the music wasn't right for my psyche.

I gave a haircut to a brain surgeon from Pakistan. He asked for a cut like the movie star, George Clooney, but I didn't tell him that Clooney cut his own hair with a *Flowbee* vacuum. Before I raised my comb and scissors to his head, the brain surgeon vehemently insisted that I turn off the stereo.

"Why?" I asked him.

"Because I prefer not to listen to your music," he said without further explanation. He eyed me in the mirror with a touch of condemnation.

American music didn't jive with his world view, and he considered music to be a sinful influence. Music was banned in barber shops and hair salons in various Muslim countries; if caught playing music, stylists were beaten or even condemned to death. The brain surgeon was also not happy about sharing the salon with my Corgi. In Pakistan, dogs were considered vermin. Against my better judgement, I silenced the stereo as he requested, and ushered my Corgi into a back room. Then anxiety surged immediately in my body.

The brain surgeon barraged me with personal questions. "Do you believe in God?" he asked. "How many times a day do you pray?...How can you be alone with women?...Why do you want to touch the hair of women?...Are your parents ashamed of your profession?...Why did you not study for a better career?...Why aren't you married?...Are you in a lot of debt?"

As he spoke, I wondered if he had to wrap his enormous, bushy beard in a hairnet in order to perform brain surgery. And then I suspected the hospitals could not safely conduct brain surgery during the pandemic, which might anger a brain surgeon.

"Did you come to America because you could make a better living here than you could in Pakistan?" I countered.

The brain surgeon could not look me in the eye. He chose to avoid answering the same way I ignored his rapid-fire questions. Instead, he ran his fingers through his freshly cut hair and nodded at his reflection in the mirror. "The haircut is satisfactory. I will need another appointment in precisely four weeks."

The Climate of Truth

I answered him succinctly: "I will schedule you again on two conditions."

"Excuse me?" he said, squinting his eyes.

"First, I will not remove my dog again from this room to appease you. This is Irma's house, and she comes to work with me every day."

"What is the second condition?" he asked in a patronizing tone.

I calmly flipped the switch on my computer to bring music back into the room. I could breathe easier once the classic rock sound of *The Doobie Brothers* caressed my ears. Songwriter Tom Johnston described the 1972 hit *"Listen to the Music"* as a call for world peace:

> *"Don't you feel it growin' day by day?*
> *People getting' ready for the news*
> *Some are happy some are sad...*
> *Oh...we got to let the music play*
>
> *...Whoa oh whoa...*
> *Listen to the music*
> *Whoa oh whoa...*
> *Listen to the music"*

"No one has ever asked me to turn off the music in my shop before," I said to the brain surgeon. "I will not do that again. If you prefer not to listen to the music, then perhaps this isn't the right place for you to get a haircut."

The brain surgeon tossed cash on the front counter without saying another word. I never saw him again.

❖

Tara arrived 45 minutes early for her noon highlight appointment. She was in her usual state of nervous agitation. While I finished with another woman's service, Tara seated herself in a lobby chair and hunched herself forward with her long blonde hair covering her face. She sulked, fidgeted and fumbled erratically with her cellphone while chewing her cuticles. Glancing at her through the reflection in the wall mirror, I knew she was working herself up to a

Judgement

frenetic tizzy. It always took the first half hour of Tara's scheduled time to calm her down before I could even begin to spruce up her hair.

When she first started coming to me, Tara was accompanied by her husband. He was a mild mannered, respectful fellow who helped anchor his wife's behavior as a positive influence. She frequently caught his gaze in the mirror as her way of comforting herself. He did not speak much, but just smiled or nodded at her. That seemed to keep her calm. Over the course of several months, Tara gave various unintentional clues that she was a recluse, if not agoraphobic. It was difficult for her to leave home, and she often required her husband's presence to sustain her when she was out in the world.

After collecting payment from my other client, I was the only human in the room with Tara. It was unfortunate that she came alone that day. She submitted to rocking back and forth while clutching her abdomen.

I gathered the broom and dustpan from the closet, swept up the cuttings from the floor, and retrieved a coloring cape and two towels for Tara's service. I placed the cutting shears made with surgical Japanese steel back in their leather case and stowed the used combs and brushes in the bottom drawer of my service caddy for future sanitizing. All was ready. I noticed the familiar sensation of mild nausea in my stomach that always accompanied the presence of a difficult client.

"Come on over, Tara," I motioned.

Irma, my Corgi, stood ready, her bunny-bump of a tail wagging excitedly as Tara hung her coat on a wall hook and walked deliberately to the styling chair without paying tribute to the dog's friendly customer service. Irma didn't seem to mind as she sneezed her greeting with a shake of her head and pranced adorably to her "couch potato." Her bed had a raised cushioned rim upon which Irma could effortlessly rest her chin and watch the proceedings from a few feet away.

"What do you want to tell me about your hair today?" I asked Tara, bracing for her customary critique right out of the shoot.

Tara stared blankly at herself in the mirror. She grabbed repeatedly at her long blonde hair, fluffing it forcefully with a wide scowl on her face that made her look much older than her actual

The Climate of Truth

years. Her eyes were a vacant, pale blue, and the rims of her eyelids were noticeably red and puffy as if she had been crying all morning.

"Whatever you've done before, I don't want you to use the same colors ever again!" Tara barked unexpectedly.

Irma's head lifted off her chin rest while her radar ears swiveled sharply in Tara's direction.

"Ok then, let me get your color file so I can better understand what you want me to do for you," I said in a purposefully calm tone. I exited the room to find Tara's color recipe card from the formulary in the back of the house. I cautioned myself to breathe slowly and remain optimistic. I returned to the styling chair and pulled out the color swatch book from the center drawer of the antique secretary desk that was my workstation. The desk was masterfully hand-carved in the 1870's (the reconstruction period after the Civil War) out of solid crotch mahogany. A hammered copper medallion of George Washington's face was inlaid on the inner side of the left-front dove-tailed drawer. It was a private emblem of patriotism I treasured and no one else noticed. Many clients complimented my use of an antique desk instead of institutional salon furniture. Tara was not at all impressed by the desk; she barely noticed anything beyond the point of her own chin. She continued to stare glumly at herself in the mirror while chewing her cuticles. Her chin quivered slightly. The purplish half-circles beneath her lower lash-lines were swollen, and her facial muscles twitched involuntarily.

"OK," I said, taking a deep breath to steady myself. "According to my notes, we used bleach the very first time I highlighted your hair. We were trying to match what someone else had done before. You later asked not to use bleach anymore because you wanted to use pigment instead to keep it from getting too light."

I looked Tara in the eye but got no response.

My recitation continued, "Then each consecutive appointment since, we have used a combination of high-lift blonde and medium blonde for a more natural blend on your fine hair. And we have also added some gentle lowlights to tone down the bleached ends. Everything seems to be growing out very nicely. It's well-blended without a prominent line of demarcation." I reported the facts as I knew them. "And I have a notation that you do not at all like cool-based blondes, only warm blondes."

Judgement

    Tara did not offer any assistance with the consultation. Her chin quivered even more noticeably. She resumed bending sideways while grabbing frantically at the length of her hair, attempting to fluff it mechanically. She stared at herself in the mirror with a severely angular frown and squinted eyes. I did not mention my notes where I wrote that Tara's hair clearly exhibited signs of chronic hair pulling because significant patches had been yanked out at the root or snapped off in emotional fits. However, after having worked with Tara for the past two years, I helped bring her hair back into a healthier state. Her gentle layers had regained shine and elasticity that softened the harshness of her nervous face.

    "I don't know the first thing about hair color!" Tara blurted out. "Every other place I've ever gone, all I do is sit down and they make me blonde!"

    "Why are you frustrated?" I asked gently.

    "Nobody else ever asks me all these questions!" Tara shouted. Large wet glossy pools filling the orbs of her eyes, making them glow with the reflection of the shop lights facing her.

    "I ask questions so that I can better understand how to help you," I replied.

    "I don't know!" Tara shrieked as she rocked back and forth in the styling chair, slapping at her abdomen.

    "Well," I continued cautiously, taking three steps backward to allow her plenty of room, "according to my notes, you have been pretty happy with the colors that we have used thus far. And your hair grows out just fine without harsh contrast. It looks lovely and very natural. No horrible grow-out, even after three months." I stood at the far corner of the desk, holding the swatch book as a protective shield between myself and the styling chair. "You don't want bleach, and you don't like cool blondes, and you don't want me to use the same colors I have used before which are warm blondes. So…can you point to any of these color swatches that you <u>do</u> like?"

    "I don't know! I don't know!" Tara yelled out while starting to hyperventilate. "I don't know if I can do this right now!"

    "You have asked to book two-and-a-half hours of my time. That's not fair," I said calmly.

The Climate of Truth

"Don't you understand! I have anxiety! I never leave the house! With this virus thing going on, I'm really afraid to be here!" Streams of snot began to flow from Tara's nose as tears flowed freely down both sides of her face.

"I've been very patient with you," I replied. "And I have been very supportive. I'm just standing here trying to figure out how to help you with your hair color. I'm sorry that you're not feeling very well at the moment. I think we are all worried about the whole virus thing. But whatever this is, whatever is happening with you right now -- it has nothing to do with me."

"Who are you, MR. PERFECT!? Mr. 'I never have a bad day!' Mr. 'everything's wonderful every day of your life!'"

I glanced at the clock overhead and realized Tara had already blown through twenty minutes of her appointment time as usual. "Well, let's see, maybe we can focus on bringing the color down a few notches. Let's just talk about picking two colors that you like from this swatch book so we can get something accomplished here for you today. That would really help to make you feel better."

"I just want to sit here and relax! I come here to relax, and you just won't let me do that! I don't get it! Nobody else has ever treated me like this before!" Tara cried as she was in full blown nuclear meltdown mode.

At that moment, I realized that Tara had probably worked herself up to the point of being escorted out of several other salons in town before she came into my life. "OK then," I said as I quickly and adeptly removed the color cape and towel from around Tara's neck in a sweeping motion while still maintaining a separation distance of at least three feet. "I don't need to be standing here while you yell at me. That is not productive, and you don't seem to be able to let me help you. So now it's time for you to gather your things and leave."

Tara leapt out of the chair and gasped. "I'M REALLY TRYING TO BE NICE TO YOU!"

There were many snappy retorts that sped through my mind in that instant, such as, 'if this is you trying to be nice, I'd hate to see your full-on bitch mode.' But I caught a look of desperate concern on Irma's face with her ears drawn straight back against the top of her head. It was the same fearful look she had on the Fourth of July with fireworks blowing up the sky. I knew it wouldn't be good to escalate

Judgement

the tensions beyond what was necessary to protect the shop. It wouldn't be good for Irma, especially.

"Please just gather your things and go," I said. I spread my arms wide to usher Tara toward her coat hanging on the rack at the front door. Tara looked about the shop as if she were searching for something to smash -- the vase of sunflowers on the front desk, the crystal water fountain, or maybe she would knock over the hand hewn cherrywood magazine rack that I designed many years ago. Copies of *"Martha Stewart," "Oprah," "Time"* and *"People"* magazines could go flying.

I was able to corral Tara toward the front door, where she cowered in the corner. She faced the wall while she donned her coat, sniffling and choking on her runny nose. I knew to avoid a threatening posture by leaving her plenty of room to exit without blocking her path. I opened the front door and took a few steps backward. When Tara finally turned toward the door with vibrantly florid body shivers and twitches, I interjected a final comment.

"Please hear me," I said while raising the palm of my hand in a "stop" gesture. "Please do not return here again."

Tara's face instantly exploded in snapping fangs with her head shaking from side to side, her long blonde (and beautifully colored) layers slashing the air and hitting her face as if she were caught in a slow-motion windstorm.

"Just shut up! You just shut up!" she bellowed, her fists raised toward her chin.

"No," I said gently with my palm raised again, "You need to hear me. You can't come back here again."

"Just shut up! You shut up Mr. Perfect! Ahhhhhhhhhhh!" she howled.

With my arms spread wide, I ushered Tara out the front door and onto the porch as her banshee attack continued. Directly across the street on the opposite corner, a group of three male contractors were busy operating a jackhammer to remove an old cement slab from the neighbor's front stoop. Tara's tirade was loud enough to be heard over the pummeling jackhammer. All three of the men stopped their work as they stood in amazement to watch her. She stomped the full length of the porch toward her car parked in the lot at the rear of the house. The three contractors offered a sincere long-distance look

The Climate of Truth

of general sympathy in my direction. I responded with a shrug of my shoulders. The three contractors all nodded in agreement as Tara sped off in her oversized sport utility vehicle with mudflaps that bore the chrome-plated silhouette of the nude female form. What looked like two stainless steel testicles swung violently in nylon sacks from the trailer hitch on the back end of the vehicle. I wondered if the roads would be safe for other drivers that afternoon but realized it was useless to contemplate such things.

Without wasting anymore time, I shut the front door, drew the letters "CXL" across Tara's name on my schedule book, wrote the phrase *"Never Book Again"* on her client card, and immediately filed it away in the closet after describing her tirade in shorthand. I then went to the bathroom to grab a can of air freshener, and generously sprayed the scent of cinnamon and apples, thinking it would dispel the contrails Tara left in her wake.

I looked at Irma. "I think we better smudge the shop with sage tonight. What do you think, pookie?"

Irma sneezed in acknowledgement. Or maybe she sneezed because of the spicey air freshener.

"Do you wanna go outside and cleanse? Go do a nice big pee to release all that nonsense?" I asked the bright-eyed red and white Pembroke lass.

Irma barked and headed straight for the patio door. I let her out, and she barked all the way down the stairs. She was in search of wayward squirrels that she did not allow on her patio. I followed her down to get some fresh air and let the sunshine on my face. It was difficult to regroup after such a flagrant bout of negativity.

After a few minutes, Irma came to where I was standing, and licked my hand. I smiled at her and said, "Aren't people fun, Boo-boo-doo? Well, at least now we can have a nice long lunch! You want some cookies?"

Irma cocked her head to one side as she smiled and sprang into action at the mention of the word "cookies." She trotted jubilantly up the patio stairs (a difficult feat for a girl with stubby legs) and headed straight for the kitchen to await her treat. She stood looking directly at the kitchen cabinet that housed her plentiful stash of doggie snacks. Peanut butter and chicken with rice cookies were her absolute favorites, unless there were turkey jerky bites or lamby-tots. It always

Judgement

amazed me that Irma never once attempted to nose the cabinet open, though she was perfectly capable of doing so.

No matter how hard I tried, I couldn't help but take the altercation with Tara personally, as if I was the sole cause of her pain. I replayed the scene of Tara's meltdown over and over in my head, wondering if I could have handled it any differently for a better outcome. I questioned whether I had behaved inappropriately toward her. I could have given in to a baser nature. As written in Alexandre Dumas' story, *"The Woman with the Velvet Necklace,"* I could have eviscerated Tara with a razor tongue so sharp that that her head could have been severed from her neck and fallen to the floor. The image of the severed head intrigued me until the guilt set in. It was difficult for me to fathom how I was the one to pay the steepest price for an unprovoked client meltdown -- physically, emotionally, and financially.

"I wonder if this is the new normal with this virus thing?" I asked Irma, as she licked her lips after having devoured her snack. "I wonder if fear is going to make people crazy. What do you think, Irma dog?"

Ironically, I remembered two clients who preceded Tara that day. I told them both that I was lucky my shop was functioning so well and that I had so many wonderful, quality clients. It was as if Tara was determined to test my resolve when I least expected it, as if the universe sent her specifically to challenge my faith in good fortune.

Those contemplations kept me awake for four straight nights. I hated to be tested. Because, inherently, all tests posit two distinct outcomes – success or failure. Fighting the war of duality always proved to be a real bummer.

Staring at the ceiling on those four sleepless nights, I contemplated how it was even possible for Tara and her husband to be missionaries when she couldn't leave the house. I remembered that she told me they used chatrooms and webcams to preach their beliefs all around the world. She explained to me that all baptized members of the *Jehovah's Witnesses* were considered to be ordained ministers, and they all became missionaries who worked to share their beliefs with outsiders. And then I realized that Tara had not attempted to proselytize me.

I sat up in bed in the middle of the night, wondering if Tara's diatribe had less to do with her anxiety, and more to do with bigotry.

The Climate of Truth

I went straight to the computer to do a 2:00am dive into the question and came across the following answer: *"Jehovah's Witnesses do not hate homosexuals; they hate the practice of homosexuality. Jehovah's Witnesses think that homosexuals are in need of salvation, just like everyone else on the planet. Homosexuals can choose to change their lifestyle and live God's way."*

Since it was not my practice to openly discuss my lifestyle with hostile clients, the subject of homosexuality did not come up in conversation with Tara. Nevertheless, it seemed to me that most observant people would have been able to determine my orientation without having to dig too deep. When I was younger, I was mortified about being outed. But at the age of 58, I attained the state of being where I didn't advertise, but I couldn't hide my identity. I stared at the computer screen, reading what others preached about who and what I was. It was enough to keep me from sleeping the rest of the night.

❖

On March 16, 2020, Canada closed all borders to the US. The state of Washington had 904 confirmed COVID cases, more than double the tally from five days earlier. There had already been 48 deaths, most of them from nursing homes in the Seattle area. State officials told the public to assume that everyone had been exposed and was, therefore, potentially infected.

A term that became commonplace at the time was the phrase "flatten the curve," which referred to the various safety precautions that were implemented (lockdowns, social distancing, and mask wearing). They were intended to keep people apart, thereby lessening the degree of exposure to the virus and the rate of infection. "Flattening the curve" of infection was the goal used to prevent hospitals from being overrun by a surge of COVID patients. At first, the public adhered to the safety protocols, and the spread of disease was slowed. But the public soon grew weary of confinement and the economic disaster it was causing. Little did we know at the time that safety protocols would become flashpoints of controversy that would eventually lead to armed insurrection.

Also on March 16, the state of New York (which became the early American epicenter of infection) reported 950 cases. By the time New

Judgement

York went into lockdown exactly one week later, more than 12,000 cases were reported, compared to more than 2,200 cases in Washington state. The shocking New York surge was later determined to have been caused by travelers arriving from Europe; COVID hopped international flights from Asia to Europe, and then jumped on connecting flights to New York, home to some of the busiest airports in the world.

European outbreaks occurred about two weeks ahead of the American timeline. For example, the nationwide lockdown in Italy went into effect on March 9, 2020. By the time New York followed suit on March 23, Italy had surpassed 56,000 cases and the hospitals were overrun, unable to handle the COVID surge. Patients died in the hallways of Italian hospitals without receiving care.

"All of us have to recognize for the next several weeks, normal is not in our game plan," the Governor of Washington said. He compared the COVID crisis to battles in World War II. "This is bigger than all of us," he said. The Governor used emergency powers to shutter all non-essential businesses and to ban social gatherings of 50 or more people. Eventually, all social gatherings were banned. The business closures were initially planned through the end of March, but would be extended for nearly three full months.

Too afraid to go to the grocery store alone, a friend agreed to accompany me. We had to make sure we had ample food stored for the lockdown. Unfortunately, everyone in the region had the same idea, and the store was packed with terrified people who stared at each other with suspicion. It was the first time I wore a mask in public. My mask was custom sewn for me by another friend, Tiffy. It was stuffed so full of filter papers that I nearly suffocated. The mask was also so tight that my ears were nearly ripped off both sides of my head.

"There ain't nothing gonna get through that mask, Mike! Not a single spore!" Tiffy said.

I wore vinyl gloves and goggles to go shopping and carried portable packs of hand sanitizer. There was so much fear in the air that I'm sure it wilted the lettuce in the produce section. Having survived my first COVID shopping experience with a friend by my side, I figured I could handle solo shopping from then on.

I remember seeing a married couple at the grocery store that day. Both wore matching black T-shirts with white lettering. They were

The Climate of Truth

both heavy-set and defiant, marching through the store with their chins jutted toward the ceiling as they tossed all manner of goods into their caravan of four grocery carts. They were both maskless. It was odd to see them cram at least ten multi-packs of toilet paper into their carts. Their matching T-shirts read: *"Recall Governor Inslee! He's NON-ESSENTIAL!"* It was because of people like that couple that toilet paper disappeared from store shelves for months on end. It was an infestation of angry hoarders.

❖

The problem in my region was the public's impression that emergency lockdowns were intended only to take place in Seattle, the epicenter of the outbreak in Washington state. The state government never contacted businesses directly about the lockdown, though it had the means to do so. State emergency proclamations were confusing, and accounts in the media provided conflicting information. The closure of non-essential businesses took effect at midnight on March 17, 2020, but it took a whole extra day for me to realize that hair salons in my region were included in the state-wide lockdown. I opened for business as usual on March 18 at 9:00am. Neither I nor my clients were aware that my shop was supposed to have been shuttered that morning. Only essential businesses, such as grocery stores, pharmacies, banks, and hardware stores were supposed to remain open.

I was still dragging from four sleepless nights because of the dust-up with Tara. I was a little punch-drunk. March 18, however, would prove to be another momentous day in the annals of my COVID journey. It was not only the day my business went into lockdown, it was also the day that Dylan was coming for his second haircut.

Dylan was tall and trim, solidly built but not lanky, bespectacled in tasteful frames, with salt and pepper hair. He was 49 years old. The instructions from his first haircut were seared into my memory; his hair should never feel the touch of clippers. Scissor cutting only for that elegant and well-dressed professional male specimen who wore khaki trousers and brown soled shoes with the stitched outline around the edge, not a scuffmark to be seen. He preferred just the right amount of styling paste and a tousled blow-dry with the sides brushed gently forward toward his face.

Judgement

The only thing out of place about Dylan was a round, red, glass bauble that hung from a leather strap around his neck. The glowing pendant housed a white crystalized substance, which he later identified as a portion of the cremated remains of his deceased husband. I shuddered but tried not to show it. And then I got goosebumps, because I'd learned from the red bauble that Dylan was not only the marrying kind, but he appeared to be unattached and available.

Dylan worked for city government in the Human Resources department, meaning he could size up anyone's personality in mere seconds without registering his findings anywhere on his face. He was a human super-computer devoted to instantaneous psychological, sociological, and pathological analyses of any living, breathing mass of muscle and bone with a brain and a subconscious. I found this attribute to be thrilling, frightening, and annoying all at the same time. But he was my type, and that seemed to dispel my concerns over his profession.

During the first haircut with Dylan four weeks before, the banter was effortless and nearly giddy. Irma seemed to give the "two paws up" look of approval when I telepathically asked for her opinion of the new man in the styling chair. This communication was achieved through interpretation of her specific eyebrow movements and the trajectory of her tail wag.

On the date of Dylan's even more important second haircut, I arranged for him to arrive early in order to be able to spend more time with him. This made me apprehensive, but in a good way -- a way that I hadn't felt in quite a long time. The shop bell rang, and Dylan entered, wearing a genuine smile. His eagle eyes were so expressively focused on me that I worried he would notice the tremble in my hands caused by nerves. I could feel the tips of my ears turn red with searing heat. I caught his gaze in the reflection of the mirror as I dusted the hair clippings from the back of a woman's neck who was about to leave.

Dylan winked at me as he sat in a lobby chair to wait his turn. My face grew flush with a hot flash to match the redness of my ears. I quickly used the technique of breathing to the count of ten in order to calm myself. The specter of COVID was wholly absent from my conscious awareness, as if I were under a spell.

The Climate of Truth

"Hello Miss Irma," Dylan called out to my Corgi. She came immediately to him and nudged his open hand with her nose in welcome. "She likes me," he announced. "She really likes me!"

"You do a great Sally Field," I said, laughing.

"Any man who's worth his salt can do Sally Field," he declared.

"Good to see you again, Dylan," I said, trying to portray clinical professionalism. "But you have to know that Irma is expecting you to pet her. She doesn't work for free."

"My apologies, Miss Irma," Dylan said as he caressed the top of her head.

"Careful not to touch her ears," I warned.

"Yes, I remember, Mike. You told me the last time."

After the lady client exited the shop, I quickly neatened my workstation and then invited Dylan to the shampoo bowl.

"Come on over! How did your first haircut work out?" I asked, hands clasped in front of me.

"Perfect. Couldn't ask for better. Do it again," he said with another wide smile.

"It's hard to be perfect twice in a row," I said coyly.

"Not according to your reviews," Dylan countered, raising his eyebrows invitingly.

"Please undo your top button," I instructed with a poker face.

"But it's only the second date!"

"So I can tuck your collar," I said, ignoring the innuendo.

Dylan quickly undid the button with another wink. I motioned him to sit in the shampoo chair, tucked and draped his collar with a towel, leaned him back into the sink, and began to test the water for warmth. In his reclined position, I could see the outline of a tattoo peeking out from the opening in his collar as it slightly exposed his chest.

"Oooooo. What's your tattoo about?" I asked, looking further than maybe I should have. "May I reach to see more of it?"

"Sure," Dylan said, "but it's not a very good tattoo."

Judgement

I discreetly pulled the fabric of Dylan's shirt aside to reveal more of the ink amidst a swath of fine chest hair. A strong pulse constricted my throat, nearly causing me to choke. "It's a lion," I said meekly. "Reminds me of *'Aslan'* from C.S. Lewis, *'The Lion, the Witch and the Wardrobe.'"

"Nobody gets that. How did you get that!" Dylan exclaimed. "That's exactly what it's supposed to be, but it's too blah I think."

"Are you a Leo?"

"No, I'm a Cancer," Dylan replied.

"Thank goodness you're not a Leo. That would be too tough on a Capricorn like me. Cappies are upside down and backwards Cancers. Your inside is my outside and vice versa."

Dylan laughed loudly, nearly bouncing his head out of the sink.

"Keep it clean, Mister!" I warned jokingly. "Being six months apart, Capricorns and Cancers make the best of friends. I have a lot of friends who are Cancers."

"Do you now? What a line!"

"That's not a line," I protested. "It's in the music of the spheres."

"Nobody has ever said right off the bat, 'hey, that's *'Aslan!'*"

"Well, I could tell right away. I am an artist, you know…And it wouldn't take a lot to make that tattoo pop better. A little contrast here and there, deepen the shadows. I could take a photo, mock it up, you could take it to someone for a retouch. To make you feel better. And *'Aslan'* could leap right out of your shirt. It would be fierce!"

"Could he now?" Dylan said with a subtle grin.

I took my time massaging Dylan's scalp under the warm water as he relaxed his neck. He closed his eyes. I studied his face as I ran my fingers through his hair, until I realized my shameless reenactment of Warren Beatty's scene of sudsy seduction in the classic film, *"Shampoo."* I turned off the water nozzle and dabbed Dylan's head with a towel. It would be the last time I gazed romantically upon anyone's face during COVID.

The two of us returned to the styling chair where the haircut commenced. I draped Dylan in a striped cutting cape and sprayed some leave-in conditioner into his hair to make the comb glide better

The Climate of Truth

through the cut. We looked at each other now and then in the mirror, something I never really did as a matter of practice. My heart began to race.

The magical moment was interrupted by the shop doorbell. As I turned my head to peer at the video monitor, my mood crashed directly into PTSD sensations when I saw the image of a familiar face. It was Tara.

"I need to speak with you!" she squawked over the intercom.

I froze, not knowing what to do next. Then Tara walked sideways toward the front window and stared at me through the glass. We were only a few feet apart. I could feel my chest tighten with a wheeze. I couldn't look toward Dylan, who, with his expert analytical abilities, could instantly have quantified the "Uh-oh!" pheromones emanating from my aura.

"I'm busy right now," I said to Tara through the glass. I couldn't believe that particular woman would show up at that specific moment in time, on that important day of Dylan's second haircut, after I had clearly banned her from my shop.

"I'll come back later!" she yelled through the glass.

The sickening idea of her returning yet again forced me to excuse myself from Dylan's haircut. I headed toward the front door of the shop, opened it slowly, and stepped out onto the porch. Thankfully, I was out of Dylan's line of sight.

"I think you'd be more comfortable talking privately out here," I said cryptically. "How can I help you?" I quickly shut the door behind me so it would lock, just in case things were to get out of hand.

There was a long moment of silence as Tara collected her thoughts. "I just wanted to apologize for my behavior last week," Tara said with pursed lips.

That was not the opening volley I expected in the exchange. She stood in front of me looking as if she was in physical pain. Her shoulders were hunched forward. Her handbag hung like a barbell from her stiff fingers that were clasped in front of her.

"I'm a *Jehovah's Witness*," Tara announced. "And we always counsel our congregants not to lash out at other people. I am sorry that I raged at you."

Judgement

I stood very still, thinking the word "rage" was an accurate representation of her behavior the week before. It was much like another situation I witnessed on the freeway once, when a man was wildly tailgating a four-by-four truck while waving a hammer out the driver's side window, yelling profanities at the driver of the truck ahead of him. The hammer went flying into the back window of the truck, smashing the glass. A lot of honking and swerving occurred. Road rage. Salon rage. Same animal.

"I am very sorry that I raged at you," Tara repeated. "I should never have done that. It wasn't right."

I noticed Tara's face was eerily still. Her eyes were clear and fixed on mine. Her breathing was steady. Her hair was neatly styled and lovely even though she hadn't had it recolored elsewhere yet. I had never seen her style her own hair before, and it still looked good despite the grow-out. I took comfort in looking at the quality of my work in her tresses.

But there was something not quite right about this situation. It wasn't the same face that I witnessed during the nuclear meltdown five days before. She presented an entirely different personality. Perhaps she finally took her meds. But something was off. It bothered me that our chat resembled a twelve-step program from *Alcoholics Anonymous*. It seemed that I was Tara's current challenge, her attempt at making amends according to an outline.

Tara continued, "You have taken excellent care of my hair. You do really good work, and I wanted you to know that. Especially at a time like this when the world looks like it's coming to an end and people are going to die."

Stunned, I answered her indignation the only way I thought possible. "I don't believe in the end of the world."

"You can choose not to believe all you want, but you may come to a different understanding when bodies start dropping. That's how it's written in scripture. Those are God's words, not mine. But beyond all that, I want you know that I do care about you, more than you can possibly understand. I care about you because it is God's commandment that I do. I keep you in my heart."

I was afraid she was gearing up for a handshake, or worse yet, a hug. But then it happened -- a squint of her blue eyes. She narrowed

The Climate of Truth

her fixed gaze upon me where a glimmer of mean girl escaped with her next words.

"Maybe we just don't <u>MESH</u> very well," she said coolly, pursing her lips even tighter. "Maybe that's why things went the way they did last week."

The wind gently blew her bangs across her forehead as her long layers caressed the corners of her mouth. With the unsettling tone of her voice, I realized her "apology" was probably the result of her husband's admonishment. I wondered if she was forced to repeat such apologies several times before as a show of penance for her sins and to confirm obedience to her Kingdom Hall. I couldn't help but ask myself how an anxiety ridden, manic-depressive, agoraphobic person like her could successfully counsel, comfort, and convert others to her way of thinking as a missionary. I couldn't find a viable answer for that one.

There were all kinds of things I wanted to say to Tara on the front porch in that moment. But in my experience, when you really want to rattle off a litany of grievances, it's usually best to remain mute. I concluded that Tara didn't really want to apologize. She truly thought I had harmed her. Tara interrupted my private mental soliloquy by reaching into her purse. My heart skipped a beat because I thought she might have pulled a gun. Instead, she fished out an envelope and handed it to me.

"I brought this for you. I think you should look it over," she said, looking down at her toes rather than at me.

I opened a tri-folded letter that read in print: *"I am one of Jehovah's Witnesses, and I am reaching out to invite you and your family to join us for the memorial of Jesus's death. The night before he died, Jesus asked his followers to commemorate his sacrifice, he said, 'Keep doing this in remembrance of me.' (Luke 22:19) At this meeting, you will find out why his sacrifice was so important and how his promises affect you. This event will be held on Sunday, March 28 at 7:30pm. I hope that you will join us! Sincerely, Tara."*

Inside the folded letter was a screed, the front of which featured a colored caricature of Jesus with his hands beckoning the reader. The screed included a scan code to watch an online video entitled *"Why Did Jesus Die?"* The narration of the animated video began:

Judgement

"Billions of people have died throughout history. But the death of one person stands alone. That of Jesus Christ. Why did he die? Did his death have a purpose? To find the answer, we need to go back to the beginning of human history. The Bible explains that God created the man, Adam, perfect, without sin. He was free to eat from all the trees in the Garden of Eden, except one. God gave the simple command not to eat from that particular tree. This tree symbolized God's right to set the standards of good and bad. As long as Adam remained obedient to Jehovah, he had the prospect of living forever on a paradise Earth..." I had no desire to learn what the *Jehovah's Witnesses* thought about Eve.

As a student of art, I had a much different interpretation of the story of Adam and Eve. It took me 25 years to get there, but I finally flew the 13 hours to Rome. Within an hour of landing, I hailed a cab straight to the Vatican where I met a private tour guide. My exhaustion wouldn't stop me. The guide took me to a separate entrance where we bypassed the thousands of people waiting in line. We entered a long hallway decorated with painted maps of the world, jammed shoulder to shoulder with other tourists, all of us waiting to enter the Sistine Chapel. We stood upon mosaics that were cannibalized from the massive Colosseum. It was the first time I heard the Colosseum was in ruin because it had been deconstructed to build the Vatican.

I held my breath as I entered the Sistine Chapel, a place I had wanted to visit ever since I was a child. I was dumbfounded by the fact that one of the most famous spots on planet Earth was so small. Like everyone else jammed into that compact space, I tilted my head back to view the frescoes on the ceiling. I felt my breath escape my throat with a rush of awe. I was jarred by an ominous bass voice that bellowed like *"Jabba the Hut"* in *"Star Wars," "Nooooooo Foto!"*

Goosebumps flared all over my body the second my eyes took in the central panel, *"The Creation of Adam."* God's outstretched finger nearly touched the fingertip of Adam, the firstborn. To me, the panel depicted an ancient ritual, when the *Wisdom of Truth* was transmitted through the Divine spark of life through God's finger -- an act the Hindu mystics referred to as *shaktipat*, when the spiritual teacher initiates the student with a zap of conscious self-awareness. I understood the story of Adam and Eve to be more than just two people standing alone in a garden. To me, it was about the Genesis of two distinct races of ancient humans.

The Climate of Truth

Along with a few renegade cardinals and friends, Michelangelo formed a secret society known as the *Spiritulali*. Though the *Spirituali* were not successful in their goal to reform the teachings of the Roman Catholic Church, the Sistine Chapel frescoes remained the primary evidence of their liberal rebellion. Michelangelo, among other artists of the Italian Renaissance, attempted to dispel the archaic myth that made independent thought the root of evil and the downfall of the righteous. Within the Sistine Chapel frescoes, he depicted equality among races, equality between men and women, and the celebration of homosexuality, ideas steadfastly labelled as heresy by the church. However, Michelangelo had become so famous that the cardinals who opposed him dared not to destroy his frescoes. They did, however, hire other painters to cover several of Michelangelo's nude characters with fabric and loose-fitting underpants because they complained the frescoes were too risqué for the church to abide. But how would they explain the creation of Adam and Eve without nudity?

I was slammed back into reality on my front porch as Tara cleared her throat with a sound of agitation. It was then that I remembered the Vatican had just been closed to the world when a priest became infected with COVID. There were 12 cases at the Vatican in the first wave of infection that struck Italy. The Pope became ill as well, but the world was told he just had a cold. I thought the Pope was a rockstar when he said, "If a person is gay and seeks God and has good will, who am I to judge?"

"Why are you handing this to me?" I asked Tara, puzzled by the trifold screed entitled *"Why did Jesus Die?"*

"Because the plague is among us," she said sullenly. "The virus is intentional. Not accidental. It is God's judgement upon the sinners of this world. There is a penalty for sin. *'For the wages of sin is death.'* It will be very interesting to see who lives and who dies from this plague, because there is no stopping it. The virus will show us who is saved…I know what you are, Mike. You may think of me as just a dumb blonde, but I saw you through the window with the other man in your chair. You have eaten the forbidden fruit, and it is not what God intended. If you don't want to suffer eternal death in a place called Hell, then I hope you will join us. It is in your best interest to come."

Judgement

After hearing Tara's words, I had a sort of out-of-body experience. My mind was instantly transported to a job where I worked on the 99th floor of the *World Trade Center* in Manhattan. In my twenties, I was an administrative assistant in the education and training department for a national insurance corporation. I had two bosses, one a Jewess, the other a *Jehovah's Witness* who was overly fond of accordion pleated skirts. Directly outside the window of our office, across the East River and beside the Brooklyn Bridge, the *Watchtower Building* could be seen below. It was the world headquarters for the *Jehovah's Witnesses*, where they designed screeds like the one Tara had just handed me.

My boyfriend at the time stopped by the office one day to take me out to lunch. From then on, my accordion skirted boss followed me around with a contemptuous can of *Lysol* and a pair of rubber gloves. She sprayed everything I touched because she was certain I was going to spread AIDS around the office.

One of the hijacked planes on 9-11 soared right into the 99th floor and slammed into a sea of claims adjusters as well as the education and training department where my desk once sat. The national insurance company I worked for at the time lost more workers that day than any other company in the twin towers. I wondered if my accordion skirted boss had enough time to calibrate her sins before she was incinerated.

My attention snapped back to Tara standing in front of me, and the screed I was holding. I was careful not to register any emotion on my face. I thought to myself, "Nothing I say is going to make a hill of beans difference to her in any way. Just nod as if to say thanks, back up, take the keys out of your pocket, unlock the door, go inside and quickly lock the door behind you." And that's exactly what I did.

Tara left quietly without further incident. I never got an angry call from her missionary husband demanding to know why I made his wife cry at her ill-fated appointment. Tara never posted anything profoundly negative about my salon online. I didn't have to preserve all the security footage of Tara's meltdown in full bloom. In that situation, I knew that I avoided all kinds of unpleasantness by keeping my mouth shut. And most importantly, I knew I would never attend a religious event like the one advertised in Tara's trifold letter that was designed to make me hate myself.

The Climate of Truth

❖

When I reentered the shop and locked the front door, my mind was reeling. I couldn't speak, and I felt a bit dizzy. I dumped the trifold letter and the screed in the garbage can beside me. My ear caught the sound of a familiar song on the stereo that helped ground me back into reality. The soothing voice was John Lennon:

> *"Imagine there's no countries*
> *It isn't hard to do*
> *Nothin' to kill or die for*
> *And no religion, too*
> *Imagine all the people*
> *Livin' life in peace"*

It was as if John Lennon was the antidote to a venomous snake bite when I had only minutes to live.

"What was that all about?" Dylan asked, snatching me out of my paralysis.

I blushed with a pronounced hot flash of embarrassment. "Nothing really. I don't want to bore you."

"Bull!" Dylan quipped.

"You deal with all kinds of people in Human Resources. You know how it is."

"Just spill it," he insisted. "You know, Capricorns and Cancers make the best of friends. So lay it on me, <u>friend</u>."

"Jeeze. That's rich."

"You better not be distracted," Dylan said. "I'll hold a grudge if you screw up my haircut!" He stared at me as though he might storm out of the shop.

I was instantly horrified, but he started to laugh uproariously. "You should see the look on your face right now!" he hollered.

"What's happening?" I said, thoroughly confused.

"You think I'm serious?" he shouted.

"I dunno. I can't figure you out."

Judgement

"Lighten up," Dylan said with a smile. "What's the difference between a good haircut and a bad haircut?"

"According to Lily Tomlin in '*Search for Intelligent Signs in the Universe*'…"

"You saw it on Broadway?" Dylan interrupted.

"Absolutely."

"Every self-respecting homosexual has made the pilgrimage to Broadway to see Lily," he said. "So, you already know the answer. The difference between a good haircut and a bad haircut is…?"

"Only two weeks," I said, completing Dylan's thought. "Don't you know it's not kosher to dis a stylist with scissors in his hand?"

"I like to live dangerously," Dylan said with yet another wink.

As I continued the haircut, I poured out the wretched story of Tara and her alleged apology. Dylan offered that, according to the tenets of her faith, God wouldn't let Tara enter Heaven if she had harmed someone and hadn't made amends. In his opinion, Tara's apology was geared toward her own salvation at the moment of judgement because she thought the world was coming to an end with COVID.

"Gross," I said.

"But predictable," Dylan said warmly. "To each their own."

"I'd rather eat socks," I said with a smirk.

Just then, a cheesy old song came on the stereo that caught Dylan's attention.

"Rumor had it that Tom Jones used to stuff socks down his pants to look more impressive when he sang this song," he said.

"What?"

"I'm surprised that you, a fellow queer, don't know that famous factoid!" Dylan jiggled in the styling chair as he crooned along with Tom Jones:

The Climate of Truth

*"Pussycat, pussycat, you're delicious
And if my wishes can all come true
I'll soon be kissing your sweet little pussycat lips"*

I noticed more tattoo ink poking out from beneath Dylan's left shirt sleeve. He was surprised to hear me easily identify the symbol of the tree of life, the symbol of the human soul, and the symbol of the alchemic heart that adorned the cover of Kahlil Gibran's *The Prophet.* All three symbols were emblazoned on his inner forearm in geometric progression.

Dylan stared at me in the mirror. "You're quite the find," he said tenderly. "And you look handsome with your new haircut. Who cuts your hair?"

"I do."

"How in the world do you do that?" he asked.

"Carefully," I said with a shy grin. I didn't mention that I hurriedly performed the haircut on myself the night before in preparation for his visit. I wanted to make a good second impression. I blushed with yet another hot flash.

"Maybe you can get my other Mike to quit shaving his eyebrows off with the clippers," Dylan said with a sigh. "You'll school him up, right?"

I stiffened, bewildered. "Your <u>other</u> Mike?" I repeated, gobsmacked. Suddenly, Dylan was uniquely oblivious for a man with supposed superpowers in personal observation.

"He's my very handsome fiancé. We're newly engaged…How funny is it that his name is also Mike!"

"Yeah, too funny. How about that." I felt like I had been slapped by a wet fish.

From then on, Dylan referred to this fiancé fellow as "my other Mike," a statement that induced a peculiar sensation of physical pain in me. Just when things were going so well, two perfectly suitable blokes were enjoying the ritual of a great haircut experience. The music was playing, the dog was smiling, the sun was shining on that beautiful March day, the birds were singing, the windchimes were tinkling in the breeze, I'd just spent an hour laughing at his jokes –

Judgement

and then Dylan had to go and blow a perfectly beautiful thing. Instantly, the image of Tara's vulgar scowl brought the dread of COVID back into my mind, as if she had somehow cursed me.

When alone contemplating my misfortunes, I stared at the sky (or the ceiling if it's in the way of the sky at the exact moment of tangible crisis) and demanded that God answer for the dysfunction of the fates, or destiny, or whoever it was that kept track of those kinds of things. It was neither right nor fair that my perfect match was otherwise engaged, literally. Thank God I didn't hear a classic 1977 lyric, or I would have bashed the stereo with my own fists. It was bad enough the song was playing in my head as if on cue:

*"Oh, it's sad to belong to someone else
When the right one comes along"*

Dylan and I, both lonely, shared the same city for quite a while but never found each other until it was too late. As Dylan explained, his first date with "my other Mike" lasted an incredible 14 insatiable, life-altering days in Michigan, after which "my other Mike" packed up his life and followed Dylan home to my town. They were already busy redecorating. In the scope of social reconnaissance, it was never a good sign when the redecorating stage ensued. My dream was crushed. I wondered why I bothered thinking about disastrous love triangles in the middle of the COVID storm anyway.

In the midst of my reverie, Dylan whistled like a coo-coo clock and gestured with his index finger, pointing it up at the ceiling and then bending it to the right. He stared at me intensely.

"What?" I asked, holding T-blade edging clippers in my hand.

Dylan repeated the gesture with the coo-coo whistle.

"I don't get it," I protested.

"I am a true-blue homosexual," Dylan proclaimed.

"So?" I shrugged.

"I am a trained box-watcher."

"A box-watcher?" I said, confused.

"Yes. A box-watcher," he said with a nod.

The Climate of Truth

"What the heck are you talking about?" I said.

"I was trained to observe…packages."

"At *UPS*?"

"Not exactly," Dylan said as he repeated the coo-coo whistle and the weird finger gesture.

"I don't understand!"

"Ahem," Dylan said as he cleared his throat. "Because Capricorns and Cancers make the best of friends, I am obliged to tell you that you might wanna fix that." He pointed down. "That's what friends are for."

"Fix what?"

"Look down," he insisted.

"What, did I drop something on the floor?"

"Oh, you're too cute," Dylan said. "Check your fly."

Right about then my blood pressure spiked into my ears. I turned my back to Dylan and zipped up my fly.

"You were watching my box?" I asked, frantically.

"Always and forever. I'd tell you if you had toilet paper stuck to your shoe or broccoli in your teeth. I'm that kind of friend."

"Great. I didn't do that on purpose you know! I hate it when a new pair of jeans has a loose zipper."

"Bet you tell that to all the boys," Dylan said with a grin.

"Stop it already. You're killing me here!" I said in a loud voice, waving the clippers.

"I thought I specifically told you that clippers were not supposed to touch my head."

"I'm not clippering your hair-hair. I'm just edging around the edges! If you don't edge around the edges, you'll look like a dork, neck fuzz and all."

"Alright then, I've got my eye on you," he said with a chuckle.

"And to think I was out there on the porch with that horrible woman, my fly hanging in the breeze! No wonder she hates me!" I

Judgement

said with a moan. "She thinks I'm a total perv. Some devil that might lure her husband to the dark side."

Dylan commended me for my composure. "I don't think I could have handled it any better," he said, placing his hand against my cheek to comfort me. His hand was warm to the touch. The intimacy startled me. That was the last time I remember being touched after COVID lockdown day.

❖

On the day my shop was shuttered, I received a frantic phone call from two of my favorite lady clients on a party line. They knew me for at least 25 years and found me to be solemnly single but hopeful in love. Nathalie and Sadie were a married couple who helped me move into my shop. After we addressed their fears of having bad hair for months to come because of the COVID lockdown, I relayed the story of Dylan. Both ladies insisted that I pray for divine intervention that would deliver Dylan into my waiting arms. Of course, I said it wouldn't be the right thing to do, bad karma and all. I explained that I couldn't handle being a homewrecker.

"It's a Jewish thing called guilt," I said to my gal pals.

"Hey, Jews don't have anything on us Catholic girls when it comes to guilt," Sadie said.

"'*Sexy Sadie, What a lady!*'" I sang. "The Beatles wrote that song about you, didn't they, Sadie my love!"

Both of my lady friends insisted that I should fight for Dylan's affections. "You're such a nice guy," Nathalie said. "Why are you still single?"

"Question of the century," I replied in exasperation. "There must be a good reason. It's just that nobody's told me yet."

"As soon as the government let us, we got our marriage license," Sadie said. "And we never know if it's going to stick. Trump's trying to reverse marriage equality as we speak!"

"We worry about you being all alone. Especially at a time like this," Nathalie said.

The Climate of Truth

"People are dying out there from the dreaded plague. It's not like anyone can really date right now," I said. "What was I thinking with this Dylan guy? How could I be such a dumbass in the middle of a catastrophe!"

"There is still hope for you, my dear hair husband," Nathalie said.

"Looks like I'm doomed to suffer through this COVID crap alone," I sighed.

"You have us," Sadie said quietly. "You will always be our family. We've got you!"

"Hey! I have an idea! You should write a book!" Nathalie shouted into the phone.

"Yeah! It will keep you busy during lockdown!" Sadie agreed.

"What else have you got to do?…'Alone, alone, all, all alone, alone in the deep blue sea,'" Nathalie said with a laugh.

"No! No! That's not the way it goes," Sadie insisted. "It's 'Alone, alone, all, all alone, alone on a wide, wide sea.' If you're gonna quote literature, do it right."

"Pardo-nay moi!" Nathalie said. "I like my version better! The point is, some sweet man out there will fall in love with you…eventually. Maybe when he reads your book!"

"Oh, come on! Who'd want to read it?" I countered.

"We would!" they said in unison.

"At the very least, it would be incredibly entertaining," Nathalie said. "And so juicy!"

"All the strange people you meet!" Sadie said.

"The stories you could tell!" Nathalie chimed in. "You can write all about us! Because you love us, right? And you think we're wonderful!"

"I remember the infamous words of Truman Capote," I said. "At least I <u>think</u> he said it. I've been looking for the quote for years, and I just can't find it anywhere. But I swear I heard him say it out loud, maybe on Johnny Carson all those years ago." I mustered the mush-mouthed, twangy voice of Truman Capote (that sounded a lot like the cartoon character *"Deputy Dawg"*): "If you don't want to be in my

Judgement

book, don't invite me to your party. Bowsy-wowsy-wowsy-woooooooo."

Main Street

❧

Originally, my Corgi was a surprise from friends of mine. I was very depressed at the time because my beloved Boston Bull Terrier, Archie, had been suffering with cancer. He'd had three operations to remove tumors the size of hard-boiled eggs from his underbelly. It was October, and I knew in my heart he was going to pass by Christmas. Knowing that Archie's end was near, my friends, without my knowledge or consent, took it upon themselves to go puppy shopping for me.

My landlady was sipping tea from a china cup while reading the newspaper. She accidentally knocked the cup from its saucer, causing tea to spill across the newsprint. The wet stain drew her attention to an advertisement for a litter of Corgis. Being the superstitious Irish type, she hollered, "It's a sign!" She remembered that I once befriended a baby Corgi while on a trip to Wales. My landlady then hijacked my housemates, and together they drove for several hours to meet a dog breeder. I was told the litter of Corgi pups had been born somewhere near the Canadian border.

I lived in a house I shared with four other people. I was alone when my cellphone rang.

"Where are you?" my landlady demanded.

"In my room, why?"

Main Street

"Come out to the driveway right away!" she said, as she quickly hung up on me.

I climbed the stairs from the basement and saw my housemate's car parked on a diagonal in the driveway with the headlights on. My landlady was sitting in the front passenger side of the car. The motor was running as I approached. The electric window rolled down on the passenger's side, and there was a red and white Corgi splayed across my landlady's chest. At four months old, the puppy's tongue was hanging out and she was panting with excitement.

"Look at the size of those feet!" my landlady said with a squeal, pointing to the Corgi's white-mittened paws. "Aren't they adorable!"

"Very cute," I said, wondering what was going on.

"Here!" my landlady said. "This is for you!" She handed the puppy to me through the car window.

"What!" I gasped.

"I raided Stanley's piggy bank, so you owe him $800." Stanley was my landlady's toy chocolate brown poodle.

Before I could say another word, my housemate's *Ford Taurus* quickly backed out of the driveway and sped off, leaving me with a hunk of Corgi in my arms. Everybody knew I was a "love at first sight" kind of guy when it came to dogs, so I was smitten on contact. I hauled the girl pup down the stairs and into my bedroom, where Archie was convalescing on my pillow. He growled once. The puppy growled once. My geriatric black cat could have cared less as he trotted through the room, thinking the puppy was just another piece of furniture. The goldfish wiggled and giggled in their tank as if to say hello. Uther, the Irish Wolfhound came bounding down the basement stairs, followed by Baby Elvis, the Border Collie – they belonged to my housemates upstairs. Both of the bigger dogs sniffed the puppy, then turned tail to run back upstairs. And that was that. A Corgi was officially part of the family.

I thought of a few names that seemed to suit the Corgi's face. "You look like you could be an Eydie, as in Eydie Gormé. Do you like Eydie?"

The puppy just sat there staring at me while panting. Archie looked on, unimpressed.

The Climate of Truth

"How about Katherine Zeta? Because you're Welsh, like Katherine Zeta Jones?"

Nothing happened with that one either.

A song came to mind about a famous redhead, Lynn Redgrave in the film *"Georgy Girl"* about the "Swinging 60's" in London. "*Georgy*" is tempted to walk into a hair salon to get a newfangled style. Once she sees the finished product on her head, she dashes out of the salon in a panic and runs through the streets until she finds a public restroom where she drenches her head in a sink full of water. "*Georgy*" preferred the "au naturel" look to the frou-frou she got at the salon. I sang my own version of the Academy Award winning title song from the film, written and performed by the Australian folk band, *The Seekers*. I danced around the room as I sang:

> *"Hey there, **'Corgi'** girl*
> *There's another **'Corgi'** deep inside*
> *Bring out all the love you hide and,*
> *Oh, what a change there'd be*
> *The world would see a new **'Corgi'** girl"*

"Do you like the name Georgy the Corgi, little one?" Both Archie and the puppy stared at me without moving a muscle. "Dang! You guys are a tough crowd tonight."

And then I remembered a famous redhead, Shirley MacLaine in a wonderful movie with Jack Lemon, *"Irma La Douce."* Irma with the green stockings sang:

> *"When lovers crowd the Seine*
> *Who wants to go again?*
> *They'll steal a kiss and then*
> *Irma La Douce will sing!"*

"Can you sing, little Corgi?" I tilted my head back and let out a howl.

Without hesitation, the puppy closed her eyes and tilted her head back to yodel.

Main Street

"What a good girl!" I cheered, patting her on the head. "Do you like the name Irma? Should we call you Irma after "*Irma La Douce*," because you're a redhead like Shirley MacLaine and because you're sweet? *'La Douce'* means 'the sweet one' you know."

To my amazement, the Corgi pup let out a little yip, and licked me quickly on the tip of my nose.

"We have a winner!" I said, prancing around the room some more.

I took Irma's first photo while she was standing next to Archie on top of my bed. Her radar ears were bigger than her head, and her tongue hung out of her mouth like ribboned candy. A few days later, it was Halloween, and I dressed Irma in a Merlin's cape and matching conical hat emblazoned with the moon and stars. I stood her on a dresser next to an electric jack-o-lantern and snapped her photo. The following year, I dressed her as a ladybug in a red and black polka-dot flamenco dress with wings and antennae on springs. The year after that, she was a pink damsel in distress with a veil across her face. From then on, Irma flat out refused to wear Halloween costumes.

❖

Above all else, Archie loved to play dominos at the family table every Friday night. He had his own chair, and his own rack of tiles. He wore a green visor like a card shark, and had his own plate of snacks. He literally reached his paws out to move the dominos around, and I helped him finalize his moves. He enjoyed receiving the applause earned as a domino champion. Irma was not allowed to play because it was Archie's special time.

Archie had trouble breathing on Christmas Eve. Scores of bright red, bulging tumors covered his underbelly. They sprouted overnight. We were both terrified. I called my landlady to tell her I had to take Archie to the vet.

"Tomorrow is Friday. He wants to play one more game of dominos. It's Christmas!" she insisted.

"No, he's suffering. It's time," I said. I could barely get the words out.

The Climate of Truth

My landlady sent over one of her expensive scarves to wrap the body. Alone, I held Archie while the vet administered the pink shot. Through the ceiling speaker in the vet's office, I heard *"Silent Night."* Archie was gone within seconds. I wrapped his pug-nosed face in the scarf, and crisscrossed the ends around his torso. The body was taken from me to be sent for cremation. When I left the vet's office, I collapsed in the parking lot, sobbing my guts out. It was one of the worst days of my life. But at least I had Irma to go home to. She sat by me and licked ice cream from my finger, and that helped.

Irma was the reason I became a solo hair stylist. Corgis are working dogs, and they go insane if they don't have a job to do. Irma went to work with me from the very first day that I had her. In all of her 13 ½ years, she never missed a single day of work. Neither did I. I was working with another woman in a two-person shop at the time. At first, my workmate was happy to accommodate a puppy. After a few days, she hated the idea, and told me I had to ditch the pup or leave. I chose the latter and established a one-man studio where my pup could come to work.

I registered my solo business as a corporation with the state, and Irma's pawprint was registered as the "director of entertainment." Her job was to tell jokes and laugh with all my clients, which she did with ease. As a herding dog, she barked whenever the timer went off, guided every client back and forth from the shampoo sink, and remembered every client who used the treatment room to have their eyebrows waxed. If Irma thought I spent too much time yacking, she would interrupt with her barks to demand payment, and then promptly ushered each client out the door. There was no question that Irma was a dedicated salon professional and that she wore the furry pants in the family.

❖

It was the first of July 2020, and everybody was wondering how bad the pandemic was going to get with the Fourth right around the corner. People were tense. The air was hot and muggy. A summer COVID surge had already ransacked some hospitals because people insisted on having raucous parties for Memorial Day. The states were arguing about when and how schools should be reopened because children were depressed and floundering without social interaction. Some states tried to reopen the schools in May, only to close days

Main Street

later when COVID filled the hallways. Teachers were understandably frightened about going back into the classroom, preferring to teach online instead. Several families sued universities for failing to allow their kids to play football, despite the fact that COVID cases were raging across college campuses.

Misinformation was being widely circulated in social media that the virus only infected the elderly and not young people. The data showed that 40% of all COVID cases were asymptomatic, meaning we were in the grip of a silent pandemic where victims had no idea the virus was being transmitted until several days later. Across the country, college students held COVID parties where they gathered in crowds with the specific intent to infect each other. They held betting pools where the jackpot was awarded to the first person infected. Health officials were testing sewer outflows to detect COVID infections when toilets were flushed in fraternity and sorority houses on college campuses. The caseload remained manageable in my area, which made a lot of people wrongly conclude that the pandemic was being blown out of proportion by the media.

When George Floyd, an unarmed black man, was cruelly murdered in broad daylight by a White police officer in Minneapolis on Memorial Day, violent protests erupted in cities all across the country. Businesses were vandalized and looted by angry mobs. Various buildings, including hotels, stores, and police precincts were torched. Thousands of people took to the streets in the middle of the pandemic to draw the world's attention to the racism that claimed so many lives of people of color in America. The rest of the world responded with simultaneous protest marches to show their solidarity with the cause. Millions of people were involved in the global demonstrations.

Economic analysis at the time revealed a deeply disturbing trend; whenever a person of color, like George Floyd, was killed by police and the case became a national media sensation, the American stock market experienced a steep increase in value. With his lack of empathy fully on display, Trump offered an unsettling eulogy for George Floyd on the day of his funeral: "Hopefully George is looking down right now and saying this is a great thing that's happening for our country. This is a great day for him. It's a great day for everybody." Trump's comments shifted awkwardly to claims that his administration had managed to gain economic superiority over China despite the pandemic, arguing the US economy was roaring back like

The Climate of Truth

a "rocket ship." Trump implied that George Floyd's death was a catalyst for record gains in the stock market. Analysts dubbed the phenomena "The Trump Bump."

The Trump administration did not take any steps to hear grievances from the various leaders of protest movements. There was no offer to problem solve in order to alleviate racial disparities in any way. Instead, the Trump administration loudly and repeatedly proclaimed there was absolutely no institutional racism in America, and insisted that law and order would be protected at all cost. Those pronouncements were described as "pouring gasoline on the fire" of civil rights. Especially when COVID cases hit Black people two and a half times more than White people, and people of color died more than twice as much and twice as fast as Whites.

❖

It was time for Irma's after-dinner walk in the neighborhood following a long and busy day at the shop. It was July 1st, around 8:00pm. I harnessed Irma, and we headed south two blocks, where she inspected the grassy corner next to a telephone pole. Irma was not much of a walker. As part of the queen's court, she automatically assumed her royal duties included sniffing and peeing on every blade of grass she encountered. The ritual could be somewhat tedious, so as a matter of course, I often used the time to call friends on my cellphone.

I happened to be speaking with my former housemate, Patty, who moved to San Francisco. I was facing the sunset at the time. One block west, I saw a white minivan waiting to turn left at a stop sign. The left turn signal was on. Through the back window of the minivan, I could see the driver's head swivel back and forth to check for cross traffic before turning into the intersection. The setting sun outlined the silhouette of the driver. Out of nowhere, a white *Jeep Grand Cherokee* smashed into the minivan at full force. The sound of the impact was deafening. The force of the crash spun the minivan completely around in the opposite direction, where it slammed into a black pickup parked at the curb. White crashed into black. The white *Jeep* then careened directly into the sharp corner of a three-foot cement retaining wall. The *Jeep* seemed to fold into itself from the force of the impact. Car alarms sounded off in the surrounding area, caused by the concussive noise.

Main Street

"What was that!" Patty shrieked into the phone.

"Oh God," I said. "It looks bad. I gotta go!"

"Call me back and let me know what happened," Patty insisted before she hung up.

"Come on Irma, we gotta go down there!" I said as calmly as I could, knowing my dog would not respond well to yelling. Spooked by the sound of the crash, Irma instantly planted all four paws in defiance, and morphed into 500 pounds of "no!"

"We have to go, Irma! It's our duty to help!" I pleaded. But Irma wouldn't budge. I had to bend down and scoop her 34 pounds into my arms in order to jog the block toward the scene. I held her against my chest for the entire encounter that unfolded.

As I approached, I could tell the airbags had deployed in both vehicles. Smoke was pouring out of the minivan's engine block. The driver, a White woman with her hair piled on top of her head into a messy bun, was already on her cellphone arguing with her insurance company. She wore a waitress uniform. She sat herself on the curb opposite the destruction and lit a cigarette to calm her nerves. She was holding her injured arm. She was in shock. As if we had known each other for eons, the White woman turned to me and said "My insurance company wants me to give them my social security number over the phone. That's jacked up isn't it! Should I give it to them?"

Irma turned her head to look at me. I felt her breath against my face. She wanted me to say something.

"They already have your social," I said. "No biggie. They're just trying to make sure you are who you say you are according to their records," I explained.

"Oh yeah, that makes sense," the waitress said. The muscles in her back relaxed a bit.

"Do you need an ambulance?" I asked.

"I'm fine. I'm OK. I'll be alright. My arm is killing me. I think it's broke, but I'll deal with it later," she said, her voice trailing off in frustration as she went back to conversing with the insurance company.

A large, dark brown van with tinted windows rounded the corner and pulled up right next to where I was standing. The

The Climate of Truth

windows of the van were painted in white letters: *"Black Lives Matter!"* and *"I Can't Breathe!"* Names of victims of alleged racist violence also covered the glass: *George Floyd, Breonna Taylor, Trayvon Martin, Eric Garner, Ahmaud Arbery, Michael Brown, Tamir Rice* – those were the names I could see from where I was standing, but there were more names on the opposite side of the van.

A beautiful woman with a cocoa-toned skin and long, layered black hair stepped out of the van and walked right toward me. It was then I realized I wasn't wearing a mask, and neither was anyone else. Slammed back into reality, I took a few steps back to keep my social distance.

My eyes shifted to the white *Jeep Grand Cherokee*, the cause of the accident. The *Jeep* was going far faster than the posted 25mph speed limit in a residential neighborhood. The *Jeep* had Oregon plates, and a large 'O' decal that covered the back windshield, representing the University of Oregon football team. A six-foot American flag lay atop the roof of the *Jeep* in a crumpled heap. The heading edge of the flag was hoisted atop a makeshift pole that split in half upon impact with the minivan. The collision caused the front two wheels of the *Jeep* to snap clean off. The front end of the *Jeep* was compacted into a 'V' shape where the metal met the cement retaining wall. Gasoline and radiator fluid were leaking like a geyser.

Then I noticed the driver of the *Jeep*. He was White, quite tall at about 6'4", bald as a bowling ball, shirtless, and angry. His six-pack abdominal muscles were clenched like boulders under his skin. He wore drab army camouflage fatigues. I noticed his eyes follow the lady from the *"Black Lives Matter"* van as she approached me, and then his eyes seared into mine. I noticed the swastika tattoo that crawled up the side of his neck, and the double lightning bolts that adorned the base of his skull. The flash of his eyes was a clear sign that violence could erupt at any moment.

I looked quickly to the *"Black Lives Matter"* lady and whispered to her while holding my hand up to stop her in her tracks to keep her distance. "I support what you are doing, but you need to stay on this side of the street!"

The Black woman's eyes searched the accident scene based on where I was looking, and she recognized the threat posed by the driver of the *Jeep Grand Cherokee*.

"Skinhead," I said calmly. "We don't want this to get ugly."

Main Street

"What can I do?" the Black lady asked me, as if I was suddenly in charge.

"Take care of the waitress," I said. "She's in shock. Whatever you do, keep away from the angry White guy over there," I whispered.

"Got it!" The Black lady sat down on the curb and put her arm around the waitress.

I shuddered to think the Black lady might have been at local protests against the police, and she might have been setting fires without wearing a mask. I thought better of it, because she didn't look like the violent type. But I wondered if COVID was going to infect the scene of the accident because people weren't being careful.

I saw a nervous Black man with an afro standing on the sidewalk, observing the scene of the accident. He was shivering in fear at the sight of the skinhead. Another fellow, a sweet-faced White man with a ginger beard, appeared from the house behind me.

"Would you like some raspberry peach bubbly-water?" he asked with a genuine smile, holding an aluminum can in my direction.

"No thanks, I'm good," I said, as the man tried to hand out beverages to anyone who wanted one at the scene of the accident.

Once again, Irma looked at me as if she were instructing me to do something more. I hugged her close to my chest. My arms were aching from the weight of her, but I carried her toward the skinhead. He was breathing very heavily with his hands on his hips. He looked right at me with a scowl. I approached him slowly. Irma was facing him as I held her tightly.

"Are you hurt?" I asked the skinhead sincerely, noting the gasoline pooled around his ankles.

Observers were standing all around, and several of them were smoking. I watched the thought enter the skinhead's mind as he realized that he could easily drop a lit cigarette into the pool of gasoline at his feet. His eyes locked on me, the gay Jew, the very type of person a skinhead was sworn to despise.

Irma stared in the skinhead's direction, and he stared right back at her. Their eyes locked. She exhaled. The scowl suddenly left the skinhead's face.

"I hit my head," he said gruffly.

The Climate of Truth

"Do you need an ambulance?" I offered.

"No," he said.

I watched his fist curl into a ball and his fingers turn pale from the lack of circulation. Without warning, he punched the hood of his defunct *Jeep Grand Cherokee* with his bare knuckles. Irma did not flinch. He punched over and over at full force. With each punch, the dent he was making in the hood of the *Jeep* grew more cavernous. With each punch, he yelled "Fuck! Fuck! Fuck! Fuck!"

The skinhead then marched up and down the street, waving his arms at passing traffic like a madman while yelling at the air. An older woman appeared wearing a tube top and overalls, her messy blonde hair teased into a sloppy ponytail. She argued with the skinhead, but I couldn't hear what was said. Infuriated by the older woman, the skinhead marched back to the *Jeep* and punched it some more. More expletives fired off like mortars.

I dialed my cellphone.

"9-1-1, what is the nature of your emergency?"

"There's been a bad accident." I gave the address on the corner of Main Street.

"Is anyone injured?"

"I asked, but both victims said they did not need an ambulance. The lady may have a broken arm. Please send an officer," I said.

"All officers are currently responding to other calls."

"Ummm…you might want to escalate this situation faster. The guy who caused the accident is a skinhead. He's got swastika tattoos. He's punching holes in the hood of his *Jeep* with his bare knuckles and he's shouting. He's dangerous. There's gasoline everywhere. People are smoking. One spark, and this whole corner could go up in flames. I'll hold up my cellphone so you can hear the skinhead shouting and punching."

The skinhead saw me hold my cellphone up to record the noise he was making, and he stared me down with his teeth clenched, his abdomen heaving. I put the phone back to my ear.

The dispatcher replied, "Is the man violent, or is he just mad that he wrecked his car?"

Main Street

The absurdity of the question took my breath away. "It's pretty clear that he's being violent right now. Punching holes in the hood of his *Jeep* with his bare knuckles is not a normal behavior. A lady pulled up into the middle of all this driving a *"Black Lives Matter"* van. She's Black, he's a skinhead. There are other people of color here who look terrified. Gasoline is pouring into the street. Fire and smoke. Potential boom-boom. You get the picture?"

A single officer was dispatched, but it took quite a while for him to arrive. He meandered slowly toward the skinhead, walking bowlegged with his hands on his holster like John Wayne in *"True Grit."* The officer didn't have a mask on either. He talked to the skinhead like they were both old drinking buddies. The skinhead laughed.

Right then the *"Black Lives Matter"* lady stood up to ask me a question, but she suddenly stopped to sneeze and did not cover her mouth.

"Oh God," I said to myself, "COVID!"

Irma looked at me once more. This time it felt like she was telling me to scram.

I held my hand up to stop the *"Black Lives Matter"* lady from getting any closer. "I've done what I can here. I need to get home."

The White waitress turned toward me. "Please don't leave me here like this! I need you! You're a witness!" She was visibly shaking.

"The police will take care of it from here. I gave my contact information to 9-1-1, so if they need to reach me to give a statement, I will gladly do so."

"I just paid off my minivan, and now it's totaled!" She began to weep.

"That really sucks," I said gently. "I'm so sorry."

"And today was my first day back to work since the lockdown. I wait tables down at the waterfront. And now I have no way to get to work because I have no wheels. My kids are gonna go hungry. Looks like I won't be able to work for a while because I think my arm is broke."

"Your insurance will help you with all that. I'm sure you'll get damages," I said.

The Climate of Truth

"Really?" she said, searching my eyes for reassurance. She took a long puff on her cigarette.

"I think it will work out," I said in a soothing tone. "You need to have someone look at your arm. You might ask the officer to send an ambulance."

"That dude's crazy over there. He's all jacked up on something. Like meth," the waitress said.

"Let the cop deal with it. He'll call you a tow."

The waitress suddenly stopped shaking when she caught Irma's gaze. "What kind of dog is that?"

"A Corgi."

"A what?"

"A Corgi. Like the Queen of England has," I said.

"Oh," the waitress said with a smile. "She's 'totes adorbs.'"

"And she knows it too!" I said, laughing a little.

"All girls know when they're beautiful," the waitress said with a maskless smile.

"You have beautiful hair too," I told her. "I notice things like that because I'm a stylist."

The waitress smiled at me and blushed. "Thank you."

"My Corgi girl needs to get home now. She's had a long day. So good luck to you. You'll be OK."

"Thank you for your help, you guys. I really appreciate it," the waitress called after me.

As I turned to head home with Irma in my arms, I whispered in her ear, "You are a very good girl, Irma Lu! Corgi magic saves the day."

Irma turned to look me in the eye, then she rested her nose against my neck with a sigh. I carried her all the way home. The adrenaline coursing through my veins made my arms and legs quite wobbly. I barely made it up the back steps with Irma in my arms.

I went straight for the stereo to put on some soft rock music to calm my nerves. To my surprise, the mellow voice of "*Sweet Baby James*" Taylor caressed my sensitive ears in his rendition of "*Our*

Main Street

Town." He sang about Main Street, the street upon which I had just witnessed the traffic accident.

> *"Main Street isn't Main Street anymore*
> *No one seems to need us like they did before*
> *It's hard to find a reason left to stay*
> *But it's our town, love it anyway*
> *Come what may, it's our town"*

I gave Irma a few chicken and peanut butter cookies for all her hard work. She chewed them down gratefully as I contemplated the music that filled the room. When the intensity of the car crash wore off, I remembered to call my friend Patty back in San Francisco. I told her the details of the events down the block. To my astonishment, Patty laughed, thinking the story was humorous the way I told it. Her reaction confused me. I suppose she didn't understand the rawness of what happened, how close we all came that day to a flashpoint event that could have erupted into lethal violence.

I didn't tell Patty that that accident triggered an episode of post-traumatic stress. Directly across from the scene of the accident, I could see the building where my old salon used to be on Main Street. Hearing James Taylor sing about Main Street made the hair stand up on the back of my neck.

❖

Twenty years prior, the *Southern Poverty Law Center* identified the town where I lived as a hot zone for White supremacist activity. Residents found pamphlets with swastikas tucked under the windshield wipers of their cars parked on the street. When little kids opened their brightly colored plastic Easter eggs gathered from the town square, they discovered the candy inside had been replaced overnight by tightly folded Neo-Nazi propaganda. Teenagers would even go missing, having been abducted and taken out of state to be trained in supremacist ideology at militant camps.

I heard that skinheads were frequenting the antique stores on Main Street, a block from where I worked at the time. The skinheads shopped at those stores to find Nazi memorabilia. I went to

The Climate of Truth

investigate one antique mall, a large corner building with a faded replica of the stars and stripes painted on the cinderblock façade. The young ladies who worked the front counter there said they were intimidated by the supremacist types who came into the store. I roamed the aisles of that antique mall and found several Nazi medallions, a Hitler youth knife, battle helmets and swastika arm bands. I didn't have a lot of money at the time, but I managed to scrape up more than $200 to purchase all the Nazi memorabilia I could find to get it off the street. In my opinion, the memorabilia should either have been destroyed or placed in a museum. It shouldn't have been available for sale to people with questionable motives. I displayed the memorabilia on a framed board and brought it to a televised City Council meeting where I gave a speech. The camera zoomed in on the display I was holding.

"I bought this Nazi stuff on Main Street, USA. This shouldn't happen. We've got to do something," I said in front of an audience who gasped audibly.

That action led to my participation in a committee to establish a *Human Rights Commission* in our region to deal with hate crimes. The commission was endorsed by the Governor of Washington state. Funding and office space were allocated to the project.

Within a few days of my televised speech, the owner of the antique mall walked down the block on Main Street and into the hair salon where I worked. I was alone at the time, folding laundry in the back of the shop. Without warning, the man, a retired Veteran, snuck up behind me and slammed me up against the wall. He pinned my arms behind my back and placed his mouth close to my ear.

"I hope you have deep pockets, you little fucker! Because I'm going to sue you for every penny you've got!" he grunted in my ear. The spittle from his hot breath hit the side of my cheek. He smelled of whiskey. He shoved my face into the wall, then turned and quickly exited the building out the front door. I did not report the incident to the authorities. Instead, I committed myself to further investigate hate crimes in the region, and found there had been documented cross burnings, acid attacks, and violent bullyings at elementary schools that were all fueled by racial bias. I brought this information before the City Council and the formation of the *Human Rights Commission* was approved.

Main Street

In response, local church groups mobilized a campaign to derail the effort, declaring from their pulpits that the proposed *Human Rights Commission* was nothing more than an agency of "the thought police." The church groups levied threats against me personally. On several occasions, 40 or more people gathered on the sidewalk in front of my home while waving *Bibles*. They shouted that they were going to eradicate my "Satanic homosexual agenda." The church groups swarmed future City Council meetings to protest. In the end, the *Human Rights Commission* was scrapped under this political pressure.

Some weeks later, I was driving down Main Street in rush hour traffic at about 8:00am. Suddenly, a large, black, standard Poodle sprang into the street right in front of my car. This happened directly in front of the antique mall. I slammed on the brakes and swerved to avoid hitting the dog. Several other cars also slammed on their brakes and a traffic jam ensued. Fortunately, there were no collisions. At the same time, the owner of the antique mall, the man who attacked me at the hair salon down the block, came walking around the corner.

Still hyperventilating from the near miss, I jumped out of my car and stood in the middle of the intersection. "Is this your dog?" I called out to him.

"What of it!" he yelled back, clearly recognizing me.

"Well, he just ran in front of my car here, in the middle of Main Street, and I nearly hit him. You should have him on a leash for his protection!"

My statement triggered a reaction in the man. He ran toward me. He was wearing a baseball cap, embroidered with the logo that showed he was a Vietnam Veteran. He bared his teeth beneath a bushy mustache. When he reached me, he raised his fist toward my face and attempted to push me backward into oncoming traffic with his other arm.

"Fudgepacker! Fudgepacker! Fudgepacker!" he screamed at me. He wound up his fist preparing to punch me in the face.

Cars swerved to avoid hitting me. I felt the backdraft from a passing white pickup truck within inches of my spine.

The incident was suddenly interrupted by a tall, barrel-chested, bald man, the proprietor of another antique store on the opposite corner.

The Climate of Truth

"What is WRONG with you, man!" the bald fellow yelled at the Veteran. "Stop that!"

The Veteran stopped cold, then suddenly turned back toward his antique store. "Heel!" he shouted at the black Poodle, and the two of them disappeared behind the cinder block building with the faded stars and stripes.

"I'm very sorry this happened to you. I don't know what's gotten into him," the bald man said quietly. He gave an eye-witness account to the police that resulted in the Veteran being hauled off to jail. The hate crime charge was compounded by another case against the Veteran, and he ended up in federal prison.

Just prior to the altercation on Main Street, the Veteran decided to set up a barstool in front of an open screen-door at the back of his house. He was drunk at the time. Upon the stool, he stacked several tiers of empty aluminum beer cans. He backed away from the stool, down a long hallway to the opposite end of his house. Once there, he raised his arm to take aim with a semiautomatic rifle. He fired several shots down the long hallway to knock the beer cans from their perch. The bullets flew out the back screen-door toward a cedar fence in the backyard. On the opposite side of that cedar fence was the play-yard for a children's daycare. There were children present in the play-yard at the time of the shooting.

It was several years before I was brave enough to walk into the antique mall again. The Veteran's wife was still running the place, though she was preparing to sell the business. The wife was a kind-natured lady with long, black, curly hair that contrasted sharply with her aquamarine eyes.

She smiled at me. "Haven't seen you in a month of Sundays. How are you?"

"OK, I suppose." I thought for a moment before speaking again. "I've been wanting to ask you a question."

"It must be about what happened that day," she said. "But you don't have to worry. We're divorced now and he's long gone."

She wanted that to be the end of it, but I had to continue. "I just want to know…why?" I could feel the surge of pressure building in my chest and the heat rush across my face.

Main Street

"Who knows?" she said with a shrug. "There's no explanation for insanity. The man's just mad at the whole world." She leaned on the counter facing me with an intense look. "I got him out of my life…You need to get him out of yours too. That's all I can say about it." She spoke the absolute truth.

❖

Many years later, another dear client of mine was moving out of the neighborhood. She was downsizing her home and was trying to get rid of the bulk of her belongings. Without mentioning it first, she brought a framed original painting to show me.

"For some reason, I think of you when I look at this piece. I would like you to have it," Tessa said. We had been good friends for 22 years.

She unwrapped the brown paper to reveal a beautiful watercolor behind glass, painted by a well-known local artist. It was a collectible. But more importantly, the painting was a street scene depicting the very corner of Main Street where the Veteran backed me into oncoming traffic. However, the vantage point was looking from the antique store toward the shops across the street. The antique store was not visible in the painting. It was a very peaceful scene, looking out at a bead shop and a bakery that were no longer there. And driving down the middle of Main Street in the painting was a white pickup truck, just like the one that whizzed past me when the Veteran tried to kill me. The significance of the watercolor was earthshattering for me. The painting allowed me to look away from a scene of horror in my life toward the rest of Main Street and the rest of the world.

As it turned out 20 years after the hate crime, I bought an old Victorian house a few blocks away from the antique mall. My one-man hair salon was situated in the front parlor. I hung the watercolor in my new home, in a spot that I walked past several times every day. The painting of Main Street reminded me that random acts of kindness brought *Peace* that saved my life. Ever since, it has been my perpetual goal to offer kindness to help others.

The corner of Main Street where a white *Jeep Grand Cherokee* collided with a white minivan could have made the national news in a summer of protests, just like Minneapolis did after the murder of George Floyd. You never know when it could happen. You could be

The Climate of Truth

out walking your dog without a mask and find yourself drawn into a cataclysm. As the calming influence on that fateful July 1st, Irma helped people make a different choice to avoid the cycle of human conflict. *Grace* allowed us all a better outcome than violence. I firmly believed that our presence helped keep someone from getting killed that day. I knew that in my bones, and so did Irma.

Eyes

⤙ ✤ ⤚

A masked man wearing a dark hoodie and sunglasses entered Democrat Party headquarters in Spokane, Washington, with a large pack strapped to his back. Wires were visible, connected to a push button switch he held in his hand. He thrust a two-inch stack of typed paper entitled *"Democrats and Republicans"* into the quaking hands of a female Congressional aide and demanded his "manifesto" to be published immediately, or he would blow up the office with everyone in it.

"I don't want to hurt you. I do have a bomb. Please read this manifesto and share it widely," the masked man said, as he demanded to speak with the Democrat Party Chairman.

When the office staff escaped out the back door, the domestic terrorist set fire to the interior of the building, causing extensive damage. He then walked calmly outside toward the police who were waiting for him with guns drawn. Police did not find a bomb.

Elected officials in seven states warned about the accelerating threat of politically based violence as Trump continued his attempts to overturn the election with unsubstantiated claims of voter fraud. In Georgia, an election technician in his twenties received death threats and a noose and was told he should be hung for treason. The Secretary of State in Georgia experienced armed caravans in front of his home, and his wife received sexualized threats on her cellphone.

The Climate of Truth

In a televised press conference, a top election official in Georgia warned that "Someone's going to get hurt, someone's going to get shot, someone's going to get killed…Mr. President, you have not condemned these actions or this language. Senators, you have not condemned this language or these actions. This has to stop." But the threats of violence continued, unabated.

In Michigan, armed protesters threatened the Secretary of State as they amassed in front of her house. In a separate October 2020 sting in Michigan, the FBI and state authorities arrested 13 members of two right-wing anti-government groups. Charged with terrorism, conspiracy, and weapons crimes, the militias had devised a complex plan to abduct and try the "tyrant" Governor for "treason," and then intended to torture and murder the lady Democrat. Those involved in the Michigan plot intended to blow up a bridge and fire upon law enforcement, acting out of anger for the COVID lockdowns imposed by the Governor in her attempt to slow the spread of the virus. Federal charges would bring a sentence of life in prison for some of the extremists.

Trump did not condemn the violence of White supremacists and hate groups like the two militia groups in Michigan. Instead, on national television during a Presidential debate held over the summer before the 2020 election, Trump told the militia groups to "stand back and stand by," a phrase immediately emblazoned on T-shirts by Trump's extremist supporters. Trump's words were taken as a clarion call for these militants to escalate violent acts against the government.

Christopher Krebs, Trump's appointed Republican Director of Cybersecurity, called the election "the most secure in American history." Krebs publicly declared that, even though he personally voted for Trump and was disappointed in the outcome of the election, it was more than clear that Trump had lost, and there was no evidence that any significant form of election fraud had taken place anywhere in the nation. To secure the vote, Krebs cited unprecedented interagency cooperation between the Department of Homeland Security, FBI, CIA, Defense Department, US Postal Service, all Secretaries of State and their associated election officials and armies of volunteers, the US Elections Commission, both major political parties, social media companies, and election technology companies, among others.

In order to boost the meritless claims (dismissed by 60 courts, including twice at the US Supreme Court) that the Presidential

Eyes

election was stolen from him, Trump broadcasted that Krebs' statements were "highly inaccurate" and then fired him on *Twitter*. The lead attorney for the Trump campaign then appeared on a right-wing news program, saying Krebs should be "drawn and quartered" and "taken out at dawn and shot." The attorney's public statements amounted to Krebs being falsely accused of high treason, which resulted in a barrage of death threats made against Krebs and his family.

Through social media, the Arizona Republican Party openly asked its supporters if they were willing to "give their lives" to overturn the results of the election. They did so while using the battle-cry "*Stop the Steal*," a phrase penned four years prior by Roger Stone, the self-described "dirty trickster" and strategist for three Republican Presidents, including Trump. Although Stone, the last vestige of Nixon's *Watergate* scandal, was convicted of seven felony counts in the investigation of Russian meddling in the 2016 Presidential election, Trump pardoned him, fully commuting Stone's sentence of 40 months in federal prison.

Eighteen Republican State Attorneys General, supported by 126 Republican Congressmen, all joined a lawsuit filed by the State of Texas before the US Supreme Court in a desperate bid to toss out millions of legal votes cast in Michigan, Pennsylvania, Georgia and Wisconsin. The goal of the lawsuit was to disenfranchise Democrats, subvert the will of the voters, and flip the final results of the election in Trump's favor.

Ted Cruz, a Republican Texas Senator, agreed to argue the case on Trump's behalf before the US Supreme Court. However, during the 2016 Presidential election, Senator Cruz called Trump a "pathological liar," "utterly amoral," and "a narcissist at a level I don't think this country's ever seen." The hypocrisy was dumbfounding.

Without dissent, the US Supreme Court rejected the case brought by Texas and declared there was no demonstration of *"a judicially cognizable interest in the manner in which another State conducts its elections."*

In response to the court's decision, Trump tweeted, *"The Supreme Court really let us down. No Wisdom. No Courage!"*

The Supreme Court's decision effectively rendered moot any further attempts brought by Trump or his allies to overturn the

The Climate of Truth

results of the election through lawsuits. Regardless, Trump refused to concede and continued his promise to fight, implying he would encourage state legislators to swap electors to those who were loyal to him. This pointed to the existence of an autocratic caucus within the ranks of the US legislature that had the political will to fully destabilize and shred Democracy. A conservative based news poll further revealed at the time that, without credible evidence of any kind, 77% of Trump voters thought he actually won the election, and 68% of all registered Republicans believed the election was stolen from Trump. Neither of those opinions were true. The phenomena became widely known as "the big lie."

Five weeks after the 2020 election, on December 12, thousands of unmasked pro-Trump demonstrators, including White supremacists and neo-fascist, armed militia groups wearing bullet-proof vests, marched on Washington DC as a show of force to support Trump's baseless claims that the election was "rigged." This happened just three weeks before the *Electoral College* was to convene to formalize the final tally of the Presidential election. Those pro-Trump demonstrators clashed with anti-Trump demonstrators on the streets of Washington DC, resulting in beatings, stabbings, and 33 arrests.

In response to the violence, Trump tweeted: *"Wow! Thousands of people forming in Washington (D.C.) for Stop the Steal. Didn't know about this, but I'll be seeing them! #MAGA."* Trump feigned surprise despite knowing the demonstrations had been planned for weeks.

Trump's increasingly desperate *Twitter* posts were fueling the violent public conflicts. An "enemies of the state" list began to circulate on the dark web, publishing home addresses of public officials who rejected Trump's wild claims of election fraud. Photos were circulated on social media of the public officials with red targets over their faces, bearing the hashtags "*#remember their faces*" and "*#NoQuarterForTraitors.*" Those officials were harassed, stalked and threatened by armed protestors who gathered in front of their homes and at their offices.

Credible threats of violence caused police to close the state legislative campus in Lansing, Michigan when the *Electoral College* was in session. Across the country, various members of the *Electoral College* (especially people of color) received death threats. They had to be escorted to their chambers by armed guard through secret entrances, and some even met in undisclosed locations due to the escalation of threats against them. Such threats loomed for months,

Eyes

following Trump's bold pronouncement on national television to "Liberate Michigan" from the lockdowns. State Capitol buildings across the country were boarded up to prevent violent mobs from breaking in.

Meanwhile, the rates of divorce and romantic breakups were at record highs; state unemployment funds dried up without hope of replenishment; evictions were poised to soar with rent moratoriums expiring at year's end; businesses reported record numbers of layoffs and closures; numbers of homeless individuals and families more than doubled; mental health emergencies, drug overdoses and suicides surged 30% (the highest jump in three decades) because of COVID isolation; and COVID infections and deaths were skyrocketing. Trump offered little comment about these simultaneous disasters, except to denounce a news story about a COVID surge overflow unit built into a hospital parking garage in Reno, Nevada. Trump labelled the story "fake" and "a scam," despite the fact that news crews filmed the unit's operations.

❖

"I can't go on living like this!" Ruby Jean shouted while sneering at her masked face in the styling mirror. "I understand that you have to wear a mask because you have asthma," she said as if I had a life-crushing weakness to be ashamed of. "But there's nothing at all wrong with me! I don't need to wear a stupid mask!"

She flailed her arms about and whipped her head back and forth to punctuate her irritation, making it difficult for me not to smear hair color where it didn't belong. I reminded her to pull her mask back up from where it fell below her nose during all the commotion. She obliged, but only after releasing a great gust of hot breath out of the top of her mask that whooshed toward my face with her loud sigh of disgust.

"Besides," she bellowed, "it says right on the CDC website that masks are useless! If masks can't stop smoke particulate from the wildfires, they sure as hell can't protect you from virus spores that are even smaller!" Her self-described Clark Gable ears turned as red as her name. "Nothing is going to prevent us from catching COVID! It can't be stopped! It's going to have to run its course. It's just the

The Climate of Truth

culling of the herd because there are too many freaking people on the planet! Amen-God-period!"

Ruby Jean's pronouncements made no medical sense to me. During the regular flu season in 2019, there were 38 million cases of the flu reported. When the flu season came around again in 2020, while people were wearing masks and practicing social distancing and hand washing because of COVID, there were only 2,000 cases of the flu reported. Clearly, something was working to keep the regular flu at bay, and that would have included wearing masks.

"Please hold still," I said calmly, trying like mad to keep the foils on Ruby Jean's head as she writhed about in her fury. "It's hard to hit a moving target."

"Sorry!" she answered, whipping her head again with emphasis. "As God is my witness, I'm ready and willing to be arrested because I just can't wear a useless mask anymore! It's ridiculous!"

I didn't think of Ruby Jean as a horrible person; I saw her more as a tortured soul and I pitied her. On the brighter side, I appreciated that she was consistently punctual, and often told me how she would never miss "a sacred hair appointment." She marked the event in her digital calendar with neon yellow to make it appear imperative.

Ruby Jean despised having her name abbreviated. To her, being called Ruby alone was too common. The sound of her name might conjure the image of a woman who painted herself with candy-apple red lipstick and matching nail polish, but Ruby Jean never wore a bit of makeup. Her skin was as pale as the full moon in January, and her disposition could sometimes be just as frosty. She appeared to command the attitudes of a staunch southern belle, having been born and raised in the deep south. Given that many of her views were diametrically opposed to my own, I couldn't grasp how she tolerated sitting in my styling chair. I guess her devotion to having beautiful hair took precedent over her conservative wrath, but not without my having to witness the depths of her own political unrest.

Ruby Jean's barnstorm shifted to declaring the Governor of Washington State a depraved fascist because of his mandated lockdowns designed to help stop the spread of COVID. They were the same kind of lockdowns employed by various other Governors out of deference to common sense public health and safety measures. All non-essential businesses were shuttered during the year, including mine for three months. A renewed state-wide lockdown during the

Eyes

holiday season would kill off restaurants and bars that were barely hanging on. One out of every three small businesses had already closed permanently nation-wide because of pandemic restrictions.

Ruby Jean refused to acknowledge that the whole reason lockdowns were imposed was because the masses, overall, were not behaving in a way to halt the spread of the virus. Great numbers of people were refusing to wear masks. They were also travelling, partying, and gathering in crowds against constant warnings from weary health officials. But resentful factions defied safety protocols to dispute any restriction of personal liberties. Rampant selfishness overwhelmed the urgent need for global humanitarian cooperation.

The immediate result of this defiance was a daily flood of American COVID deaths that surpassed the loss of lives on September 11, 2001, the deadliest terrorist attack in modern history. By early December 2020, more than 3,000 Americans were dying from COVID every day. The numbers were expected to double over the next four months. Overwhelmed hospitals were forced to turn away patients because there were no more beds available. There weren't enough doctors and nurses to treat the infected throngs. All because entitled people refused to wear masks and practice social distancing.

Practically levitating with anger right out of the styling chair, Ruby Jean lifted her clenched fist toward the ceiling. "You can go to Main Street any day of the week and buy yourself a whole pile of funny marijuana stuff, but you can't go to church on Sunday and sing a hymn! Imagine that!"

The US Supreme Court had recently reversed itself by declaring that state governments could no longer enforce COVID lockdowns or attendance limits on religious institutions. The conservative majority of the court opined that such restrictions were a violation of religious freedoms because they *"single out houses of worship for especially harsh treatment."* How trying to save lives could be interpreted as *"especially harsh treatment"* was beyond me, but that's how the power of the court shifted with Trump's three new conservative justices.

Ruby Jean applauded the court's decision. "Finally!" she said with her arms crossed tightly against her chest. "We have a hint of morality! Glory-hallelujah! God always wins in the end!"

❖

The Climate of Truth

I woke up early that Friday morning with a severe tension headache. I didn't get much sleep the night before, partly because I worried that Ruby Jean might be in a combustible mood. I took a dose of *Tylenol* at 4:00am, hoping to blunt the throbbing in my brain before dawn.

One of my other clients, the manager for a medical clinic, insisted that I only use *Tylenol* for pain relief. "The virus kills people who take *Advil* and *Aleve*!" she yelled at me over the phone. "*Ibuprofen* is like crack cocaine to COVID!" That opinion turned out not to be true, but I didn't know it at the time. I followed the advice I was given, even though *acetaminophen* didn't really touch my headaches. Thus, my experience of the COVID age was synonymous with pain. That was probably true for a lot of people.

I tried to start my workday with a cup of coffee and television news, followed by a regimen of 40 vitamin supplements to boost my immune system (as prescribed by my doctor). Health officials explained that those who died from COVID were deficient in Vitamin D3. Zinc supplements were usually sold out, but if you could get your hands on a bottle, they said it could actually kill the virus. Something called NAC could help prevent the cytokine storm caused by COVID in the lungs; N-acetyl cysteine is an amino acid commonly used to treat chronic lung conditions and the flu.

The nurse at my doctor's office, who was prone to believe in conspiracy theories, told me that NAC was taken off the market because it was proven to be an effective treatment against COVID. "They got rid of NAC to force everyone to take the vaccine," the nurse said, emphatically, "because they know it works and they don't want us to treat COVID naturally with vitamins." The nurse also believed that Bill Gates, the prominent philanthropist, secretly put microchips in the COVID vaccine "to screw with people." She ignored me when I said that it was unlikely for microchips to pass through the eye of a hypodermic needle, and that a nurse should know such things. I was able to find NAC readily at the vitamin store, but felt it best not to mention it to her. She also believed in the use of *Ivermectin* to treat COVID infections rather than taking a vaccine. Many doctors warned against human consumption of *Ivermectin* because it was a veterinary medicine used to treat parasites in cows, pigs and horses. Several people were poisoned by the unapproved drug. The FDA urged the public not to take *Ivermectin* "Because you are not a horse."

Eyes

My headache made the vitamins smell like vomit that day. I forced myself to swallow them anyway, but could only do it slowly, one pill at a time while plugging my nose. New medical studies showed that plant-based immunonutrients found in green tea, dark chocolate and muscadine grapes could also fend off COVID infection. I already consumed those things on a regular basis.

When I tried to turn on the news on that throbbing Friday morning, I found the cable box was completely dead. "Noooooooooo!" I yelled at the black screen with my hands grabbing my hair. The words *"No signal"* appeared, followed by *"connection error."* Television was one of my only comforts. It was the main connection from my hermitage to the outside world. With my blood pressure spiking and my head pounding like a jackhammer, it took 45 minutes to fight with the automated robot voice at the cable company to initiate a reset to my cable box. The robot voice refused to allow me to speak to a human.

Finally, the cable box rebooted, and the news came on just in time for me to hear that with nearly 200,000 new COVID cases daily (and someone's death every 30 seconds) America, the wealthiest and most powerful country, now had the distinction of having more COVID and more death than anywhere else on the planet. COVID had surpassed every other illness as the leading cause of death. There wasn't enough room for all the corpses to stack into refrigerated semi-trucks that lined up outside hospitals.

The caseload had yet to peak after millions of people got on airplanes for Thanksgiving, despite the dire warnings from health officials not to do so. As COVID cases climbed further, 33 million people went back into lockdown in California, where hugging and all social gatherings (even those outdoors) were banned. Hearing this news, I dumped my fresh cup of coffee down the drain, turned off the television, and collapsed my pounding head onto the kitchen counter in a fit of nervous laughter. It was all too much to take in. I would be seeing Ruby Jean in less than an hour.

❖

A few days prior, I had a sort of premonition that I needed to get myself to the warehouse to stock up on supplies for my trade. I always tried to listen to my hunches. Because supplies were getting

The Climate of Truth

harder to find by the day, hunting them down was becoming a full-time job. My work for clients like Ruby Jean required the use of great quantities of disposable gloves, folded sheets of aluminum foil, and continuous rolls of paper towels and disinfectant to sanitize all the surfaces and equipment in the shop. When I got to the supply warehouse, there was not a glove or sheet of foil to be had. Neither police, emergency medical technicians, hospital staff, nor food handlers could find gloves to use on the job as needed. Gloves were not manufactured in the US. The warehouse manager griped that there wouldn't be any gloves in stock for another four months.

    Because hundreds of millions of people were all stuck at home with nothing better to do, they were busy guzzling unprecedented amounts of soda pop and beer. Statistics showed that 1 in 3 Americans were binge-drinking alcohol during lockdown. The beverage canning industry was notably ten billion cans behind demand, and this problem caused the shortage in the supply of aluminum foil. This sent me into another panic because I couldn't work without gloves and foil. I spent $1000 for the last few wholesale cases of powder-free gloves and boxed foil that I could find anywhere in the metro area. It was five times the normal price, but I was the lucky one to grab it off the shelf. I could only use powder-free gloves, because I was allergic to those that were coated with cornstarch. At least I had enough supply of gloves and foil to keep working through the new year, so I couldn't complain. There wasn't a shred of spooled cotton to wrap a perm or remove hair color stains. It was impossible to find household spray cleaners, so I settled on $650 for ten gallons of hospital-grade spray virucide.

    I plowed through a jumbo 12-pack of paper towels every four days, and they too were usually missing from store shelves. I had several people hunting for paper towels on my behalf whenever they went shopping. Other business staples like liquid bleach, disinfecting wipes, laundry soap, and the infamous bundles of toilet paper were all on frequent backorder or unavailable due to hoarding. Many of the haircare products that I'd carried for the last 20 years were out of stock for months on end. Trump's trade war made it difficult to acquire any products that contained components sourced from China – which was practically everything. I had to spend a fortune to stockpile supplies just to stay in business.

    I only ventured out to the supply warehouse, a high-end grocery store where everyone was known to wear masks, my post office box,

Eyes

the drive through at the bank, curbside pickup from a burger joint every now and then, and my doctor's office twice monthly for my life-saving asthma injections that cost $5000 a pop. Meanwhile, the Trump administration was attempting to annihilate the *Affordable Care Act* in a case before the US Supreme Court. Trump sought to destroy my ability to keep my much-needed health insurance in the middle of a global pandemic. This literally meant that I could lose my ability to breathe at any moment.

I hadn't had any social contact with any of my friends in the prior ten months and didn't see that changing any time soon. Health officials were warning that the next four to six months would be the worst ever experienced with COVID. I always declined invitations to socialize because I believed it was my responsibility to remain in isolation to protect my clients from getting infected. I also wanted to survive. My only companions were my two fan-tailed goldfish and my 13½-year-old Corgi. I didn't count my clients as social contacts.

I stayed away from all big-box stores because they were known to be primary vectors of infection that caused nearly 40% of all new COVID cases. Those stores were also the targets of anti-mask protesters who swarmed in to expose their naked faces in defiance of state mandates. The more aggressive protestors even ripped the masks from the faces of other unsuspecting shoppers. Propaganda signs popped up all over town that read *"Unmask your smile!"* Ruby Jean found herself in the middle of an anti-mask protest at *Walmart*. She willingly pulled the elastic from her Clark Gable ears and applauded with gusto. The excitement of her rebellion made her cry with a sense of personal triumph.

❖

Three years prior, Ruby Jean was "exceedingly late to the marriage game," as she put it. She was the last of her large family to marry at the age of 48. I didn't sleep the night before because weddings always made me nervous. Ruby Jean's hair was quite long and very heavy. It took a great deal of architectural design and a vast pile of concealed hairpins for me to secure her bridal updo without making it look like the ancient goddess Athena's crested battle helmet. Ruby Jean's honeymoon was her only foray away from home in many years, spent camping in the frigid, rustic backwoods of Iceland for two weeks.

The Climate of Truth

She ordered her one-of-a-kind wedding ring on her cellphone while sitting in my styling chair. The center stone was a rose-cut, opaque, grey diamond. It was surrounded by a ring of tiny, clear, pavé diamonds in a thin, filigreed rose-gold setting.

"Most people think my wedding ring is from an estate sale," Ruby Jean said proudly. "The grey diamond sparkles with overcast skies and thunderstorms. It's so strange that it looks very dull in the sunshine." Those words seemed like a testament to her outlook on life overall.

Ruby Jean also purchased a new car for herself from my styling chair. Her old car was near the end of its days, and she needed something more reliable that better represented her new marital status. She arranged to pay cash for a model that matched the antique grey stone of her wedding ring. I had to slam the foils in and out of her hair to get her off to the dealership in time to close the transaction. Shortly after her excited drive home from the dealership, she managed to bottom out on a cement barricade, causing thousands of dollars in damage to the brand-new car.

Regardless of what befell her, Ruby Jean lived with her convictions firmly opposed to the potential for giving in to failure. "I'll only go down swinging," she said, referring any crisis, obstacle, or liberal idea.

After the wedding, she moved into her new husband's house. She described her new abode as something worse than a man-cave with fudge brown carpet and a slovenly fat cat. Moving into that house made her aesthetically glum, but marriage required sacrifice. As a newlywed, she arrived with a box of rubber gloves and disinfectant, much like the supplies I used to sanitize against COVID every day. She resigned herself to tolerate the avocado-colored appliances and to ignore the enormous crack in the outdated and heavily stained porcelain bathtub. The newlyweds would have to scrimp and save to afford modest home improvements.

It was her new husband's second marriage. He came to the union with two adult sons. This made Ruby Jean an instant grandmother, a title she wasn't sure she could live up to, being childless herself. Her husband worked full-time for a shipping company. He sustained on-the-job injuries to his ankles, knees and toes. He chose to quit deliveries in favor of an indoor graveyard shift in the sorting station to earn more money for the house remodel and retirement. He made

Eyes

those choices knowing he would see little of his new bride with that kind of work schedule. Their financial plan was for him to retire within five years, because his body might not last any longer than that. His shiny bald head was a striking contrast to Ruby Jean's long, thick tresses that were, in reality, silver-grey that were magically disguised as creamy blonde silk. Her husband would have preferred if she could sit on her hair, but she complained that the bulk took forever to dry, especially in the frozen tundra of their honeymoon in Iceland spent in a camping tent.

Her husband nearly fainted when she threatened to cut her hair above the shoulders. He got down on his knees and begged her not to do it. "Boys are silly," she said with a sardonic smile at the recollection.

Once, Ruby Jean delighted in showing me a cellphone photo of a surgical tray covered with at least a dozen large, fatty lipomas that were removed from her husband's backside. She observed the medical procedure in person. Her husband wanted the painful lumps to be excised so he could lie in bed with his new bride without wincing. The extracted yellow globules were pictured all lined up in a row, each at least two inches in length, laid out beside a pair of stainless steel forceps, aside a wad of blood-stained gauze. I couldn't imagine why anyone would want to show me such an image.

Without warning, another long-term client texted me a photo of her recent brain scan that showed a ghostly image of her entire skull with two large tumors. The expression of the neon green skull seemed to be screaming while red laser beams shot out from its eye sockets. The shock of the image made it difficult to keep working the whole rest of the day. Nevertheless, I made a point to visit that client at her hospital bedside following both brain surgeries.

Several other clients sent me disturbing notices by text while I was at work. One client wrote: "*My mother* [also one of my clients] *just died while I was rubbing her feet,*" or "*Ollie had a heart attack and died in my arms twenty minutes ago. I knew you would want to know.*" It got to the point where I was afraid to read my texts or emails.

There were several texts from clients that read *"Cancel my appointment. I got the COVID."* Some clients were hospitalized. Some were intubated. Some had less severe symptoms. Others were "long-haulers" with extensive side effects that refused to abate. Several of them complained obstinately that they had no idea how they got infected, but continued conversation revealed how they chose to attend an indoor dinner party with friends or sat next to someone who coughed on them at a bar or at church. Several clients infected other people, but never in my shop. Some of my clients died from COVID. I bore witness to all of it.

Ruby Jean was astonished when I relayed the news of one COVID related death. "Really!" she said with her chin retracted into her neck. "He was only 33 and was supposed to get married next week? Sounds like he was going to die anyway from something else. People die of all kinds of things, but nowadays, they say EVERYONE dies of COVID!" She turned her head toward me with her eyebrows raised in mock dismay. "Funny, I don't know a soul who's gotten it. Perhaps media sensationalism is just making this out to be worse than it really is. It's a good reason to boycott the news!"

Ruby Jean vehemently supported the theory that "herd exposure" was the only way to achieve "herd immunity" from COVID. She gave no consideration to the assured increase in the death toll that would follow suit with that line of thinking.

Another female client, a bank teller, insisted that hospitals were paid more money by the federal government when COVID deaths were reported.

"Where did you hear that?" I said, aghast. "Doctors wouldn't incentivize COVID. That's creepy!"

"I know it to be true," the teller objected. "One of my cousin's friends -- his wife died of cancer. When he got the death certificate from the hospital, it wrongly said his wife died of COVID. He went to the hospital administration and asked them to correct the death certificate. 'My wife never had COVID,' he told them. The hospital refused to make the correction. It made him furious. So you see, hospitals get paid money to fudge their COVID numbers."

❖

Ruby Jean's new husband was an avid Civil War reenactor who owned various historically accurate uniforms for the Confederate team. He spent many a weekend in the forest and field, fighting Yanks amid the sulphury smell of powder horns and cannon fire. Her wedding gift to him was to fulfill one of his life-long dreams. He'd

Eyes

always wanted to learn to parachute from a plane, so she sent him off to a special camp where he would train to jump in a weekend. It was a curious thing that a man with severe injuries to the lower half of his body would want to feel the full force of falling from the sky to the ground. But his dream was to jump in a Confederate uniform while shouting the high-pitched "Wa-woo-woohoo, Wa-woo-woohoo!" -- a true-to-life Confederate battle-cry said to conquer the warrior's fear of death.

When it came time for her husband to cut loose from the open bay door of the airplane and deploy the parachute, he froze in abject fear. He returned home, sullen, his dream unfulfilled. He complained of the waste of money. Ruby Jean rubbed his head with her slender fingers to soothe his self-loathing. She noted the large lipoma that still needed to be extracted from the crown of his bald pate. Scientists later determined that bald men were twice as likely to suffer severe COVID symptoms, would spend twice as long in the hospital because of those symptoms, and were more likely to require intensive care. They also discovered traces of COVID in male genitalia many months after recovery from the virus, a condition that was believed to cause erectile dysfunction.

❖

2019 was a very rough year for Ruby Jean. Her aged parents insisted on building a new house, and she stage-managed the design, construction and move-in while maintaining her full-time job as a corporate accountant. Within weeks of project completion, her mother developed dementia, followed by a severe pain in her thigh that left her wheelchair bound. The pain turned out to be an aggressive cancer. Simultaneously, Ruby Jean's father experienced the metastasis of prostate cancer to the liver, followed by double pneumonia that failed to heal. Privately, Ruby Jean wondered if the lingering pneumonia may have been an early, undetected case of COVID.

After six decades never being apart, both of her parents were sent off to different care facilities. They grew despondent in their separation. Ruby Jean's mother died first. A few months later, at the height of the first spring COVID surge, her father insisted on dying at home in his own bed while looking at a photo of his beloved wife on the nightstand.

The Climate of Truth

"He just gave up…because he was too tired," Ruby Jean said of the father she adored. As she spoke, she looked even paler than the color white. The one-two punch of her parents' deaths nearly destroyed her. She managed all their medical care and fought with all the doctors on her own while the rest of her family criticized her efforts. Understandably, this made her even more bitter.

Ruby Jean's head whipped back and forth again while I was attempting to foil her hair. "I'm ready and willing to be arrested and go to jail because I will not be <u>forced</u> to pay for *Obamacare* that I don't want or need!" She never acknowledged how the health coverage provided by the *Affordable Care Act* extended the medical benefits granted to both of her parents during their critical illnesses. Nor did she consider how the social safety net put more money in her pocket from her parents' estate instead of having to pay excessive medical bills.

To soften Ruby Jean's mood, I often told her that she was one of the strongest, most dedicated, and most gracious daughters I had ever known, and that she couldn't have done a better job in taking care of her ailing parents. My consolation seemed to help keep her from spilling out of her skin. I cradled her masked head in my arms as she wept in the styling chair. I called her "*Ms. Blue Eyes Cryin' in the Rain*," one of Elvis Presley's refrains. She gazed at me through a pool of tears with a look of quiet desperation.

Ruby Jean planned and managed both of her parents' funerals, only to have her father's service canceled because of mandated COVID restrictions. It infuriated her for months to come. She was appointed coexecutor of her parents' estate, along with her brother, who turned into a tyrant in his hour of grief. Stuck in a feud with his siblings, her brother refused to attend the last family Thanksgiving while his parents were still alive. His guilt over that decision devoured his remaining humanity. The whole affair caused huge patches of Ruby Jean's hair to fall out from high levels of stress. I prescribed a therapeutic shampoo and conditioner to nurse her hair back to health. It took several long COVID months for new sprouts of hair to grow in long enough to blend over the bald spots. But it worked, and she was grateful.

As I was foiling Ruby Jean's hair on the day of my horrendous headache, two ambulances raced past the front window of the shop, followed by two firetrucks. The sound bounced off my throbbing forehead, but I tried not to show Ruby Jean that I was in pain. I knew

Eyes

the sound of the sirens reminded her of the death of her parents. They reminded me of more COVID cases being rushed toward a ventilator.

I always encouraged Irma to howl at the sirens as a way to sooth her anxiety from the noise. We often howled together, tilting our heads toward the ceiling while closing our eyes. That time, though, Irma put both of her front paws over her eyes and buried her nose in her "couch potato."

❖

It had been a long and tense month since the Presidential election. Lately, I hadn't seen any of the troubling four-by-four trucks that sped past my house with giant *"Trump 2020"* flags snapping in the slipstream. An entire legion of those trucks had been frantically traversing the county for months as a form of voter intimidation. I'd never seen anything like it before, and neither had many of my clients. Several of the trucks displayed oversized American flags with the image of Trump's face superimposed over the stars and stripes. Other flags presented the image of Trump as *"Rambo,"* a franchised character from bloody action films that were written, directed, and starred Sylvester Stallone, where he played a muscle-bound special forces Veteran who fought and killed vast swaths of the Viet Cong, corrupt cops and drug cartels.

At the height of the Vietnam conflict, my father was shipped stateside from the jungles of the Mekong Delta to attend special officer's training at Quantico, under the mission *"Operation Ranch Hand."* My father was allowed a brief day's leave to visit home before he was shipped back to front lines outside Huế City. I was a toddler at the time, and my mother was holding me in her arms in the master bedroom. Out of his army duffle bag, my father produced a capped glass vial that looked like it was full of maple syrup.

"With this, we can win the war and drive those bastards out of the jungle!" my father shouted, waving the glass vial at my mother's nose, threatening her.

She turned her body sideways to shield me from the vial, covering my face with her free hand.

The Climate of Truth

"If the Communists bring the war to America, all the women and children should head for the hills and the men will defend the country!" he commanded.

My father had brought a vial of *Agent Orange* into our family home. But he swore his psychological evaluations were off the charts, and that he would one day make the rank of General. That glass vial is what precipitated my parents' divorce when I was four. I'll never know for sure, but I wondered if the confrontation in the master bedroom was one of the many traumas that contributed to my mother's mental illness.

Eleven million gallons of *Agent Orange* rained down on Vietnam to defoliate the jungle and expose the Viet Cong hidden there. In addition, it was used to poison the civilian water supplies and crops. The biochemical weapon also ate a cancerous hole in my father's throat, and his esophagus had to be replaced with a splice of his small intestine. He suffered a bleeding stomach for the rest of his life.

I discovered a stack of *Polaroids* in my father's desk drawer. They were snapshots of dead American soldiers lined up in a grassy field in Vietnam. Scores of dead bodies laid side by side. A Huey helicopter was in the background. Some of the bodies were dismembered, some with their pants blown off and their genitals exposed to the sun. All of them were face up, some with eyes open, some with bloody trails across their foreheads. Their camouflaged uniforms were in tatters, their undershirts ripped open. As a boy of only 12, I couldn't understand why my father, a survivor of the Holocaust, would keep those dreadful photographs.

I remembered the televised Congressional hearings on the Vietnam War, when the public heard that American soldiers raped and tortured Vietnamese civilians, cut off their ears and their heads and electrocuted their testicles. That's why I joined the *Union of Conscientious Objectors* in high school. Those were the thoughts that suddenly filled my mind when I saw Trump's image as *"Rambo"* fly past the front window of my shop. Thinking the 2020 election was long behind us, I felt like I might breathe a little easier. I was wrong.

❖

I took Irma out for her nightly constitutional. It was dark, around 8:30pm. It should have been a peaceful time for a leisurely

Eyes

neighborhood stroll after work, when Irma could sniff every blade of grass and tree trunk as she liked to do. But as we headed down the sidewalk, something made me turn to look back over my shoulder toward the corner where my house fronted the busy boulevard. I looked just in time to see a monster truck with jacked up wheels roar past my house with six Trump flags audibly billowing in the wind, each of the six flagpoles ablaze with a string of bright red Christmas lights. Several similar trucks followed in a honking caravan. The drivers were all yelling profanities out their open windows.

I caught myself saying "Oh God!" out loud.

There were many such trucks in the coming days, taken again to the streets to show their support for Trump's wild conspiracy theories. Trump railed vituperative attacks against various public officials. He called members of his own party "enemies of the people" when they disagreed with him. He fired many federal officials who disputed his false claims that the election was stolen from him.

I walked Irma to the southern end of my block where I discovered six police vehicles had cordoned off the intersection around the corner. There were also two fire trucks and an ambulance, all with strobe lights flashing. Another police car slowly rolled up beside me with its driver's side door wide open while in motion. Once parked, an officer stepped out. Irma would normally bark at such an apparition, but she was steadfastly silent. The officer was quite tall and lanky, dressed entirely in black with all manner of shadowy combat gadgets strapped to his *Kevlar* flak jacket. I could barely see his angular face in the glow of a distant streetlamp.

"Officer," I called out, waving my hand at him. "I live right around the corner here. May I ask what's happening?"

The officer approached me with his hand touching the grip of his sidearm. I was horrified, never having had the occasion to experience an officer grip his service weapon in close range. I said nothing. I was an unarmed hairstylist out for a walk with his low-rider dog that was built like a kielbasa sausage. Clearly, we weren't a threat. But the COVID age made a lot of people jumpy, suspicious, and paranoid. The officer released the grip of his gun once he convinced himself that Irma and I were harmless.

The officer's voice was subdued, as if to avoid making too much noise. "There's a man on the roof of the blue house," he half-whispered. "He won't come down." The officer pulled the folded

The Climate of Truth

brim of his wooly cap further over his ears to guard against the sting of the cold.

"The massage place with the prayer flags?" I asked in hushed disbelief. How could I have missed hearing all the tactical equipment and emergency personnel dispatched within mere feet of my kitchen window? Thankfully, the massage business was closed. I shuddered at the thought that the man on the roof could easily have chosen to climb my house instead.

"We are going to pull back and maintain a low profile for the time being," the officer explained. "Hopefully we can keep from spooking him any further."

"How long has he been up there?" I strained my eyes in the dark but could not see anyone on the roof because the offender was on the back side.

"A few hours," the officer replied matter-of-factly. "We've got some social workers around back trying to coax him down."

"Why did he climb up there?"

"He's taken a large quantity of methamphetamine. He's also removed all his clothing." The officer cocked his head in response to a signal in his earpiece. He then spoke quietly into the radio mic strapped to his shoulder, "Copy that."

It was about 39 degrees, and a light rain had started to fall. The naked man on the roof might have caught his death from hypothermia instead of COVID, and I wondered if I should run home to offer some hot tea to the cause. I quickly thought better of inserting myself.

"God bless him," I said to the officer. "Is he armed?"

"Only with a few large tree branches," the officer said looking toward the roof in question.

"Holy cow," I said shaking my head. "Everyone's just gone bonkers. I'm sorry you have to deal with something like this. There are probably a million other things you could be doing instead."

"It's the job," the officer said.

"Thank you for your time, and for filling me in."

Eyes

"Thank you for saying thank you," he said with a quick nod of his head as he disappeared into the dark.

My neighbor learned the naked man's name was Michael. It startled me that we shared the same name. Neither the police nor the fire department were going to haul the naked man off the roof. He was going to have to come down on his own. That finally happened at 1:00am. After seven hours of his screaming into the winter night sky, Michael was tucked into the ambulance and hauled away. That sleepless night before the morning of Ruby Jean's appointment was the reason for my pounding headache at 4:00am.

A week before that, a fleet of six full-sized SWAT vehicles (some from different counties), several battalion command vehicles, four fire trucks and three fire marshals, three ambulances, more than a dozen police cars, and a chopper overhead all went racing past the picture window at the front of my house where I was cutting hair at the time. I called 9-1-1 to inquire, but the incident was simply described as "a public safety concern." I called the local newspaper to see if they knew the nature of the emergency, but the newsroom was shuttered due to COVID with all reporters working from home. I called a television station, and they knew nothing of the situation but thanked me for the news tip. I called a neighbor who lived in the direction of the chaos, and she went online to "*Nextdoor.com,*" where someone posted comments about a crazed drug dealer who'd gone berserk in broad daylight on the roof of a house about half a mile down the road. He'd stripped off his clothes and would not come down. This fellow was waving automatic rifles at police officers. The SWAT team staged a response from a parking lot mere blocks from my house.

Through her *Ring* doorbell camera, another client of mine witnessed her neighbor across the street strip off all her clothes while dancing on her front porch in the middle of the night. The woman was also high on meth. She was released from the hospital some days later. Apparently, stripping off one's clothes and screaming in public while high on meth were regular things in the COVID age.

Around the same time, an old man a few blocks away doused his house in gasoline while his terrified wife tried to talk him out of dropping a lit match. He too was waving a rifle. All the same emergency vehicles sped past my house again. There was a stand-off for several hours. The old man stood yelling at the sky before he successfully torched his own house. He cheered as his life was destroyed, firing a few random shots into the air. The fire crews could not move in until the police were able to tackle the old man and seize his cache of weapons. He was taken away to jail in handcuffs where he received a psychological evaluation. The fire crews had to let the house burn to the ground. They turned their focus to protecting the surrounding properties instead.

Days later, the old man's wife was still sitting where her house once stood, her head in her hands, staring at the charred debris. "For months, I tried to get him some help," she cried to anyone who would listen. "He's been my soulmate for more than 50 years. But with all the lockdowns, he just snapped. I don't recognize him anymore."

She wiped the tears from her eyes. Her fingertips left a trail of dirt caked on her face. The dirt was all that was left of her front yard. The elderly couple could not afford homeowner's insurance, but it didn't matter since the act of arson would not be a covered loss.

❖

All summer long, I knew Thanksgiving would be a critical turning point in the pandemic. I worried about it for months, knowing that family gatherings over the holidays would cause infections to soar exponentially. I was surprised to see costumed trick-or-treaters going door-to-door at Halloween, but not surprised to hear of the COVID surge that happened two weeks later. One of my clients sent me a photo of a contraption her husband built so he could hand out candy to the trick-or-treaters while preserving social distance requirements; it was a long section of plastic pipe that started at their front door and stretched 12 feet at a downward slant, attached to the wall beside the front walkway of the house. A barricade was placed across the front walk so no one could get within several feet of the front door. A sign was placed at the end of the pipe that read: "*Put your candy bucket here*" with an arrow pointing to the opening. When a trick-or-treater arrived, my client would insert a piece of candy into the mouth of the pipe, and it would roll down the long tube and into the child's waiting jack-o-lantern bucket. Everyone clapped to celebrate each successful deployment of candy.

I contemplated closing my business until after the first of the year to protect myself. But many of my clients were strictly adhering to the safety protocols, and I decided to remain open to serve them. The day

Eyes

of my terrible headache, Ruby Jean's appointment was only a week after Thanksgiving; that was the prime COVID incubation period following exposure from a family gathering. Given her history of large family events, I was pretty sure Ruby Jean would flout the COVID safety protocols and risk infection. Being a hairstylist made me a reliable predictor of human behavior. Therefore, I sent text messages well in advance to all my scheduled clients; the texts were designed to defend my business against those who were not in compliance with public health and safety requirements for COVID:

> *"PLEASE NOTE THAT SAFETY PROTOCOLS HAVE INCREASED…Please read the instructions below and respond to this text to CONFIRM AND KEEP this appointment while adhering to all protocols. The state mandated business closures have been extended, but they do not include hair salons at this time. So, I am able to honor your appointment as long as COVID protocols are followed. If you have traveled more than 50 miles from home, or if you have kept company with out of state travelers, a 14-day quarantine waiting period is required prior to service. If you have spent time indoors while unmasked with people outside of your household, the same 14-day waiting period is also required, and you will need to reschedule accordingly. If you have symptoms of COVID, a cold, or the flu, or have been directly exposed to someone with symptoms, the same 14-day waiting period applies. You must wear an ear-loop mask for the duration of your service. All food and drink are prohibited. You are required to wait for your appointment outdoors, so please remain in the parking area, and I will come out and get you when ready. Please come to your appointment alone as extra guests are prohibited. Feel free to contact me if you have any questions. So far, we have successfully prevented viral transmission at Blow Your Top, and we will continue to employ these common-sense protocols to keep everyone safe."*

The Climate of Truth

Most everyone responded to this straightforward text with gratitude for my dedication to public health and safety. Knowing Ruby Jean as I did, I dreaded her response. She usually ignored my texts or confirmed her appointments after making me wait for several days. To my surprise, she answered quickly. Her response read:

> *"I will be celebrating Thanksgiving quite safely and have every reason to believe that I can attend my hair appointment next week without incident. I will definitely see you on Friday. Thank you and have a blessed holiday."*

My heart sank in reading Ruby Jean's words. It seemed like her clever way of telling me to get my nose out of her family's holiday plans, and a rejection of what she considered to be the state's unlawful attempt to trample on her personal freedoms. But my COVID safety text had nothing to do with politics. Several of my clients told the truth and moved their appointments willingly to remain in compliance with the protocols. Ruby Jean was a whole other matter.

The night before Thanksgiving, I called a friend with a long history as a legal assistant in a high-powered firm. I read Ruby Jean's response over the phone to Tiffy, who interpreted Ruby Jean's words as another way of saying "Up yours!" Tiffy also suggested that I should close my shop until after the holidays to avoid this type of conflict and to prevent myself from getting infected. She explained, "You don't need this woman! You have asthma for goodness sake! You should fire her as a client for doing this to you. I will find three other clients to replace her for you! You can't allow this to stand. You have to call her out!"

The following day, Thanksgiving, I didn't change out of my sweatpants. I didn't shower. I didn't speak with anybody. Instead, I nervously stared at the ceiling in my office for hours, writing several draft text responses to Ruby Jean in my head. I wondered how one woman could make me feel so bewildered. Exhausted, I put myself back to bed until I could summon the courage to continue. Ruby Jean had connections to several of my clients. Creating a conflict with her could cause more harm to my business. I had to tread carefully.

Eyes

  After a solo Thanksgiving meal of four homemade chicken tacos, I typed a draft response on my cellphone. Dealing with Ruby Jean had thoroughly soured what remained of a COVID holiday. Out of professional courtesy, and because I was generally thoughtful (even when others were not), I decided to wait until the day after Thanksgiving to press "send." My text to her read:

> *"Ruby Jean, if I am interpreting your words accurately (please correct me if I am wrong), you are not able to adhere to the COVID safety protocols I outlined in my text to you. Out of respect for the many businesses that are now closed while mine is not, and in order to protect the many vulnerable clients who rely on me to help keep them safe, respectfully, I will need to push your appointment further out as mentioned if you spent the holiday indoors while unmasked in the presence of people outside of your immediate household. Health officials have determined that family gatherings, such as those at Thanksgiving, are primary vectors for viral transmission. Please know that I struggled greatly in writing this text, because I did not want to upset you."*

Once again, to my surprise, Ruby Jean replied swiftly:

> *"Heavens to Betsy! I had no idea that my lack of absolute clarity would cause you to suffer so much added stress and anxiety! Bless your ever-loving heart! (Emojis: smiley face, smiley face, smiley face, red heart, red heart, red heart) Yes, of course I have adhered to, and will continue to adhere to all of your protocols. I only meant to say that my appointment was a week out, and that I had no idea what could happen between now and then. Barring unforeseen circumstances, I will most certainly be at my appointment next Friday."*

  I knew the phrase *"bless your ever-loving heart"* was southern belle code for "go screw yourself!"
  It seemed like Ruby Jean was rearranging her own words in an attempt to tell me what she thought I wanted to hear, as if I was a

The Climate of Truth

panting Poodle that needed to be calmed. I called Tiffy again to relay the next round of back-and-forth with Ruby Jean. My friend told me that my verbiage was specific, clear, reasonable, professional and non-confrontational.

Tiffy tried to bolster my spirits. "Everybody loves you, Mike! Because you are awesome every day of the week! At least it sounds like she's trying to be reasonable."

I wrote back to Ruby Jean:

"Thank you for the clarification. See you Friday."

By the time Ruby Jean pulled into the parking lot in the new (repaired) grey car that matched the color of her grey diamond wedding ring, I was nauseous. I desperately needed another dose of *Tylenol* to subdue my blinding headache but had to wait a few more hours to prevent an overdose.

I unlocked the white, wrought iron gate. "Good morning beautiful!" I chirped.

Ruby Jean sighed and gruffly wrapped her mask around her protruding ears as she passed. She wore a stylish, belted trench-coat in a black-and-white houndstooth print with a matching muffler knotted about her neck. Her long hair hung down the back of her coat, blonde against the sharp, staggered houndstooth pattern. Once again, the sharp juxtaposition of black against white was profoundly noticeable.

"Wow," I said enthusiastically. "Your hair grew out quite nicely. Look at that, it drapes beautifully. The color change we did is very smooth, even after six weeks."

"I know a guy!" she laughed with a toss of her hair.

"I'm sorry," I said looking down at the patio pavers, "but it's my job to ask the COVID screening questions every time."

"Yes, of course," she said evenly. "That's why God created the word 'polite.'"

I repeated the various COVID safety questions by memory. Ruby Jean answered each with a simple "no" and a slight nod of her head.

Eyes

When I got to the final question, I looked directly at her pale blue eyes. "Have you been indoors while unmasked in the presence of people outside of your immediate household?"

She returned my gaze with a relaxed poker face. "No," was her prompt response.

"Up we go," I said, gesturing toward the stairs to the shop. "Everything has been sanitized for you." As she ascended ahead of me, I asked, "Is your stepson still living with you? I think we talked about him last time."

"Unfortunately, yes."

"How is that going? Is he clean and sober?" I asked.

"It's a total dumpster fire," she said, turning to face me from a few steps above. "I'll tell you all about it."

❖

Ruby Jean settled in for her two-and-a-half-hour appointment, during which time she filled me in on how her brother was making her life miserable regarding the disbursement of her parents' estate. "Even though he's been so unpleasant," she said, "I still invited my brother and his family to Thanksgiving dinner."

My heart skipped a beat, because Ruby Jean had already reported that no one outside of her immediate household had attended her Thanksgiving feast. I caught a brief glimpse of my angst-ridden expression in the mirror, and quickly relaxed my eyes to avoid any appearance of dread. I continued to apply foils to her hair.

Noticing my course correction, Ruby Jean countered masterfully, "None of my family members came for Thanksgiving."

I breathed a sigh of relief while looking only at my hands. "Why invite your brother if he's being such a dick?"

"It was the first time in 35 years that my family did not gather for Thanksgiving," she said. "All because of COVID… I had to invite my brother, knowing full-well he would refuse to come…I've decided to take my parents' house, the one they recently built, as my part of the inheritance. So that I can say goodbye to my husband's fudge brown carpet and that horrible crack in the bathtub. I invited my brother to

The Climate of Truth

Thanksgiving so he wouldn't block my plans to keep my parents' house. I did it to keep the peace."

The conversation was interrupted by the shop phone. I answered to a frantic woman.

"My hairstylist just cancelled my standing appointment on December 19th!" she shrieked. "Without an explanation!"

"I don't know if I can help you. Let me check my schedule. What service do you need?"

"An updo!" she said, sharply raising the pitch of her voice to a shrill quiver.

"Is it a wedding?"

"Yes!"

"Are you the bride?" I asked.

"Yes!"

"I didn't think weddings were being allowed right now, because of the pandemic," I said succinctly.

After a few seconds of silence, the woman started to cry. "I don't know what I'm going to do with all my bridesmaids!"

"I am so sorry. I feel for you, truly. But I am already fully booked that Saturday. As a one-man shop, I tend to book up well in advance, especially during the holidays. And I can't accommodate an entire wedding party."

My inner voice wanted to yell at her for planning a potential super-spreader event. I wanted to get indignant and in her face. I wanted to announce to her that I would never book a damned wedding with a bridezilla in the middle of a pandemic. But I was not an ass. That's never good for business. I used the gentlest phone voice I could muster. "I am so sorry that I cannot help you right now, but I really hope you can get it all sorted out so you can be happy."

"That's OK. Thank you anyway," the woman said while wailing. "Have a nice daaaaaaaaaay!" She quietly hung up the phone.

"Oh dear," Ruby Jean said with a smirk that could be interpreted from under her mask. "I could hear her from all the way over here."

"It takes all kinds of denial," I said, as I returned to my foiling.

Eyes

"Where were we?" Ruby Jean asked.

"Your new house," I said. "Are you going to bring the stepson along when you move?"

The corners of Ruby Jean's mouth turned quickly down, as indicated by the shift in her mask. "The jury is still out," she said smugly, her eyes heavy.

"Why is he living with you in the first place?"

"He had a terrible breakup with his male lover some months back," she said. "Lord knows, I try to understand these things. I try to be flexible and forgiving, but I'm a Christian first and foremost."

"Has he had counseling?" I asked.

"I've paid for his therapist for the past three years. One would think that regular and expensive therapy could cure him of rash behaviors. Guess I'm not that lucky…That purse string needs to close."

The "therapy" the stepson received was the type offered by a conservative church, intended to reprogram gay people into a heterosexual lifestyle.

"Did the counseling help?" I kept my eyes firmly focused on my work, avoiding the tempest brewing on Ruby Jean's face.

"In order for him to live with us," Ruby Jean said, "the rule was that we were all going to have a dry household. It was no big deal for us, the parents, to give up an occasional glass of wine or a cocktail at the end of a long day. But his father found a whole pile of empty bottles in the recycling bin, as if they wouldn't be discovered."

"Uh-oh…Is the kid working?"

"Barely. It's iffy," she said.

"What does he do? I don't remember," I said.

"He's a medical assistant who also happens to be an out-of-control alcoholic. Not a good combination."

The thought of an alcoholic working in a medical office made me wonder about the potential for risky behavior and unsafe choices during COVID. "Sounds like he needs a lot of structure," I said.

The Climate of Truth

"Absolutely. But we can't get the baby boy out of his bedroom. I'm sure he's close to losing his job. Seeing that he doesn't show up for work a lot. Because he's drunk. I don't know if he's able to arrange for a leave of absence until he can pull it together. He's using our home as a hammock. He's lazy and ungrateful. An entitled brat." She tilted her head down to comfort herself by looking at her wedding ring.

"Trying to talk to an alcoholic in distress is like trying to have a meaningful conversation with a wet baggie full of flour," I said.

"He's been to rehab four times already. I paid for that too."

"Have you tried a heart-to-heart?" I asked.

Ruby Jean grew more poised. "I sat him down. I told him that I had my own nervous breakdown in my twenties. I, too, suffered anxiety attacks. I nearly killed myself back then, but I came out the other side."

It was one of those moments when I wished I never heard what was said. My tendency to care about people often caused bombshells to land in my lap.

As if in a trance, Ruby Jean mouthed her words without expression. "It took an awful lot of hard work. But I was <u>willing</u> to do the work. Whatever it took. I did it all by myself. And if I could do it, then the baby boy could certainly do it. All it takes is being completely <u>honest</u> with yourself. It's useless to do the work without <u>honesty</u>. So I asked the baby boy, point blank, if he was 'unwilling' to do the work, or 'unable.'"

"What did he say?"

"'I dunno,' In that mopey, cowardly voice of his. Which was a fairly accurate response." She folded her hands in her lap and continued to gaze upon her wedding ring.

"Your husband is working graveyard, so he's not around for these important discussions. You're the one stuck dealing with it?" I asked.

Ruby Jean sighed heavily. "It's really a thankless task to be the bad cop to someone else's kid…I see so much of his father in him. He's the child of his father's heart. They are so much alike in many ways."

Eyes

I couldn't help but wonder if Ruby Jean was admitting to buyer's remorse in her choice of a husband. From the look in her eyes, she seemed to be coming to the same conclusion, but she tried to shrug it off.

"Well, at least the baby boy was somewhat presentable for Thanksgiving," she said with a slight grimace marked by the creases in the fabric of her mask. "It was a holiday miracle…Did you cook for Thanksgiving?" she asked.

"Nah," I said, wrinkling my nose, remembering how Ruby Jean filled my holiday with angst and stress. "I just made chicken tacos. Nothing special. I prefer to eat out for a traditional Thanksgiving meal. But, as we all know with COVID, there's no fine dining right now."

"There's takeout."

"Not my thing for Thanksgiving," I said.

"I would have invited you over," she said with a pout.

It was a strange offer given the need for social isolation during COVID.

"Thanks, but I've got a perfect quarantine record," I said. "I haven't socialized with a single soul this entire year. Can't stop now. I'm on a roll!"

"Well, we had a lovely time at Thanksgiving," she said. "My mother taught me it was always important to set out the good china for the holidays. It always makes me feel better to have everything look so pretty."

I was nearing the end of my color application with just a few foils to go. "Did you have a turkey with all the fuss?"

"Oh yes, it was a marvel to behold," she said. "Everything was timed very well. Turkey with stuffing, mashed taters, green bean casserole, cranberry sauce, cornbread and pumpkin pie. All the trimmings."

"I hate green bean casserole," I said. "With the cream of mushroom soup and the French-fried onions?" I asked.

"My family loves that stuff. They gobble it down."

The Climate of Truth

"Sounds like you made enough to feed an army," I said. "Leftovers?"

"Heavens no. The baby boy showed up and brought a friend of his from work unexpectedly. I had to rearrange the table and make room for an extra place setting."

Her words sent a shock of electricity up my spinal column. She continued, seemingly unaware of my hidden apprehension. "It was the first time in 35 years I didn't spend Thanksgiving with my family. So, I was very happy that I could host my husband's family," she said.

My hands instantly grew clammy and started to shake. "Who all came to sample your cooking?"

"My husband's eldest son, his wife and three children. His sister and her four kids. Both his parents. And his youngest son brought the unexpected guest from work. It was a full table."

From what I could tell with a fast mental count, there were 16 people at Ruby Jean's Thanksgiving table. I found this out half-way through her long appointment, after all the back-and-forth texts trying to prevent this very situation. After she told me to my face, while she stood on my patio, that she hadn't been unmasked while indoors with people not in her immediate household.

I swallowed the tidal wave of anger that dumped into my chest. I couldn't tell if she simply lost track of her lie about celebrating a "Safe Thanksgiving" or if she was messing with my throbbing head.

The phone rang again. It was a woman who I'd only seen once before for a haircut. A week prior, she had to reschedule her upcoming appointment because she said she was infected with COVID.

"I'm so sorry to hear this news," I told the woman on the phone the week before. "You must be really stressed right now, but I hope you have a speedy recovery." I tried to be as reassuring as possible and allowed her to reschedule the appointment after the required quarantine period. The same woman called back the second time at the precise moment Ruby Jean confessed to hosting a mass gathering at Thanksgiving.

"I need to cancel my rescheduled appointment," the woman on the phone said firmly.

Eyes

"May I ask why?" I asked politely.

"I just got back from Cabo, and I had my hair done down there."

"Oh…Thank you for letting me know," I said as I hung up the phone.

I erased the woman's name from my schedule and turned back to Ruby Jean. "It takes all kinds," I said. "A week ago, that lady said she had COVID. Now she says she just got off a plane from Cabo. Either she lied to me, or she's been busy infecting all kinds of people in two countries."

I searched Ruby Jean's eyes for recognition of my deeper meaning, but she kept her poker face in check. I stood silent for a moment, dumbfounded as Ruby Jean met my gaze over the edge of her mask. The classic harmonies from the *Eagles* drifted out from the stereo:

> "You can't hide your lyin' eyes
> And your smile is a thin disguise
> I thought by now you'd realize
> There ain't no way to hide your lyin' eyes"

I looked quickly away from her, having finished the color application. I gathered all my materials and carried them into the back room, behind a closed door, where I could privately hyperventilate. The feeling of betrayal was overwhelming. My anger made my face feel like a fever blister. I couldn't think. I felt violated.

"I hate being right about people!" I whispered to myself.

It took nearly the entire 35 minutes of Ruby Jean's processing time for me to collect myself. My volcanic stomach shot wads of acid into my throat. I decided it was in my best interest to contain my feelings and not allow her to know the extent of my fury.

The timer bell rang out and Irma barked to announce it was time for me to rinse Ruby Jean's color. I covered my face with a mask once again as I emerged from the back room. Irma escorted Ruby Jean to the shampoo sink. I removed Ruby Jean's headful of foils, and then handed her a COVID safety towel.

The Climate of Truth

"Please hold the towel over your eyes and nose when you recline in the sink," I said in a clinical, professional tone. She shimmied her hips toward the back of the chair and laid gently back into the sink with the towel over her face.

"Please lift your feet," I said. She followed my instructions as I hoisted the footrest. Grateful that the barrier towel prevented me from having to look at Ruby Jean's eyes, I began to wash the color from her head. Her long tresses filled the entire sink like a coiled, blonde snake. I scrubbed, rinsed, and conditioned her hair, then squeezed the water out of it. I then took the towel from her face to pat her hair dry.

"I'll meet you back at the styling chair. You wanted a trim, right? A quarter-inch?" I asked not looking her in the eyes. I scooped a wad of her shed hair out of the trap in the sink, wrapped it into my vinyl gloves, and threw the bundle in the trashcan.

"Correct," she said. "Quarter-inch. My hair lays so nicely right now. Especially the second and third day after a wash. I really like the length. It's so much easier now that my hair is growing back in."

"Good to hear."

"It's always a great day when it's 'sacred hair appointment' day!" she said with a nod of her head.

We settled into the haircut. I decided the safest thing to do to prevent losing my temper was to circle the conversation back to Ruby Jean's stepson. I sectioned off her haircut.

"The way I see it," she explained, "I refuse to fund the baby boy's dysfunction any longer. I'm ready to buy him out – put a down payment on a house for him and ship him off to failure."

"That's pouring money down the toilet."

"I'm already pouring money down the toilet with this kid," she said with a shrug of her shoulders. "I don't know what else to do."

"Can your husband take a leave of absence from his job to deal with this?"

"We've talked about it. Don't know what good that would do because my husband just can't seem to muster the 'tough love' approach."

"Sounds like a family intervention might be necessary," I said.

Eyes

"No one else wants to deal with the baby boy either. They think if they push too hard, the kid will just up and kill himself. And I'll be the one who will have to scrub the bloodstains out of the crack in the bathtub."

"How old is this kid?"

"Thirty-three," Ruby Jean said quite sadly.

"Way too old to be skimming off his parents."

"Way too old," she said, echoing my tone. "When millennials go bad, they go really, really bad. They can complicate a one-car funeral."

"Maybe you could pack a bag and move into your parents' house, alone for a bit. Maybe the separation will help your husband commit to taking a stand."

"I hope it doesn't come to that," Ruby Jean said, her eyes welling with tears. "My husband is a good man. I don't want to hurt him. I don't ever want to force him to choose between me and his son. When my husband is away on his Civil War weekends, the kid brings some strange man into our home for a romantic romp. But he can't be bothered to go to work. I'm being held hostage in my own home."

She looked up at me through her tears. *Blue Eyes Cryin' in the Rain*," I thought to myself.

Embarrassed, Ruby Jean shifted her gaze to her wedding ring again. She eyed the ring with a touch of melancholy. "Oh drat!...I lost a diamond. I thought the ring looked paler than usual today," she said with a sigh. "Just another way that God is testing me."

The missing diamond reminded me of the gaping hole in someone's smile where they are missing a front tooth, the dark void surrounded by the white of bone.

Ruby Jean ran her fingers over her thread-bare yoga pants as my ionic blow dryer evaporated the steam from her head. "Wow. I need new leggings," she said. "You can see my knees right through the fabric."

I put my hand gently on her shoulder. "Even with your hair falling out from all this stress, and even with holes in your knees, you don't look the worse for wear, honey bear."

The Climate of Truth

She fist-pumped the air without enthusiasm. "Cheers for big ears!" she said. She wiped the tears from her eyes with the sleeve of her sweater.

❖

Within a few days, I was surprised to receive a customized Christmas card from Ruby Jean. It featured a photo where she stood with her hands on her hips beside a Christmas wreath hung on her front door. She had a pitiful look on her face. In the foreground, her gregarious husband, sporting a goatee and a wooly cap stretched across his bald head, made googly eyes at the camera from the bottom corner of the card. It would have been impossible for him not to have noticed the sadness captured in his wife's eyes. The caption on the card read in white letters, *"Decking the Halls – and – Bouncing off Walls."* The flipside of the card was a poignant statement in grey-blue print:

> "*This card says it all, right?*
>
> *We imagine that like us, your 2020 was full of ups and downs and that you are heartily sick of the coronavirus pandemic. The sadness of Ruby Jean first losing her mom, and then her dad, and not being able to hold a funeral, has been offset with the peace of knowing that her dad is reunited with her mom in their heavenly home and not cruelly locked down in solitary confinement like so many older people have been.*
>
> *The infringement of seemingly never-ending pandemic restrictions upon our freedoms has been offset with gratitude that we have both retained our jobs. The pain of various members in lockdown-induced crises has reinforced the importance of family connections and faith. And so, it goes. In honesty, we have found ourselves gritting our teeth at times while striving to fulfil the admonition of Romans 12:12 – 'Be joyful in hope, patient in affliction, faithful in prayer.'"*

Eyes

I wasn't inspired to send my usual barrage of holiday cards during COVID Christmas, but I was compelled to send one to Ruby Jean after reading her despondent greeting. I sent her a card with a glittered polar bear joyfully playing in the snow, flat on its back, feet up in the air. I wrote:

> *"Ruby Jean,*
>
> *The thing that I hold onto most these days is the feeling that it can only get better from here. I wish you all the happiness you can imagine at this time of new beginnings.*
>
> *Mike at Blow Your Top,"* signed with a cupid's heart.

Once the holidays passed, I decided to call Ruby Jean after the first of the year to reestablish my boundaries about the COVID safety protocols. To my surprise, she picked up on the first ring.

"Oh! It's you! Live and in person," I said. "I thought I would get your voicemail."

"Well, here I am, working remotely from home," she replied in a friendly voice.

"How are things in your universe?"

"Hanging in there," she said, attempting to remain positive. "How about you? Did you have a good Christmas?"

"It was a quiet rest from everything else going on in the world."

"Amen to that," she said.

"Is the stepson behaving?"

"Honestly, he hasn't been too awful lately, so there's hope," she said, sounding cheerful.

"That's a relief."

"Amen to that too," she said.

"Well, I needed to talk to you about something important," I said as excruciating pressure built in my stomach.

"What about?"

The Climate of Truth

"It's difficult for me to say…I was very disheartened when I saw you last."

"Oh no! Whatever for?" she said, dismayed.

"You told me about the large number of people you had over for Thanksgiving."

"It was just my husband's family," she objected gently. "Didn't I explain to you that those people were all in our 'bubble'?"

"There was no mention of a bubble. You said your stepson brought a stranger home from work unexpectedly."

"Oh heavens! I'm so sorry that I wasn't abundantly clear. My husband's parents are both 78 years old. Everybody had to get COVID tested before they could come to Thanksgiving. Everyone wore masks until we sat down at the table. We were as safe as we could be. My in-laws would not have come if a stranger was at the table, so when my stepson asked to bring his friend from work, the answer was no. Thankfully, my stepson didn't over-react – he was rather cordial, which was unexpected."

It wouldn't have made any difference for me to point out the glaring inconsistencies in her revamped account. "Well, just as long as we are clear from here on in, if you are indoors while unmasked in front of people that you don't live with, including friends and family, then we will have to reschedule your appointment for at least ten days out. All of my other clients are doing the same thing because they don't want me, or anyone else to end up in the hospital…or worse." As soon as I said those words, the pressure in my stomach disappeared because I spoke my truth.

"I understand," Ruby Jean said, audibly inhaling heavily into the receiver.

"With everything else happening in your life, I didn't want to pile on," I said, sincerely. "I was worried about speaking to you about this."

"I would expect nothing less of you, Mike. You have to protect your business. You are all you've got."

I was amazed by her aura of calm and her obvious effort to deescalate. "Thank you for acknowledging that," I said. "We all have to be extremely careful right now to protect everyone in our lives."

Eyes

"Absolutely," Ruby Jean said. "No worries on my end, Mike. I will be happy to see you for my appointment. Thank you for calling." She quietly hung up the phone.

Ten days later, the night before her next appointment, Ruby Jean sent a text at 10:00pm:

> *"UPDATE: Someone in my bubble was exposed to COVID today. Sorry for this being so last minute, but given what has happened, I have to cancel my appointment at 9:00am tomorrow morning. No need to reschedule. Hopefully I will be able to keep my appointment six weeks from now, but if not, you know I'll only go down swinging. Since I won't be seeing you tomorrow on your special day, I wanted to at least say Happy Birthday to you."*

There was no way I could find someone else to take Ruby Jean's spot in my schedule on such short notice, so I lost two and a half hours of work. But I preferred that to risking COVID exposure on my Birthday.

I texted a response: *"I am very sorry to hear this news. My heart goes out to you. I hope everything turns out OK."*

"Thank you," she replied.

That was the last I heard from Ruby Jean on the subject, and I did not press for more details. From that point on, however, she did not complain about wearing a mask. She also seemed to be a calmer person who refrained from raising her voice and using incendiary language.

When she married her husband, Ruby Jean promised that he would not have to retire with a mortgage payment. She kept her word. She used her inheritance to pay off the mortgage to their new house and settled the rest of their debts. That was a lucky move, given that her husband required full-knee replacement surgery. Her husband also wanted to retire someplace on a coast because he always loved the water. Ruby Jean insisted that they must retire in one of the seven states that did not have income tax. Of those seven states, only four had coastlines: Alaska, Florida, Texas and Washington. Ruby Jean's other deciding factor was to live in a state

The Climate of Truth

that did not impose quarantine restrictions and closures because of the COVID pandemic. I suppose that last qualification took Washington state, the place where she had lived most of her life, out of the running.

An epidemiological study released by *Columbia University Mailman School of Public Health* showed that 103 million Americans (31%, or 1 out of every three people) had already been infected with COVID by December 2020. Large metropolitan cities showed even higher infection rates from 42% to 52%. More than 60% of the upper Midwest and the Mississippi Valley were estimated to have been infected. The number of active COVID cases were known to have been severely underreported and were estimated to have been ten times the official count. Comparatively, the CDC only reported a COVID positivity rate of 12.3%. Three-quarters of all infections were undocumented because they were asymptomatic or only caused mild symptoms and were not reported. Undocumented cases caused the virus to spread quickly through the population, which revealed that COVID was a very dangerous and highly underestimated pathogen in the first year of the pandemic.

It took several months for the truth to come out. Ruby Jean's stepson was arrested for drunk driving. Soon after, he was infected with COVID. As a result, both of Ruby Jean's in-laws were infected, and her father-in-law was admitted to the ICU where he was intubated and died. The science showed that bald me were more susceptible to COVID, and Ruby Jean's husband was predisposed to contract double pneumonia as a result. He survived but developed "long hauler's syndrome" that included impotency. He was forced to retire early. Ruby Jean was laid off from her job because of cutbacks caused by the pandemic and she could no longer afford her "sacred hair appointments."

Flowers

It was yet another Friday, the week before Christmas 2020. The day began with a call before the shop was even open. I was brewing my morning coffee when I answered the phone. A panicked voice oozed through the receiver like a whistling kettle that was boiling over on an overheated stove.

"I have to cancel my appointment!" a woman's voice squealed in a thick, languid drawl the moment I answered. "Did you hear me!" she shouted. "I have to cancel my appointment this morning!"

"Mavis? Is that you?" I asked.

"I know it's very short notice and you're gonna hate me, but I have to cancel!" She sounded as though she might shatter into a million shards of glass at any second.

"I don't hate anybody, Mavis. Are you alright?"

"No! No, I am not!" she spewed.

Mavis was a transplant from Houston. She was usually out of breath for the first half of her haircut due to her severe asthmatic condition, a "touch of diabetes" as she called it, and a weak ticker. She was frequently hot and sweaty, a side effect of her various maladies and medications. On top of that, COVID terrified her, which tended to magnify her symptoms. She was morbidly obese with very bad ankles and knees that made it difficult for her to climb the stairs

The Climate of Truth

to my shop. She walked gingerly, wincing with each step as if she were barefoot while treading over a bed of razor blades. Advanced osteoporosis caused her to shatter three vertebrae simply by rolling over in bed. Though she needed emergency surgery, Mavis decided to allow her pulverized spine to fuse on its own. That very painful choice would take years to heal. Her acute level of agony made her temperament appear hostile.

Mavis nearly gave herself a heart attack the first time she showed up for a pandemic haircut in June 2020, when the shop first reopened after lockdown. She was almost too afraid of COVID to leave her house, and I spent a great deal of time calming her down before I picked up the scissors. I coaxed her into conversation about her bold color choices in quilting fabrics. That helped to refocus her attention long enough to allow me to snip away her locks. While cutting her coarse, unruly hair that she rarely combed herself, I looked over her shoulder as she scrolled through hundreds of photographs of the quilts she kept on her cellphone. With continuous flicks of her finger, the geometric images flashed over the screen so quickly that I became dizzy and had to look away.

"Looky here!" she said, suddenly stopping to enlarge an image. "I made this one special, just for my granddaughter. All her favorite colors!"

I must have said "gorgeous!" dozens of times.

"I could just quilt all-the-day-long!" she said. Her fingers trembled when the thought of COVID returned to her. She set her cellphone down when her shaking hands made it impossible for her to scroll through the photos any longer.

I put my hand on her back reassuringly as her asthmatic cough flared with escalating anxiety. "Take it easy on yourself, sugar-plumb," I said.

"It's the dang mask – makes it harder to breathe!" she wheezed.

"I know how you feel. I wheeze all the time too," I said.

The last time I saw her in the shop, she had me cut her shoulder length hair into a cropped pixie. She never asked me to do that kind of style before. I usually advised not to do drastic haircuts at a time of crisis, such as a global pandemic. Against my better judgment, I gave in to her demand to chop it all off.

Flowers

"Ooooooooo-eeeeeee! That's short!" she gasped, eyeing her new profile in the mirror.

"You insisted," I countered with a chuckle.

"I know, I know! It seemed like such a good idea at the time."

"I think you look pretty snazzy with short hair. And it helps control the frizz," I reassured her.

"Is <u>that</u> what it does?" she asked, tilting her head to one side like a cockatiel.

"You've been updated!" I announced to the room. "I think it makes your eyes and your cheekbones stand out."

"You think so?" she said, tipping her head in the opposite direction.

"Absolutely."

"You're so full of shit, pardon my French. I'm too fat to have cheekbones," she said, matter-of-factly.

"Look right here," I said, pointing to a spot just below her eye and just above the top edge of her mask. "There's a shadow-line on your face…That, my dear, is clearly the topmost part of your cheekbone. And your new haircut accentuates the hollow of your cheek. It makes you look thinner. That's why they call me 'Magic Mike!'"

"I will never be able to make my hair look as good as you do, 'Magic Mike'," she said, squinting her eyes. "I'm just no good at it."

"If I can do it, you can do it!" I said with sincere optimism. "It's pretty easy, low maintenance, not rocket science."

"If it's that easy, it can't be all that magic, 'Magic Mike,'" she said bluntly. She stared at herself in the mirror for a moment. "I think I might like it."

"It's super cute!" I said.

"I'll take your word for it," she said, finally breathing at a rested pace. "It's really hard to tell, wearing a damn mask and all."

Three months later, her call interrupted my morning coffee. It was the week before Christmas. She spoke in a hysterical whisper, as

The Climate of Truth

if an intruder had just broken into her home and she feared for her life.

"Did you hear me!" she shouted. "I have to cancel my appointment this morning!"

"What's wrong, Mavis?" I asked, concerned.

"It's my finger!" she screeched into the phone, sounding as if she were about to cry.

"OK? What happened?"

"You know I broke it, right? I know I told you!" she insisted as she began to hyperventilate.

"Yes, I remember now," I said, even though I didn't recall at all.

"Well, I fell on it! Smack-dab right on it, you know, and I broke it. You know me, I trip over my own two feet all the ding-dong time! Me and my bad knees."

"Oh no!"

"Snapped my finger clean through," she said. "My husband had to rush me to the emergency room. My poor little finger was all sideways from my hand, hangin' by a thread!"

"Eeesh." I winced.

"Smashed it up real good!" she said, her voice trembling.

The image of her enormous body landing on a single finger made a jolt of electric sympathy pain shoot up my spine.

"I had no choice," she continued. "I just <u>had</u> to go to the emergency room! It hurt so bad! It made me cry!" she groaned, breathing heavily to force the air into her lungs. "It's gonna need pins!!!"

I waited for the bomb to detonate.

"I broke my dang finger…and now I spiked a fever!!!" She sobbed hysterically into the phone. Her breath made whooshing noises.

"You think it's COVID?" I asked, cautiously.

"The emergency room is the only place I've been. I was right next to all them sickies! Otherwise I haven't set foot outside of this house! Except to see you!"

Flowers

"Have you been tested?" I asked.

"The doctor says the fever might be because of my finger," she said with a sniffle. "He says they don't have enough COVID tests for everybody anyway. So I didn't get tested."

I'd never heard of it before, but according to the internet, an infection can develop in a broken bone, and that can cause a fever to spike.

"Let's hope you just gave yourself a hot-flash from all the excitement and pain, that's all," I said. I wondered if the doctor fibbed to help prevent Mavis from rocketing into a complete nervous breakdown. There are times when that caliber of white lie is humane.

"Anyway, I have to cancel my appointment because of the fever," she fumed. "I am so sorry to do it to you last minute like this. And I really needed a haircut right now too. Dang it!" Her breath sounded like turbulence at 40,000 feet.

"I understand, honey. We gotta stay safe," I said as calmly as possible.

"I don't know -- I just don't know…when I might be able to come back to see you…" Her voice trailed off in tears.

"Don't worry about it. Just call me when you can. We'll figure it out," I said.

"Uh huh," she answered quietly, though it seemed like there should have been more words. "I just can't breathe," she said. I could hear the mewling of her lungs. She hung up the phone slowly without saying anything else. Her goodbye was a click of the dial-tone.

I remembered thinking that I wouldn't get to see how her short pixie cut grew out.

An ambulance suddenly sped past the shop window going 70 miles per hour. I wondered if EMTs would have difficulty hoisting a very large woman like Mavis onto a gurney. I shook my head to get the vision of it out of my mind. The hyper phone call about her broken finger was the last time I ever spoke with her. I worried about her for months and assumed she became a statistic when she didn't return any of my calls.

The Climate of Truth

❖

After I hung up the phone, I noticed two homeless men on the church lawn across the street from my front window. I immediately redialed.

"Police non-emergency," the operator said.

"My name is Mike."

"What are you reporting?"

"Two homeless guys," I said, looking out my front window as I spoke. "Camped out on the lawn across the street. There is a no-trespass agreement with the police department. I need to have an officer dispatched to remove these people from private church property. They are right in front of a sign that says *'no-trespassing.'*" I provided the address.

"Physical description of the men?" the dispatcher asked.

"Both White males. One in his early thirties, I think. Long, dark hair, bushy beard. The other, an older guy, maybe in his mid-fifties," I said as if I'd reported such things 500 times over the past few years.

"What are they wearing?"

"Well, right now I can tell you they are NOT wearing pants," I said. "They are both squatting on the church lawn to take a dump right in front of me and everyone else driving by. They are chatting with each other. Both of them are holding a cup of coffee," I said as plainly as I could. "At least I think it's coffee."

The operator continued, unphased by the account. "On the south side of the building?"

"Yes. On the east end of the south side, toward the white house next door. The older guy has a white baseball cap and the younger one has a navy-blue wooly cap and a blue plaid lumberjack jacket. They've got their gear spread out in the bushes. Tarps and bedrolls and such."

"Are they armed?" the operator asked.

"No idea," I replied.

"Have you approached them?"

"You guys tell me never to do that," I said.

Flowers

"Yes, good, we don't want you making contact with them, for safety reasons."

"Yes, of course," I said, overly familiar with the instructions.

"Do you want the officer to contact you?" I could hear the dispatcher typing notes into the computer system.

"Sometimes they call me, sometimes they don't. I've been a caretaker for the church for the past three years. This happens all the time," I said, well-rehearsed. "We just need the police to move them along."

I took up the frequent task of reporting encroachments at the church because the church members rarely did. If I didn't report it, the problem would increase and spread across the street to my front porch as it had before. The church members felt guilty about calling the police to deal with trespassers, especially if they were arrested for refusing to leave. I explained to one of the board members that it didn't serve the homeless to allow them to camp on the porch of the church without care of any kind. I clarified that if the church wanted to serve the homeless, it should invite them into the sanctuary, give them a cot and access to a shower and a toilet, and hot food. The church members didn't want to be involved at that level -- it was far too much responsibility.

The police dispatcher asked, "Do you have any symptoms of COVID?"

The question startled me. No operator had ever asked me that specific question before. "The responding officer can call me if he needs to," I said. "He doesn't have to meet me face to face. And to answer your question, no, I don't have any symptoms of COVID. I always wear a mask."

"I will pass all the information along. You have a good day now, ma'am," the dispatcher said as she disconnected.

Operators commonly mistook me for a woman on the phone, even when I plainly told them my name was Mike. It made me cranky when people who were trained to listen didn't hear. But these were jarring times that numbed everyone's senses. I asked various people sitting in my styling chair if they thought I sounded like a woman, and they always said no.

The Climate of Truth

I later discovered the emergency call center was having serious staffing trouble. Call volumes were soaring with COVID related issues. Emergency operators were getting burned out and they were quitting in droves. A skeleton crew was all that was left to operate the 9-1-1 system. Call volumes were so heavy that callers had to wait on hold for up to half an hour. The panicked public screamed their COVID fears at emergency operators who truly wanted to help. But there was only so much help a sane person could give before they reached the breaking point. Police departments were also struggling to keep enough officers on staff; entire police units in metro areas resigned en masse because of the risk of being exposed to pandemic violence.

Luckily, two officers responded to the church across the street within a few minutes of my call. Sometimes the police were too busy with other crises to respond, and I would have to call back several times to request assistance. Sometimes the trespassers refused to leave, and they got carted off to jail because they wanted a warm bed for the night. But in this case, the two homeless men laughed, pulled up their pants and walked away without resistance. They left a barrage of plastic bags, newspapers, cardboard, chewed food and other refuse for someone else to clean up. The officers decided not to cite them for indecent exposure because it was nearly impossible to enforce infractions against the homeless. The officers carefully stepped away from the used toilet paper bundled amid the piles of excrement left on the church lawn.

❖

My front doorbell suddenly rang, and I almost jumped out of my skin at the sound of it. Since COVID protocols began, I didn't allow entry to my shop through the front door. I unbolted the door to find a rather nervous looking Latino man wearing a mask.

"Deese eeze por jew!" he whimpered in a thick accent as he thrust a vase of flowers right at my masked face. In his attempt to hand off the flowers, he turned his face away from mine as far as he could while he kept one squinted eye trained on me. He was leaning backwards to get as much airspace between us as possible. It struck me that the poor guy was petrified every time he rang a doorbell, thinking he could catch COVID from any of the flower deliveries he made to total strangers. His mask was black, making the whites of his

Flowers

horrified eyes stand out against his golden-brown skin. Once he handed me the flowers, the delivery man scrambled away as if to escape being shot. His running steps clomped all the way down the long deck to the back stairs by the parking lot. The scent of fear was in the air. Bewildered by the interaction, I shut and locked the front door.

    I glanced down at the bouquet in my hands and immediately noticed several white chrysanthemums throughout the arrangement. Every chrysanthemum was wilted, their petals falling to the floor. The edges of the red roses were turning black as if scorched by a lighter. The white pearlescent lilies were bruised and crumpled with black and purple cracks, and the center of the blooms near the pistils were turning brown. In the middle of the carnage were two felt reindeer antlers. Had the bouquet been fresh, it would have been a jolly holiday treat. But looking at the deplorable condition of those flowers made me loathe humanity.

    I set the vase on the front desk and stared at it in disbelief. The attached card had my name on it, along with a holiday message of love and hope from one of my dearest clients and her husband. They sent holiday flowers to me annually, and I was sure they were costly. The name of the florist was missing from the card; I'd never seen an incognito delivery before. The mood of injustice gurgled in my gut and added to the calamity of the day.

❖

    Logan arrived for his appointment soon after the fatal flowers were delivered. The first thing to know about Logan is that he was a retired police investigator. His professional expertise overtly defined his perceptions. He was an impenetrable fortress of skeptical suspicion. In his mind, that made him reliably flighty-proof. He was very protective of those he chose to welcome into his circle, and he regarded our friendship with warmth.

    At 6'4", he knew to slouch way down in the styling chair so I could reach the top of his head while standing on my tiptoes. He hired me for the unpleasant task of wrapping the tiniest yellow perm rods into his short, broomstraw hair every eight weeks. By the time I was finished, I could barely feel my fingers. But I enjoyed his company and our philosophical banter while I agonized to serve him.

The Climate of Truth

"The first time I met you, Mike, I knew you were the perfect person to give me a perm!" he said with bravado.

Logan had to perm his hair his entire adult life to avoid appearing like a thistle bush, a look that he thought would have destroyed his credibility as an expert witness. I was the first person he hired to work on his hair when he moved away from San Francisco with his second wife. He told me he did a deep dive and background check on my business and was convinced I would proficiently shield him from any form of hair catastrophe. We'd been friends ever since, something I did with only a few clients over my career.

Together with his wife, Mary, we enjoyed fine-dining excursions in the city. Logan insisted on being the chauffeur. I was amply impressed by the masterful way he could speedily navigate his giant SUV within inches of various cement columns in a parking garage. Around and around we raced floor to floor in search of a parking spot. The tires squealed against the cement of the parking structure with sharp radial turns. It was a fine-motor skill Logan learned at the Police Academy. With a huge grin, he informed me that he could also do the maneuver in reverse. From the backseat, I begged him not to.

I was amused by the way Logan sat with a knife in one hand and a fork in the other, a napkin tucked in the collar of his shirt, ready and waiting for his hunk of cow to be served. He liked to wash it down with a cocktail. He disavowed vegetables and bread as a waste of real estate in his stomach. He always refused the cash I handed him to pay for my supper, so I had to slip it discretely into Mary's purse. She pretended not to notice. We hadn't been out to dinner together since the pandemic began, and I missed it greatly.

When my old washing machine galloped across the floor at midnight and exploded, spewing gallons of soapy water throughout the main level of my house, Logan delivered and installed a brand-new washer the very next morning. With all the breakdowns of the supply chains in manufacturing, it was an absolute miracle that I could find and replace an appliance on an emergency basis during COVID. There was at least a two-month delay for home deliveries of appliances (six months or longer as the pandemic progressed), so Logan's kindness kept my shop open because my salon couldn't function without a working laundry.

When I couldn't find the bulk rolls of paper towels needed to sanitize the shop between every client as required by the *State*

Flowers

Department of Health, Logan was the first to make special trips to the store to nab the newly arrived 12-pack shipments that kept me stocked up. Being an asthmatic, it was too dangerous for me to risk shopping at a super-crowded *Costco.* Due to the limited supply, the stores would only allow one pack per customer.

It was always a fight for Logan to accept reimbursement. "Don't worry about it," he said coyly. "I need to make sure you stay open so you can do my perm. It's purely selfish motivation."

I always managed to stuff money into his pocket while he protested with his arms up. "You make me feel like a stripper!" he complained.

"Don't flatter yourself, honey!" I said, laughing. "You're not at all my type!"

I told Logan how unsafe I felt when right-wing protestors marched, shirtless, in front of my home with American flags strapped to their backs. About 30 of them, wearing camouflaged army surplus pants, gathered on the sidewalk just outside the front window. They slammed their open palms repeatedly with clubs and metal pipes as a sign of intimidation. I had no idea why they chose my Victorian house to menace during the first COVID summer, but I knew there were some far-right extremist organizations based nearby. Protests and counter-protests were becoming more frequent. There was always a chance that random violence could erupt, but fortunately, violence didn't find its way to my corner of the city. Nevertheless, the intimidation tactics used by the shirtless men in camouflaged army pants scared off the client who was sitting in my styling chair at the time.

"If anything happens, call me right away, and I will be at your house in five minutes!" Logan insisted over the phone. "I'll take care of it, whatever it is!"

Imagining him, one ex-cop with a perm, against a crowd of rowdy, supremacist hooligans, gave me pause. But Logan truly meant what he said. As a man living alone at a time like that, I could sleep better at night because of his promise to defend me, though I would never hold him to it.

Logan retired at the age of 56 from a life-long pursuit of law, order, and politics (all synonyms for deceit and dysfunction

The Climate of Truth

according to him). "How could you afford to retire so early?" I asked him in disbelief.

"White privilege," he said abruptly. "That, plus I worked my ass off, and my beautiful wife is bringing home the bacon all on her own." He further explained that he chose to retire early because the justice system often aided hardened criminals to escape from prosecution. He'd had enough of paying exorbitant San Francisco taxes to support what he thought of as a failed bureaucracy.

Even after retirement, Logan was summoned by those he described as "shifty-eyed district attorneys" to testify in murder cases that made national news. He was the investigator assigned to those cases. Logan wasn't at all fond of the lady Attorney General with whom he was forced to work on several occasions; she would later become Vice President Harris, the first woman of color elected to such a high office in the US. Logan was proud to make Ms. Harris uncomfortable because he detested her brand of liberalism.

When his cases came before the court, Logan testified to the evidence he collected and processed years before. He then suffered being branded a liar by criminal defense attorneys. That always made Logan's face turn bright red in the witness box. His face turned even more red when I showed him news articles about the trials he attended. Without generous amounts of hairspray to glue his brushed perm into place, his resentments over the lack of accountability in the courts would certainly have caused his tight perm to spring from his head like sprouts from a *Chia Pet* planter. That would not have been a good look for him as an expert witness.

Logan's general philosophy was rooted in a scorched-earth Libertarianism, meaning any form of government was too much government for him, because <u>all</u> government was invasive and tyrannical. To me, that seemed like a strange sentiment coming from a guy who spent his entire career working <u>for</u> the government. This meant that I often had to converse with him carefully, or risk unleashing a political debate that pitted liberalism against conservatism, always a losing prospect in my view. It was disconcerting for me to be unable to tell when Logan was joking and when he was sincere. And he seemed to revel in my struggle to discern the difference, what I considered the mark of a cynical man. In my view, his cynicism was born of deep-rooted pain. I waited

Flowers

patiently to see if Logan's hard shell would crack open to release the real, gentle and caring soul that I knew he carried inside of him.

❖

    Logan and Mary pulled into my driveway on my day off. It was the middle of June 2020, and I had just been back to work after lockdown. I hadn't seen Logan in the shop for months, first because of the mandated COVID closure for non-essential businesses like salons, and second, because out of desperation, he took the clippers to his own head to shave off his thistle bush since I couldn't give him his much-needed perm. The buzz-cut combined with the N-95 mask strapped to his face made him look like an endangered platypus. All three of us wore masks as we spoke, even though we were standing outside in my driveway.

    "Special delivery!" Logan said merrily, handing off two jumbo packs of paper towels, laundry detergent, bleach wipes, and spray cleaner.

    "Whoa! Your hair looks even shorter in person!" I laughed into my mask.

    "This is what happens when the Governor destroys the economy with lockdowns. Stupidity takes over!" Logan crossed his arm over his midsection and bowed deeply to give me a clear view of the handywork on top of his head.

    "Stand up, man! Don't force me to look at your mutilation!" I yelled. "It's going to take months for that to grow back out before it's long enough to perm again."

    "Can this pandemic get any more tragic!" Logan yelled to the sky.

    "How did you manage two packs of paper towels? I thought they enforced the limit," I said.

    "I bought the first one, took it out to the car," Logan said. "Then I went back inside and bought the second one, and nobody noticed. I don't call that cheating, because it's going to a good cause -- you!"

    "Awwwww…You got the receipt for the goods?" I said, bashfully.

The Climate of Truth

"Drat!" he said with feigned absent-mindedness while patting his pockets. "I guess I must have dropped it in the parking lot at the store." He gave himself a squirt of hand sanitizer and massaged it into his skin. He offered a squirt to his wife.

"Haven't seen you guys in months!" I said, stuffing cash into his pocket as usual to pay for my supplies.

His tender wife, Mary, kept her social distance. She nervously squeezed the metal strip over the nose-bridge of her mask to make it fit more snuggly on her face. "We miss your foody little self so much!" she said. The quiver in her voice gave away the fact that she was scared to death to be out in public with the virus on the loose.

"Don't make me hungry talking about food," I replied. "We never made it to the steakhouse downtown before the lockdown. I'm so bummed. God only knows when we will be able to enjoy fine dining again."

"There won't be any restaurants left anywhere in this country," Logan said smugly.

"More than 100,000 closed down for good so far," I said.

"What a waste!" Logan shook his head, resentment building pressure within him.

Personally, I couldn't see why anyone would want to sit, unmasked around strangers, just for the right to eat out at a restaurant during a pandemic. In my mind, takeout was as far as it should go until things were under control. But my heart went out to the restaurant workers who were losing everything while COVID hammered that sector of the economy. Several of them used to be my clients, and they could no longer afford my services. I purchased take-out at least once a week to help support the restaurants in their time of need.

Logan and Mary stood on the bottom rung of the back staircase to my house. I stood on the top landing facing them both. We talked without moving from those positions for the better part of an hour. Then Mary ascended the stairs to stand closer to me while facing her husband below. The conversation had turned to the civil rights protests that had been taking place across the country in response to the murder of George Floyd.

Flowers

"I can't talk about this!" Logan protested through his N-95 mask, his arms raised in the air.

"Why not?" I asked.

"It's click-bait! They feed this crap to you, and you eat it right up! Click, click, click! Money, money, money! And that's why cities are on fire!" He grew red-faced with anger. His reaction was quick triggered like a flash-bang grenade.

"Not every protester is a vandal or a looter," I offered in a measured voice. Until that moment, I had never seen Logan lose his temper.

"I'm not going there! I can't do it! Not happening!" He backed away from us with his arms still in the air. In that stance, Logan looked exactly like the protesters who marched against police brutality with their arms raised in the "don't shoot!" pose. "You don't want to hear it from me! You don't want to see me like this!" Logan shouted.

"Hear what? I'm talking with you because I care about you," I said.

"Why can't you talk about this with us, honey?" Mary asked her husband, sounding hurt.

"No, I won't do it!" Logan repeated, violently shaking his head.

"There's institutional racism in this country," I said.

"Ack! Ack! Ack!" Logan snapped as he whipped his hands in wild gestures.

I was undeterred. "People of color are not getting the same level of treatment for COVID that White people can get. People of color are dying a heck of a lot more in this pandemic. COVID itself is showing us the institutional racism in our country, and something needs to be done about it. We have an entrenched caste system, and Whites think they are at the top of the food chain. Sometimes protests are the only way to motivate necessary change."

"It's not a good thing when cities burn! That's the bottom line! That is not the answer!" Logan said, raising his voice to a loud growl like a bear defending its cubs from trespassing humans.

"Then what IS the answer?" I demanded.

The Climate of Truth

"It ISN'T *'Black Lives Matter,'*" he muttered. "That's for damn sure!"

"Are you saying it's *'ALL lives matter?'* I'll have to slap the White privilege right out of you," I said jokingly.

"Don't go there!" Logan warned.

"I know! It's 'BLUE lives matter' for you, right?" I shouted. "Because you're an ex-cop. It's the Blue Wall. The Thin Blue Line. I'm totally hooked on the cop TV show, *'Blue Bloods!'* You know blue is my absolute favorite color! Seriously!" Logan stared at me intensely, but I continued. "Come on, you always tease me about this kind of stuff. Don't stop now because you got your knickers in a knot."

"Just keep pushing and see what happens!" The look in Logan's eyes said he wasn't kidding, but I kept at it.

"Wait! Wait! I know!" I said. "It's 'Black Olives Matter!' They even have T-shirts for that one! You gotta admit, that's good timing on that joke."

"Meh," Logan said.

There was a long pause while Logan caught his breath.

"Do you think they should make the choke hold illegal for cops to use?" I asked.

Logan's fuse was suddenly lit again. "THE CHOKE HOLD SAVED MY LIFE MANY TIMES! I WOULDN'T BE STANDING HERE TODAY WERE IT NOT FOR THE FUCKING CHOKE HOLD!" Logan seethed, grasping the air with his fingertips.

"Do you think it was a crime, the way George Floyd died?" I asked.

"He died because he had a heart attack from a fentanyl overdose!" Logan said sharply, sounding annoyed. "It's all right there in the medical examiner's report!"

"Come on!" I objected. "You deflected my question. Like the politics of the situation didn't find its way into the jurisdictional medical exam. Yeah, right. You're better than that! George Floyd was recovering from COVID. He got it back in March. His lungs were very weak. The pressure on his neck, because a cop was kneeling on it for almost nine minutes, and his inability to breathe caused things that looked like blood clots to explode in his lungs. He suffocated

Flowers

with his face smashed into the asphalt with that cop riding him. George Floyd's family had an independent medical exam that showed he died of traumatic asphyxiation caused specifically by that cop kneeling on his neck!"

"Any narrative can be manipulated to suit any agenda," Logan said abruptly.

"The asphyxia caused his heart to stop. Murder is murder," I said.

"George Floyd was a felon! He aimed a loaded gun at a pregnant woman's belly when he committed armed robbery!" Logan shouted. His passions were roused to the point that his head shook from side to side. He had to adjust his mask several times to put it back in place.

"It's far too convenient to assassinate the character of a dead man to cover for officers who committed grievous crimes," I said, pointedly. "Did you follow the evidence to come to your conclusions? Like you always tell me to do? Or are you simply offering opinion?"

Logan did not respond. He shifted his gaze to the cement at his feet.

"Just the facts, man," I continued, plainly. I opted to push through his resistance. "I don't accept that you think it was justifiable for an angry White officer to suffocate a handcuffed Black man while the whole world watched in horror…While three other officers had their hands in their pockets like you have right now, and then say George Floyd had it coming. That a Black man died like that over a stupid twenty-dollar bill. He didn't attack anybody or hurt anybody. He didn't commit a felony. It should never have gone where it went. Children on the sidewalk and passersby witnessed a murder! No one should ever have to see such a thing. George Floyd was denied basic human dignity. Is twenty dollars all that a Black man's life is worth? That, my friend, is the reality we are living in! That is the reality of White privilege."

"Media click-bait!" Logan snapped.

"No! I won't let you do that to me!" I insisted.

Mary shook her head, looking incredibly sad.

"I won't let you dismiss my thoughts and my feelings as 'click-bait,'" I said. "That just makes you sound jaded and ignorant, which I know you are not."

The Climate of Truth

Logan looked up at me, which was encouraging, but he remained mute.

"There was clearly some history between George Floyd and that cop, Chauvin," I continued. "Maybe something happened between them in the past. They worked security at a nightclub together. Maybe there was an altercation that we know nothing about that would give context to Chauvin's motive. Besides, there was nothing in the reports that said the woman in George Floyd's robbery case was pregnant. Everything becomes a meme these days, even when it's not true. Even you, the great detective, fell for click-bate on that one. You were primed and ready to believe that a Black man held a gun against a pregnant woman's belly." I performed a dramatic bow toward Logan. "Thank you very much. I'm here all day!"

"I agree with Mike," Mary said.

Her pronouncement startled Logan. "I knew this would happen!" he shouted at the both of us. "The two of you liberals against me! You won't be able to take it, I'm telling you. It won't be pretty! When I get going on shit like this, it makes me so angry!"

"Nobody's against you, Logan. We're just trying to understand," I said. "And by the way, as I've told you countless times before, I'm an Independent."

"You need to tell him, honey," Mary said quietly.

"No!" Logan backed up again. "You don't want to see me like this!"

"Just tell him. He's your friend," she pleaded.

Somehow the conversation had pushed Logan directly into flight or fight. He stared at the cement beneath his feet again. He was counting on his fingertips, a move I assumed to be a self-soothing, coping mechanism.

"I was just a kid…" he began, barely audible amidst the traffic noise on the boulevard.

"Go on, honey. It's OK," Mary said. "You are safe here."

I realized Logan was going to bare his soul, in my driveway of all places. That is where COVID brought us.

Logan began, "I was in San Francisco, the godforsaken town I left to come here. It was raining. I was wearing a yellow rain slicker." His

Flowers

eyes welled up, and then he forced the fluid back by blinking rapidly. "I was just a kid…I was walking home. It was dark. All of a sudden they were right on top of me."

"Who?" I asked.

"The '*Death Angels,*'" Logan said.

"What's that?"

"Have you heard of the '*Zebra Murders?*'"

"No," I replied.

Logan laughed. "How many people did Charles Manson kill?"

"Five or six, I think."

"Interesting," Logan said. "So, you've heard of Charles Manson?"

"Everyone's heard of Charles Manson," I said. "He had a swastika tattooed on his forehead for chrissake. He was a deranged hippie, high on drugs. He was delusional."

"You repeat those details because he was infamous, because the case was heavily reported. But Charles Manson never killed anybody. He had other people do it. Yeah, he was a rapist and a racist, and a drug addict. But the media called him a murderer, and it stuck for more than 50 years. But what is the truth? What really happened?"

"Why are we talking about Charles Manson anyway?" I said. "He was locked up his whole life. Obviously, he did something heinous. So, he conspired with others to commit murder. Why are we nitpicking semantics?"

Logan laughed again, nervously. "Don't you think it's interesting that you have a bold impression of a man you thought was a murderer, though he may or may not have killed only five or six people…but you know nothing about a group of serial murderers who killed more than 200 people around the same time?"

"You're referring to the '*Zebra Murders?*'"

"Yes," Logan said, his face turning pale.

"200 murders?" I asked.

"Do you doubt me?"

"Why would I doubt you?" I replied quickly.

The Climate of Truth

I could see that Logan was having an argument in his head – whether or not to speak out loud about his demons. He chose to continue. "The *Death Angels* were aligned with the *Nation of Islam*. They were a Marxist Black gang that claimed it was dedicated to eradicating racism by overthrowing the government…The *'Zebra Murders'* was a term coined by the media at the time. 'Zebra' was the call sign on encrypted police radio calls."

"You mean like '1-Adam-12'?" I asked.

"Yes. 'Zebra' happened to be the call sign assigned to police units that were dispatched to investigate the *'Death Angels.'* When the media got ahold of it, they hammered the whole Black against White theme, and they made it stick. So, it was forever remembered as the *'Zebra Murders.'*" Logan's shoulders were raised three inches toward his earlobes. It was more than evident that he was on the verge of an anxiety attack.

"Take a deep breath. It's OK. Tell Mike the whole story," Mary said coaxing him with her soft, soothing voice.

Logan spoke slowly and clearly. "People in the Bay Area were terrified. You never knew when or where it could happen. Businesses shut down early. Us kids would call in sick to school because we were too afraid to go. Downtown was dead before it got dark. Everybody packed it up and bolted their doors shut out of fear. The whole city was in lockdown because of the *'Death Angels.'* The mayor instituted the first 'stop and frisk' of Black men at random to try and find these punks, but that got shot down too because it was, oh yes, of course, discriminatory and against their rights…To the *'Death Angels,'* White people were devils who deserved the pain of violence…The *'Death Angels'* scored points, like an initiation. So many points to knock off a White grandpa. So many points for a White housewife. Extra points for a skinny little White kid…They had me, the skinny little White kid. I was walking home in the dark. It was raining. They grabbed me by the back of my rain slicker. They had those afro pick things in their hair. They were going to slit my throat with a switch blade. But my slicker was wet and slippery from the rain. I was able to quickly slide right out of the sleeves to escape. I ran through a hedge behind me like a jack rabbit. The branches sliced my eye and half of my face, but I kept running. I ran all the way home…I'd be dead if it wasn't raining that night…The rain kept splashing the blood in my eyes."

Flowers

Logan looked at his feet, where his teardrops stained the cement on the driveway.

"Is that why you became a cop?" I asked, finally understanding the cause of the scars on Logan's face.

"Obviously," he said, almost in a whisper. "So go ahead and kill the choke hold. Take away another useful form of self-defense. And watch the cops drop like flies."

With the backdoor to the house open behind me on the landing, Irma came out to stand beside me. She looked at me intensely as if to prompt me to pay close attention.

I faintly heard Bruce Springsteen's plaintive voice on the stereo. In his ballad *"American Skin (41 shots),"* Springsteen sang about the memory of Amadou Diallo, a young Black immigrant from New Guinea who was mistaken for a serial rapist, and fatally shot by four plainclothes New York City police officers. It happened in the Bronx in February 1999. The officers shot at Diallo a total of 41 times; 19 of the shots hit the innocent, unarmed Black man who was only reaching for his wallet. The officers mistook the wallet for a gun. The four officers were charged with second-degree murder but were acquitted at a trial that centered on police brutality and racial profiling.

The backlash against Springsteen was immediate. The police union called for a boycott of his concerts, and a union president publicly labelled Springsteen a "dirtbag" and a "floating fag." Springsteen was booed onstage.

In 2012, Trayvon Martin, a Black 17-year-old, was killed by a White vigilante in Florida. When that murderer was also acquitted, Springsteen dedicated his song to Trayvon Martin at a concert in Limerick, Ireland.

> *"Is it a gun, is it a knife*
> *Is it a wallet, this is your life*
> *It ain't no secret*
> *It ain't no secret*
> *No secret my friend*
> *You can get killed just for living*
> *In your American skin*
> *41 shots*

The Climate of Truth

41 shots
41 shots
41 shots"

That "random" song in my playlist just happened to coincide with the events unfolding in my driveway. The thought of it gave me the chills.

After listening to the lyrics for a few moments, I said, "Good girl, Irma. Stay right here by me." I returned my focus to Logan, saying, "I don't know why anyone would want to be a cop in this day and age."

"Me either," Mary said softly. "I'm relieved you're off the streets, Logan."

"Me too," he said, appreciative of his wife's sympathy.

"I don't know what I would do if I ever lost you," she said, trying not to cry.

"That's all over now. No need to worry anymore," he said, happy to be protective of her again.

With Springsteen's song haunting me, I was compelled to keep working the problem before all of us. "Please tell me truly, what do you really think of *'Black Lives Matter?'*" I asked Logan.

"Go on their website and see for yourself," Logan said. "It's all Marxist propaganda. Just like the *'Death Angels.'* Yeah, 'Power to the People,' man. Fist-pump, fist-pump. We're so cool! And now we have officials painting the words *'Black Lives Matter'* in giant yellow letters all over the streets, calling it a freedom plaza. What a joke! It's like the *'Zebra Murders'* of 1973 all over again, but this time it's much worse. It's national. It's acceptable! Hell, it's even worse than the race riots of 1968 during the Nixon campaign, and they were horrible."

"Do you have any Black friends that you talk to about this?" I asked.

Logan looked at me with piercing eyes. "I was one of only three White kids at an all-Black high school in Oakland. What do you think?" he said with a sneer.

"It wasn't meant to be a pointed question," I said.

"Like I said, I was one of only three White kids at an all-Black high school, and the other two are already dead."

Flowers

"I don't have any Black friends," I said calmly. "That's why I was asking. Not because I was accusing you of racism."

"Oh," Logan said, bewildered. "I do keep in touch with my Black friends who were on the force with me."

"What do they think of *'Black Lives Matter?'*" I asked.

"They're mad as hell about it too," Logan said. "They call it what it is, Marxist bullshit burning down our cities. They want nothing to do with it."

I paused for a moment before I spoke. "I disagree with you," I said. Logan looked at me as if I had betrayed him. "You're painting it with very broad strokes. *'Black Lives Matter'* is not the same thing as a gang of serial murderers," I said.

Logan's face turned bright red as he shouted. "Our cities are burning because of a carefully constructed narrative that is intended to brainwash you! Because a bunch of people got all excited about the death of a single drug-addled felon named George Floyd!"

"That's a false equivalency," I said calmly.

"Is it?" Logan shouted. "People have died because of the *'Black Lives Matter'* protests!"

"Opportunists come out anytime a catastrophe happens," I said as I kept my eyes on Logan. "Opportunists thrive on chaos…But there have been thousands of peaceful demonstrations all across the country in honor of George Floyd. There have been marches all around the world -- what is it up to now, 60 countries have joined in? All because they saw the same video of George Floyd's murder on the internet. All those millions of people around the world believed what they saw with their own eyes. They saw the truth. The facts of this case are very clear, detective. That many people all over the world couldn't have got it all wrong. It's not some giant conspiracy."

"It's not good when American cities burn!" Logan objected.

I thought for a moment before I continued. "Trump was holed up in a security bunker because the protesters got too close to the White House," I said. "The protesters called him 'bunker boy' and that pissed him off. So, what did he do? He got vengeful. He stood in the Rose Garden the very next day and told the world he was the 'law and order' President, by golly. And that he was going to send the National Guard out to squelch the protests if Governors didn't do it

The Climate of Truth

first. Then he made a show of it and strutted across the street to Lafayette Square with the Attorney General, the Secretary of Defense, and General Milley in his camo-fatigues all in tow. So, it looked like the military brass was behind Trump's promise to 'dominate the streets.' The Metropolitan Police used force to clear the George Floyd protesters out of the Square who were there to demonstrate against police brutality. Cops in riot gear clubbed and punched protesters and knocked them to the ground. People were attacked by their own government right outside the White House. They used tear gas, rubber bullets and smoke bombs. The protesters were shoved back and knocked over with riot shields. Even reporters were clobbered in the face. As a show of force, helicopters were ordered to hover very low over the protesters and hit them with air blasts from the rotor blades. Tree branches snapped off and went flying. One of the helicopters had the Red Cross insignia -- that's against the Geneva Conventions."

"You're saying it's OK for the protesters to burn our cities, but it's not OK to make them stop?" Logan said.

"One of my clients is a member of the Episcopal church up the block here," I said. "She told me about what happened at *St. John's Episcopal Church* at Lafayette Square. Without warning of any kind, the Secret Service stormed into St. Johns Church and teargassed innocent people there. The Secret Service claimed those violent and hostile Episcopalians were rioting like '*Antifa*.' But all they were really doing was handing out bags of food to hungry people on the back porch. The Secret Service came onto private church property and teargassed a priest, two deacons, and a bunch of hungry homeless people. One Deacon was slammed to the ground so hard that she was injured. Two people were taken to the hospital because of the teargas. Everybody was yanked off the back porch of the church, a place where several US Presidents have gone to worship. All so Trump could strut across the street from the White House to pose in front of the parish house of that church, so he could hold up a *Bible* that Ivanka whipped out from her oversized *Dolce & Gabbana* designer purse. Trump held the *Bible* up in the air, upside down as it turned out -- as if he ever cracked it open. All that mayhem so Trump could whip up his Evangelical base, because strongmen don't abide looking weak. All that affrontery to 'life, liberty and the pursuit of happiness' because Trump didn't like being called 'bunker boy.' How petty! *St. John's Church* even sent an official grievance letter to the Secret Service by the way. All they said in return was that Trump ordered them to do it and they had no choice but to follow the President's orders. End of story. Not so much as an apology…So yeah, I suppose there are always people with ulterior motives and alternate agendas who infiltrate and hijack the spirit and intent of events to suit their own narrative…By the way, the FBI found that some of the violence at the George Floyd protests in Minneapolis was perpetrated by White extremists who were masquerading to make it look like '*Antifa*' was doing the smash and grab. But it wasn't '*Antifa.*' It was really the '*Boogaloo Bois.*'"

"I know all about 'Umbrella Man' and the sledgehammer at the *AutoZone*!" Logan shouted. "People were screaming that the 'Umbrella Man' was a cop at first. Because of George Floyd, all cops are bad! All cops are evil, fascist pigs! Ew! Bad Cops, bad cops!"

"Why would you conflate my own words to my face? I did not disparage cops," I said, evenly.

Never had I seen a closeup of a cop in distress. The façade of the great protector fell away again, and a man, fully human, stood in front of me quaking in the trauma of his psychic pain.

"NOW you want to be literal!" Logan scoffed.

"I'm the one you are talking to right now, Logan. I'm the one listening," I said. "Don't drag me into a fight with the ghosts of unreasonable people stuck in your mind."

"Whatever," he said with a shrug.

"That horrible George Floyd murder video was taken by a teenage girl on her cellphone," I said. "The whole world is involved because that brave, innocent girl had the courage to record a snuff film! Can you imagine, as a young person, having to live with that realization for the rest of your life? Can you put yourself in that child's shoes?"

Logan's face softened. That was a good sign that his heart was somewhat open still.

"George Floyd was a powerless Black man," I said calmly. "That's the way a lot of angry White folk like it…How can there be peace when our nation's top leaders refuse to correct such injustice?"

There was a long, uncomfortable silence.

The Climate of Truth

Logan cleared his throat. "There was a young Black man -- not that it should matter what color he was. He wanted to go down and see the '*Black Lives Matter*'protests to support George Floyd…He never made it home that night in Minneapolis. He was missing for weeks, and his family searched and searched for him. Because the violent protests overwhelmed the city, investigators didn't have the resources to look for a missing person. Two months later, they finally found a body in the charred remains of a pawnshop that was torched by one of the protesters…What a horrible death, to be burned alive. The family didn't know what happened to him. They didn't know why he was in that pawnshop. They may never know. They held a funeral with a life-size cardboard cutout of this young man because they didn't find the body in time. Where is the outcry for justice in that case? Huh? I spent my entire career on the streets, fighting for the rights of the disadvantaged. They shouldn't have to worry about being burned alive in a protest."

I chose my words carefully. "As tragic as that story is, Logan, it's not the same thing."

"Mike's right," Mary said softly.

Logan shot her scathing look. "It is the same thing, and you both know it! You just don't want to admit it! It's never a good thing when cities burn!" Logan inhaled deeply and looked at his feet again.

"I agree, it's not a good thing to witness the burning of our cities," I said. "But with all due respect, that young man's death in the pawnshop fire is not the same thing as the murder of George Floyd. It's about intent. All you had to do was see the look of depraved indifference on Chauvin's face as he choked the life out of George Floyd. The sunglasses on his head, his hands in his pockets, nonchalantly rocking his knee back and forth across George Floyd's neck. Chauvin enjoyed it. It was sadistic…And the other three cops watched him do it…We're all better than that!"

"Yes, we are," Mary said. "We have to be better than that!"

"But it happens over and over and over, this thing where subjugated Black people die a senseless death by the hands of White people," I said. "That's White privilege…It's an epidemic brought closer to light in the middle of a pandemic. The outrage of the protesters…my friend… is justified…No wonder our cities burn."

Logan stood extremely still for a moment.

Flowers

"What are you thinking, honey?" Mary asked him. "Talk to us."

"Emotionally, I agree with you," Logan said straightforwardly. "But intellectually, I'm angrier than ever before in my entire life."

"What a shocker! You actually admit you agree with us!" I said with a dramatic flair.

"Miracles do happen every now and then," Logan said with a sigh.

"Well, at least you and the '*Death Angels*' have something in common," I said, my eyebrows raised in anticipation.

"How's that?" Logan was suspicious.

"You both hate the government," I said, laughing a little. I was satisfied that my teasing had hit the mark.

"Good one," Logan said. By the movement of his mask, I could tell that he was smiling.

❖

Darnella Frazier, the 17-year-old Black girl who captured George Floyd's murder on her cellphone, was awarded a special *Pulitzer Prize* in journalism for "the crucial role of citizens in journalists' quest for truth and justice." She described the murder as a "traumatic life-changing experience," and testified at the trial that she spent sleepless nights apologizing to George Floyd for "not doing more." Her video that showed police officer Derek Chauvin kneeling on George Floyd's neck for 9 minutes and 29 seconds, was the most important evidence used to convict Chauvin of unintentional second-degree murder, third-degree murder, and second-degree manslaughter. Darnella's video was also the spark that ignited global protests against police brutality, and was described by another journalist as "one of the most important civil rights documents in a generation." It was important to remember that three teenagers and a nine-year-old child bore witness to the murder. Darnella was on the scene because she accompanied her nine-year-old cousin to the *Cup Foods* store. Video evidence taken from the crime scene showed a female clerk from the *Cup Foods* store as the only person involved in this historic event to wear a mask. The female clerk was sent out into the street to bring George Floyd back into the store, but he refused.

The Climate of Truth

The intersection where the murder occurred became a permanent memorial and protest site known in the community as *"George Floyd Square."* The makeshift shrine was visited by countless thousands of people. The intersection, also the center of a Black-owned business corridor since the 1930's, became an active installation of flowers, murals and sculptures that symbolized the *"Black Lives Matter"* movement. Several of the murals and sculptures were vandalized by those who opposed memorials to racist violence. A two-block stretch of the avenue was later named *"George Perry Floyd Jr Place"* by the City of Minneapolis, and the memorial area became one the city's cultural districts, designated to promote racial equity, cultural identity, and economic growth for people of color. It was also important to remember that George Floyd was murdered on Memorial Day.

The manager of the *Cup Foods* store was interviewed on camera a few weeks after George Floyd's murder. The manager reached under the front counter behind the cash register to retrieve a giant wad of counterfeit twenty-dollar bills that had been confiscated by his staff in recent weeks. The fake currency had flooded into the community. The appearance of only one of those fake twenty-dollar bills was used to justify lethal force by White police officers against a single, unarmed Black man.

❖

In June of 2021, a year after the incidents at Lafayette Square, an Inspector General released a government report that concluded federal police did not clear the park across from the White House so Trump could conduct his photo-op. Instead, the report determined the US Park Police and the Secret Service removed the protesters from in and around Lafayette Square for contractors to install a circle of barricade fencing all around the White House. The reasoning seemed far-fetched. Shortly after the report was released, Trump issued a public statement thanking the Inspector General "for completely and totally exonerating me in the clearing of Lafayette Park! As we have said all along, and it was backed up in today's highly detailed and professionally written report, our fine Park Police made the decision to clear the park to allow a contractor to safely install antiscale fencing to protect from *Antifa* rioters, radical *BLM* protesters, and other violent demonstrators who are causing chaos and death to our cities."

Flowers

It must have been presumed to be pure coincidence that Trump began his stroll through Lafayette Square only 11 minutes after the park and the surrounding area was completely cleared of peaceful protesters by the use of force. There was no mention in the report about the Secret Service assault on innocent people at *St. John's Episcopal Church*, who had nothing to do with the protests. There was no reference to General Milley's presence as he observed protesters being routed with helicopters and the National Guard.

In his keynote address to the *National Defense University Class of 2020*, delivered just ten days after the incidents at Lafayette Square, General Milley said, "I am outraged by the senseless and brutal killing of George Floyd. His death amplified the pain, the frustration, and the fear that so many of our fellow Americans live with day in and day out. The protests that have ensued, not only speak to his killing, but also to the centuries of injustice towards African Americans. What we are seeing is the long shadow of original sin in Jamestown, 401 years ago. Liberated by the Civil War, but not equal in the eyes of the law until 100 years later in 1965. We are still struggling with racism, and we have much work to do. Racism and discrimination, structural preferences, patterns of mistreatment, unspoken and unconscious bias have no place in America. And they have no place in our armed forces."

The General continued, "As many of you saw the result of the photograph of me at Lafayette Square last week, that sparked a national debate about the role of the military in civil society. I should not have been there. My presence in that moment and in that environment created a perception of the military involved in domestic politics. As a commissioned uniformed officer, it was a mistake that I've learned from, and I sincerely hope we all can learn from it." General Milley's associates knew he considered resigning because of Trump's aggressive moves against the George Floyd protesters and the photo-op scandal, but he chose not to.

In September 2021, Bob Woodward released his third book about the Trump Presidency with his co-author Robert Costa, entitled "Peril." Two days after the January 6 attack on the US Capitol, Woodward and Costa described how General Milley acted in secret to prevent Trump from entering a war or from launching nuclear weapons. The authors wrote how Milley *"was certain that Trump had gone into a serious mental decline in the aftermath of the election, with*

The Climate of Truth

Trump now all but manic, screaming at officials and constructing his own alternate reality about endless election conspiracies." According to Woodward and Costa, Milley worried that Trump could *"go rogue."*

"Peril" detailed how General Milley called his Chinese Counterpart, Gernal Zuocheng, on January 8, 2021. General Milley specifically told the Chinese General, *"We [the US] are not going to attack or conduct any kinetic operations against you."* Milley added further that he would notify China in advance of any potential US attack so it would not be a *"surprise."* There were 15 people on the videoconference calls General Milley held with General Zuocheng, including personnel from the US State Department.

Trump released a statement in response to the revelations in *"Peril:" "If the story is true, then I assume (Milley) would be tried for TREASON in that he would have been dealing with his Chinese counterpart behind the President's back and telling China that he would be giving them notification 'of an attack.' Can't do that!"* Trump also referred to Woodward, who was twice honored with the *Pulitzer Prize*, as a "sleaze." When the news broke, General Milley came under fire, but he defended his secretive actions as being "perfectly within the duties and responsibilities" of his rank as the chairman of the Joint Chiefs of Staff. He reserved further comment until he would be called to testify before Congress on the matter. Perhaps then General Milley would be able to provide further details of Trump's erratic and dangerous behavior during his last days in office.

I was among many people who were grateful for General Milley's intervention under those circumstances. It was frightening to think what might have happened had a Trump loyalist been seated in Milley's position instead. I suppose the whole world could have gone up in flames because, according to US intelligence reports, China firmly believed the US was prepared to attack at the time. China viewed Trump's antagonistic rhetoric, including his repeated references to COVID as the "China Virus," as a sign that a US attack was imminent.

❖

Logan was in a much better mood come Christmas, even though he still had to wear a mask in my shop. He arrived for his eight-week

Flowers

perm on December 18th, 2020. Immediately, he started in with his teasing.

"You're madly in love with sleepy Uncle Joe, aren't you?" he said, referring to the new President-Elect, Joe Biden.

"Gimme a break," I said, standing on my tiptoes, wrangling Logan's bristly hair into the tiny yellow perm rods again. "At least I don't wake up in the middle of the night thinking Biden's going to start a nuclear war. Hey, scootch down, will ya? I'm short and you're killing my back."

Logan slouched in the styling chair so I could better reach the top of his head. "Yes, the majority agree, the orange Satan had to go," he said, referring to Trump. "But anybody with a lick of common sense would have voted for Jo Jorgensen."

"Who?"

"See! You've never even heard of a national hero," Logan said. "The Libertarian chick from Libertyville, Illinois, who wants to liberate the US from all wasteful foreign wars. Who called out Social Security for the 'Ponzi Scheme' that it is! Who called the COVID lockdowns 'the biggest assault on our liberties in our lifetime!'" Logan seemed quite proud of himself.

"Who voted for her? You and the pugnacious Libertarian Senator from Kentucky?" I countered.

"I'll have you know, Jo Jergensen came in third!"

"How many votes?" I asked.

"A few," Logan said slyly.

"Like a hundred?"

"One-point-eight million," he said as if he'd just won the lottery.

"One-point-eight million compared to 80 million for my guy. I don't waste my vote like you do just to make a point," I said. "But at least you finally admit you didn't vote for Trump. Why the heck was it such a secret?"

"Your brain has been devoured by the amoeba media you consume," Logan objected.

"Not today, please," I said.

The Climate of Truth

"You've been thoroughly programmed and brainwashed, just the way they like it."

"For the last time, I am not a sheep!" I said. "I get my news from many different sources. I even quit using *Google* like you suggested, and the computer stops hundreds of trackers every day."

"Isn't it wonderful to be liberated! You might make a good Libertarian yet!" Logan applauded. "Hey! Have you seen the 'Corn Pop' video? "

I could tell that Logan couldn't wait to set me up with another whammy. "The what?" I said.

"You need a good laugh at sleepy Uncle Joe's expense." Logan took out his cellphone to locate a *YouTube* video. "You've got to see this! It's a riot. It shows Biden is truly demented. He must have Alzheimer's. He can't keep a single thought straight in his head. He can't form a cogent sentence. The man is insane. It's all right there in this video."

While I continued to wrap Logan's perm, I looked over his shoulder as he played a video clip of Biden giving a speech at the dedication ceremony of a Wilmington, Delaware swimming pool in 2017. Biden spoke to a crowd of Black people, including a bunch of Black children wearing swimsuits:

> "This was the diving board area, and I was one of the guards. And they weren't allowed to -- it was a three-meter board. If you fell off sideways you landed on the damn -- the <u>darn</u> cement over there. And 'Corn Pop' was a bad dude…"

Logan howled with delight. "'And Corn Pop was a bad dude!' You can't make this shit up!"

> Biden continued: *"And he ran a bunch of bad boys. And I did -- and back in those days -- and to show you how things have changed, one of the things you had to use, if you used pomade in your hair, you had to wear a bathing cap. And he was up on the board, wouldn't listen to me. I said 'HEY ESTHER! [referring to Esther Williams, the film star of 'aquamusicals' in the 1940s*

Flowers

and 50s that featured synchronized swimming] YOU! OFF THE BOARD! OR I'LL COME UP AND DRAG YOU OFF!' Well, he came off, and he said, 'I'll meet you outside.' My car -- this was mostly -- these were all public housing behind you. My car -- there was at the gate out here. I parked my car outside the gate. And I -- he said, 'I'll be waitin' for you.' He was waiting for me with three guys with straight razors. NOT A JOKE! There was a guy named Bill Wrightmouse, the only White guy, and he did ALL the pools. He was the mechanic. And I said, 'what am I gonna do?' And he said, 'Come down here in the basement.' Where mechanics, where all the pool filter is. You know the chain? There used to be a chain went across the deep end. And he cut off a six-foot lump of chain – he folded it up. He said, 'You walk out with that chain. And you walk to the car, and you say, you may cut me man, but I'm gonna wrap this chain around your head.' I said, 'you're kidding me.' He said, 'No. If you don't, don't come back.' AND HE WAS RIGHT! So, I walked out with the chain. And I walked up to my car. And they had in those days -- used to remember the straight razor, you'd bang 'em on the curb, get 'em rusty, put 'em in a rain barrel, get 'em rusty. And I looked at 'em. But I was smart, then. I said, first of all I said, 'When I tell you get off the board, you get off the board. I'll kick you out again. But I shouldn't have called you Esther Williams. I apologize for that.' I apologized but I didn't know if that apology was going to work. He said, 'YOU APOLOGIZING TO ME?' I said, 'I apologize, not for throwing you out, but I apologize for what I said,' and he said, 'OK,' closed the straight razor and my heart began to beat again."

Logan laughed and slapped his thigh. "Uncle Joe, the king of gaffes. This is <u>your</u> President now!"

My ears perked up at the song on the stereo playlist. The hair stood up on the back of my neck when I heard Jim Croce's number one pop hit of 1973, "*Bad, Bad, Leroy Brown.*" It was Croce's only number one single, and it was still at the top of the Billboard Charts the day he died in a place crash on September 30th that same year. It was also the second number one song to include a curse word ("damn") in the lyrics. Biden uttered the word "damn" in his "Corn

The Climate of Truth

Pop" speech too as he told the story of his encounter with a street gang that carried straight razors.

>*"He got a custom Continental*
>*He got an Eldorado too*
>*He got a 32 gun in his pocket full a fun*
>*He got a razor in his shoe*
>
>*And he's bad, bad Leroy Brown*
>*The baddest man in the whole damn town*
>*Badder than old King Kong*
>*And meaner than a junkyard dog"*

"Sounds to me like Biden was telling a story about race relations when he was a young man," I said. "You say he sounds insane. But I'd say he has a hard time with extemporaneous speaking because he stutters."

"'Corn Pop was a bad dude!' Come on!" Logan howled.

"Corn Pop" was a real person, also known as William L. Morris, who died in 2016. Morris was a member of the "*Romans*," a Black street gang in Wilmington that was prominent in the 1960s. Biden's "Corn Pop" speech occurred in 2017 at a ceremony where a municipal swimming pool was renamed the *Joseph R. Biden Aquatic Center*. Many people regarded Biden's time as the only other White person at that segregated pool as the genesis of his understanding of race relations. At the time, Biden said he didn't know any Black people. He took the job as a lifeguard at that pool because he wanted to overcome his lack of experience with Black culture. The Black community in Wilmington thought so highly of Biden, they named the remodeled aquatic center after him. At the dedication ceremony, the former president of the Delaware *NAACP* said of Biden, "Joe understands Black folks, poor folks, all folks. He loves people."

I inhaled deeply before I addressed Logan's antics. "My senior year in college was the first time I had a female roommate. Her name was Rozz. She also happened to be Black."

"Was she a gangsta!" Logan laughed. "Did she call herself 'Corn Poppie?' Was she a baaaaaad dudette?"

Flowers

I was put off but tried to ignore Logan's taunts. "Actually, Rozz was quite beautiful, gregarious, and a very talented performer."

"So now you're going to tell me that you are an expert at cohabitating with Black people?" Logan said.

"Rozz and I worked together in *New Salem State Park*, Illinois, after I graduated from college. We performed in a historical play about Abraham Lincoln at an outdoor amphitheater. There were only two Black people in a cast of about 40 -- Rozz and another young man named Clayton. The play was about the Civil War and the abolition of slavery, but there were only two black people on the stage every night."

"This sounds like it's going to be good!" Logan said, rubbing his hands together.

"It was a very strange summer. We saw Lincoln's tomb, and the house where he lived when he was a Congressman. When we sang *'We Shall Overcome'* onstage, sometimes giant june-bugs would fly down our throats, and we would practically choke to death."

*"We shall overcome,
We shall overcome,
We shall overcome, some day.
Oh, deep in my heart,
I do believe
We shall overcome, some day"*

"It was a gospel song from the turn of the 20th century that Pete Seeger made famous as a 60's protest anthem for civil rights," I said. "It didn't have anything to do with the time of the Civil War, but hey, it was art."

Logan slapped his thigh and laughed. "You're killing me!"

I continued, undaunted. "But I came to understand the vision…When we weren't onstage, there was nothing to do in New Salem except to watch the corn grow or go to the local swimming pool. I was already at the pool this one day. Rozz told me she would meet me there. And boy, she made an entrance. She walked onto the pool deck and struck a pose like a supermodel. She had on a brand-new electric-blue one-piece that made her skin glow. She had Jackie-

The Climate of Truth

O sunglasses that made her look mysterious. Rhinestoned flip-flops, coral colored lipstick, her hair all swept up and back, and a white beach towel wrapped around her waist. She was stunning. Everyone in and around the pool suddenly stopped to stare at her. It got really quiet. People quit splashing in the water…There she was, a Black woman who didn't belong at the all-White swimming pool in 1985. But it didn't even phase Rozz. Right about then, Clayton showed up. Now there were two, count them, <u>two</u> Black people at this otherwise all-White pool. I guess Rozz asked Clayton to meet her there. She looked at him through her sunglasses, and this huge smile came over her face. Her teeth were white as snow in the sunlight. Then, very slowly, she unfurled that beach towel for the big reveal. And there, in all her glory, two giant bushes of fluffy black pubic hair stuck out of either side of her swimsuit like crowns of burnt broccoli."

"You're making this up, right!" Logan yelled, turning red in the face with glee.

"As soon as they all saw the spectacle, people started screaming. Women grabbed their children. Everyone cleared the pool. They all ran to the locker room. Cars started pulling away from the parking lot…Rozz put her arms around Clayton's neck and gave him the most sensual kiss I'd ever seen on stage or screen. Let's just say that Clayton was more than impressed. So was I…Rozz could sure clear a swimming pool. So yeah, man…'*We Shall Overcome.*'"

"OK," Logan said. "I've got a good one for ya. You're going to think I'm a racist, but hand to God, this really happened."

I had a bad feeling about what he was about to say.

Logan began, "I'm on a call to *Geneva Towers*, one of the most dangerous housing projects in San Francisco. Right up there with *Cabrini Green* in Chicago. People died in gang fights at *Geneva Towers* practically every day. Stabbings, shootings, overdoses. You name the crime, it happened there…So I pull up in my squad car. Three other officers met me there because you never go to *Geneva Towers* alone. We come upon an older Black woman. She's the one who called 9-1-1. This woman is clearly drunk and probably stoned as we roll up. 'How can I help you, ma'am?' I said. The Black woman was so out of it."

Next, Logan impersonated the Black woman with the voice of "Mammy" from "*Gone with the Wind.*" "That bitch daughter of mine, she done broke into my apartment, and she done stole all my clothes,

Flowers

and all my makeup and stuuuuuff. That crack-ho done stole all my shit, took all my weed!"

Logan cleared his throat and spoke as himself. "I was completely professional. 'Do you want to file a report?' I asked her."

He spoke in the voice of Mammy again, fanning himself: "Hell yes!"

"Let's start with your daughter's name," Logan said in his own voice.

As Mammy, he said, "Fah-<u>mah</u>-lee."

Logan furrowed his brow. He spoke as an officer, "Can you repeat that please?"

"Fah-<u>mah</u>-lee!" he said once again in his Mammy voice.

"That's an unusual name," the officer said. "Can you spell that please?"

He spoke slowly, slurring the sounds as Mammy: "F, E, M, A, L, E. Fah-<u>mah</u>-lee."

My heart sank. "You're going to say she named her daughter 'Female Black' because that's what it said on the birth certificate?"

"Well, at least she could read!" Logan howled.

"You're straight up telling me the family name was 'Black' in this story?" I asked.

"Hand to God, this really happened!" Logan insisted. "I told you, you were going to think I'm a racist," he said nonchalantly, with a twinkle in his eye. "Hand to God," he went on, "The perp's name was 'Female,' and her last name was really 'Black.'"

I attempted to hide the look of disappointment on my face. "What happened next?"

"When you hear something like that," Logan continued, "you have to bite the inside of your cheek to keep a straight face. You take the report like a good soldier, then go to the squad car, where you shut the door and roll up the windows. And then you let loose and laugh your guts out. But thanks to George Floyd, all cops are evil, racist, fascist pigs! Because that's what they say about us on the news."

The Climate of Truth

There was an uncomfortable pause in the conversation.

"I can't do this with you today," I said.

Logan seemed to be surprised by my tone. I struggled to secure a perm rod on the shortest hair on the side of his head.

"What's happened?" he asked sincerely.

"I guess you'd have to say that today I've lost my sense of humor. I hope it's not permanent. But right now, I can't take a joke. So, I can't do this with you today."

"Why?"

"I'm angry," I said.

"At me?" Logan seemed perplexed.

"Rozz was a free spirit. I learned a lot from her."

"What do you want to teach me today, Mike?" Logan's voice was thick with condescension.

"I had no idea that Black women used cocoa-butter in their hair with a curling iron," I said. "It sizzled. The unusual smell of fried cocoa-butter filled our apartment. There were a lot of strange cultural things like that – things I knew nothing about – how Black people lived. You've got difficult hair, Logan. Maybe you can relate."

Logan bristled at the thought. "I'd never resort to a curling iron or cocoa butter! So no, I don't think I can relate."

"Like me, Rozz had a rough upbringing," I said. "She wasn't at all close to her family. We had that in common. Neither of us had any place to go home to for Thanksgiving. My mother had disappeared, on the run from the IRS, or some such nonsense. But my senior year in college, for the first time ever, my uncle, my mother's brother, invited me to his house in Chicago for Thanksgiving dinner. It was a total surprise because I hadn't seen him in a few years. I didn't want to leave Rozz alone over the holiday, and again, to my surprise, my uncle invited her to join us. My uncle had never met Rozz. So I drove to Chicago with her, and rang the doorbell. My Aunt Lydia answered the door. She took one look at Rozz and said 'Oh!'"

"Your *'Guess Who's Coming to Dinner'* moment!" Logan said, slapping his thigh again. "See, I told you this would be good."

Flowers

"As you already know, Rozz was used to that kind of rudeness. But she kept her chin up, didn't flinch or even blink. She kept a smile on her face. She held out to shake my Aunt's hand and said, 'Hiya! I'm Rozz! I'm very pleased to meet you.' My Aunt made a face like she was shaking hands with a pile of dog shit."

"Ah, so you're admitting that you hail from a long line of racist pigs yourself! Brilliant!" Logan howled. "I love this story. Welcome to the club!"

"We're at the formal dining room table. I don't know why there's a fancy laced tablecloth because they had two toddlers at the table, both in highchairs. Aunt Lydia giggled every time her little princes sent a gob of cranberry sauce flying onto the laced tablecloth, because it was so cute. So, I'm sitting next to Rozz, and she's sitting next to my uncle, who's at the head of the table. My uncle hardly said a word the entire meal. Things were…"

"Tense?"

"More than tense," I said. "To break the silence, Aunt Lydia cleared her throat, so I knew something was coming."

"Is this the good part?" Logan asked.

"Aunt Lydia had this obnoxious voice. She was a big woman who could be heard clear down the block." I used a high-pitched, nasal voice to emulate my aunt: "'So, Michael! You're graduating from the University next semester. Rozz here is a sophomore…Are you two going to maintain a long-distance relationship?'"

"Oh no!" Logan cried.

"Rozz had just put a wad of turkey and gravy in her mouth," I said. "When Aunt Lydia popped the absurd question, Rozz couldn't help it. She spat out the turkey and it went flying all over the white lacey tablecloth. Some of it landed in other plates of food. Some of it landed in the gravy boat. Rozz let out this enormous guffaw. She leaned forward to pound her forehead on the table, she was laughing so hard. And every time she banged her head, the smell of fried cocoa-butter wafted up from her hair. My uncle didn't look up from his plate, but he wrinkled his nose in disgust – probably because he could smell the cocoa-butter too…Aunt Lydia dropped her fork on her plate. She grabbed my baby cousins right out of their highchairs and stormed out of the room, and up the staircase to her bedroom. The boys were screaming. She slammed the bedroom door. It was the

The Climate of Truth

last time I ever saw my baby cousins. My uncle didn't say a word. He pushed his chair back away from the table, got up, and disappeared upstairs too. Rozz and I just sat there trying not to laugh, but we couldn't help it. We were abandoned at the holiday table. So, we did the only logical thing – we got up and left. I grabbed a bunch of crescent rolls for the long drive home. Didn't get to have any pumpkin pie. As soon as we got to the car, Rozz said, 'Don't you dare apologize for what just happened in there. You might as well be Black like me'…Funny how the last words my father ever spoke to me, he referred to me as 'the black sheep of a black sheep'…so I guess Rozz was right…I remember my aunt once said that Black people smell funny because they have copper in their blood, and she thought that's what makes their skin dark…On the long drive home, Rozz said, '<u>That</u> was freaking hysterical! I will never forget it as long as I live, and I wouldn't have missed seeing that for the world!'…My aunt and uncle didn't speak to me for another 35 years. And that's why I hate Thanksgiving."

"How sad for you," Logan said.

"The best part of the story is that on the drive up to Chicago that Thanksgiving Day, Rozz and I had been arguing in the car. Both she and I were interested in the same cute guy back on campus. We were arguing about whether he was gay or not. He was quite the hunk with his black curly hair and his black cowboy boots. He was an actor. Can't remember his name…Anyway, Rozz won the argument because she seduced that White cowboy right in front of me. It was absurd for anyone to think that Rozz and I were a couple. I mean, it's rather obvious. So we were arguing in the car over a man we both wanted, and that's why Rozz lost it all over the Thanksgiving spread when my evil aunt was scoping out our relationship."

"Why are you telling me this story?" Logan asked.

"Because Rozz was the first person to honor me for who I really was. Because she helped me to feel like I belonged in my own skin."

"Ah-so, grasshopper," Logan said with a flicker of animosity. "So, what you're really telling me is that I'm like your evil racist relatives because I rant about protesters burning our cities."

I did not take the bait. "You don't have the right to politicize my coming out story."

"You brought it up," Logan said, defensively.

Flowers

"What I'm telling you, man, is that my own family couldn't even pronounce the word 'homosexual.' They were never interested in an honest conversation," I said.

I was nearly finished wrapping the perm, ready to proceed with the cotton halo.

"Hey, sidetrack for a second?" Logan said, catching me off guard. "What do you do with those little bottles of perm solution when you're done with them?"

"They're garbage," I said, confused.

"Do you mind if I take them?" he asked.

"No…That's a first."

"I want to use them to apply Mary's hair color."

"Oh," I said.

"She asked me to color her hair. We need a squeeze bottle."

"The nipple's too small," I said. "You'll have to cut off the tip. And make sure you rinse it out thoroughly. Doesn't seem like a good thing to combine perm residue with hair color."

"Trust me, I'd wash it several times. It would be grounds for divorce if I made her hair fall out," Logan said.

"Why doesn't she just come here to get her hair done?" I asked in disbelief.

"She wants to very badly. She loves you to pieces. But she has this tremendous guilt because she quit seeing this other stylist, who was way the hell far away in Gresham. She has the greatest excuse in the world not to go there anymore, COVID! But she's paralyzed with guilt because she quit going, and therefore, doesn't think she can go anywhere else instead, even though she wants to come see you."

"That makes no sense," I said.

"Tell me about it," Logan said, slapping his thigh while laughing.

"Why use crap hair color when I can use the good stuff on her?" I asked, even more confused.

"We use the good stuff!" Logan griped.

The Climate of Truth

Over-the-counter hair color included applicator bottles in every box, so the whole topic was a ruse. It was Logan's clumsy attempt to change the subject by insulting me.

"What brand are you using?" I asked, finally on to him.

"It's a really good brand, that's all I know," Logan insisted, straight faced.

I handed him my business card.

"Tell Mary she can call me anytime. I'm happy to see her if she changes her mind," I said.

"Now where were we?" Logan said, sarcastically. "Oh yes, your terrible Thanksgiving dinner."

❖

As if on cue, the voice of Pete Seeger gently filled the shop after I had already mentioned *"We Shall Overcome."* I paid close attention to the lyrics, wondering at the strange timing of the coincidence. It felt like *Pandora* had somehow summoned him. Blacklisted during the McCarthy era, Seeger was one of my heroes. He was strumming the guitar, singing one of his many famous songs about the cruelty of war -- how the graves of fallen soldiers were strewn with flowers, put there by the women who loved them:

> *"Where have all the flowers gone,*
> *Long time passing?*
> *Where have all the flowers gone,*
> *Long time ago?"*

I pointed to the wilted floral arrangement sitting on the front desk, the one that had just been delivered that morning.

"What do you see over there, Inspector?" I asked Logan.

"Pretty flowers," Logan said, seeming disinterested.

"Look closer."

"Correction. Some pretty spent flowers," Logan announced.

Flowers

"You wanted to know why I'm angry. You're looking at some of my anger over there," I said.

"Flowers are picked. And then they die. That's what they're for. So what?" Logan said with a shrug.

"They were delivered in that state just this morning," I said, plainly.

"Oh!" Logan said, somewhat astonished. "That changes everything."

"Some really nice people I know spent good money on those flowers as a Christmas present," I said. "My friends were taken advantage of. It makes my blood boil. My friends are at the hospital as we speak. The husband had a double hip replacement surgery in the middle of a COVID pandemic. He's trying to learn to use a walker. With all of that stress going on, they still stopped, like they do every year, to buy Christmas flowers for me. And that is the result."

"I can see why you'd be upset," Logan replied.

"I took photos of the bouquet and sent them to another friend of mine who happens to be a wholesale distributor to all the local florists. He said my bouquet was worse than anything he'd ever seen and that it never should have been delivered."

"You allow yourself to be devastated by a bunch of bad flowers?" Logan asked.

"My florist friend said there's no flower shortage, even with COVID. There's no excuse for it. He said it was a scam. When you buy FTD, some florists intentionally use crap product to save money."

"But why let it ruin your day? Especially when I'm here to cheer you up," Logan asked.

"What if the flower shop is struggling, barely making it because of COVID? What if the little Latino family…"

"Stop right there!" Logan interrupted. "How do you know there is a 'little Latino family?'"

"Because the delivery man was Latino. He even had an accent to prove it. And when I called his shop to complain, because I investigated and found the perpetrator of this calamity, I recognized his Latin voice on the answering machine. There was a baby crying in the background of his recorded message," I explained.

The Climate of Truth

"There's no such thing as a <u>little</u> Latino family! They don't believe in birth control!" Logan laughed.

"What if the family can't make a living because no one is buying flowers right now?" I said. "There are no weddings. There are no funerals because of lockdowns. Everyone hates Christmas this year. Which means that all my ranting about wilted flowers is just petty nonsense!"

"And there it is – what triggered this crisis in you today," Logan said. "COVID is no reason for anyone to do less than their best. Always your best foot forward when it counts the most."

"Doing your best doesn't seem to be enough to make people happy," I said, feeling helpless.

Logan put his hand on my shoulder. "I'm very happy with you, or I wouldn't be here, Mike."

"My bouquet was a 'dump and run!' Merry fucking Christmas!" I misted Logan's perm rods with water, then doused his head in perm solution. "Don't forget your drip towel," I cautioned him. "I upset my friends in the hospital because I felt I had to tell them they got gipped, that they should demand their money back. They wrote a bad *Yelp* review. The flower shop loses business. The baby goes hungry. One bad thing after another. And I can't bring myself to throw the flowers out because someone paid good money for them…But does any of this really matter?"

Logan jumped out of the styling chair, grabbed the vase of wilted flowers, and threw them in the garbage can.

"What was that!" I yelled.

"That was your problem solved," Logan said, wiping his hands.

"Sit down, will you! I'm not done squirting the stuff on your head!" I said.

"Why don't you tell me what is really bothering you?" Logan insisted.

As I applied perm solution to each of the tiny yellow perm rods, I told Logan about the defecating homeless men at the church across the street, Mavis and her broken finger, and the story of Ruby Jean. By the time I finished, it was time to rinse the perm. I ushered Logan to the shampoo sink.

Flowers

"Good God, man, why didn't you lead with the lady who lied to your face about the crowd she had over for Thanksgiving? No wonder you're upset. I'd be fuming mad too if someone pulled that on me…Mike, you're someone who has to be honest. It's your nature. You're innocent, and you don't really know how to deal with liars. My wife and I love that about you…I'm truly sorry that you've been so mistreated."

"Everyone is being mistreated in this pandemic. It's breaking my heart," I said, trying not to lose my composure.

"I've gotten myself in a lot of trouble with my big mouth," Logan said. "It cost me a lot over the years. But it never kept me from speaking out."

After letting Logan's perm oxidize for a few minutes, I applied the neutralizer, the final rinse, and removed the perm rods from his head. I led him back to the styling chair when I saw something on my security cameras -- an unauthorized car parked in my driveway next to Logan's SUV.

"That car is not supposed to be there!" I said. I quickly unbolted the front door and went out on the porch to get a better look. Logan whipped past me as the great protector, his purple perm cape fluttering in the breeze.

A woman appeared on the sidewalk. She had on a baseball cap through which her waist length ponytail protruded out the back. She held a *GrubHub* food delivery sack in her hand. She headed for the mystery car in my driveway, having just made a delivery to the neighbor next door.

"You're parked right in front of a sign that says, 'private parking' or you will be towed!" I hollered after the delivery woman. "I've told you this before! Don't do it again! Do you hear me!"

The delivery woman kept her eyes below the bill of her cap. She did not engage. She silently ducked into her car and backed out as quickly as possible and drove away. I walked Logan back into the shop.

"The nerve!" I said to Logan. "She skulked right past the front window here and saw us. But why the hell do I feel so petty having to yell at her? Because if I didn't yell, I'd have the drug dealers back using my driveway to make deliveries in the middle of the night!"

The Climate of Truth

"You did what life has forced you to do," Logan said. "Some would call you a hateful, racist xenophobe, like me," Logan said with a wink.

"I just want to be left alone."

"There are two kinds of people in the world," Logan mused as I resumed cutting his hair.

I rolled my eyes.

"There are 'the get off my lawn' types, and there are 'the rent is too high' types. I'm a loud and proud 'get off my lawn' kind of guy. My wife is a 'rent is too high' type of gal. That's why she is always paralyzed with guilt."

"I'm afraid to ask," I said.

"You, Mike, are just like my wife. But you have also learned that you have no choice but to defend your driveway, or else you will have no more driveway. I hope you will learn to respect yourself for that," Logan said. "I never apologize for yelling at anyone to get off my lawn. And I never will. This is America."

❖

Exhausted by another relentless Friday, I began the process of closing the shop for the night. There was laundry to do, combs and brushes to clean, surfaces to sanitize, hair to sweep, accounting to record. Hours later, the smell of Logan's perm still hung in the air.

I had to drive to the bank to make a night deposit, and to the post office downtown to retrieve the day's mail. It was long dark by the time I entered the lobby of the post office while wearing a mask. I saw a bright red *Target* shopping bag in the middle of the floor right next to where my post office box was located. Just behind the automated vending machine, a homeless man was huddled over the shopping bag, rummaging through its contents. I froze in place.

"Rubber-band-rubber-band-rubber-band-rubber-band! All I need is a rubber band. And a piece of wire!" the homeless man yelled as he slapped himself repeatedly on the forehead.

The homeless man jerked his head up and looked at me through strands of stringy, shoulder-length, dirty-blonde hair. A bright pink carnation was tucked behind his ear. The flower seemed woefully out

Flowers

of place on a winter's night. The homeless man's eyes were bright blue, but vacant. His face was flush from the winter cold. He was barefoot. His feet were caked with mud. He wore a motley coat with pockets full of refuse.

"Don't mind me," he said with a maskless smile and bad breath that I could smell ten feet away. "I talk to myself all the time. Rubber-band-rubber-band-rubber-band-rubber-band-rubber-band! Do you want to use the machine?" He gestured graciously toward the automated postage vendor.

I did not engage but stood perfectly still.

"Are you afraid of me?" he asked with a wide-eyed grin, pulling his hair out of his face to give me a better look. He snatched the pink carnation from behind his ear and shoved it into his mouth. He chewed ravenously, sending bits of pink flower petals to the cold tiled floor.

"Because I am going to make a bomb? Tee-hee-hee!" he shouted, his voice echoing off the tiled walls. He stomped his muddy feet and danced in a circle. "Or are you gonna call the cops on me? Rubber-band-rubber-band-rubber-band-rubber-band!"

I turned my back to him, unlocked my post office box, and quickly retrieved my mail.

"Goodnight, sleep tight, don't let the bed-bugs bite!" the homeless man called after me in a sing-song voice as I left the building.

Once, I saw another homeless man urinate all over the front door of the post office. Several others had attempted to pry the locked mailboxes open. From what I heard, they were trying to steal the federal stimulus checks everyone got as emergency COVID relief. Eventually, the post office put a padlock on the front door at 6:00pm to lock the homeless out, which made it impossible for me to get my mail after work.

When I got back in my car for the quick drive home, the song playing on the radio startled me. The tune was written by a member of the Musicians and the Songwriters Halls of Fame, the Jamaican-born Thom Bell. The song was recorded by the *Spinners* in 1976.

The Climate of Truth

*"Hey ya'll, prepare yourself for the rubberband man
You've never heard a sound
Like the rubberband man
You're bound to lose control
When the rubberband starts to jam"*

I gasped when I heard that song, having just experienced my own version of the "rubberband man" in the post office. I rolled down my car window, stuck my head out and yelled at the sky, "Oh, come on, will ya! Enough already!"

I drove my car around the corner from the post office to a stoplight. A man was headed my direction on the adjacent sidewalk. He was accompanied by a very plump Golden Retriever. The two of them entered the crosswalk in front of my car. The dog had a large plastic "cone of shame" around its neck to keep it from biting itself. The man, as pudgy as his pet, ambled slowly and carefully while the dog limped along beside him. The man had a huge barrel chest and exceptionally large thighs. I observed the quirky scene while *"Rubberband Man"* continued to play on the radio.

As they passed directly in front of my car, I saw something I had never seen before. The man wore a dark polo shirt, a dark baseball cap and tan cargo pants. Strapped to his muscular thigh was a drop-leg holster holding a nine-millimeter *Glock*. The man stopped in front of my car, turned to face me, and put his hand on his gun. He flinched to make it look like he was going to draw his weapon.

I winced in the driver's seat. The man laughed at me, then continued on his way.

I dialed my cellphone.

"Police non-emergency. What are you reporting?"

"Is 'open carry' allowed inside city limits these days?" I asked.

"Yes," the dispatcher said. "It is allowed."

I swallowed hard. "I didn't know that. Thank you," I said as I hung up the phone.

❖

Flowers

Three other clients sent flowers to me in the coming weeks. All three purchased bouquets through FTD, and all three orders were assigned to the same flower shop that delivered the wilted Christmas arrangement. The first of the three deliveries was a colorful bouquet that arrived fresh and lovely, and it resurrected my faith in humanity. My security cameras showed the same Latino man crept up the side stairs to deliver the second bouquet; he left another wilted arrangement sitting on the front doormat and never rang the bell. I didn't find out about the third bouquet until one of my clients called several weeks later to ask why I never acknowledged the gift. Thoroughly embarrassed, I explained that the security cameras did not show a delivery was ever made. My disappointed client went directly to the flower shop and demanded a fresh bouquet to be made on the spot. She said she wouldn't leave without the flowers she paid for weeks earlier. She delivered the fresh bouquet to me herself because she couldn't allow the scam to prevail. She reported the pattern and practice of floral fraud to the *Better Business Bureau,* the *Secretary of State,* and the headquarters of the *Florists' Transworld Delivery* service based in Downer's Grove, Illinois. News reports at that time showed the floral industry was going bankrupt because of COVID.

When spring arrived following the COVID Christmas of 2020, I promised myself I could find joy in the pandemic by admiring the flowers in my garden. I spent hours cultivating the blooms, gently supporting the stalks by tying them to plant stakes with green ribbon. My clients lovingly referred to my yard as "The Park." I went out into the garden one morning to discover almost all my flowers snapped from their stems and strewn all about the lawn and sidewalk like refuse. The plants were brutalized. My security video showed a homeless woman who wore a black skirt and a pink bandana on her head. The homeless woman had rampaged in my garden at 11:05pm the night before. She attacked my flowers because I would not allow her to pitch her tent on the church lawn across the street.

"This is not your lawn!" she yelled at me. "This is God's lawn! A lawn is a part of nature, and nature is free! I have every right to be here!"

Of all the things to focus on while she was yelling at me, I noticed she was wearing coral colored lipstick. It was a shade very similar to the one that Rozz wore on that fated day at the swimming pool. I couldn't help but wonder why a homeless woman, whose life was

The Climate of Truth

stuffed in a collection of plastic garbage bags, would persist in the application of lipstick.

Patriots

꒰ ❖ ꒱

    I was yanked out of a magical dream where I was playing with Irma in a field of wildflowers. It was around 4:00am when my cellphone rang. Thinking it was an emergency involving one of my friends, I sprang out of bed in the dark to answer the call. Gymnastics were involved to make sure that I didn't squash Irma where she slept on the floor at the side of my bed. My dismount landed me against the corner of the bedframe, where I managed to stub my toe at full force. I cursed as I hobbled down the hall toward my cellphone, where it sat atop the writing desk in my office.

    "Hello! Hello!" I said, breathlessly into the phone. The pain in my toe was throbbing like a hot piston engine.

    A robotic voice on the other end of the line said, "Your social security number has been hacked!"

    It was only a scam. Once awakened, I could not get back to sleep. That was how the fateful work week began on Tuesday morning, January 5, 2021 (hairstylists commonly have Mondays off). The coffee didn't kick into my bloodstream until Harper, my first client of the day, arrived.

    "My hair is dull," Harper complained. "Should I tone it?" Her natural hair color was a flat pewter.

    "You could use a toner tune-up," I said, grimacing a little as I limped around the back of the styling chair because of my throbbing

The Climate of Truth

toe. "Advanced technology has made an express toner that is quick and easy. It takes only five minutes. It should last until your next haircut."

"I want to make it lighter and brighter," she insisted.

"It's not possible to lighten natural color with a toner. It's more like adding a watercolor wash to your hair to give it more pizzazz. A toner will add a lot of shine and sparkle to your silver, and it won't show a grow-out line. That's the beauty of it."

"Do it!" Harper ordered. "I want my cut to be choppy and spikey…Are you OK? You're limping."

"I'm alright. Just smashed my toe this morning and it's giving me fits."

After the shampoo, I lathered the silver toner over her wet hair while Harper was reclined in the sink. A Neil Diamond classic was playing on the stereo. Harper hummed along with the music:

> "Hands, touching hands
> *Reaching out, touching me, touching you*
>
> Sweet Caroline
> *Good times never seemed so good"*

As I massaged the color into her scalp with my gloved fingers, whimpers of delight floated out from beneath the COVID safety towel that covered Harper's face.

"That feels so goooooood!" she moaned. "You are the only one who has physically touched me in the last ten months because of COVID."

"I live alone," I said, "So I understand." I sang along with Neil Diamond in a dramatic voice, *"Reaching out, touching me, touching you!"*

Harper joined me to sing the chorus, *"Sweet Caroline!"* and the sound of the trumpets, *"Bah-Bah-Bah!"* We laughed together as I swirled the toner deeper into her roots.

"How do you feel about not being touched except when having your hair done?" I asked.

Patriots

"I'm ambivalent," she said flatly. "I'm used to it. But right now, I really notice that you are touching me. It feels so strange and unfamiliar. Like I'm sensory deprived or something."

"Please continue to lie back in the sink as you are for five minutes, and then we'll rinse again."

"OK," she said.

"Personally, I can't stand it if anybody touches my head," I said. "But I was like that even before COVID. People always want to grab hold of my curls, and it freaks me out."

"It's not fair that you have such amazing curly hair."

"I'd give it to you if I could," I said. "I was walking down to the corner this morning to mail a letter, and some guy was standing next to a trashcan smoking a cigarette. He had long, stringy, salt and pepper hair. Older guy. He moved right in front of me to cut me off. I thought he was going to try to rob me or something. But he looked right at me and said, 'Dude! You have the most awesome curls!'"

"Heavens," Harper said.

"Then I went into the drugstore to get some mouthwash, and this little old lady with a snow-white ponytail came right up to me, got right in front of my face. We're the only two in the whole store wearing a mask. And she said, 'Can I please touch your gorgeous curls?' She reached up to my head, and I had to duck. And I told her that it creeped me out to have people touch my hair. She said she understood, and she walked away…When I went to the grocery store, this lady working at the meat counter just rested her chin in her hands on top of the counter and stared at me. 'I want you to know that you have the most beautiful curls that I have ever seen.' She said it with a mesmerized look in her eyes. I've never been fashionable a day in my life. Now, all of a sudden, everybody wants my hair. I get several calls a week, men and women both, and they all want perms. We can't even keep perms in stock anymore. There's a national shortage of perm chemicals. It's the strangest thing. Everybody wants my hair."

"Who cuts your hair?" Harper asked, her face peeking from behind the safety towel.

"I do it by feel."

"I can't imagine. That must be difficult," she said.

The Climate of Truth

"Yeah, it would be easy to lose an ear."

"Mike van Gogh!" she said with a laugh.

I rinsed the express toner and conditioned Harper's hair. "Please let go of the safety towel," I instructed her. I took the towel from her face and used it to pat her hair dry. I motioned for her to sit up, and we were face to face.

"I'm very nervous about the run-off election today in Georgia," Harper said, looking at me intensely over the top of her mask. Her 70-year-old eyes looked weary.

"You mean 'War and Peach?'…or 'Georgia on all of our minds?'"

"Clever," Harper said.

"If the Democrat contenders don't flip those senate seats, Biden will be hamstrung," I said. "What a fluke that it's 'do or die' in Georgia. Half-a-billion dollars pumped into a runoff election, all to pay for negative ads on television. What a waste."

"What half-a-billion could have done to treat COVID in Georgia alone," Harper said.

"If the Republicans win Georgia and retain control in the Senate, the government won't function. It will be nothing but obstruction on Capitol Hill."

"Do you think there will be violence?" she asked with a quiver in her voice.

"I don't know. But you can sure feel it in the air."

We went back to the styling chair, where I snapped a cutting cape around her neck.

"I got so many compliments on my last haircut," Harper said. "Do it just like last time. It's so easy to take care of. I just love it!"

I began to section and snip her sporty, layered fringe. As usual, I thought out loud in conversation as I worked. "The National Guard is being called out in several states," I said. "Capitol Buildings all over the country are being boarded up because of the threat of violence. Militants say they will storm the Capitol in Olympia tomorrow to protest the certification of the election. They claim it's unconstitutional for Congress to meet virtually because of COVID protocols. They say there might be more race riots. Businesses are

Patriots

boarding up their windows in DC because pro-Trump rallies are happening there tomorrow to protest the certification of the Electoral votes. The police posted signs all over DC that say carrying a weapon is illegal."

"Like that's going to stop anybody," Harper interjected.

"The Defense Department said the military won't get involved like they were called to do last summer with the *'Black Lives Matter'* protests. But the police are on standby with special response teams to deal with chemical or biological weapons."

"Violence is a popular choice," Harper said looking like she might be ill. "Why am I not surprised?"

"Republican senators in Pennsylvania refused to seat a Democrat who won reelection. They tried to seize control of the session away from the Democrat Lieutenant Governor. It's like they're on fire to overthrow everything across the board. It's total anarchy."

Harper looked at me through the mirror. "Why not? Trump gets away with it all the time! 'Monkey see, monkey do'… I never thought I would live to see this kind of thing…If you ask me, the Democrats are too polite. They need to bust some heads! They need to make arrests."

"This kind of thing hasn't happened since the Civil War," I said. "Several southern Senators objected to Abraham Lincoln's election. Those Senators were expelled from Congress. They were charged with sedition."

"That's when politicians had some guts," Harper said. "They practiced what they preached."

"Well, really, that's when the southern states began to secede from the union. Almost all of the Senators who were expelled helped to lead the Confederacy."

"It's like the Civil War never ended," Harper said. "Here we go again."

"But I don't think anybody's going to get booted out of Congress this go around," I said.

"We could end up split into three countries," Harper mused. "Pacifica and Atlantica – I don't even know what they'd call the red states in the middle."

The Climate of Truth

"Midlandia?" I offered, waving my scissors in the air.

"I kind of like the name Pacifica," Harper said. "I could live with that…You heard about Trump trying to strongarm the Secretary of State in Georgia to switch the vote tally?"

"To magically find 11,780 Trump votes that don't exist. Weird how the actual number is burned into my brain," I said.

"What the heck is it about Georgia?" Harper said, brandishing her arms. "Thank God they recorded the phone call with Trump making his threats, so there is irrefutable proof that he was trying to cheat with fake votes. It's a crime to interfere with an election! Trump committed treason! He thinks he's above the law!"

"Please hold still so I don't gouge your haircut," I said.

"Sorry. Can't help it. It makes me furious," she said, shaking her head in disbelief. "Trump should be arrested. But nothing ever sticks to him."

"I don't think he will ever be arrested. It would start a Civil War for sure."

Harper's eyes drifted to a painting that hung above my workstation. "Did you do that one too?"

"I did almost all the artwork in this room, except for the American flag with the poppies. That was painted by a friend of mine," I said.

"What's the story behind that incredible piece? It looks historical," Harper said, looking at a framed colored drawing high on the wall over my workstation.

"That's Benjamin Franklin playing chess with the French widow, Madame Helvétius, while they took a bath together."

"How risqué," she said. "Politicians are always screwing someone."

"The last two of Ben Franklin's personal 12 commandments were to 'increase and multiply, and replenish the Earth,' and to 'Love one another,' even at the taxpayers' expense. That sort of says it all," I said with a laugh. "Ben Franklin was really a colonial hippie who believed in free love."

Patriots

"I never would have thought to put Benjamin Franklin in the same 'grab 'em by the pussy' scale as Trump loves to say. It just reinforces the fact that men are pigs," Harper said.

"Present company excluded!" I whined.

"Of course. You're a unicorn," Harper said with a wink.

Harper didn't know that I had a tattoo of a unicorn on my right shoulder.

"That bathtub piece is my rendition of a scene from the *HBO* miniseries about John Adams," I said. "Madame Helvétius was said to be so beautiful that a 100-year-old man once told her, 'Ah, Madame, if only I were only 80 again!'"

"Yuck! Those French!" Harper said. "She looks like she could stop a dump truck with that face. That 100-year-old man must have been blind as a bat."

I offered a brief history of early American diplomacy. "The *HBO* series took liberties with historical accuracy in that famous bathtub scene. It didn't really happen that way. The real story is that Ben Franklin was taking a bath and playing chess with another man."

"You mean…?" she said.

"The bathtub belonged to one of Ben Franklin's French lady friends, but it wasn't really Madame Helvétius. She was around at the time, but not in the bathtub in this instance. She was a widow. Ben Franklin was a widower by then, and he was in love with her. She was 60 when they met. He proposed to her, but she turned him down. But then, Franklin was in love with just about any woman in or out of a skirt, and all the women of France were all madly in love with him too -- much to the dismay of the Puritan prude, John Adams. Madame Helvétius had ties to the French court when Ben Franklin was the first Ambassador appointed by the colonies. Ben Franklin got Madame Helvétius to whisper in the ear of the commanding General of the French Army, and that led to the General having a chat with the King of France, and that is how French troops were sent to help win the American Revolution. Because the French really hated the British too. So, if Ben Franklin didn't flirt with the ladies of the French court, we wouldn't be standing here today as Americans."

"Amazing," Harper said.

The Climate of Truth

"And it's fun to know that Ben Franklin slept in the nude and spent the night in the same bed with John Adams once in New Jersey. The things that happen in New Jersey!"

"You're a crack-up," Harper said.

"So, I'm told."

"The way you use layers of color in your artwork, the stroke marks. What medium is that?" Harper asked.

"Watercolor pencil."

"The perspective is remarkable. Even the reflection in the standing mirror," she said.

"I did that piece in 2008 when I was sick in bed with a really bad flu for two weeks. I was in quarantine to keep my housemates from catching it…If only people would do that kind of thing nowadays, maybe COVID wouldn't have killed so many people…It took me three days just to do the upholstery on the armchair by Ben Franklin's bathrobe."

"I love his one sock and shoe in the middle of the floor there. And the little white dog poking out from behind the bathtub," Harper said.

"That's a Bichon Frisé. A French breed, of course," I said.

"Oui-oui Monsieur!" Harper said with a giggle. "That's about all the French I know."

"I've even been to Ben Franklin's townhouse in London, by *Charing Cross Station*, where he lived for 17 years. The *British Historical Society* turned his townhouse into a museum. When they started renovations, they discovered 28 bodies buried in Ben Franklin's basement."

"He literally had skeletons in his closet?" Harper asked, astonished.

"Not what you would expect, huh? Carbon dating showed the bodies were buried there while Ben Franklin was in residence. The skulls were dissected, and limbs were sawed off. Six of the bodies were children, but that's a whole other story about grave-robbing for cadavers, all to train medics for the Revolutionary War in secret."

"Ben Franklin had a dark side!" Harper said. "How unexpected."

Patriots

The styling chair was facing out the front window. Both Harper and I looked up in time to see a four-by-four truck speed past my corner with several *"Trump 2020"* flags, American flags, and Confederate flags waving from poles attached to the bed of the truck. A message was painted along the side of the truck in giant black letters: *"Democrats are Evil."*

"Who does that!" Harper said, aghast.

"It's got to be one of the *'Proud Boys'* or the *'Patriot Prayer'* guys. They've been beating on *'Antifa'* all year. This guy's been driving around trying to run people off the road like they did with Biden's campaign bus in Texas. It's been going on for months."

"I don't get it," Harper said.

"When asked if America was a republic or a monarchy, Ben Franklin wisely answered, 'A republic…if you can keep it.' No truer words. Makes ya wonder if we can keep the republic the founding fathers created…It sure feels like our republic could slip away at any minute."

"I guess if you repeat the lie long enough, the lie becomes truth to a lot of people," Harper said.

"The guy in the truck is one of the people of the lie. But he thinks he's a true American patriot…I don't think he's worthy of polishing Ben Franklin's silver-buckled shoes."

"How did we even get here?" Harper asked, sounding dejected.

"At least 12 Republican senators will definitely try to overturn the Electoral vote tomorrow because they insist the election was stolen. Because Trump said so."

"Treason is a capital offense!" Harper shouted. "How can they do that!" She pounded her fist on the arm of the styling chair. "Have we all gone mad? How can we let this happen?"

"In <u>their</u> minds, God gave them the mission to take over the government and to make America a White, Christian nation. To heck with anybody else. So now we've got this weird dynamic, a perfect storm where the *'QAnon'* conspiracy freaks hooked up with Trump's *'Make America Great Again'* red hats, who cater to the 94 million Evangelicals who literally make up half the electorate. Pump it up with White supremacists and *'Alt-Right'* extremists like the guy in the truck with the flags who just drove by, and we've got a fat chunk of

The Climate of Truth

funky Dominionism in the mix here. They truly believe that anybody who doesn't agree with them is Satan, and that God's going to lead his loyal Christian soldiers to take back 'dominon' over the Earth. That's how twisted interpretation of biblical law 'trumps' the law of the land, pardon the pun. That's how Nixon's '*Silent Majority*' turned into Regan's '*Moral Majority*,' and we ended up with bombings at abortion clinics, gay bashings, school prayer, and people like Anita Byrant and Jerry Falwell screaming about sexual deviants who were 'destroying family values.' It's called the '*southern strategy*,' an echo of the Confederate mindset…But Dominionists miscalculated this last election. The real reason why angry White folk are the ones who want to toss out the Electoral votes is because Black people showed up to the fight – in numbers they never thought possible."

"'Do unto others.' Did they conveniently forget that part of the *Bible*?" Harper asked in exasperation.

"Trump supporters believe that voting machines made by the *Dominion Corporation* were mysteriously reprogrammed to flip votes to Biden. Dominionism undone by *Dominion*. The irony is thick. 'Trumpers' are pissed as hell about it, and right-wing media wants to keep them pissed, so they yammer about how *Dominion* supposedly cheated Trump in some global conspiracy, even though there's absolutely no evidence. That's propaganda for you, the stuff of wars. So now, you watch -- *Dominion* will sue God, the networks, and Trump's personal army for defamation and slander."

"Trump is a cult," Harper said.

"It's like the Crusades on the road to Jerusalem again," I said. "Or the Spanish Inquisition. No wonder we have Muslim extremists who want to blow us up."

"I don't think we've ever had an outgoing administration block the incoming one from accessing the government before," Harper said.

"It's dangerous."

"And childish, and embarrassing," she said. "I'd even say it's criminal…Funny how Scotland won't let Trump in to play at his own golf course. They tell him he should concede the election and move out of the White House."

"The world thinks we've gone bonkers," I said.

Patriots

"They're right on that score," Harper replied with a sigh. "It's frightening."

"Our adversaries are watching. Congress isn't paying attention, and we are vulnerable to attack."

Three days after the conversation with Harper, the *Dominion Corporation* filed the first of several billion-dollar lawsuits against Trump's cronies, specifically for defamation. The first case was filed against Sydney Powell, one of Trump's former attorneys and one of the loudest right-wing conspiracy theorists on record. Ms. Powell attempted to have the *Dominion* case thrown out of court, arguing that her claims of voter fraud were so outrageous that "reasonable people would not accept such statements as fact." A federal judge sanctioned Ms. Powell for filing frivolous lawsuits in an attempt to overthrow the election. Ms. Powell was made to pay the legal fees for the states that had to defend themselves against her false claims of election fraud. The judge also referred the matter to state Bar Associations for them to consider the revocation of her licenses to practice law.

❖

The night of January 5, 2020, the runoff election for the two senate seats in Georgia was too close to call, but the Democrats were leading. The outstanding votes were all in counties held by Democrats where the Black vote was predominant.

At a final campaign rally in Georgia, Kelly Loeffler, one of the incumbent Republican senators, was drowned out by the crowd that chanted, "Fight for Trump! Fight for Trump!" She dropped her own campaign speech, and said instead, "I have an announcement to make. I will be voting against the Electoral votes in the Presidential election!" The crowd cheered.

Loeffler was under fire for posing in photos with a known leader of the *Ku Klux Klan*. She claimed not to have known of the man's affiliation. During campaign rallies in the Georgia runoff, *Klan* members were seen wearing black and white placards on their backs that read *"Do not Certify."*

Police clashed with Trump supporters at *"Black Lives Matter Plaza"* in Atlanta when the Democrats were both projected to have won the Georgia runoff election the following day, January 6. For the

The Climate of Truth

first time in Georgia's history, both a Black man and a Jew were elected to the Senate, miraculously defeating both incumbent Republicans.

Republicans answered the 2020 election loss by introducing 361 bills in 47 states that would restrict voting access. Most of the restrictions were aimed at eliminating mail-in voting, early voting, and drop boxes that were widely used to help people cast their ballots safely during the pandemic. The voting restrictions, specifically intended to impact voters of color, were described by the *"Washington Post"* as *"potentially amounting to the most sweeping contraction of ballot access in the United States since the end of Reconstruction"* just after the Civil War. People of color were forced to wait in longer lines at polling stations; laws were passed to disallow the voters to access food or beverage while they waited to vote, some of them having to wait for 12 hours or more.

❖

Silvia worked as a cashier at the local *Bi-Mart* for many years. She was fond of her job because, as she explained, it allowed her to lead an uncomplicated life. I didn't know how old she was, but she told me she had grandchildren.

On several occasions, I had to pound loudly on the hood of her truck, where she sat waiting for her hair appointment in the parking lot. She had the tendency to fall into a deep sleep anytime she sat still for a few minutes. Even calling her name through the truck's window did not rouse her.

I saw Silvia at 8:00am, on January 6. At the time, I didn't know how infamous the date would become. I began her haircut, a stacked bob. Silvia was the kind of dithery client who asked a gazillion questions about her hair and repeatedly complained that she was ill-equipped to master the techniques of hairstyling at home.

"I have a friend, the partner of a guy I work with, he's a hairdresser too," she announced.

Silently, I questioned why she was sitting in my styling chair when she had a "friend" in my line of work. "We are stylists honey, stylists," I said in a light tone. "When you call us guys 'hairdressers', it makes it sound like we're all named Flo, we have rollers in our hair

Patriots

and a cigarette hanging from our lips. I'm nothing like that, so we're stylists, not hairdressers. OK?"

"Sorry, no offense," she said with a wrinkled forehead that made her look like she was in pain.

"No offense taken," I said laughing. "I was just kidding with you."

Silvia was sometimes touchy and took most everything personally. "So, this other <u>stylist</u> I know, he's barely making it with COVID and all," she said. "He can't even get any walk-ins to come into his shop."

"That's why I don't do walk-ins," I said.

"I tell him that you have such a beautiful shop here, inside and out. I showed him your website and all your artwork. He loves Irma!"

Irma barked upon hearing her name, and Silvia nearly jumped out of the chair, as if she had been tased.

"Is she mad at me?" Silvia fretted, trying to catch her breath. She checked her pulse by placing her hand against her carotid artery.

"No, she's not at all like that. Irma's just a very smart dog, and she knew you were talking about her, so she wanted to put in her two cents."

"What kind of dog is she again?" Silvia asked.

"A Corgi"

"Does she bite?" she said, sounding afraid.

"Where did that come from?" I said, trying not to be annoyed.

"I don't know, I'm just nervous."

"Irma's never bitten anybody," I said. "Corgis are the smallest herding dog in the world. If you were a cow, a sheep, or a horse, you would know exactly what her barks meant. She's saying, 'Do exactly what I tell you to do, Silvia! Go to the shampoo bowl when I tell you to go.' Irma is a professional. Right Irma Lu?"

I bleated like a sheep and mooed like a cow, and that made Irma smile.

"That fat little thing can herd horses?" Silvia said.

Irma tilted her head sideways and let out a yip.

The Climate of Truth

"First, you need to apologize to Irma for calling her fat," I said. "She's built like a sausage on purpose."

"Oh, I'm very sorry, Irma," Silvia said sincerely. "I didn't mean to hurt your feelings."

"She's a very sensitive girl, and she completely understands every word you are saying. She's part of the Queen's court, after all."

"I stand corrected," Silvia said.

"Well, you're sitting, actually. But I get your point," I said, but my joke went over Silvia's head. "Did you know, Corgis can actually run in between a horse's hooves while the horse is galloping? And I've even seen a Corgi jump from the ground up onto a horse's back. Granted, it was a short horse, but it was still impressive. Irma is not inclined to be a circus or rodeo dog, but Corgis are rather amazing performers."

"Wow," Silvia said, "I didn't know."

"We're all about education here at *Blow Your Top!*" I noticed a bright red spot on Silvia's forehead. "Did you burn yourself with a curling iron?"

"I sure did. It even sizzled. I'm such a nervous Nelly with a curling iron. I can't do my hair like you do."

"Here, let's put some magic goo on it," I said. I grabbed a bottle from the stash of styling products from the shelf beside my desk and gently dabbed a bit of balm on her forehead. "That should make it feel cooler almost instantly."

"How amazing! What is that stuff?" Silvia said.

"It's a special lotion that stimulates hair growth, but I found it works really good on curling iron burns too. It's kind of a miracle cure."

"I'm not going to sprout hair out of my forehead, am I?" she asked, looking panicked.

"Oh dear," I said.

"That was a stupid question, wasn't it?" Silvia turned red in the face.

"I've heard worse," I said with a chuckle. "Another trick you can use is to keep your comb flat and hold it in between your face and the

Patriots

curling iron, like a buffer to protect your skin. If you practice, it becomes second nature."

"I guess I burned myself because I'm kinda punch-drunk these days. I haven't been getting much sleep. I toss and turn all night, thinking about everything that's happening to us, to the whole world. And then I have to get up way early, long before dawn, because I have to be at the store at 5:00am."

"Eeeew," I said. "What a ghastly hour to start the day."

"They line up at 5:30 in the morning because they all know the ammo only comes on Thursdays. You can't really tell how old they are because everybody has to wear a mask these days to get in the store. Everyone looks younger with a mask, so I have to check all their IDs. The law says they only have to be 18, but our store policy says you have to be at least 21 to buy bullets. It's a two-box limit per customer. There's a huge demand for ammo for the 22-caliber long rifle, the AK-47, the 9-millimeter -- we carry all of it. That's what kids want these days. We sell out of ammo in only 20 minutes, each and every week…Did you know that you don't have to pay sales tax on a gun safe?"

"Didn't know that, but I'm not in the market for one."

Uncannily, the stereo was playing a song that mirrored our conversation. *"Pumped Up Kicks"* by the indie band *Foster the People* was written about the tendency of "isolated, psychotic kids" to turn to gun violence, and how teenage mental illness was a primary driver for mass shootings in schools. The lyric describes how a disturbed teen could shoot and kill his classmates just to steal their $600 "pumped-up kicks" (designer basketball shoes).

"Yeah, he found a six-shooter gun
In his dad's closet, in a box of fun things
And I don't even know what
But he's coming for you, yeah, he's coming for you

All the other kids with the pumped-up kicks
You better run, better run, outrun my gun
All the other kids with the pumped-up kicks
You better run, better run, faster than my bullet"

The Climate of Truth

"We do charge sales tax on the bullets, though," Silvia continued. "I have another friend who owns a gun store. He's busier than ever. Can't keep the darned things in stock. There's millions of them out there…I think that's why I'm kinda jumpy these days. Makes ya wonder what all these kids are doing, walking around with all them bullets…So I rush home after work every day to be with my cats, and I lock the front door right away. I turn up the music so I don't have to hear what's going on out there in la-la land. I sort of drown it out with my music. I listen to the same kind of music that you have on in here, Mike. I really love your playlist. It's awesome."

"Thanks. It took me years to perfect it," I said, noticing that Silvia couldn't keep her hands from shaking. She had a far-away look in her eyes.

"I didn't sleep last night," Silvia said. "I got up at 2:00am because I got bored staring at the ceiling. So I made a fresh pot of coffee and decided to go to town painting the cabinets in my garage. They were a nasty shade of dark brown, so I decided to do a cool shade of grey instead. I was out there painting away in the wee hours until I heard this voice outside from a bullhorn. 'We've got you surrounded! Come out with your hands up!'…I tell you, I've never heard those words ever before in my life unless it was some cop show on television. 'Come out with your hands up' in the cul-de-sac right across the street from me. I was too scared to even peek out the living room curtains…It was some punk kid with a bunch of automatic weapons. There were cop cars everywhere…Mike, do you think we're going to be safe in our homes? Safe from all the people who have guns?"

"I don't know, Silvia. I sure hope so…I stay home and mind my own business." I wiped her face with a towel and took the cutting cape from around her neck. "There you are my dear. Good for another three-thousand miles. Is a little hairspray, OK?"

The conversation with Silvia took place at the same time the first 300 protesters marched to the reflecting pool near the west side of the Capitol Building in Washington DC. They arrived just minutes after Trump's personal lawyer, Rudy Giuliani, used loudspeakers to excite a crowd of thousands gathered at the "*Save America March*" behind the White House on January 6.

Giuliani said, "Let's have trial by combat!" The crowd roared in approval.

Patriots

Trump spoke to his adoring fans at the rally for over an hour, when he urged his own Vice President to overthrow the Electoral process. Trump ended his speech by instructing the primed and impressionable crowd to march down Pennsylvania Avenue to the Capitol Building.

Trump clamored, "If you don't fight like hell, you're not going to have a country anymore." He told the crowd he would march along with them, which he didn't do, and encouraged them to act with "boldness" in order to "take back our country." The intent of his speech was unmistakable – he was calling for the use of violence to retain his hold on power.

❖

My next client, Samuel, was an elder man who preferred his hair to be firmly parted from left to right and frozen in place with hairspray like "*Ken*" from the "*Barbie*" doll collection. Samuel always sported wild patterned socks in psychedelic colors. He had a pair of custom-made bright purple socks adorned with the fluffy face of his own white Persian cat. He wore candy-colored button-down shirts that were neatly tucked with the help of a color-coordinated belt. He usually wore wing-tipped shoes with jeans.

"Do you know what's going on in DC right now?" Samuel asked, looking frightened.

"Is it bad?"

"It's terrifying," he said as he pressed his mask tighter against the bridge of his nose. "Is there a way you can turn on the news, Mike? I was listening on the drive over here, and I'm worried."

"Absolutely."

I turned off my playlist and switched to *CNN's* livestream on my laptop. As I cut his hair, Samuel and I watched footage of the riotous mob as they clashed with officers at the Capitol. The soundtrack wirelessly transferred to the stereo on the opposite side of the room, making the mob fill the space with digital surround-sound. We could hear the rioters cursing on live television. We could hear their heavy breathing, grunting, threatening, and screaming. We could see the Trump flags waving in the wind, and people climbing the scaffolding to rip apart the equipment being set in place for Biden's Inauguration.

The Climate of Truth

We could see blue flags emblazoned with the phrase *"Fuck Biden!"* We waited for signs that it would all stop. But the longer we watched, the worse it got. And the worst was yet to come.

The light in Samuel's sparkling blue eyes dimmed to a milky grey as he witnessed the carnage. He turned his face away from the video screen to look at me. I resumed cutting his hair.

"They should arrest Trump, right now, this very minute!" he said in a sudden fit of uncharacteristic anger. The dark circles under his narrowed eyes grew even denser in color as the blood pooled in his face. "And then they should tie him up and cut off his balls with a rusty old razor!" I remembered President Biden's story of "Corn Pop" and the rusty switch blades.

Samuel was impassioned as he spoke. His words were intentional, stemming from deep, personal pain. His prostate had been removed due to cancer. He had to inject his penis with needles in order to have sex. It bothered me that I knew these intimate details about his life, but he confided them to me so that I could encourage other men who might have found themselves in the same predicament. He also confided in me to prove to himself that a man who experienced prostate extraction needn't feel emasculated.

"You can still lead a normal, healthy sex life," Samuel insisted. "It's important never to give up hope. You need to tell other guys, Mike."

As he continued to watch the insurrection unfold on television, Samuel fully embodied the pale aura of hopelessness. "They should rip off Trump's disgusting hair. And then they should shoot him in the head!"

I never knew Samuel to talk like that before. He was normally a gentle man who adored Broadway musicals. We spoke at length about the film version of *"Cats,"* the soaring arrangements and the delightful costumes, and how the cattails in group dance numbers moved in perfect synchronization with the orchestra. We both agreed that it was a lovely film that didn't deserve to be eviscerated -- "useless kitty porn," as reviewers called it.

I told Samuel that, every day, I had to walk past the *Wintergarden Theatre* on Broadway where *"Cats"* was performed, on the way to my New York apartment in Hell's Kitchen. I told him that I had many friends who worked on that show, and how one of the dancers I knew

Patriots

complained about the exhausting choreography – "all the sus-sous up the poop-a-doos!" as he put it. Samuel loved that one.

Though COVID made performance art seem like a dream from long ago, I told Samuel how Betty Buckley's thunderous voice could be heard through the cement wall of the *Wintergarden Theatre*, clear out onto the street. I told him how she practically burst my eardrums when she sang "*Grizabella's*" showstopper, "*Memory*," at an outdoor concert in the Catskills:

> *"Touch me*
> *It's so easy to leave me*
> *All alone with the memory*
> *Of my days in the sun*
> *If you touch me*
> *You'll understand what happiness is*
> *Look, a new day*
> *Has begun"*

Ms. Buckley stood on a floating platform in the middle of a lake, accompanied by a 40-piece orchestra, and sprays of multi-colored water danced from fountainheads positioned all around the platform. Those were the kinds of things that made Samuel appreciate living. Not a riotous horde who called themselves patriots.

Staring at the images of the mob attacking the Capitol, Samuel confessed that he was forced to quit speaking to his daughter and her entire family because they had all turned into rabid "Trumpers." He said they were all brainwashed, and that they probably welcomed the violence we were witnessing. The thought of it made Samuel tear up in my chair. It was not the America that either of us wanted to live in.

President-Elect Biden was scheduled to speak on his plan to provide financial relief for small businesses struggling from the pandemic. Instead, the nation saw Secret Service agents draw their weapons on the Senate floor, hooligans rifle through and toss government documents found on Senators' desks and then sit with their feet upon the dais. Terrified Congressmen wore gas masks while huddled together in the upper balcony of the House chamber. Capitol Security Guards tried to calm and usher the rioters out of the chamber, calling it a "sacred" space.

The Climate of Truth

Because Trump remained silent during the chaos, Biden went on national television to call for the "mob to pull back to allow Democracy to go forward." He also called upon Trump to go on national television, to "fulfill his oath and defend the Constitution, and demand an end to this siege." Biden made that demand in the name of "honor, decency, respect and tolerance." Reports came through the news that suggested certain members of Congress were considering the 25th amendment to remove Trump from office.

❖

Vivian was my next client that fateful day. She was a retired nurse who contracted Hepatitis by accidentally stabbing herself with a dirty syringe while on the job. She persisted in treatments and finally achieved full remission after many years of suffering. Bravely, Vivian opted for a simultaneous double knee replacement surgery and never once complained about the pain. She lived just a few blocks from my house, and I often saw her walking the neighborhood to strengthen her newly implanted titanium knees.

Vivian was not one who liked to plan for hair appointments. Her usual pattern was to call after waiting three months for a haircut. By then, she was severely agitated by bangs that were stabbing her in the eyes. After knowing me for 25 years, she didn't change her hair appointment habits, but she was always very excited to sit in the styling chair.

She watched the newsfeed on my desk as I cut her bushy grey hair into a Dorothy Hamill wedge. From the livestream, we could hear glass breaking, police being beaten with hockey sticks, baseball bats, and American flagpoles. Bear spray and tear gas were being spewed at officers trying to hold the mob back, and smoke alarms blared in the background.

"It's really hard for me to stand here and do my job, knowing that our country is under attack," I said. "It's making me question reality."

"It's days like this that I wonder if I still have a husband," Vivian said with profound sadness. "Earl says 'hello', by the way."

Vivian handed me Earl's calling card. She kept her eyes focused on the floor when she spoke, as if it was too much to for her to

Patriots

observe the violence unfolding on the screen. It was strange to converse while we heard people being beaten.

"He wanted me to give you his card," Vivian said. "He would like it if you'd email him sometime. Or maybe a *Zoom* call."

"I've never done a *Zoom* call in my life. Don't even know how to do it."

"It's pretty easy," she said. "You just push a few buttons."

I wasn't interested in contacting her husband. The thought of it made me bristle internally. "Where is he again? Some ghastly hot and humid place if I remember."

"Costa Rica. I know you'd hate it there because of the heat," Vivian said.

"They have mosquitos the size of chickens there," I said. "And I'm sure there are tons of nasty snakes in the jungle…I prefer the coolness here, and I never get tired of the rain."

"I love the rain here too," she said, wistfully. "I could never move down to Costa Rica with Earl. He wants me to, but I couldn't handle the heat either…But Earl loves it there. Don't know why, but he really loves it…He's made some good friends down there. He has a very cheap housekeeper who cooks for him. What more could a man want? He's very happy with the life he's created there."

"Are _you_ happy, Vivian?" I stopped cutting her hair for a moment to look her in the eye.

She adjusted her mask, and then pondered a moment. "I'm not sure…But I think so."

"Earl moved to Costa Rica to get away from Trump, right? I think he called it the 'kakistocracy,' where a country is run by the worst of the worst, the most unqualified."

"What a word, eh?" she said.

"Is he going to stay in Costa Rica?"

"I don't know," Vivian said, keeping her eyes downcast. "Things are simpler down there. Calmer. There is no standing army to attack its own people. Earl likes that a lot. But who knows what he's going to do…It's not like what I thought was going to happen with my life. It's unusual, I know."

The Climate of Truth

I paused, wondering if I should speak any further on this sensitive subject, but was compelled to continue. "I don't mean to get too far into your private business, but are you angry that he left you up here, alone?"

She looked up at me over her mask. "Sure, I was angry. You bet."

"Did you <u>tell</u> him you were angry?"

"We had words…But time has passed. Feelings subside," she said.

"But marriage vows don't subside, do they?" I asked.

The haircut was interrupted by the front doorbell. Irma barked ferociously because no one was supposed to enter the building that way. I excused myself to answer the door. I was shocked to find my friend, Dominick, standing there wearing an ascot with a blue blazer, and a mask. He was holding a Christmas bag that was decorated with an old-fashioned Santa, candy canes, and pink tissue paper. It was unsettling to behold Christmas trappings while the Capitol was under siege.

"This is your belated Christmas present!" Dominick announced merrily, thrusting the bag in my direction.

"Are you OK?" I asked, overwhelmed to see him.

"I'm pretty good," he said with a nod.

"Are you <u>really,</u> OK?" We locked eyes for a moment.

"Yes, I'm fine. I'm back to work. These are my work duds, see? So, Merry Christmas!" Dominick said.

"Thank you for going out of your way, with everything going on," I said.

"I don't want to keep you from your other client," Dominick said, waving goodbye. "Miss you, friend!"

"It was an even better Christmas present to see the whites of your eyes!" I yelled after him as I shut and locked the door. I put his gift, a bottle of peach infused white wine, in the kitchen. I appreciated the effort even though I didn't drink. I returned to Vivian at the styling chair.

"Sorry for the interruption," I said.

"That's quite all right, Mike. He sounded like a nice fella."

Patriots

"He's a good friend, and a client, like you. It was surreal to see him just now. I can't get over how he just appeared at my door. I texted him just this morning to see how he was feeling and didn't expect to see him standing there just now. He's a health clinic manager. One of his nurses infected him with COVID. He was so incredibly sick, he couldn't even stand up. It went on like that for a few weeks. He was barely able to make it to the bathroom. He had to force himself to stand up and walk around a few rooms in his house. It came on so suddenly, and he gave it to his husband, but his husband didn't get a bad case. It's strange how everybody has different symptoms…He went through all that, and still took the time to bring me a Christmas present…I was afraid for him."

"He won't be the last you will know to have COVID, I'm afraid," Vivian said.

"I know a lot of people who have been infected."

"Your friend sounds like a lucky one," she said. "I was reading about a young woman this morning. Six months after COVID, she still has severe symptoms and no control over her body. She still can't breathe or carry on a conversation. At first, she did everything right. She was completely isolated for months. But then came her 21st birthday. She said she wanted to feel normal for just that one day. So, she visited some friends in Boise and they went to bars and restaurants, typical for a 21st birthday. Her friends assured her that the bars and restaurants followed all the precautions, and that the cases were low. But outbreaks happened at three of the bars she visited. Six months later, she barely has enough energy to stand up. Was it worth risking her life to make her birthday seem normal? Your friend there, he's a lucky one, already back to work."

I looked at the laptop screen in time to see a man walk through the statuary hall of the Capitol Building with a large Confederate flag hoisted on a pole slung over his shoulder. My blood ran cold.

"Have you thought about divorce?" I asked her.

"For like five seconds," Vivian said, fluttering her eyes. "It's too complicated…Things are restricted with COVID down in Costa Rica too. Earl can't come home right now even if he wanted to. They won't let him into the US."

"I'm asking out of concern for you, not out of judgement."

"I know this about you, Mike."

The Climate of Truth

"It seems like Earl's decision…was…well…extremely selfish," I said. "It doesn't seem like he fully considered your well-being with his politics. He's left you alone in the middle of COVID, now in the middle of an insurrection too. That has to hurt."

"It hurts like hell…But I love him," she said firmly. "And he loves me…We *SnapChat* or *Facetime* at least an hour every day."

"That's a tough life," I said.

"No tougher than yours, Mike. You're all alone too."

"But I'm not married. Not that I haven't tried!" I said.

"Earl asks about you all the time," she said. "We remember all the work you did to protect the drinking water here in our county. Earl says, 'That Mike, he's not afraid to go into the belly of the beast.' We both respect you for that."

"Yeah, well it nearly destroyed my reputation," I whispered.

"Yet here you stand. And pretty straight up from what I can see right in front of me."

"Never straight!" I said with a laugh. "Gayly forward. Gayly forward!"

We were both quiet as excited voices reported that the mob was climbing in through broken windows and pouring into the Capitol Rotunda. Shortly thereafter, a woman was reported to have been shot while attempting to climb through a broken glass door into the Speaker's Lobby, mere feet from where members of Congress were hiding. The woman had a *"Trump 2020"* flag strapped to her back like *"Superman's"* cape. She later died from her wounds and posthumously became a recruiting tool for right-wing militants.

"At least you have your grandkids here, Vivian. And you have your adorable dogs," I said. "I wish you nothing but peace and a happy heart in this new year. In all this violence, we have to find peace."

Vivian wiped a tear from her eye. "Thank you for your words of encouragement. You help give me strength to keep going, and I will never forget it."

Exactly one year later to the day – January 6, 2022 – the first anniversary of the insurrection, Dominick sent a text at 7:30am: *"Sorry for the late notice, but I need to cancel my appointment tomorrow. Yep, I got*

Patriots

COVID a second time. I have no idea how it happened. I'm fully vaccinated and boostered. We follow all the rules. I just don't get it. Mom and brother are fine so far. Hubby just has a sore throat. Maybe I can take the new COVID pill. Not sure. We'll see what my doc says in the morning. I'm congested but my throat is fine, and the cough is no different than it has been for the last year, so there's that. I'm well enough to work remotely, LOL! (Emoji smiley face with a wink) We stayed home and watched movies on New Year's, so I don't get why this happened to me again. We did go to the van Gogh exhibit in Seattle, but we were all musked the entire time, as was everyone there."

❖

When Roger called for an appointment, it was usually because he was exasperated with his bushy hair after waiting for several months for a haircut. He was consistently astounded when I explained that my soonest opening was a week or two out for a gentleman's cut. Regardless, he always declined to book his appointments in advance. It was particularly tricky when he called me the day before his daughter's wedding, and I chose to rearrange my schedule to accommodate him. In my experience, his pattern of behavior was consistent with people who had difficulty making commitments. Years before, I saw a sign on a fellow stylist's station that addressed this problem, but I didn't have the nerve to post it myself: *"Poor planning on your part does not constitute an emergency on my part."* Roger mistook my practice of being accommodating as a sign that I was a pushover.

Once in the styling chair, Roger would customarily apologize for waiting until the last minute to get a much-needed haircut, and then he showered me with compliments about the quality of my work. He always did this with a gentle voice and soft-focused eyes in an attempt to display humility. However, the effect was more like he was impressed with his own ability to be congenial while his mind was elsewhere. He usually wore a feigned smile with the corners of his mouth turned slightly upward, as if he were fighting off a bout of heartburn. It seemed like he had to do an awful lot of extra work to be inauthentic. Luckily, I was relieved of his feigned smile on January 6 because it was covered by the required mask.

The sights and sounds of the insurrection were still playing over the laptop.

The Climate of Truth

"How are you feeling today, Mike?" Roger asked with his usual reverent tone.

"I feel like we're all going to need the 'morning after pill,'" I replied. "Because of today's giant rape and pillage." I began to saw away at the gnarly mess on his head.

"You're always so busy, Mike. So business must be booming for you?"

"Not exactly," I said, trying not to sound put off by the abrupt change in subject.

Roger raised his eyebrows, as if I was shining him on. "Isn't your calendar full? I mean, you tell me you are always booked out for several weeks?"

"I'm fully booked, sure. But every day is a logistical nightmare with COVID. You got in today because of a last-minute cancellation. Someone called because they are infected with COVID and they had to cancel. So I am constantly having to reconnoiter. I've lost a lot of clients too. Some are too afraid to come, some are too pissed about wearing a mask or having to answer safety questions. Some are mad about being rescheduled because they chose to take a trip and risked exposure – which means they have to wait the quarantine period for a haircut. And some cancel because they've been laid off and can't afford to come. Then there's always the medical emergency, the personal emergency, a death in the family, the alternator in the car blew up. Some cancel without notice. Some just decide not to show up for their appointments and don't bother to call. I won't hear from them again."

"Interesting…I figure that you are having to work at least 25% harder with all the extra safety steps you have to take," Roger said.

"That's life with COVID. Work harder and make less." I maneuvered quickly through the angles on his head. Wads of his bushy hair hit the floor in clumps.

"I'm sorry to hear that. It surprises me," Roger said.

"At least I'm working, so I can't complain. I'm paying the bills. A lot of people can't say that right now."

"True…I suppose you are aware of what happened today?" Roger asked blithely.

Patriots

"It's playing out right in front of you on the screen over there."

"I can't watch it. It's too much." Roger's eye drifted away from the screen on the laptop facing him.

"What do think about all this?" I asked. "What do you have to say about anyone or anything?"

"Well, I really wanted the conservatives to remain in control of the Senate, so there's that. I wanted to protect the corporate tax cuts."

Taken aback by his avoidance of the obvious, I said, "Well I, for one, am relieved that a Black pastor from Martin Luther King's pulpit and a young Jewish kid successfully flipped the Senate in the Georgia runoffs. And they did that in the heart of *KKK* land where both Jews and Blacks have been lynched. I'd call that karmic justice. It means that Biden might actually be able to lead the country without having both of his hands tied behind his back by the likes of 'Moscow Mitch' in the Senate. So, I'm fine with the way the election turned out, with Kamala Harris serving as the historic tie breaker with a fifty-fifty split."

Roger thought for a moment, furrowing his brow off and on. "But without a low corporate tax rate, American corporations can't remain competitive with the rest of the world. Without the tax breaks, the corporations will leave again, siphoned off by any other country that offers zero corporate tax incentives. We need the corporations to stay put because they employ the people."

"But do they pay a living wage?" I interjected.

Roger sidestepped my question. "All the gains we have made over the past four years under Trump could be completely upturned by the new administration. It makes it very difficult for me to determine where to invest. I try to watch the investment news, but that's all I can handle. I turn off the rest. I'm really worried about the markets and where to make a good yield."

Though completely flabbergasted by his choice of conversation, I held back. "I'm sorry Roger, but I'm just a guy who does hair all day. I don't have any investments and don't understand anything about the markets. I'm not the right guy to ask about how to diversify your stock portfolio," I said plainly. It appeared that my comment hit a nerve, because Roger turned his head away from me. "Please keep facing forward, sir."

The Climate of Truth

"Oh yes, my apologies," he said.

"No worries." I continued to snip his burly brown hair, careful not to further expose the balding donut at the crown of his head. "I would also venture that volatility in the markets may reflect that we are now, what, 28-trillion in debt? Due in part to the huge corporate tax cuts Trump put through that benefit himself and all the golden parachute CEO's who don't pay taxes at all…Because they are so much 'smarter' than all the rest of us. All the 'very stable genius' types and all…I'm sure us lowly hair guys are in a higher tax bracket than the mega-corporations, like *Amazon*, who pay zero. I'd say that's what got us in this deficit mess long before the new administration had anything to say about it. No sir, I just put my meager savings in the bank because I work far too hard for a living and can't afford to speculate. I would puke my guts out if the market crashed, as it should any day now to self-correct, and I lost all my savings. That's a lot of haircuts down the drain, Roger. I'm not well suited to that kind of risk. Besides, I would think today's chaos at the Capitol would cause far more market uncertainty, given our sudden turn toward being a banana republic. I'm sure <u>that's</u> going to jeopardize our triple-A credit rating. That's the price you pay for the tyranny. All you had to do was see the images all over the television to get the point."

"I didn't see any images. I don't watch television so I can't really comment," Roger deflected.

"Heck, let me fill you in on the images you've missed, Roger!" I said. "Where to start? Let's see, an angry White man carrying a giant Confederate flag through the marble rotunda of the Capitol. A mobster hanging from the Senate gallery like a chimpanzee – I think he turned out to be a marketing executive from Boise. And another sitting with his feet up on Nancy Pelosi's desk – I think he helped to steal her computer and her official mail, so now we have a breach of national security and state secrets. Another yahoo sat his rear in Pence's chair just minutes after Pence was evacuated. Then there's the terrified Congress people with thick plastic bags over their faces – those were supposed to be gas masks – but they looked like extras in a cheesy sci-fi film about bioweapons. A voice came over the Senate chamber's audio system – 'The protesters are in the building.' The Senate stopped the Electoral debate and vacated the chamber. That's when a woman who wore a Trump flag like a cape was shot in the in the hallway and her blood pooled all over the white marble floor. While those around her yelled 'Hang Mike Pence!' It's surprising that

Patriots

only one insurrectionist was shot and killed. I don't know why this one image in particular stands out in my mind, but this goofy guy jumped up onto the pedestal of the bronze statue of Gerald Ford and put a *'MAGA'* hat on the statue's head and put a *'Trump 2020'* flag in the statue's hands, and then took a selfie with his arm around Gerald Ford as if they were frat buddies in *'Animal House.'"*

"I don't watch the news because it inflames and sensationalizes everything," Roger said. "It's like the whole country has an autoimmune disorder, and it's attacking itself. You can never tell what's true anymore."

"The media doesn't have to embellish a mob riot. That's inflamed enough as it is."

"I disagree. The media is culpable. It foments dissention," Roger said.

I continued cutting and edging, moving the elastic straps of Roger's mask from around his ears with ease. My fingers flowed smoothly and were not impacted by the content of my words. "What is the media supposed to do, look away when three jumbotrons with Trump's angry face, big as a house, is ranting about election fraud? 'You will never take back our country with weakness!' he shouted. Oh, sure, it's a peaceful demonstration, right? And Donald Junior is frothing at the mouth, warning anybody in Congress who didn't vote to overturn the election, saying 'We're coming for you!' Trump looked out at that crowd and saw the Confederate flags with his Trump flags. He saw the *'Camp Auschwitz'* T-shirts marked with '6MWE' – an abbreviated version of 'six million wasn't enough,' because you know, it wasn't enough to murder six million Jews in the Holocaust. A lady Representative from Illinois spoke at Trump's *'March to Save America'* pulpit, and said, I kid you not, verbatim, that 'Hitler was right about one thing…whoever has the youth has the future!' Trump said <u>these</u> were his people! Not the rest of us -- <u>these</u> were his special people that he loved, the ones who were destroying the seat of Democracy. So, he tells them he's gonna march on down to the Capitol, along with the grandpa from Alabama who's got 11 napalm Molotov cocktails in his truck and some pipe bombs and a long-gun and some automatic pistols, so he could, you know, put a bullet in Nancy Pelosi's noggin on live TV. This grandpa said he was going to walk around DC, randomly yelling 'Allahu ak Bar,' just to screw with people, because Trump is America's savior. Because, you

The Climate of Truth

know, Democrats created COVID to steal the election. Convicted criminals who Trump pardoned, Roger Stone and Michael Flynn, told the crowd at the rally that they were fighting the greatest battle between good and evil, and that they were on the side of the good. Then some of the so-called 'patriots' were going to head right for Congressman Clyburn's office, a Black man, so they could string him up on the gallows that were erected on the Capitol steps with a big fat noose. And they'd lynch him right next to the traitor, Mike Pence, because the Veep didn't vote to overturn the election. And as the riot broke out, the Trump family is watching the goings-on from inside a staging tent. The Trump family were literally dancing for joy as the windows were being smashed at the Capitol, as the pepper spray went flying. They were dancing when people were being beaten and when people died. They danced to the once fabulous song, *"Gloria,"* a song that's used to fire up crowds at football and hockey games. That once fabulous song is now stained by the memory of a bloody coup, and I'm sure the estate of Laura Branigan is going to have something to say about that.

> *"Gloria, I think they got your number*
> *I think they got the alias*
> *that you've been living under*
> *But you really don't remember,*
> *was it something that they said?*
> *Are the voices in your head calling, Gloria?"*

I continued, "'*Gloria*' is about a woman who's messed up in the head, on the verge of insanity, all because she fell for a guy who used and abused her. Sound familiar, Roger? Do we know a powerful guy who lives in a big White House in Washington DC who would do something like that? We know they were playing '*Gloria*' because Donald Junior videoed the whole thing and put it on his *Instagram*. Rather than condemn all the violence, Trump told the mob, 'We love you. You're very special,' while the mob literally took a crap on the Capitol floor and trailed shitty brown footprints all over the building. That's our shining symbol of freedom. And guess who got to clean up the shit and the blood and the broken glass? Uniformed janitors, and, of course, they are all Black men. Trump knew exactly what he was doing. Where were all the troops to defend the Capitol? They knew a mob was coming. But the leaders of the free world didn't

Patriots

want the 'optics' of an armed guard against a crowd of angry White people. But last summer, a whole phalanx in full riot gear filled the steps of the Capitol when '*Black Lives Matter*' were protesting, and those people were attacked by our own forces. I spent all day scanning the video footage of the attack and saw maybe six Black people in all that catastrophe unfolding before our eyes. Two of the Black people I saw were Capitol Police officers trying to keep the mob from killing lawmakers. The other four Black people I saw were janitors in uniform mopping up the shit from angry White people inside the Capitol Building. So, Roger…the media is just supposed to look away and not record an attempt to overthrow the federal government because it could be seen as too sensational?"

"I didn't know any of that was going on," Roger said with a shrug of his shoulders and a glassy film coating his eyes.

"I learned about all this in a single afternoon. Because I choose to pay attention to historically significant events…It might be a good idea for everyone to observe the free press, as provided by the Constitution, when history of this magnitude is in the making." I edged the nape of his neck with T-clippers in silence and buzzed the stubble from his earlobes. "Is a little bit of styling paste OK, Roger?"

"Whatever you think is best, Mike. I love what you do to my hair."

I wasn't quite done making my point. "As usual, Trump sucked up all the oxygen today, while another 4000 people died of COVID. For all those who still insist that COVID is a fake conspiracy that Democrats are using to take over the whole world, they should be forced to go stack dead COVID bodies into the refrigerated trucks…But instead, today we witnessed our own countrymen attack our Democracy…the first time since the British tried to burn the Capitol down in the War of 1812!"

"I didn't mean to upset you," Roger said meekly.

I rubbed in some styling paste and combed Roger's hair. "You didn't upset me, Roger. What happened today has upset me. I would think you'd be upset about it too."

I wiped the cuttings from the nape of his neck and blow-dried his hair with my fingers. I did not use a brush. I could tell Roger was trying to figure out how to regroup without having to change his position.

The Climate of Truth

"Well, one thing is for sure," Roger said calmly. "We live in an unprecedented time with multiple crises hitting us all at once. Financial crises and unemployment, businesses going under, drought, fires, hurricanes, violent protests and vandalism caused by '*Antifa*,' election fraud, and a plague called COVID. Any of these was bad enough on their own."

It struck me how money was at the top of Roger's list of woes and COVID was at the bottom. And both were sandwiched in between debunked falsehoods.

Roger paid double for his haircut to leave a hefty tip. "I appreciate all that you do," he said, before he raced down the stairs to exit as quickly as possible.

"Thank you for your kindness," I called after him as I shut and locked the white, wrought-iron gate.

❖

Melissa arrived for her cut and color looking sullen.

She first came to me the year before with frizzy hair that was way too dark and too drab for her complexion. I corrected her color and tamed her messy hair to make her look what I called "devastatingly casual."

Melissa was another retired police officer from California. She told me that she used to be physically stronger when she was working the streets, and that she was still stronger than most other women. She described how she would practice the carotid hold with the elbow across the main artery in the neck until the target lost consciousness. That way, an officer could subdue and cuff a suspect safely before he or she regained consciousness in less than two minutes. Melissa described how she often came close to passing out during those practice sessions, but she always tapped out before she dropped. She also told me about the bruises she sustained while performing all the various handcuff maneuvers.

I began her hair color session by applying a medium brown formula with a brush to her grow-out, and a matching toner to rebalance the pre-colored hair with a liquid color in a squeeze bottle.

Patriots

 Melissa stared at the laptop screen on my desk as a reporter announced that someone in the mob had thrown a fire extinguisher at the head of a Capitol Police officer. I decided to reengage my playlist so we could have some background music rather than listening to all the hatemongering being livecast on the television. It was incredibly strange to see the images of insurrection while music played. The stereo turned to the catchy 1972 tune by the Scottish band *Stealers Wheel*, "Stuck in the Middle with You." Director Quentin Tarantino used that song in a disturbing scene in "*Reservoir Dogs;*" a sadistic man wielding a razor blade tortured a police officer he was holding hostage. While singing and dancing along with the catchy tune, the sadist sliced off the officer's ear, and then wiped the blood on the officer's shirt as he said, "Was it as good for you as it was for me?"

> *"Well, I don't know why I came here tonight.*
> *I've got the feeling that something ain't right.*
> *I'm so scared in case I fall off my chair,*
> *And I'm wondering how I'll get down the stairs.*
>
> *Clowns to the left of me!*
> *Jokers to the right!*
> *Here I am, stuck in the middle with you."*

 Some swore the song was about the ridiculous battle for power between the left and the right, the Democrats versus the Republicans.

 "Never repeat what I am about to say to anybody," Melissa said with an intense stare. "If I were a member of the Secret Service, I would put a bullet in Trump's brain."

 "You're not the first person to say something like that to me today," I said.

 "This kind of violence in the name of an ideology, it's the textbook definition of domestic terrorism. Trump's cronies won't admit it, but he committed high treason today. Case closed. The police were completely outnumbered, like lambs to the slaughter. Where was National Guard!"

 "Pelosi, Schumer and McConnel were on the phone from wherever they were hiding in the tunnels, begging for troops when Trump didn't make the call," I said.

The Climate of Truth

"So, Trump cans Mark Esper, the freaking Secretary of Defense, on *Twitter*," Melissa said. "Because he refused to let armed troops slaughter the *'Black Lives Matter'* protestors last summer. Then Trump replaces Esper with one of his whacko loyalists, Christopher Miller. And, surprise, no one could get Miller on the phone during the riot to get the National Guard deployed. It took hours, HOURS for Miller to approve a proper defense through the chain of command. The troops could have been there in minutes to put a stop to this shit show!"

"There had to be a lot of coordination to pull off this kind of thing." I said.

"They found pipe bombs at the headquarters of both the Republican and Democrat national committee offices. That had to be a decoy to draw law enforcement resources away from the Capitol. It's an absolute miracle that the police only shot one person so far. Because it could have been a massacre. A total bloodbath. It's a miracle that nobody in the House or the Senate was murdered by these freaks. They were being hunted," she said.

"Did you hear about the six women that had the foresight to pack up all the Electoral certificates in lock boxes, and hide them away? So the Electoral process could still be certified later. They did not take those certificates to the Parliamentarian's office, where the mob went looking for them. Those amazing ladies hid the Electoral certificates where they could not be found. Can you imagine what would have happened if that 'shaman' guy with the buffalo horns got ahold of the Electoral certificates?"

"Exactly!" Melissa shouted. "How did the rioters know where the Parliamentarian's office was in the first place! They went right to it, looking for those certificates!"

"They had help from the inside. Someone had to feed them information," I said.

"Who are the real winners in this attack?" Melissa asked. "Vladimir Putin, and Xi Jinping. That's who. America crashes and burns with international humiliation, and dictators fill the empty power void." She stared blankly at the video screen as I finished the last rows of color application near the nape of her neck. "The last time I was in DC, I couldn't believe how the main buildings were all right there on the street, completely accessible. I thought they should have been more blocked off to prevent this kind of thing from happening. It's all too open. It was bound to happen sooner or later."

Patriots

The vault of my memory was suddenly opened by Melissa's words. "The last time I was at the Capitol, it was for *'The March on Washington,'*" I began. "It was a peaceful march for Gay Rights in October 1987. The National Mall was completely filled with people, elbow to elbow, from the Capitol all the way to the Washington Monument. The newscasters said there were only 20,000 people in attendance. They tried to play it down. But the police reported there were 750,000 of us. People were waving their rainbow flags at the biggest Gay march ever seen. Nobody smashed windows or clobbered police officers with flagpoles. The Gay folk held hands and sang songs. The AIDS quilt was laid out in the middle of the mall for the first time. There were the embroidered names of Freddie Mercury and Rock Hudson, among thousands of others. I remembered how my uncle said they should flush Rock Hudson down the toilet – but wait! They couldn't do that because he had AIDS and if they flushed him, it would give AIDS to everybody else! The quilt panels were unfurled one at a time, row by row, each of the individual pieces representing the size of a grave…There was an organized protest on the steps of the Supreme Court, because the court voted to make it a crime to be Gay. The march itself was led by Cesar Chavez, Jesse Jackson and Whoopi Goldberg. People with full-blown AIDS were pushed along in their wheelchairs with their IV drips rolling right beside them. And there I was, just a kid in my twenties who worked at an AIDS charity, standing in the VIP section in front of that huge crowd, right up against the stage. Whoopi Goldberg trashed Reagan. Ooooooo, she hated him because he refused to acknowledge the AIDS pandemic, the Gay plague. Whoopi got bleeped on television because she called Reagan the 'fucking President.' Jesse Jackson was running for President at the time. He showed up to give a speech, driving a powder blue *Dodge K-Car*, wearing a matching powder blue three-piece suit and an afro. He was introduced by a tiny lesbian in khakis and a kelly-green polo shirt, who raised her fists with the cheer, 'muff-divers of America, unite!' Jesse Jackson didn't know what to do with that – he looked scared to death. But the crowd roared in a wave of approval and Jesse started laughing. I stood in the front row of history in the making and didn't know how I managed to do that. But nothing that day got my attention more than one overlooked thing. There are metal grates inlaid in the sidewalk in front of the Capitol Building, just behind where we were standing. Steam came out of those grates. With the chill of fall in the air, a homeless man set up a cardboard box to sleep in right over one of those steam grates. He

The Climate of Truth

was living like that, right on the Capitol steps -- mere feet from Congress, celebrities, candidates, and 750,000 people marching for civil rights. No one else noticed that homeless man's suffering. But I did."

❖

The sun had set long before on January 6. Rain was falling at a sharp slant due to the heavy wind. It seemed fitting that a violent day would end with a winter rainstorm.

Daphne was the last client that terrible day. I brought her up to the patio door overhang to allow her to wait under cover, away from the rain. She wore a fur-trimmed parka with the hood drawn closely about her face. The hood seemed more like a place to hide than a way to shield herself from the weather. Above her mask-line, the upper bridge of her nose was bright red from the chill in the air. She sniffled a little. She might have been crying in her car.

I knew Daphne practiced meditation. She attended a Buddhist temple somewhere across the Interstate Bridge. I didn't know if she was a full-fledged Buddhist, but it would be a safe bet that she was because of her outlook on life. However, her usual serene vibe was absent that day.

The prior fall, she attended a symposium at the Buddhist temple about White privilege. As a young, beautiful, gentle, White woman, she professed to having escaped the agony of discrimination by default. She could not personally grasp the concept of being on the receiving end of hatred. The thought of it frightened her. She sat in that symposium over the course of two months in order to educate herself on the blight of racism. She shared her thoughts on her quest toward enlightenment over several haircuts, and I was touched by the depth of her sincerity.

The sound of the insurrection was still blaring over the stereo. I asked Daphne all the COVID safety questions as she stood outside the patio door. She answered with a soft voice that I could barely hear. At her prior appointment six weeks before, she admitted that she lost her conscious awareness and spent time in a car with a few friends without wearing a mask. It upset her that she didn't contemplate the risk until she'd been in the car with them for half an hour. She

Patriots

explained that stress was making her brain-dead, and she apologized for being careless. She swore she would never do it again.

"I've had the news on all day, Daphne. Is it OK to keep listening to it?" I asked gently while taking her temperature.

Daphne stomped her foot lightly to signal polite frustration. "I guess we can listen to it if you really have to." The rest of her face turned as red as her nose.

"Are you OK, honey bear?"

"No…I know there's a lot happening right now…But I don't think my constitution can handle listening to the news." Her voice trembled. Her heavy breath fogged up her glasses.

"I'll turn it off and put on some music, no problem. Give me a sec here." I disconnected the livestream news and plugged in my *Pandora* playlist. Don McLean's iconic ballad filled the room with a very familiar refrain. I listened as I sprayed virucide to sanitize the various stations in the shop while Daphne waited for me just outside the patio door.

*"But February made me shiver
With every paper I'd deliver
Bad news on the doorstep
I couldn't take one more step*

*I can't remember if I cried
 When I read about his widowed bride
Something touched me deep inside
The day the music died…*

*So, bye-bye, Miss American Pie
Drove my Chevy to the levee, but the levee was dry
And them good ol' boys were drinkin' whiskey and rye
Singin' 'This'll be the day that I die
This'll be the day that I die'"*

I couldn't help but shudder when I realized that Don McLean sounded like he was bidding farewell to our Democracy, the day the music died at the Capitol on January 6. *"Bye-bye Miss American Pie"*

The Climate of Truth

took on a whole new meaning. By the look on her face, Daphne seemed to come to the same conclusion.

"Is the music better than the news?" I hollered out to Daphne as I sanitized.

"Yes. Thank you, Mike," she answered plaintively.

I finished wiping everything down. "Come on in, lady friend."

She stepped into the shop sedately.

"You can go ahead and put your purse on the left side of my desk here, Daphne. Please hang up your coat by the front door. And then head into the restroom to wash your hands with soap and water," I said.

Daphne performed all the tasks silently, except for her tiny sniffles. I grabbed some clean towels from the cabinet. She met me at the shampoo station and sat down. I handed her a towel, and without further instruction, she knew to cover her face with it. She made sure to keep the upper corners of the towel out of her hairline so I could scrub freely. She did not speak while I washed her hair.

"Please let go of the towel, Daphne," I said as I completed her final rinse.

Her hands moved away, but her fingers were tensed. I took the towel from her face and dried her hair with it, squeezing the excess water into the shampoo bowl.

"Lift your feet, please," I said as I lowered the footrest.

Daphne sat up. I placed my hand on her shoulder to keep her from moving. "You are safe here. Just relax and get your haircut. You don't have to think about anything else."

Irma walked over and looked up at Daphne. She then nudged Daphne's leg with her forehead, so Daphne patted Irma sweetly.

"I'll be OK," she said as she rose to walk to the styling chair. "Irma looks a little tired tonight."

"Today's news has wiped her out, I'm afraid. Irma's a sensitive girl," I said.

"I know the feeling," Daphne said.

Irma followed and placed herself at the foot of the styling chair so she could make eye contact with Daphne to comfort her.

Patriots

I put a cutting cape around Daphne's neck while Don McLean continued to strum his guitar. He sang about God, the *Bible*, Rock and Roll, Satan and Hell while Daphne stared at herself in the mirror.

"My ears don't have the crevice at the top to hold the elastic in place," she said. "Remember, last time, the loops kept flying off?"

"I've heard of sloping shoulders, but sloping ear loops?"

"I've got a new mask this time," she said. "Hopefully it will stay on better for you. It has these little loop tightener thingies on the side here. It feels more snug at least."

"I can work around it. Thank you," I said.

"You're welcome," she said, avoiding eye contact.

"What do you want for your haircut today?"

"Just a light trim, please. I want to grow it a little longer. Do the layers. Texture the bangs. I really love my hair now. It's so easy to handle."

"That's great, honey. Do you want it straight or curly today?"

"Oh…just curly today. I'm just going home and going to bed," she said wearily.

"Ok, got it." I began to section her hair with clips. "We can talk if you like, or if you want to just sit and be quiet and listen to the music, we can do that too. Whatever you want is fine with me."

Daphne sat with her eyes closed for a moment, and then popped them open quickly. "Oh my gosh!" she exclaimed. "I haven't seen you since before Thanksgiving!"

"It seems like the holidays were light years ago already, doesn't it?"

"For Christmas, all we did was eat," she said. "We didn't go anywhere or do anything."

"Me either," I said.

"I was all worried about our traditional Christmas breakfast, French toast dipped in ice cream."

"What?" I said.

"Yes! It's so fun! It has all the flavors already in the ice cream. And then we had hash browned potatoes and ham," she said.

The Climate of Truth

"I love fresh hash browns dipped in blue cheese dressing! A little salt and pepper."

"It was too much to have French toast and potatoes and ham, and then have prime rib for dinner too," she said. "It was just the two of us, me and my husband. So, he came up with the idea, 'Why don't we just have breakfast for dinner!'…What a superb idea that was!"

"You're so cute," I said.

"So, I took a bubble bath, and I stayed in my pajamas all day. I didn't have to worry about all that extra cooking, so it took the pressure off. Except the pressure went back on because there were so many one-on-one *Zoom* calls all day. It was exhausting," she said.

"I was glad to unplug. I think I may have had two or three phone calls over Christmas weekend, but nothing on video. I don't even know how to do video calls."

"It normally doesn't happen that I get so many calls," she said. "So, I finally got to making breakfast for dinner. And my wonderful husband took my photo and said that I looked 'adorable' in my pajamas…I prefer to think about positive things." Light began to return to her eyes.

"Positive is really all we've got to hold onto. Positive is change for the better," I said to encourage her. "Positive is being kind to one another."

"Like for Christmas, the neighbors got together, and we all did this 'traveling elf.'"

"Is that like the traveling gnome?" I asked.

"Yeah. The elf was only $14.99 at *Tuesday Morning*. You know, they are going out of business? So sad. Because of COVID."

"I heard."

"The elf is three feet tall, and every few days, he would travel to someone's house in the neighborhood. And all the neighbors would venture out to try and find him," she said.

I could tell Daphne was smiling under her mask. And she was playfully swinging her feet back and forth in the chair.

"The neighbor kids were out doing their elf hunting too," she continued. "I'll show you a photo. I have it here on my phone." She

Patriots

leaned forward to retrieve her phone from her purse and sat back in the chair again.

I had to adjust the cutting cape from her movement.

"Sorry Mike. I'm such a pain today."

"It's all good. No biggie," I said.

"Here, here, here, see!" Daphne scrolled quickly through photos at a pace that caused vertigo.

"I can't see. Can you make it bigger?"

"Can you find the elf in the picture?" she asked, excited.

I peered over her shoulder. "Oh…how fun!...Was the elf at your house, there?"

"Not at my house, no," she said, staring at the photo in her lap.

"That's one festive elf. Sounds like a new tradition in your neighborhood," I said.

"It was a wonderful thing to do…and positive…and it brought the neighbors together." She sat quiet for a moment, then looked up at me in the mirror. "We've been looking out for each other in our neighborhood."

"Community watch is a good thing," I said.

"At 3:00am, a burgundy car drove through. They took vice grips to our mailboxes. To steal our mail. Looking for the COVID stimulus money, I guess. But they didn't get my mail because I had just gotten it that afternoon."

"It's happening all over town," I said. "I hear about it all the time. You got lucky."

"We got a kit from the locksmith to replace the lock with a smoother one that can't be gripped," she said. "The mailman came by. The Post Office was supposed to fix all the locks. But with the Post Office being all messed up these days…"

"Thank you for removing 711 mail-sorting machines, Mr. DeJoy, in your sordid attempt to stop the vote by mail. And thank you for sabotaging said machines, some of which were brand new, like the one in Tacoma, so that the darned things can't be plugged back in. And thank you for costing the taxpayers gazillions of dollars by

The Climate of Truth

pulling this stunt, and now we don't get our bills on time, or our meds on time from the US Post Office. And we can't get our vandalized mailboxes fixed either when cretins rip us off!... Does that about sum it up, Daphne?"

"I'd say so," she replied. "The mailman told us we could go get our own lock and fix it ourselves. So, we did that. And then we called the neighbor ladies to see if they wanted us to change their locks too, and they said no, because another neighbor was already doing it for them."

"Democracy at work! The miracle of efficiency and cooperation. Congress should take note!" I said enthusiastically.

"So now when the mailman comes, we text everybody in the neighborhood, and we all go out and grab the mail right away, and we say hello. We have to wear a mask, of course."

"Of course," I said.

"The security cameras caught the burgundy car. It's two people, a man and a woman, stealing the mail. No license plate on the front...So we know what they look like, but we haven't caught them yet. They've been hitting mailboxes all over town...But at least it brings all the neighbors together to look out for each other," she said.

After finishing the trim and texturizing her bangs and side fringe, I scrunch-dried her chestnut brown waves with a diffuser. I used a little bit of curl mist and soft gel for hold.

"My bangs look great, Mike! Thank you. No hairspray please."

"Do you feel better?" I looked her in the eyes, but she quickly cast her glance aside.

"Yes, I feel much better. I always feel better with such a great haircut," she said.

I escorted Daphne back to her car through the white, wrought iron gate. She turned to me in the dark and said, "Thank you for not judging me tonight. It means a lot to me."

"All we've got is each other," I said.

She gently waved goodbye and drove off.

❖

Patriots

I returned to close down the shop for the night. I drew the blinds and sat at the front desk with my head in my hands. I looked back at names of all the clients on my book that ill-fated day, and I understood that each of us were grieving for our country in a different way.

My way of grieving required me to observe, contemplate, and memorize. I turned the news back on and held my breath. The British Prime Minister called the insurrection "disgraceful." A third pipe bomb had been discovered at the Capitol Building. The first lady's chief of staff resigned because of the insurrection, and a few cabinet members would follow suit. A bespectacled Black man said that when the Black lady mayor of Atlanta told people to quit rioting and destroying the city during the "*Black Lives Matter*" protests the prior summer, they listened to her. They obeyed her. That was leadership. Where was leadership from the White House during the insurrection?

Because some people did not have the will or the strength to bear witness to the historically significant events that day, it seemed to me that systemic change would be painfully slow. Throughout my life, people told me change only happened in "baby steps." This time, I had the feeling that our country needed the leaps and bounds of Jesse Owens when he took the gold medal for the long jump at the Summer Olympics in Nazi Germany in 1936. Jesse Owens, the tenth child of a sharecropper from Alabama, and the grandson of a slave, singlehandedly showed the world that Hitler's idea of a superior Aryan "master race" was a myth.

Identity

The attack on the US Capitol on January 6, 2021, was ultimately defeated in the dark of a winter's night after hours of brutal violence and destruction. The Department of Defense declared the Senate and House chambers and all leadership offices were cleared of rioters by 7:15pm after more than a four-hour delay in large scale military deployment. The National Guard finally used flash-bang grenades, tear gas and tactical gear to disperse the mob from the surrounding Capitol grounds. What began as a protest behind the White House devolved into a vicious mob with an estimated 30,000 people who amassed at the Capitol. Over the next few days, 6,200 troops were deployed to restore order and protect the building and its occupants, but the vast majority of the troops arrived well after the attack was subdued. The deployment surged to 26,000 troops at its peak, and they remained in position at the Capitol for months at the cost of $521 million for protective services alone.

Classified as an act of domestic terrorism, the insurrection triggered what the Department of Justice called the largest criminal investigation in American history. Of the 738 rioters who were eventually charged with federal crimes (at the time of this writing), none of them were arrested on the day of the attack. A national manhunt ensued, following the trail of digital evidence from cellphones, media coverage, social media posts, and video from police body cameras and security cameras. The day after the insurrection,

Identity

the FBI requested help from the public to identify people who took part in the violence. On *Twitter*, the FBI wrote: *"If you have witnessed unlawful violent actions, we urge you to submit any information, photos, or videos that could be relevant to fbi.gov/USCapitol."* The manhunt revealed some of the attackers included Republican Party officials, former State Legislators and political donors, White supremacists and far-right militants, Evangelicals, federal agents, and personnel from police, fire and military units among others.

During the attack, several members of Congress appealed directly to Trump to send troops to defend the halls of Congress.

Kevin McCarthy, the House Minority Leader, spoke to Trump directly over the phone: "You need to get on TV right now, you need to get on *Twitter*, you need to call these people off!"

"They're not my people," Trump said dismissively. He falsely insisted the mob of insurrectionists were all affiliated with left-wing *"Antifa"* radicals.

McCarthy countered, "They just came through my windows and my staff is running for cover. Yeah, they're your people. Call them off!"

Trump said, "Well, Kevin, I guess these people are more upset about the election than you are."

Trump's refusal to defend the US Capitol was a violation of his oath of office, an impeachable offense. But 43 Senate Republicans who witnessed the mob violence firsthand (including McCarthy) voted to acquit Trump's second impeachment – the only American President to be impeached twice. The second time, Trump was charged with inciting the insurrection. Constitutional scholars described Trump's actions as the most dangerous crime ever committed by a President against the US.

Democrat US Representative Ayanna Pressley was the first woman of color to be elected from Massachusetts. Her Congressional office suite was equipped with a system of panic buttons. As the rioters breached the Capitol Building, it was discovered that all of the Congresswoman's panic buttons had been secretly yanked out, an indication that someone within the Capitol complex was complicit with the attack and had targeted Ms. Pressley personally. Two other Democrat Representatives also reported non-functioning panic buttons in their offices.

The Climate of Truth

Capitol Police advised Ms. Pressley to evacuate with her husband (who was standing guard with her during the riot) to a "safe room" where other members of Congress had been sequestered. The "safe room" was a crowded, windowless committee hearing room where Ms. Pressley observed a large group of Republicans who repeatedly declined to wear masks that were offered to them. Ms. Pressley refused to enter the room under those risky conditions. She was told she would either have to be locked in the "safe room" with everyone else, or she would be left to defend herself on her own out in the open.

"We're not going to survive a terrorist attack to be exposed to a deadly virus," the Congresswoman replied. "I will take my chances out here," she said, having to choose between being exposed to COVID and the threat of mob violence. The Congresswoman, her husband, and her staff used furniture and water jugs to barricade themselves in her office suite.

Several of Ms. Pressley's colleagues contracted COVID while locked in the "safe room." Her husband also contracted COVID that day. The Congresswoman, who suffered from alopecia (an autoimmune disease) tested negative for COVID but went directly into quarantine anyway. A symptom of her autoimmune disease, the last bit of her hair fell out on the eve of Trump's impeachment, which left her completely bald.

The FBI initiated an investigation into the missing panic buttons, including reports that Republicans in Congress were seen conducting tours of the Capitol complex with suspected insurrectionists prior to the attack. Such tours were highly irregular, given the building was in lockdown under COVID safety protocols. A US State Department appointee with a top-secret security clearance (also a former Trump campaign staffer) was charged with numerous felonies, including storming the Capitol and assaulting an officer with a riot shield. Regardless, Republican Senators obstructed justice and voted against forming an independent commission to investigate the attack against the Capitol.

At 2:24pm during the insurrection, Trump tweeted: *"Mike Pence didn't have the courage to do what should have been done to protect our Country and our Constitution, giving States a chance to certify a **corrected** set of facts, not the fraudulent or inaccurate ones which they were asked to previously certify. USA demands the truth!"* Trump was incensed that Vice President Pence refused to overturn the Electoral certification and toss out millions of legally cast ballots. In response, the violent mob of Trump supporters erected a gallows with a noose on the Capitol steps to "Hang Mike Pence!"

❖

The State Department had already issued warnings that it was not safe for US citizens to travel to Russia because of escalating political tensions at the end of 2020. US citizens, government and military personnel had been arbitrarily detained by Russian officials. Some detainees faced harassment or extortion. The cold war had returned.

On August 20, 2020, Russian opposition leader Alexei Navalny barely survived an assassination attempt with a lethal nerve agent sprayed inside the inner seams of his boxer shorts in his suitcase. The Kremlin vehemently denied responsibility for the poisoning. When questioned about Navalny, Putin himself said, "We don't have this kind of habit, of assassinating anybody." Putin's answer implied it was pure coincidence that several of his political opponents had been assassinated in recent years. However, Navalny later recorded a phone call with an FSB operative who freely admitted the nerve agent was used against Navalny in a Kremlin-sanctioned mission. Navalny unknowingly wore the poisoned boxers onto an airplane where he collapsed mid-flight. Had the plane continued on to Moscow as planned, he would have died. He only survived because the pilot made an emergency landing and Navalny was rushed to the closest hospital. Because of international pressure, Navalny was then transferred to a hospital in Berlin where he was treated for more than a month, followed by six months of recuperation. There was immediate international condemnation of Putin when lab results determined the nerve agent used against Navalny to be from the Russian arsenal of biochemical weapons.

Oddly, Trump was reluctant to condemn Russia's role in the assassination attempt. When asked about it by a reporter, Trump said "It is interesting that everybody is always mentioning Russia. And I don't mind you mentioning Russia, but I think probably China at this point is a nation that you should be talking about much more so than Russia, because the things that China is doing are far worse, if you take a look at what's happening with the world." Trump deflected further by touting his decision to give anti-tank weapons to Ukraine

The Climate of Truth

to help them resist their Putin-backed enemies from invading their country.

Navalny chose to return to Russia after his recuperation to continue his opposition campaign against President Putin. Ahead of takeoff from Berlin on February 2, 2021, Navalny said he did not expect to be arrested when he landed in Russia. However, his flight was diverted in midair for "technical reasons," and he was immediately taken into custody by the KGB when he landed in Moscow, as was his wife, his lawyer, his spokesperson, and several of his aides.

It was an act of air piracy that would be repeated six months later when the authoritarian President of Belarus, Alexander Lukashenko, personally ordered an international European flight that flew through Belarussian airspace to be diverted by his own fighter jets. This was done to intercept a dissident journalist who was aboard the plane, one who promoted the opposition during the highly contested Belarussian election. The journalist had previously accused Lukashenko of election fraud. Six crew and 126 passengers were detained from the diverted flight; they were searched and questioned in an open act of state-sponsored hijacking. The journalist and his girlfriend were both arrested. The journalist was falsely charged with inciting public disorder, social hatred, and terrorism, which was known to have brought the death penalty. Lukashenko simply followed Putin's example on how to crush his detractors by hijacking an airplane.

Hundreds of Belarusians were arrested in Lukashenko's "purge" of disloyal organizations. Those arrested included lawyers, journalists, and opposition politicians among others. Dozens of nongovernmental organizations were shuttered, including those that offered medical and hospice care. Maria Kalesnikava, the main opposition leader to Lukashenko's authoritarian rule, was sentenced to 11 years in prison. She led an uprising in which tens of thousands of Belarusians joined the largest opposition protest in the country's modern history. She was charged with conspiracy to seize power and threatening national security by organizing rebellion on social media.

Crowds gathered in cities throughout Russia to protest Navalny's arrest, including Moscow and St. Petersburg where thousands of protesters were detained and beaten. The Kremlin's shady excuse for Navalny's arrest was condemned by the European Council, various member states of the European Union, the United Nations and the

Identity

US, among others. The Russian government asserted that Navalny willfully violated the conditions of his parole when he left Russia, even though he was unconscious and near death when he was flown to Berlin for life-saving medical treatment following his attempted assassination. Navalny was originally imprisoned in 2014 under trumped up charges of embezzlement; he was falsely accused of stealing monies from the political network he built to oppose Putin's Presidency.

Vast internet and cellphone outages were reported throughout Russia during the Navalny protests, presumably initiated by the Russian government in an attempt to curtail further mobilization of the crowds. Putin told his closest allies that he feared being dragged through the streets and assassinated by the protesters, as happened to the tyrant of Libya, Muammar Qaddafi.

❖

I'd known Yelena for close to 20 years. She was a Russian immigrant and a CPA by trade. She had a college-age daughter. She was first married to an American who abused her physically, mentally and emotionally. Their divorce was brutal. Yelena and her daughter ran for their lives with only the clothes on their backs.

Even years after the divorce, Yelena never got over being skittish. It took all her inner strength to sit quietly in the styling chair, as if she expected her ex-husband to jump out at her from my linen closet. To help control her claustrophobic anxiety that was magnified by having to wear a COVID mask, she read Louie L'Amour novels that had been translated into Russian while I worked on her hair. Her latest selection was a story about a captured US Air Force pilot who was shot down by the Soviets over the ocean between Russia and Alaska.

Yelena eventually found a mild-mannered Russian boyfriend who chauffeured her everywhere, including to her hair appointments. He dutifully waited out in the driveway for a few hours while I highlighted Yelena's hair because COVID protocols did not allow for visitors to wait inside the shop. Yelena was visibly more relaxed with the new man in her life, but she still tended to be wary. Her voice was very measured and soft, and she always spoke in generalities with a noticeably thick Russian accent. She rarely gave any specific details about her own life or her feelings.

The Climate of Truth

Yelena was exceptionally thin. Her legs seemed to attach directly to her spinal column because her derriere was missing. I never knew her to wear a skirt or dress, only crisp skinny-jeans or tight-fitting slacks that were held up by the protrusion of her hip bones. She told me once that American brand jeans were a hot commodity in Russia – a new pair of *Levi's* supposedly meant you were an "A-lister." She preferred to wear polished loafers that never looked worn. Her skin always had a polished look too, appearing like she was freshly bathed in sheep's milk. Yelena sat rigidly with perfect posture in the styling chair, as if she'd spent her entire life training for the Bolshoi Ballet, waiting to be beaten across the thighs with a willow switch by a belligerent Communist choreographer.

"You're such a good hair color girl," I said, complimenting Yelena's ability to sit as still as a statue in whatever position I placed her head. She never asked me to cut her hair, only to color it. Her only answer was a slight nod that made her miniature gold-coin earrings jiggle from her earlobes. I could hear an imaginary section of ethereal violins accompany every gesture made by her long and delicate fingers as she turned the pages of her book.

Her hair was short and layered with bangs that swept sideways over her pale blue eyes. The nape of her neck was tapered to a point, and fringed tendrils escaped her mask in front of each ear. The pressures of her unsettled life had prematurely turned her sable brown hair to a sallow silver that made her look ill. The silver crop of follicles was unusually concentrated in the crown of her head instead of her temples and forward fringe. The awkward concentration of silver on top made the shape of her head appear distorted, which caused her to feel self-conscious. Over the years, I recalibrated her hair color formula to adjust for the problem as the silver became increasingly pronounced.

"Oh Mike!" she said. "I'm getting compliments on my hair color again! Thank you! Thank you!" She was grateful for the time-bending illusion that my service offered her. "Once again, you have saved my life!"

I usually worked on Yelena without speaking. She wasn't one for in-depth conversation. I filled the time by mentally singing along to the music on the stereo. Without the constant comfort of music, I would not have been able to function at my job. The stereo played Buffalo Springfield's *"For What It's Worth,"* a song inspired by the 1968 Sunset Strip curfew riots in Los Angeles where young music

Identity

fans (some who later became celebrities) clashed with police. Los Angeles County forced clubs and music venues to close at 10:00pm to curb noise and traffic congestion caused by alleged hordes of "loitering" young people.

"What a field day for the heat
A thousand people in the street
Singing songs and they carry signs
Mostly say, 'Hooray for out side'

It's time we stop
Hey, what's that sound?
Everybody look, what's going down?"

That particular day, however, Yelena looked up at me suddenly and pointedly proclaimed, "Putin's crazy, don't you agree?"

Having never discussed politics with her before, I wasn't sure how to engage her thoughts. "You know what they say about absolute power?" I said, deciding to leave it open-ended.

"I am so upset, Mike. I want so badly to see my parents in St. Petersburg. With COVID and everything, I haven't seen them in more than two years," she said, gently closing the cover of her book over her fingers that were still inside the pages. "I always used to take my vacations there."

"The world is so complicated these days," I said. "Don't you have dual citizenship?"

"Yes, I do," she replied, looking a bit frantic. "They are just supposed to stamp my passport and let me through, like I have done for years. But my parents tell me not to come right now, especially not with my daughter. Because we might be arrested at the airport."

"Why would they arrest you? You're not a criminal," I said, adding a streak of medium blonde with added boosters to cover grey.

"Because Putin has the evil eyes of Rasputin." She briefly glanced at her masked face in the mirror, then quickly looked away. "It's all very sinister…Russia is full of nothing but grief and misery. It does not understand how to evolve without deprivation and conflict." With her eyes downcast in shadow as she spoke, Yelena embodied

The Climate of Truth

the female Chekhovian protagonists who quietly wept into their sleeves but never cursed or slammed doors.

"Cruelty and oppression seem to be very popular these days," I said. "Look at China, North Korea, the Philippines, Brazil, just to name a few. Throw in the Taliban, Iran and Somalia, and we've got a full house of despots."

"Don't forget Trump," Yelena said, tersely. "And his sweet poison of lies."

Her comment startled me a little because it was unusually direct.

"Remember when Trump went to that weird summit with North Korea?" I asked.

"Only because he wanted to be nominated for the *Nobel Peace Prize*," she said. "Because he wanted to make the cover of '*Time Magazine*.'"

"Yes, there's that. But Trump was SUPER excited to see all those secret service guys running along each side of Kim Jung Un's limousine. Trump wanted his own Secret Service agents to do that for him too! He loves the trappings of a dictator."

There was a heavy silence.

"I don't know if I will ever be able to see my parents again," Yelena said, barely able to keep from bursting into tears.

"Can your folks come over here?" I asked.

"The Kremlin will never let them out, and the White House here will not let them in. So we are stuck."

"In purgatory," I said.

"All my parents can do is sit in their flat because COVID is everywhere over there, but no one talks about it. Millions of people in Moscow and St. Petersburg have COVID, at least half the population in the cities. But the Kremlin did not report it to anyone."

"Why would they withhold vital information in a global crisis?" I asked.

"Putin uses deception to make it look like the Russians are tougher than everyone else."

"Trump does that too," I said. "He must have oligarchs as mentors."

Identity

"Russia was the first in the world to create a COVID vaccine," Yelena said. "But the people are so afraid to get inoculated because they think the government put poison in the vaccine, the same way they poisoned Navalny. The vaccine came out at the same time they tried to assassinate him. It's more than stupid…The Kremlin is far more interested in selling the *Sputnik* vaccine to impress Europe and to be seen like a main player, but Europe doesn't trust Putin either…My parents are old and frail. They are afraid because the government shut down the internet, and they listen to your phone calls, and even read your mail. Anything I say to my parents could cause trouble. And now people are marching in the streets for Navalny."

"Maybe Navalny will change the world like George Floyd," I said.

"This is very dangerous. The people go to march for Navalny knowing they can be arrested just for showing up, and they could disappear into some prison colony to be psychologically tortured. But they go anyway because they say they have to fight against Putin… So, if I try to go to St. Petersburg now, my parents tell me I could disappear too. 'Are you for the motherland, or are you a stowaway rat?' They would ask me because I traveled from America. And if I explain that I am I just visiting my elderly parents, the KGB could say, 'Where is your honor? Why do you choose America over the motherland? Where is your duty to the country where you were born?…Where do your parents live?'…I never thought my parents would die without me."

Not knowing what to say, I replied, "How horrible for you." I placed my hand reassuringly on her shoulder.

"Thank you, Mike," she said, stiffening her face against the possibility of tears. She inhaled shallowly, and reopened her book, but stared blankly at the page where she left off. "A colleague of mine also has dual citizenship," she said with a far-off look in her eye. She used the word "colleague" to remain purposefully vague, as if to protect herself from potential interrogation.

"My colleague is from Germany," Yelena continued. "She brought her mother to the US from Germany to look after her…But the day after Christmas, my colleague's mother died of COVID. It was a slow and agonizing death. Her organs shut down, one by one…

The Climate of Truth

It was the mother's dying wish for her body to be returned to Germany to be buried with her parents."

"Don't tell me she tried to transport her mother's body during the holiday rush," I said.

"She did," Yelena said, looking morose.

"In the middle of the Christmas surge?"

"Americans are banned from travel to Europe because the cases are so high here," Yelena said.

"Yes, there were over 300,000 cases per day at the beginning of January."

"Because my colleague has dual citizenship with Germany, she was able to get around the travel ban. But there was so much paperwork involved, and with every one of countless forms, she had to provide a negative COVID test. She was finally able to arrange to travel with twelve members of her family...and the body," Yelena said.

"Twelve! That's a huge number. What if they all got sick?" I asked. "COVID could have wiped out her whole family."

"My colleague said, 'What am I supposed to do? It's my mother's dying wish! I'm the executor.'"

"Isn't guilt grand!" I said. "Nothing like feeling trapped by obligation...If it were me, I wouldn't do it. I would wait until it was safe. The mother's dead, she wouldn't know. It has to be about the living. Who endangers their entire family for the sake of a funeral?"

"There were very few options available for travel," Yelena continued. "But somehow my colleague was able to get everyone in her family tested and booked on a flight. But when they arrived at the airport in Frankfurt, the family was detained for more than six hours while an airport clerk reviewed all the documents. My colleague was granted permission in advance by the German government to bring the body for burial. But the airport clerk yelled at her so that everyone in the terminal could hear -- 'The corpse is infected!' During those six hours, the airport clerk was busy making arrangements to have the body sent back to the US. The clerk would allow the family to stay in Germany, but only without the body...The body, the body, the body."

Identity

"Sort of defeated the whole purpose of the trip, wouldn't you say?"

"Everyone in the family tested negative for COVID several times, and they waited for the quarantine after the mother's death. The body was zipped in a bag that was locked in a sealed coffin. The family couldn't understand why they were being detained…After six hours of all this arguing and yelling, an airport supervisor was brought in. All of a sudden, the story changed, and the supervisor approved the body to be taken to the church."

"Finally, someone rational."

"Not so much," Yelena said. "The family was not allowed to stay overnight in a hotel as planned. All twelve travelers had to quickly locate relatives where they could be temporarily housed, and police checked to make sure no one left those houses. The funeral was scheduled the following morning at 5:00am."

"Who holds a funeral at the crack of dawn?" I asked.

"It wasn't by choice," Yelena said. "The government ordered it. To reduce exposure, I suppose. They wanted to get the body into the ground as quickly as possible."

"That's cold."

"During the funeral, only one person at a time was permitted to approach the closed coffin that was double wrapped in thick plastic," Yelena said. "Police were stationed inside the church to make sure no one hugged or shook hands. The service was very short. There was no time to grieve. Everything was done in such a big hurry. Then the coffin was yanked right out of the church and taken straight to the gravesite. The family was not allowed to go. They were immediately whisked back to the airport and forced to take the first available flight back to the US…On the way to the airport, my colleague asked the driver if she could stop at a pharmacy to purchase aspirin for her severe headache. She was sleep-deprived and traumatized, and her head was splitting. When she got to the pharmacy, there wasn't a single aspirin anywhere in sight. There was absolutely no medication of any kind left on the shelves. It was as if Germany was back in wartime with people hoarding all the medications."

"Aspirin and toilet paper," I said. "Who knew?"

The Climate of Truth

"My colleague refused bereavement leave when she got home. She went straight back to work. The busy tax season was underway. She told me she needed at least eight hours a day where she could think of something other than that horrible airport clerk and the coffin wrapped in plastic…We all work from home right now, so she sat in front of her computer doing *Zoom* calls with her clients…She said making those *Zoom* calls and preparing tax returns saved her life because it kept her mind busy…I would have cremated the body here in the US and waited to transport the ashes back to Germany when COVID was over."

"I can't believe twelve people in one family agreed to go through all that torment," I said.

"I love my parents with all my heart," Yelena said while looking at the floor. "But if they were to die today, the Communists would have to bury them."

Navalny held a 24-day hunger strike to draw the world's attention to his politically motivated imprisonment. Weighing as much as he did in the 7th grade, he was emaciated when he appeared in court as he attempted to appeal his conviction. In a courtroom speech conducted by video, Navalny accused the government of turning "Russians into slaves." He declared, "I want to say, my dear judge, that your king [Putin] is naked, and it's not just one boy yelling about it, millions of people are yelling about it. Twenty years of his fruitless rule have led to this result: a crown falling from his ears, lies on television, we've wasted trillions of rubles, and our country continues to slide into poverty." Unsurprisingly, Navalny lost his appeal and he remained in prison. Navalny's nationwide network of offices was shuttered by the government. His Anti-Corruption Foundation that investigated the government was labeled an extremist organization, and all the Foundation's staff and supporters were threatened with imprisonment.

Prior to his first summit meeting with Putin in June of 2021, President Biden warned that should Navalny die in prison, it would hurt Russia's relationships with the rest of the world. In a preemptive news conference, Biden said, "Navalny's death would be another indication that Russia has little or no intention of abiding by basic fundamental human rights." Biden called for Navalny's unconditional release from prison. Putin countered, saying that he could not guarantee Navalny would survive his two-year prison term, and that Navalny's network of dissidents was "dangerous" to

Identity

Russia. Putin declared that arresting Navalny and his protesters was no different than the US arresting those in the mob who attacked the Capitol on January 6.

Russia approved the *Sputnik V* COVID vaccine in August 2020 without robust research that confirmed its safety or efficacy, the same month Navalny was poisoned. Emergency mass distribution of Russia's vaccine began in December 2020 in Belarus, Hungary, Serbia, Argentina, and the United Arab Emirates. By February 2021, following qualified trials and medical study, over a billion doses of *Sputnik V* had been ordered worldwide, and the vaccine was distributed to 59 countries. However, by June 2021, just before Putin's summit with Biden (10 months after *Sputnik V's* initial approval), the Kremlin only managed to vaccinate 14% of the Russian population because the people didn't trust their own government not to poison them. This poor performance led the Kremlin to initiate a mass COVID vaccination campaign for household pets to help prove the vaccine program was considered safe. During the summer COVID surge of 2021, Moscow reopened field hospitals, enforced mask and glove mandates, and went back into lockdowns in an attempt to slow the worst case-count since the beginning of the year. More than half of all new daily infections were reported in Moscow alone. The culprit was the more infectious Alpha variant from the UK.

When the Delta variant overtook Washington State, the Governor mandated that all healthcare workers, government employees, and schoolteachers to be vaccinated or face being terminated from employment. Many of the nurses at the local hospitals refused the vaccine outright, and therefore lost their jobs. The bulk of them were of Soviet-era Russian descent who rebelled against mandates of any kind. They thought of the vaccines as a cruel form of authoritarian rule like they'd experienced before in the motherland. Even though they sought refuge in the US, they believed the government was capable of and would attempt to poison any citizen through the distribution of the COVID vaccine.

A few months after the conversation with Yelena, I received a text from another client that reminded me of her story. The text came from a middle school teacher who had five children of her own. Her text included a photo of three recognizable figures: Vladimir Putin, Donald Trump with two thumbs up, and Kim Jong Un of North Korea, the *"Three Amigos"* standing side by side. The subtext of the display was more than obvious – a triad of authoritarian strongmen.

The Climate of Truth

The caption under the photo read: "*Tussaud's Waxworks in San Antonio removes Trump figure because people keep punching it.*" I shared the image with several other clients.

"*Thought you'd enjoy this,*" the middle school teacher wrote to me about the amusing photo, because we spent every one of her hair appointments discussing the strange politics of our world.

"*Hah!*" I replied back to her. "*Madam Tussaud screwed up! She made Trump's hair look stylish. That's not realistic! His hair never looked normal like that. And why didn't anyone punch Putin and Kim Jong Un? You would have, I'm sure!*"

"*Hell yeah!*" the middle school teacher texted back.

❖

Capitol Police Officer Daniel Hodges described having to fight through the riotous mob with his fellow officers in order to reach a defensive position at the Capitol Building. On the way up, the rioters yelled at the officers, calling them "traitors." The officers were punched, kicked, bombarded with metal objects from above, and knocked to the ground before they even reached their assigned defensive positions. The officers thought they might be killed even before reaching their posts.

Once in place, the officers were then forced to fall back into an entrance tunnel of the Capitol. The officers held the line, fighting for every inch. Officer Hodges was pinned in a metal doorframe and was being crushed by the weight of the advancing mob who shouted "Heave-Ho!" He was beaten on the head and face with his own baton. His gas mask was ripped off and he was sprayed in the face with CS gas at close range, causing him to choke and wheeze. He received chemical burns in his eyes and lungs, and his vision was blurred. Someone in the mob tried to gouge out his eyes with their thumbs. As his ribs were being crushed by the metal doorframe and blood flowed from his mouth, Officer Hodges thought he was going to die yet again.

I fell to my knees on my kitchen floor as I heard Officer Hodges scream in agony on television. Irma, my Corgi, crawled into my lap when she sensed my distress. All I could do was hug my dog. I rocked back and forth as I clutched Irma against my chest.

Identity

When reporters later asked what was going through his mind at that torturous moment, Officer Hodges said his only thought was that reinforcements would be coming any minute. That did not happen. The Capitol Police and the Metropolitan Police were woefully outnumbered and overpowered. They fought without sufficient tactical equipment or training. They were left to fight alone. Eventually, Officer Hodges was pulled free of the metal doorframe from behind by his fellow officers. The video of him screaming in agony went viral.

While Officer Hodges was pinned, Andrew Clyde, a Republican Congressman from Georgia, rushed to help barricade the doors to prevent the angry mob from entering the House chamber. Photos showed the Congressman's mouth agape as he yelled in fear. However, during a Congressional hearing of the House Oversight and Reform Committee that focused on lapses in security that led up to the events of January 6, Clyde was among a handful of Republicans who attempted to publicly rewrite the history of the insurrection. To his Congressional colleagues in the same chamber where he barricaded the door against rioters, Clyde stated: "Let me be clear, there was no insurrection. And to call it an insurrection, in my opinion, is a bold-faced lie. Watching the TV footage of those who entered the Capitol and walked through Statuary Hall, showed people in an orderly fashion staying between the stanchions and ropes, taking videos and pictures. You know, if you didn't know the TV footage was a video from January 6, you would actually think it was a normal tourist visit."

My cellphone rang as I sat on the floor, watching the coverage about Officer Hodges.

"What ya doin'?" my friend Logan asked. He sounded unusually chirpy, with a hint of aggravation. His wife had been away from home to take care of her elderly mother in Texas, and he was all alone.

"I'm devastated," I said wearily.

"Don't believe what they tell you on television," Logan insisted. "It's bullshit."

"It's clearly not bullshit," I said. "There's a lot of cop-bashing going on. It's heartbreaking."

"You mean fascist pig-bashing!" Logan jeered.

The Climate of Truth

I held my breath for a moment before I spoke. "I didn't call anybody a fascist pig, Logan."

"First cops are evil because of George Floyd. Now they're heroes because of an <u>alleged</u> insurrection. Soon they'll be back to being fascist pigs again. That's life!"

"Alleged insurrection?...Why are you so cynical?" I said.

"It couldn't have been much of an insurrection," Logan said, chuckling. "Nobody had guns."

"What planet are you on? There were guns and pipe bombs. Cops were tased and beaten."

"Tell me this – If there were guns, why weren't any of the cops shot?" Logan pondered.

There was a long pause while I thought. The sound of the angry mob continued to erupt from the television as the news replayed the scenes of the violent attack.

"You have no answer?" Logan demanded. "OK then, if the attack was so bad, why was only one rioter shot?"

"It was a miracle because the cops used personal restraint," I said. "It could easily have been a bloodbath."

"Ah, the old 'personal restraint' excuse. They don't train restraint for life and death situations. It's kill or be killed out there. So, if they used restraint, then it couldn't have been all that dangerous." Logan sighed as if he was bored. "A bunch of unhappy people brought their grievance to the government. How is that a bad thing?"

It floored me when Logan's ideas came out of Putin's mouth a few months later. Putin suggested that the rioters from January 6 were being persecuted by the US government and targeted for their dissent. "They weren't just a crowd of robbers and rioters," Putin said. "Those people had come with political demands." As if he was impersonating the Republicans who were busy whitewashing the attack against the Capitol, Putin claimed the rioters were simply taking a "stroll," portraying them as innocent folk with legitimate grievances. It didn't seem like a good thing that one of my friends agreed with a dictator, and vice versa. And I didn't know what to do about it.

"People died, Logan. Don't be so callous," I said.

Identity

"How many times do I have to tell you, it's just click-bait," Logan insisted. "I've been shot. In the shoulder. On the job. It's like getting hit with a sledgehammer and stung by a hundred hornets all at once. I have the real bullet scars to prove it. What you are watching is overdramatized theatre. It would have been far more entertaining if they knocked off a few corrupt and self-entitled Congressmen. I'd pay good money to see that!"

I looked up to see Officer Hodges screaming in agony on the television again, and instantly became nauseous. I couldn't understand how my friend, a retired police officer, could so easily dismiss the suffering of those in uniform, those who were risking their lives to defend Democracy.

"I've gotta go," I said. I hung up the phone and wept.

It was later reported that Capitol Police officers who were severely beaten in the riot reported for duty the very next day to uphold their oath to defend the Capitol. When Officer Hodges reported for duty as scheduled, he said of the insurrection, "If it wasn't my job, I would have done that for free. It was absolutely my pleasure to crush a White nationalist insurrection and I'm glad I was in a position to help. We'll do it as many times as it takes."

❖

Three hours after the Capitol breach, Trump still had not taken defensive action. According to a Pentagon report released more than two months later, Vice President Pence was the one who called the acting Defense Secretary to make a demand: "Clear the Capitol." The first SWAT team entered the Capitol Building at 2:52pm.

More than an hour after the Senate chamber was breached, Senate Majority Leader Chuck Schumer and House Speaker Nancy Pelosi called Pentagon officials to demand the National Guard to be deployed. "We need help," Schumer said over the phone from a safety bunker. General Milley, Chairman of the Joint Chiefs, announced "We must establish order." But there were two more hours of chaos and confusion as Pentagon officials strategized a military response. Strangely, there was a very swift and highly organized response to quell the George Floyd protests the summer before in Washington DC.

The Climate of Truth

At 4:17pm, Trump tweeted a video to the rioters at the Capitol: *"I know your pain, I know you're hurt. We had an election that was stolen from us. It was a landslide election and everyone knows it, especially the other side…It's a very tough period of time. There's never been a time like this where such a thing happened where they could take it away from all of us – from me, from you, from our country. This was a fraudulent election, but we can't play into the hands of these people. We have to have peace. So go home. We love you. You're very special. You've seen what happens. You see the way others are treated that are so bad and so evil."*

Anthropologists and political analysts detailed how Trump's methods were modeled after professional wrestling matches that were very popular among the working class. Trump, an avid fan of the sport, hosted *"World Wrestling Entertainment"* and *"WrestleMania"* matches himself. Professional wrestling was known to be a fake spectacle, with bigger-than-life characters "fighting" in scripted feuds under the guise of the classic "Good Guys" versus "Bad Guys" motif. One sociologist described Trump's base as a manifestation of "working-class authoritarianism," those who devoured the fantasy of staged wrestling and interpreted it as truth.

The military's response to the insurrection wasn't finalized until 4:30pm. At 4:40pm, Schumer and Pelosi accused the Pentagon of stalling and having advance knowledge of plans to sack the Capitol. The acting Secretary of Defense, a Trump loyalist, did not authorize deployment of the National Guard until 5:45pm, more than four hours after the attack began.

At 6:01pm Trump tweeted, *"These are the things and events that happen when a sacred landslide election victory is so unceremoniously & viciously stripped away from great patriots who have been badly & unfairly treated for so long. Go home with love & in peace. Remember this day forever!"*

The Department of Defense noted the Capitol wasn't fully secure until 8:00pm, as indicated by a memo from the Capitol Police. Congress resumed the counting of Electoral votes at 8:06pm. A Republican representative from Kansas tested positive for COVID during the Electoral debate and went into quarantine, missing the final certifications.

Despite witnessing firsthand the attack on the Capitol, and after nearly eight hours of floor debate over Electoral votes from six swing states, 139 House Republicans voted to overturn the election and

Identity

eight Republican Senators did the same. Regardless of the affrontery to the Electoral process, the Democrat majority upheld the election results. The few Republicans who had the courage to vote in favor of the Electoral certification, and the few who voted to convict Trump during the second impeachment trial, were formally censored by their own political party for failing to support Trump's agenda; several of them were even booed when they attempted to speak before their own members at state conventions. Evangelist Franklin Graham compared ten House Republicans to Judas Iscariot (the notorious apostle alleged to have betrayed Jesus to the Romans) after they voted in favor of Trump's second impeachment. Trump made it his personal quest to destroy the political careers of all those who voted to impeach him, beginning with Representative Liz Cheney (daughter of former Vice President Dick Cheney) who was stripped of her leadership role in the Republican caucus.

    Joe Biden and Kamala Harris were not certified as the winners of the 2020 election until 3:44am on January 7 when the Democrats carried the Electoral vote. Several Republicans voted to overturn the election solely out of fear of reprisal from the mob that attacked the Capitol. Reinforcements from the National Guard did not begin to arrive at the Capitol until 10:00am the morning after the insurrection. The attack could have been deterred within the first hour had adequate troops been deployed in a timely response. The attack could have been prevented altogether had the National Guard been deployed in advance of the Electoral count, based on the FBI's credible threat assessment of Trump's *"Save America March."* To a reasonable observer, it appeared that the Trump administration worked to curtail an adequate military presence in advance.

    On January 7, Trump posted another video statement to *Twitter*. He did not call a press conference in front of reporters. From inside the White House, he somberly proclaimed to the camera, *"I would like to begin by addressing the heinous attack on the United States Capitol. Like all Americans, I am outraged by the violence, lawlessness and mayhem."*

    Trump stood before a white fireplace mantle at a podium branded with the Presidential seal, flanked by the American flag and the banner of his office that bore the words *"E Pluribus Unum,"* meaning *"Out of Many, One."* He blatantly lied, *"I immediately deployed the National Guard and federal law enforcement to secure the [Capitol] building and expel the intruders."* Trump's *Twitter* video on January 7 was the closest thing to a concession speech following the election,

The Climate of Truth

though he never uttered the words "I concede." In the video he stated briefly, *"A new administration will be inaugurated on January 20th. My focus now turns to ensuring a smooth, orderly and seamless transition of power."*

On the day following the insurrection, *Facebook* banned Trump indefinitely, the most aggressive action taken by any social media platform. Mark Zuckerberg, the chief executive officer wrote, *"We believe the risks of allowing the President to continue to use our service during this period are simply too great."* Over the next few months, *Facebook* extended Trump's ban until January 2023. It marked a dramatic escalation of tensions between tech giants and the Trump Administration, a direct response to Trump's weaponization of the internet.

Fuming over being banned by *Facebook*, Trump flipped to his signature bombast as he used *Twitter* the following day, January 8: *"The 75,000,000 great American Patriots who voted for me, AMERICA FIRST, and MAKE AMERICA GREAT AGAIN, will have a GIANT VOICE long into the future. They will not be disrespected or treated unfairly in any way, shape or form!!!"* He followed with another tweet, *"To all of those who have asked, I will not be going to the Inauguration on January 20th."* Trump signaled that he did not support a peaceful transfer of power as he claimed the day before. Vice President Pence had already publicly confirmed his attendance to Biden's Inauguration.

Following Trump's volatile tweets on January 8, *Twitter* banned him permanently. *Twitter* made the decision *"due to the risk of further incitement of violence,"* specifically noting how Trump's choice to skip Biden's Inauguration would greatly escalate the threat level against the assembly.

Following the example of *Facebook* and *Twitter, YouTube, Tik Tok, Instagram, Spotify, Shopify, Reddit, Google, Snapchat, Twitch,* and *Pinterest* all banned Trump. Online vendors quit offering Trump products. Though Trump was incensed and dismissed these actions as *"Cancel Culture,"* the bans resulted in an immediate decrease of online threats of violence by 75%.

Regardless, plans for a second attack on the US Capitol were hatched on *Facebook* and *Twitter* by Trump supporters: *"When Democracy is destroyed, REFUSE TO BE SILENCED!"* they wrote. There was a call for another *"ARMED MARCH ON CAPITOL HILL AND ALL STATE CAPITOLS"* for January 17, the last Sunday of Trump's

Identity

Presidency. The rally cry was signed by *"common folk who are tired of being tread upon."* Fortunately, the deployment of the National Guard deterred a repeat attack against the seat of Democracy.

❖

A Capitol Police officer died from multiple strokes the day after the insurrection. Rioters who clobbered him in the head with a fire extinguisher and sprayed him with bear spray were not charged with murder because the medical examiner declared that he died from "natural causes." His ashes were displayed in a cherrywood box inside the Capitol Rotunda, and President Biden paid his respects, resting his hand upon the urn. A plaque read the officer's cremated remains had been flown over the Capitol on January 7 to honor *"the distinguished life and service of Officer Brian D. Sicknick."* Fellow Capitol Police officers sat in mourning in full dress uniform, all socially distanced while wearing masks.

Though Officer Sicknick and many other officers who fought to defend the Capitol were Trump supporters, 21 House Republicans voted against awarding all responding officers with Congressional Gold Medals to honor of their heroic sacrifice. Even though the officers saved the lives of all lawmakers, and despite noting that Republicans claimed to support law enforcement, the 21 House Republicans who opposed the honors did so because they objected to the reference of the attack on January 6 as an "insurrection." One of the rioters, a county commissioner from New Mexico said that Trump was "anointed by God," and that he didn't believe Officer Sicknick was really dead. The commissioner went on to declare that "the only good Democrat is a dead Democrat."

Four of the rioters also died. One was shot and killed by a Secret Service agent who was defending members of Congress from the mob's advance; that agent received death threats for doing his job. Another rioter suffered a lethal meth overdose, and two died of heart attacks in the melee. Approximately 140 additional officers were reported to have been injured, including cracked ribs, crushed spinal discs, stab wounds, traumatic brain injuries from blows to the head with heavy objects, being tased repeatedly (which caused heart attacks), and damage caused by chemical sprays. Several officers were nearly killed by the rioters, but somehow managed to survive. Some of the officers begged for their lives, one of them pleading while

The Climate of Truth

he was being tased repeatedly at the base of his skull, "I have kids!" About 200 National Guard and 38 Capitol Police contracted COVID from the insurrection. Four Capitol Police officers who responded to the attack committed suicide.

The FBI warned that more violent protests could spill over to all 50 state Capitols. In response to online threats, 26,000 National Guard troops were deployed to serve as security forces for Biden's Inauguration; those were more US troops than were active in the war zones of Afghanistan, Syria and Iraq combined. Barricades and unscalable fences topped with razor wire encircled the Capitol complex for the following three months.

Citing the insurrection as the cause, 16 high-ranking officials in the Trump administration resigned immediately. The House Speaker called upon Congressional staff to stay at their posts to keep the government functioning. For the second time, the House of Representatives began formulating Articles of Impeachment against Trump, noting the 14th Amendment to the Constitution "prohibits any person who has 'engaged in insurrection or rebellion against the United States'" from holding office.

A newly installed Republican Representative from West Virginia was arrested for livestreaming the insurrection to *Facebook* on his cellphone as he entered the Capitol Building with the mob. "We're in, we're in! Derrick Evans is in the Capitol!" he joyfully shouted during the live recording while wearing a helmet. The video feed had been deleted, but only after it was broadly spread across the internet. The Representative later wore a hoodie and a face mask to court after he was charged with unauthorized and violent entry to the Capitol. He did not answer questions from the press. He was released on his own recognizance. He claimed to be a journalist who was simply reporting on the events of the day and initially disputed the charges, claiming that he did not participate in the violence. He resigned from office three days later following bipartisan pressure from Congress. Upon leaving office he announced, "[I] deeply regret any hurt, pain or embarrassment I may have caused my family, friends, constituents and fellow West Virginians," and "I hope it helps to begin the healing process, so we can all move forward and come together as 'One Nation, Under God.'"

❖

Identity

    I met Ainsley as the national search for the rioters began. She arrived at my shop in a nervous and agitated state. It was her first time in a styling chair in more than 30 years, during which time she shaved her head herself every few weeks. She had let her hair grow for a few months so I had something to work with, but it was still quite short. I spent the first half of her appointment soothing her anxiety, followed by a discussion of needing enough hair to comb. I explained that, under such circumstances, I could taper the edges around her neckline and ears and fade the cut upward to allow the top to grow out more. She looked deeply into my eyes, concentrating on my every word.

    "Should I let it grow down to my shoulders?" Ainsley asked.

    "That's a huge jump for you," I said. "It would take more than a year to grow out, and given your history, I'm not certain you would last that long. It might frustrate you to have that as your goal right now. My advice is to keep it simple, let it grow a little and see how you like it. You need to get used to having it a bit longer on top, something you can style with your fingers. It might be best to keep the pressure off yourself. You may decide to let your hair grow longer down the road. But for right now, a tight, tapered cut would be a safer bet for you…Are you comfortable with that?" I asked.

    Ainsley was noticeably more relaxed. "Just do your thing," she said. "I trust you completely."

    With exceptional care, I began my work to sculpt her stubbly hair into an actual shape that complimented her kind face. Her breathing normalized as my fingers glided across her head. She watched me in the mirror with curiosity.

    "I read every word on your website," she said with a snicker. "Not because I'm stalking you! I'm just very thorough. It was a big deal for me to have someone touch my head again after all these years. I could tell that you had the right energy for me."

    Ainsley told me about her 11-acre homestead 28 miles northeast of my shop. The property was her life's dream. She lived in a humble cottage that her husband built for her, with a couch, a loveseat, and a dining room table that were all hand-crafted to last for generations.

    As a conservationist, Ainsley was dedicated to restoring her land to a more natural forest habitat. She cleared the wild blackberries and other invasive species by hand, removed debris from the forest floor,

The Climate of Truth

and thinned the tree canopy to allow for the diversification of the woods. She explained that the soil already had the necessary seeds to regenerate the various native species of trees that would restore forest diversity and would attract the right kind of insects and wildlife. Her approach was all about eco-balance. She was committed to overhaul decades of bad forest management, where the lumber industry clear-cut the landscape and replaced it with nothing but Douglas firs that were all the same age, same height, and planted too close together. An overcrowded Douglas fir forest meant that fast-moving crown fires were imminent. I couldn't help but recognize that trees were very much like people. Unbridled sameness was dangerous. Diversity was healthy and beneficial.

Once she settled back into her skin, I could tell Ainsley was smiling intently under her mask as she watched her haircut transform into something more flattering. Her eyes darted about the room, indicating that she was very interested in my artwork.

"I found a remarkable artist up by my place," she said, glancing at several of my own pieces. "He does the most amazing chainsaw art."

"Like grizzly bears?" I asked as I snipped.

"Yeah, I adore bears. Because I know I have bear medicine – they are my spirit animal. So, I hired Sunny to sculpt a giant bear for me. But not the usual hillbilly stuff. His work is hyper-realistic," she said. "I bought an old seven-foot cedar stump for two hundred bucks, and had it delivered to my front yard."

I had no idea how a chainsaw could make anything look "hyper-realistic."

"I wanted to give him a chance, to let him earn some money," she said. "I saw something good in him…He's a felon. He was just getting out of prison for the second time. Beat up some guy at a bar…He doesn't make excuses for what he did. He accepts responsibility. So, he did his time, and then he ended up by my place, living off the grid…I decided to pay him $1600 in advance to chainsaw my bear…The idea was for him to settle into a routine, give him some structure and the room to be creative. He was supposed to come to my front yard every day and work on my bear. But I came home one day and found him sitting on the lawn, staring at the cedar stump. He was totally plowed on beer… And he's a very mean drunk. That's probably what landed him in prison…The bear was roughly sketched

Identity

in. It was very stylized, like a fantasy of what a bear would look like in a dream…When I saw Sunny sitting there on the lawn in front of his sculpture, he was incredibly depressed. I took one look at him and just knew he was done, that he couldn't finish the bear. He couldn't bring himself to work on it anymore. But I loved the sculpture anyway, just the way it was. It was inspired, even though it was unfinished."

"Is it standing in your yard?" I asked.

"We built a cement pad for it, to protect the base from rotting. And there it stands, in all its raw nobility…I took photos of the bear and put them on *Facebook*. It was quite a hit…My *Facebook* page also shows that I am a proud supporter of '*Black Lives Matter*'…A few days later, Sunny shows up at my house, unannounced. He drove up in his pickup, clearly on another beer bender. This time he brought a friend with him. 'I wanted to show my friend the bear,' he said, belching in my face. Yeah, it was weird that he just showed up like that, but I decided to let it go. I turned to head back into the house, but Sunny yelled after me… 'I know all about you! I know what you're up to and who you really are!'…He was livid… 'I saw it with my own eyes on *Facebook*!' he shouted. I thought he was going to punch me," Ainsley said, looking frantic.

"Was your husband home?"

"No."

"I'm very glad to be a city mouse," I said. "I couldn't handle living in the boonies out by you. It's like a scene right out of "*Deliverance*" with the banjos playing in the forest.

"Yeah, I'm surrounded by rednecks out there, but that never bothered me before," Ainsley said. "I can usually get along with just about anybody, no matter how much I disagree with them…But like I said, Sunny is a very mean drunk." She began to knead her fingers in her lap.

"He saw your '*Black Lives Matter*' stuff on *Facebook*?"

"He said, 'You know what guys like me can do to you '*Antifa*' types!' He got right in my face. He called me a Communist," Ainsley said.

"What about the other guy who was with him?" I asked. "The friend?"

The Climate of Truth

"He looked like a long-tailed cat in a room full of rocking chairs. Totally useless and afraid. Sunny was coming at me," Ainsley said. "'You're un-American! You're a traitor! But even though I know this about you, I want you to know that I put you under my protection anyway!'"

"What did that mean?" I asked.

"I didn't know either. So, I asked him," Ainsley said. "And his response was so weird. 'Things are going to get very, very interesting around here real ssssssoon.' He hissed when he said it."

"That's a threat," I said.

"He was referring to what was about to happen on January 6th. I told him I didn't need his protection," Ainsley said. "'I beg to differ!' Sunny said. He told me that liberals like me didn't belong in those parts. He said he'd been to some meetings where he heard people talking about me."

"What meetings?" I asked.

"He said he couldn't tell me. They were secret meetings."

"Sounds like militia talk to me," I said.

"Sunny got really close to my face again. 'You are definitely under <u>my</u> protection, so you don't need to be afeared, little lady.'"

"You put up with that 'little lady' crap?" I asked.

"You gotta pick your battles," she said.

"The '*Proud Boys*' and the '*Patriot Prayer*' people are all over this region," I said. "You need to be careful. Did you tell anyone about this?"

"I called my brother in Texas," she said. "He's a cop. He asked me if I reported it. I told him I wasn't going to report it to the Sheriff because the Sheriff was probably in on it. My brother said, 'No, no! Not the Sheriff. You need to call the FBI!' 'I'm not going to call the freaking FBI!' I told my brother. 'Why get so dramatic?'…So, the FBI came to my house. They sat in my kitchen and interviewed me for an hour and a half. Sunny was arrested for violating his parole. Apparently, he wasn't supposed to live off the grid like he was. The FBI confiscated 25 semiautomatic weapons from him, and they slapped him back in jail."

Identity

"Jesus," I said.

"I know."

"Did the FBI tell him you were the one who reported him? Are you worried about retaliation?" I asked.

"The FBI swore they kept my name out of it."

"Something's wrong if a guy like that can get his hands on so many weapons," I said.

"He said people just gave them to him."

"When pigs fly!...But then, I've seen a lot of flying pigs in commercials lately," I said.

"The FBI told me they wouldn't allow Sunny to return out by my property, but he's back just the same."

"He's out of jail already!"

"He's living with an elderly couple right next door," Ainsley said.

"What are you going to do?"

"He helps the old folks out. It seems like he's pretty good to them."

"Oh, come on," I said. "How long will that last?"

"So much for the FBI keeping their promises."

"You know the one about the leopard and its spots, right?" I said.

"Will you look at that!" Ainsley stared at her haircut in the mirror. "It's just incredible! I didn't know I could look like this!"

I applied a dollop of anti-frizz cream and some styling paste and used the blow dryer to sweep her hair forward with a lifted bang. She looked quite different, an updated version of herself.

"I can already tell that you are very easy to fall in love with, Mike...All these years, and I finally have a hairstyle!" She reached out and grabbed hold of my hand, resting her cheek against my palm. "I am so lucky to have found you," she said.

The following day, Ainsley sent me a text: *"I woke early this morning to get some things done, and in my bustling about, passed my bathroom mirror and, glancing at my reflection, stopped short in sudden*

The Climate of Truth

recognition, and out loud said THERE *you are! (Emoji: Smiley Face.) This hair journey is tied to a lot of things beyond aesthetic for me, and something inside settled into its place today. I want to thank you for being wonderful at your craft, but also so astute and intuitive with people. With no intended burden, I just want you to know that in the course of you simply being you, you made a difference for me."*

A few months later, Ainsley texted me again on a rainy Sunday afternoon while I was editing this chapter. "*Hey Mike. My fully vaccinated daughter tested positive for COVID yesterday. She is asymptomatic and only found out because she had to have a COVID test prior to a medical procedure. I had a one-on-one yoga training with her, unmasked for the first time last Monday. I have been fully vaccinated since May 2nd, (as has she because she rode with us to the vaccine clinic!) and, of course, have NO symptoms, but am still getting a COVID test ASAP. There is no walk-in testing, and I can't make an appointment until tomorrow. I have an appointment scheduled with you in 9 days. Should we reschedule that?"*

I responded to her text immediately: *"Thanks for letting me know. Let's wait to see the results of your test. At least the vaccinations are working and people aren't getting sick."*

Ainsley wrote back: *"Right?!? She was so shocked that she tested positive. It was the first day that she allowed vaccinated people to be unmasked around her. It's a clear reminder that we can't be complacent. I'll keep you in the loop. (Emoji: red heart.)"*

Ainsley later told me that her sister died of COVID during the Delta surge. She was diagnosed on a Friday night and died the following Monday morning. A single mother, her sister left behind two teenage boys (one of whom was autistic), only $50 in her checking account, no food in the refrigerator, and no recorded Will. Her sister did not believe in taking a vaccine or wearing a mask. She was only 43 years old. The eldest boy had to decide how to dispose of his mother's body since there was no medical directive in place. Both boys contracted COVID from their mother. While infected, both boys went to the movies as well as to a busy laundromat to do their laundry.

❖

Identity

The University of Chicago conducted a study for the *Project on Security and Threats* that analyzed the demographics of the more than 700 people who were criminally charged after the insurrection. The study concluded that 10-12% of the arrestees were tied directly to White supremacist or militant groups. The bulk of the remaining 90% of the arrestees were educated, and they originated from counties where the majority voted for Biden, counties that also showed the most significant declines in the majority White population. The arrestees were mainly middle to upper-middle class, all White, and they included entrepreneurs, business owners, and CEOs who feared that the rights of minorities and immigrants were crowding out the rights of White people. It was an echo of the Civil War that came to be known as *"The Great Replacement,"* a belief that minorities and immigrants were taking over the country.

At least six of those arrested following the insurrection were from the metro area where I lived. One of the six, a known member of the *"Proud Boys,"* was identified by a photo taken inside the Capitol Building that was posted on social media. He was pictured flashing an "OK" hand signal (a White Power gesture) as he pushed past the Capitol Police. He wore swim goggles to protect his eyes from tear gas, a neck gaiter, and had a walkie-talkie clipped to his hoodie, which meant he was coordinating with others in the mob. Security camera footage showed he made it all the way into the Senate chamber. Online, he identified himself as a *"proud western chauvinist,"* and refused *"to apologize for creating the modern world."* He was charged with five felonies, including violent entry to the Capitol. He told friends in advance that he planned to travel to Washington, DC on January 6 to "witness history in the making," and "what you are about to see…It's going to be big." When the FBI arrested him, he had a handgun tucked into his waistband.

As it turned out, another man who was arrested from my region was the one responsible for a haunting image of the insurrection that burned into my brain – the goofy man who wore a camouflaged *"MAGA"* hat and stood atop the pedestal astride the bronze statue of President Gerald Ford. He put a *"MAGA"* hat on the statue and placed a *"Trump 2020"* flag in the statue's hand. The image was circulated around the world. Video taken inside the Capitol Building showed the same man talking on a government landline, making threatening remarks about House Speaker Nancy Pelosi and Vice President Mike Pence. "If you do not stand down, you're

The Climate of Truth

outnumbered," the man in the video said. "There's a fucking million of us out there, and we are listening to Trump, your boss!"

Reports identified the *Rule of Law Defense Fund*, a nonprofit arm of the *Republican Attorneys General Association*, as a funder and organizer of Trump's *"Save America March."* The *March* was the event that launched the insurrection from the Ellipse, a spherical park adjacent to the south White House lawn where Trump unleashed the rioters with his firebrand rhetoric. The *Rule of Law Defense Fund* was sponsored by corporations such as *Koch Industries, Walmart, Comcast, Home Depot, Amazon, Monsanto, the National Rifle Association, Facebook, Google and Coca Cola,* just to name a few. The *Fund* employed a massive national robo-call that detailed the logistics of January 6: "We will march to the Capitol Building and call on Congress to *'Stop the Steal!'* We are hoping that patriots like you will join us to continue to fight to protect the integrity of our elections." The *Fund* declared itself to be against "Lawless Liberals" and mail-in ballots.

On her *Facebook* page, Ginni Thomas, the wife of Supreme Court Justice Clarence Thomas, posted that she sent her *"LOVE"* to the thousands gathered at the *"Save America March."* Two days after the insurrection, she amended her post: *"Note: written before violence in the US Capitol."*

It was rumored that Mrs. Thomas sponsored 80 busloads of protesters taken to the *March*. The more accurate statement was that she served on the boards of directors and/or was affiliated with right-wing organizations known to recruit high school, college and university students, and those organizations sponsored the busloads of protesters. Those same right-wing organizations were also known to be anti-immigrant and anti-Muslim, and they lobbied against transgenders and women serving in the military. They also held the belief that gay marriage was destroying the social fabric of America.

Mrs. Thomas used her *Facebook* page to promote baseless assertions that George Soros, a Jewish philanthropist, was leading a *"coup"* against Trump, that philanthropist Bill Gates was using the COVID vaccines to kill people, that President Biden was corrupt, and that President Obama illegally spied on Trump's campaign.

Mrs. Thomas had frequent access to Trump's Oval Office, and she and Justice Thomas dined with the Trumps. Mrs. Thomas personally lobbied Trump to ban transgenders in the military, which he did in 2019. Despite the obvious appearance of conflict of interest,

Identity

Justice Thomas did not recuse himself from any Supreme Court case that involved his wife's lobbying activities. Mrs. Thomas even compiled lists of federal employees whom she declared to be disloyal to Trump, and urged him to fire them. Trump filled his administration with clerks formerly from Justice Thomas' office.

❖

Immediately following the insurrection, Trump supporters continued to post meritless claims online that declared personal attacks against Trump to have been *"cabal based"* attempts designed to *"push humanity toward totalitarianism,"* thus destroying *"individual sovereignty."* They asserted the *"New World Order"* would endeavor to take control of all global political and economic systems. Conservative paranoia was on overdrive. Conspiracists publicly referred to the *"cabal"* as *"the Deep State, the Khazarian Mafia, the Illuminati, the Khazarian Chabad Death Cult, the P3 Freemasons; the global, self-serving, ruling elite, whose power was <u>above</u> political parties, Presidents and Prime Ministers, Military Brass and Banking/Corporate giants."*

Trump supporters maintained the "cabal" was responsible for the "rigged" election, and that Biden's win would be overturned before the January 20 Inauguration. They also believed that national supply chains would be interrupted and the entire country would be under martial law, including a shutdown of the internet to neutralize the *"cabal-controlled"* tech companies. Trump supporters expected mass arrests of much-loved public figures to occur when their alleged affiliation with the *"Deep State"* was to become known. Trump supporters were advised to stockpile emergency supplies in preparation for revolution.

A message, claiming to originate from Secretary of State Mike Pompeo on January 9, circulated on the internet. The message announced the supposed activation of the Emergency Broadcasting System, and stated that Trump would address the public through television and cell phones. The message also warned:

"Stay indoors…Do not go out onto street…Be prepared for power outages in some cities."

The Climate of Truth

Also on January 9, the disembodied social media presence of "QAnon" "dropped" a message that was read by millions of its followers online:

> *"1. Expect the emergency broadcast system to be activated. The FCC just recently released a memorandum speaking to the requirements under Federal law to send messages from the President to the public.*
>
> *2. Expect confusion. We are in a battle for our republic against elites that are attempting the very coup that they are accusing Trump of doing. In battle, there will be disinformation but know that plans are being fulfilled.*
>
> *3. Expect high profile arrests to take place over the next 12 days and at any time. You may wake one morning to find someone in high office is no longer there.*
>
> *4. Expect this to be a bumpy ride to the very end. This is not a television show where things are resolved in 45 minutes.*
>
> *5. Expect more bombshell evidence to be released between now and Jan. 20th.*
>
> *6. Expect some sort of internet blackout or outage: Facebook, Twitter, Instagram, and Gmail are likely going to be affected. If you don't have alternate forms of communication established now, it would be a good idea to start forming them even if it's just checking on your nextdoor neighbors.*
>
> *7. Expect Trump to be inaugurated on Jan 20th!*
>
> *8. Expect the executive order from 2018 and/or the Insurrection Act to be enacted. This DOES NOT mean martial law. Remember that we have been under a state of emergency since 2018 which gives the president many powers to act.*
>
> *TONIGHT 7 PM EASTERN Emergency Broadcast from POTUS — Then the Shit-Storm Begins — President Trump Will Address the Nation. Pass this on!"*

Identity

Needless to say, the Emergency Broadcast System was never activated, and Trump did not address the nation about threats from the *"Deep State."* Instead, I found a neighborhood newsletter attached to my front door that offered information on how to prepare for *"natural or man-made disasters."* The timing of the newsletter was unnerving. It noted that western Washington was expected to experience a subduction zone earthquake between 8.0 to 9.0 on the Richter scale. Impacts could include flooding, infrastructure collapse, food and water scarcity, fire, volcanic eruption, and explosions of hazardous materials or natural gas. Residents were warned to keep a pair of good shoes, a flashlight, hard hat and gloves by one's bedside, and to compile emergency kits. Such kits should include first aid, batteries, radio, clothing, medication, cash, food and water for two weeks, maps, soap, laundry soap, can opener, tent, rope, tarps, garbage bags, family documents, extra eyeglasses and contact lenses, and entertainment items. Residents were advised to purchase these items on sale and have three kits available – one each for home, a vehicle and the workplace.

To the great dismay of millions of *"QAnon"* believers and Trump loyalists, the only arrests that happened were of the more than 700 individuals identified by the FBI as having participated in the attack against the US Capitol on January 6.

❖

After the Civil War, race-based violence was commonplace among laborers who followed the expansion of the railroad and coal mine operations. Blacks fleeing the South in the Great Migration to the North were seen as taking crucial jobs away from Whites, an ideology known as *"The Great Replacement."* Blacks had few options for employment, and they worked longer hours for far less pay. Labor organizers vehemently resisted the integration of Blacks, Chinese, southern European and eastern European workers who were all considered non-White by those who resisted diversity. Race riots frequently occurred in labor camps, and the US Army declared martial law to quell the violence. In Tacoma, Washington, an angry mob of White laborers burned Chinatown to the ground, referring to the act of destruction as the *"Tacoma Method."* Whites cheered as they witnessed the destruction.

The Climate of Truth

The ideology of *"The Great Replacement"* led to the August 2017 *"Unite the Right"* rally in Charlottesville, Virginia. White supremacists, including members of the *Ku Klux Klan*, defended Confederate statues of generals Robert E. Lee and Stonewall Jackson against planned removal, as approved by the city council. Pro-Confederate demonstrators (who were bussed in from other states) chanted "White lives matter!" and "Jews will not replace us!" They carried swastika banners and shouted the Nazi slogan "blood and soil." One chubby, incensed White man sporting a bushy gray beard and spectacles told a news crew that Charlottesville was "run by Jewish communists and criminal niggers." American Nazi websites posted a call to burn a local synagogue as part of the protest, and militants in army fatigues appeared across the street from Congregation Beth Israel, packing semiautomatic rifles. Clashes broke out in Charlottesville between the supremacists and counter-protesters. A neo-Nazi rammed his car into a group of counter-protesters, sending many people airborne; a 32 year-old woman was killed and 19 others were injured. The assailant was sentenced to life in prison plus 419 years.

Four years later, court injunctions still blocked the removal of the Confederate statues that were erected in 1924 to commemorate the Jim Crow era in the South. Also four years later, a federal jury found the neo-Nazis and White supremacists who organized the *"Unite the Right"* rally conspired to intimidate and harm others having "engaged in racial, religious or ethnic harassment or violence." The jury awarded the plaintiffs $26 million in compensatory and punitive damages, though it was unclear how the sum would ever be collected from the defendants, most of whom were not wealthy.

Joe Biden cited the events in Charlottesville as the motivation for his Presidential bid. The Supreme Court of Virginia finally overturned lower court decisions that blocked the removal of the Confederate statues, and the city of Charlottesville was ultimately able to remove the statues of Robert E. Lee and Stonewall Jackson from the public square on July 10, 2021. Crowds cheered as the statues were lifted off their pedestals with cranes. Charlottesville's first Black female mayor addressed the crowd: "(Removing the statues) is one small step closer to the goal of helping Charlottesville, Virginia, and America grapple with its sin of being willing to destroy Black people for economic gains...It is my hope that we stop taking these steps in 100-year increments and increase the frequency (of)

Identity

bold daily action and critical examination of accurate history, even when it denounces whiteness as supreme."

Trump's comments on the Charlottesville *"Unite the Right"* rally from his Tower in Manhattan were highly controversial: "You have some very bad people in that group. But you also had people that were very fine people, on both sides...You had people in that group that were there to protest the taking down of, to them, a very, very important statue and the renaming of a park from Robert E. Lee to another name." Trump continued the press conference by asking if statues of George Washington and Thomas Jefferson were to be eradicated next because both of the founding fathers were slave owners. He condemned the removal of Confederate statues as an attempt to rewrite American history and an attempt to radically change the national culture. He also said that he condemned neo-Nazis and White nationalists "totally."

At the time of the Charlottesville conflict, opinion polls showed the majority of Americans tended to agree with Trump's view that confederate monuments should remain in place. A *National Public Radio* poll showed that 62% believed the statues should be preserved as they were. When broken down by political party, 86% of Republicans, 61% of Independents and 44% of Democrats said the statues should stay. Two-thirds of Whites and Latinos agreed. Oddly, 44% of Blacks favored keeping the statues against 40% who sought removal.

At a campaign rally in Houston just over a year after the Charlottesville violence, Trump hammered his *"America First"* battle cry at his supporters. Estimates placed 16,000 ralliers inside the Houston arena, and an additional 15,000 outdoors. Trump told his boisterous crowd, "You know what I am? I'm a nationalist, OK? I'm a nationalist. Nationalist! Use that word! Use that word!" It was a strange turn of phrase given that Trump had condemned nationalism the year before. Asked why he described himself with a word that was associated with racism, Trump feigned ignorance about the etymology. He continued to flout diplomacy by saying, "I'm somebody who loves our country. I am a nationalist. It's a word that hasn't been used too much. Some people use it, but I'm very proud. I think it should be brought back."

In June 2020, Trump retweeted a video of his supporters driving golf carts in Florida. An elderly White man screamed out "White

The Climate of Truth

Power!" as he drove his golf cart past a group of *"Black Lives Matter"* protesters who were demonstrating against the murder of George Floyd. Trump thanked the "great people" in the golf carts for supporting his campaign, and wrongly predicted the "radical left do-nothing Democrats" would lose the election. The written response to Trump's retweeted video from former CIA Director General Michael Hayden was *"Holy Shit!"*

Only a few days later, the Trump campaign launched its official T-Shirt for sale on the campaign website. The T-shirt featured an eagle with outstretched wings perched atop a circlet that contained the American flag. The words *"America First"* were printed across the top of the T-shirt. The design of Trump's campaign icon closely resembled the "Reichsadler," the emblem known as the Nazi "Imperial Eagle" clutching a swastika, the main symbol of the Third Reich. The slogan *"America First"* was first popularized in 1940 by the *"America First Committee"* in an attempt to keep the US from entering World War II. The platform of the *"America First Committee"* was based on isolationism, antisemitism and fascism.

Again in June 2020, the Trump campaign purchased ads on *Facebook* that featured a red, inverted triangle with the caption *"Dangerous MOBS of far-left groups are running through our streets and causing absolute mayhem."* The statement continued: *"Please add your name immediately to stand with your president and his decision to declare ANTIFA a terrorist organization."* Trump's use of the red triangle on *Facebook* was the same symbol used by Nazis to mark left-wing political prisoners, Communists, Socialists, and trade unionists for extermination. Historians declared outright that Trump's red triangle was a death threat against leftists. On *Twitter*, The Auschwitz Museum joined the dissent: *"A red triangle that marked 'political prisoners' was the most common category of prisoners registered at the German Nazi Auschwitz death camp."*

"Antifa" was not a structured organization, and it had no leaders. It was comprised solely of local autonomous groups of individuals. One historian compared *"Antifa"* to feminists, in that both movements were conduits for activists, but neither were actualized organizations with an operational structure. Three months after the red triangle ads first appeared on *Facebook*, Trump announced his plan to designate *"Antifa"* as a terrorist organization through executive order, along with the *Ku Klux Klan*. However, the State Department never added *"Antifa"* to the federal list of named terrorist

organizations. For that matter, the *Ku Klux Klan* was never added to the list either.

Regardless, Trump continued with his *"Antifa"* charade by threatening the terrorist designation at a *"Black Voices for Trump"* campaign rally in Atlanta in September 2020. Also at that rally, Trump pledged to declare Juneteenth a federal holiday, even though he was ignorant of the date's significance to the Black community. He further denounced the *"Black Lives Matter"* movement as an organization dedicated to "mob rule," and declared the group had an "unusual name for an organization whose ideology and tactics are right now destroying many Black lives." President Biden was the one to sign the law declaring Juneteenth a national holiday in June 2021 as Republicans advanced hundreds of bills aimed to limit the voting power of people of color in almost every state.

The controversy over Trump's use of the red triangle caused *Facebook* to ban those advertisements because they violated the tech company's policy against "organized hate." The Trump campaign responded to being censored: *"This is moronic. In Democrats' America, Mount Rushmore glorifies white supremacy and the bald eagle with an American flag is a Nazi symbol. They have lost their minds."*

❖

Contrary to logic and reason, members of the Republican National Committee firmly believed that Biden would not be inaugurated, and they feverishly insisted that Trump would continue to be President for another four years. Some Republicans declared the Capitol riot to have been staged by Democrats to frame Trump, and that *"disguised Antifa people were 95%+ of the people in the [Capitol] building."* Waiting for Trump's resurrection by January 20, his supporters vowed it would be *"something to tell the grandchildren! It's 1776 all over again!"*

Some Republican officials accused Vice President Pence of being involved with the Clintons in a scheme to oust Trump with the assistance of former FBI Director Rod Rosenstein. They later claimed the insurrection was staged by the FBI, also to oust Trump. Republicans even alleged that an Italian defense contractor used lasers and digital signals from satellites to electronically flip votes in Biden's favor, and that *Dominion* voting machines were somehow

The Climate of Truth

sending the converted voting data to Germany, Serbia, China, Iran, and Rome.

After reviewing more than a quarter-million digital images taken at the Capitol riot on January 6, FBI Director Christopher Wray testified at a Congressional hearing two months later. Wray said the majority of those arrested for participating in the insurrection were classified as "militia violent extremists," some who were "racially motivated." Wray explained that there was "no indication that any 'Antifa' members participated in the Capitol assault as some Republicans have suggested." Wray identified the insurrectionists as far-right militant groups, "QAnon" members, and Trump loyalists.

Several weapons were seized from rioters on January 6: loaded 9mm handguns, a loaded rifle and loaded shotgun, a crossbow with bolts, several machetes, stun guns, 11 Molotov cocktails, a *Tavor* assault rifle with hundreds of rounds of ammunition, an AR-15 rifle, a *Smith & Wesson* pistol, knives, bats, chemicals, stolen police gear (including ammunition), flagpoles, pieces of metal and wood, crutches, a skateboard, and crowbars. Militants were also known to have stashed caches of weapons in hotel rooms and nearby parking garages. Though the vast majority of the thousands of rioters were never searched that day, investigators believed that a large number of people who assembled at the Capitol were carrying concealed weapons. According to court records, at least 85 people were charged with carrying or using weapons during the insurrection. Nevertheless, the Republican myth persisted that the insurrectionists were unarmed, peaceful protestors.

The Second Amendment, along with all state constitutions, protects an individual's right to bear arms for self-protection and for protection of their private property. But the federal and state constitutions do not allow armed members of the community to organize as vigilantes to employ lethal force en masse. Regardless of the fact that all 50 states banned private armies, militias or paramilitary groups, men with semiautomatic weapons strapped to their backs had been commonly seen at far-right rallies and racial protests since May of 2020. Due to ignorance or misunderstanding, law enforcement officers commonly failed to enforce existing anti-militia laws. That ignorance could be tied directly to a common misconception (promoted by groups such as the *National Rifle Association*) that aggressive militia activity was somehow protected under the Second Amendment. In a 2008 major gun rights case,

Identity

Columbia vs. Heller, the US Supreme Court affirmed the right of states to prohibit the activity of militia groups. Despite the Court's decision, police still refused to enforce anti-militia laws because they were either concerned about retaliation, or the officers themselves supported the goals of militant organizations and believed in a much broader (though inaccurate) interpretation of the Second Amendment.

The militia movement deemed its actions to be fully sanctioned under law, but at the same time, those armed organizations declared themselves to be free from all government control. That ideology led militias to stockpile illegal weapons and explosives, to plot the assassinations of public officials, and to destroy buildings. For example, Timothy McVeigh, associated with the *"Michigan Militia,"* used a truck bomb to destroy the nine-story Alfred P. Murrah Federal Building in Oklahoma City in April 1995. The bombing killed 168 people, injured more than 680 others, and damaged or destroyed hundreds of other buildings within 16 blocks of the blast zone, causing an estimated $652 million in damages.

Armed militia groups illegally descended on polling places across the country to intimidate and suppress the 2020 vote. During the hotly contested vote tabulation process (and the various recounts), armed militants gathered outside election offices carrying shotguns, handguns, semiautomatic rifles, *"Trump 2020"* flags, and flak jackets with walkie-talkies. Though no serious irregularities had occurred with the vote count, the armed protesters gathered in response to Trump's baseless claims that Democrats had stolen the election. Elections officials feared for the safety of their employees.

"I'm here to protect a peaceful protest," one veteran who fought in Afghanistan said while carrying a semiautomatic assault rifle, a handgun, and extra ammunition to election headquarters in Arizona.

Militia organizations were generally comprised of constitutionalists, Veterans, Libertarians, gun rights enthusiasts, survivalists, conspiracy theorists, and Confederate restorationists, all of whom were strictly anti-government. These same militias were commonly aligned with the ideology of White nationalism where they sought the creation of an all-White nation-state in the US. White supremacists were a subgroup of White nationalism. White supremacist theology declared that Aryans were God's "chosen race." Aryans only included the Germanic, Anglo-Saxon, Celtic, and Nordic

The Climate of Truth

races, wrongly thought to be the sole "true" descendants of the ancient Israelites. This system of belief was otherwise known as the *"Christian Identity"* movement.

Those who espoused *"Christian Identity"* considered the Biblical characters of Adam and Eve to be the exclusive progenitors of the White race. Conversely, the Black race, one of the so-called "mud races," was equated with the biblical term, "the beasts of the field." Adherents of *"Christian Identity"* believed Blacks and other minorities to be soulless. The Jewish race was thought to have sprung from the semen of the serpent that tempted Eve in the *Garden of Eden*. Jews were believed to have control of the government, and that political change could only occur through the use of force to overthrow the government.

"Christian Identity" believers also professed death as the penalty for race-mixing and homosexuality, and that all non-Whites were to be exterminated or enslaved as a form of devotion to Jesus Christ. Mingled with fundamentalist Evangelicalism, the *"Christian Identity"* movement predicted the yet-to-be-fought battle of *Armageddon* would include a race war, when Jews would attempt to overtake the US with the so-called *"New World Order."* These were the thoughts foremost on the minds of various violent individuals who stormed the US Capitol on January 6.

A message posted to a social media platform associated with the *"Proud Boys"* on September 7, 2020, encapsulated the fear that drove militant groups to violence, the fear of the *"Great Replacement."* The posted message read: *"The true minority in this world ARE whites. White children are less than 3% of the worlds [sic] population. I think since white majority countries are on a pathway to extinction, we should correctly refer to non-whites by their true names. Worldwide majority."*

❖

The ideology behind the *"Christian Identity"* movement infiltrated mainstream awareness during the Trump years. Pronouncements of White nationalism were the justification for the mass shooting at a synagogue in Pittsburgh in 2018, the mass shooting at a *Walmart* in El Paso in 2019, and the Christchurch, New Zealand mosque shootings in 2019. A mass shooting is defined as an attack where at least four people are killed.

Identity

On a sabbath morning, the Pittsburgh shooter killed 11 members of the Tree of Life Synagogue and wounded 6 others. It was the deadliest attack in the history of American Jews. The shooter's social media accounts were ripe with *"Christian Identity"* conspiracies that described Jews as "globalists" who sought to destroy the White race in their "traditional homelands" (namely the US and Europe) through the deliberate importation of non-Whites. One of the shooter's online rants read: *"Jews are waging a propaganda war against Western Civilization, and it is so effective that we are headed towards certain extinction within the next 200 years and we're not even aware of it. You are living in a critical time in history where the internet has given us a small window of opportunity to snap our people out of their brainwash."*

On a sunny Saturday morning in August, news reports interrupted regular programming to explain that a young man from Allen, Texas drove 650 miles to El Paso, entered a *Walmart Supercenter* with a semiautomatic rifle, and in the scope of only a few minutes killed 22 people and injured another 24 before surrendering to the police. The El Paso shooter published his extremist manifesto on the internet before the slaughter that was described as the most lethal anti-immigrant attack in US history. In his manifesto, the El Paso shooter wrote: *"This attack is in response to the Hispanic invasion of Texas. They are the instigators, not me. I am simply defending my country from cultural and ethnic replacement brought on by an invasion."* The El Paso shooter raged against "racial mixing" and specifically noted his admiration for the Christchurch shooter.

The El Paso massacre took place mere blocks from my childhood home. The elementary school that I attended from kindergarten through eighth grade (only two blocks from my front door) served as a command center for the FBI in the aftermath of the attack. The school also served as a gathering place where many stunned and sobbing people first heard news of their loved ones who were killed or injured. I couldn't help but feel personally connected to the tragedy.

Prior to the attack, the El Paso shooter's *Twitter* account included a photo of the name "Trump" spelled out in a variety of firearms. Trump wrote on *Twitter*: *"Today's shooting in El Paso, Texas was not only tragic, it was an act of cowardice. I know that I stand with everyone in the Country to condemn today's hateful act. There are no reasons or excuses that will ever justify killing innocent people…"* Despite his public condemnation, Trump's racist rants precipitated the violence. For

The Climate of Truth

years, he repeatedly referred to an "invasion" at the US southern border from immigrants seeking asylum. At a campaign rally, Trump said of the immigrants, "They're bringing drugs, they're bringing crime, they're rapists, and some I assume are good people." In a late night tweet, he repeated his refrain, *"The Democrats seem intent on having people and drugs pour into our country from the Southern Border, risking thousands of lives in the process. It is my duty to protect the lives and safety of all Americans…We must build a Great Wall…"* Trump vowed that his infamous border wall would be paid for by Mexico, but that never happened. Privately, Trump asked for the border wall to be electrified and topped with spikes that could pierce human flesh; he even asked for a price estimate. Trump also suggested that immigrants should be shot in the legs to slow them down, but he was told that would be illegal.

Trump's border policies permanently separated immigrant children from their parents and locked them indefinitely in cages. Trump even questioned why the US should allow more people to enter from "shithole countries," indicating those inhabited by people of color; he further suggested that the US should allow more immigrants from countries like Norway instead, identified by White supremacists as an origin nation for the "superior" White race.

In response to the El Paso shooting, *Walmart* stopped selling bullets for semiautomatic rifles and handguns, though it remained one of the largest sellers of weapons and ammunition in the country. *Walmart* briefly removed firearms and ammunition from its stores in June 2020, after several locations were damaged in protests following the murder of George Floyd. However, those items were returned to the sales floor after *Walmart* determined the incidents of civil unrest to be "isolated."

Within 24 hours of the El Paso shooting, a copycat in Dayton, Ohio killed 9 people at a bar and injured 27 more with a modified AR-15. Police killed the gunman within 32 seconds. An investigation showed the Dayton gunman had been disciplined in high school for planning a mass attack, and he followed social media posts that identified the El Paso shooter as a White supremacist just hours before. The double massacres in El Paso and Dayton were not enough to elicit any changes to gun control laws, but they were successful in temporarily halting the Democratic Presidential primary.

The terrorist who gunned down 51 people at two mosques in Christchurch, New Zealand, in March of 2019, used the slogan *"The*

Identity

Great Replacement" in his 74-page manifesto. He livestreamed the onslaught on *Facebook*, and the video was quickly shared on *Twitter, Instagram* and *YouTube*. The Christchurch shooter, who described himself as *"just an ordinary White man,"* denounced immigrants as *"an assault on the European people."* He further added, *"This is ethnic replacement. This is cultural replacement. This is racial replacement. This is WHITE GENOCIDE."* The shooter contextualized his massacre as a means *"to show the invaders [immigrants] that our lands will never be their lands, our homelands are our own and that, as long as a white man still lives, they will NEVER conquer our lands."* He also described Muslims as *"invaders"* and Trump as *"a symbol of renewed White identity and common purpose."*

America, New Zealand and Australia were seen as the last stand by some White supremacists who hoped to create an exclusively White homeland. Several White nationalist groups, including skinheads, *Ku Klux Klan* members, and militias had taken up the cause of the so-called *"Northwest Imperative;"* it was the notion of an Aryan nation in the Pacific Northwest of the US, comprised of Washington State, Oregon, and Idaho. Prior to stabbing two people to death on a Portland, Oregon train in 2017, the racist perpetrator posted on *Facebook* that America should be *"balkanized."* The same term, referring to breaking up a country or region into distinctly separate ethnic groups, also appeared in the Christchurch shooter's manifesto.

❖

Despite knowing the ideology of *"The Great Replacement"* had triggered racial violence for generations, right-wing public personalities began to parrot the very jargon used by the mass shooters noted in this chapter in the months that followed the insurrection. This took the inflammatory rhetoric of *"Christian Identity"* further into the mainstream. In early April 2020, Tucker Carlson, a political commentator for *Fox News*, said "In order to win and maintain power, Democrats plan to change the population of the country." Carlson told his audience that the goal of the Democratic Party was "to make you [conservatives] irrelevant." He continued, "I know that the left and all the little gatekeepers on *Twitter* become intentionally hysterical when you use the term 'replacement.'" Tucker

The Climate of Truth

Carlson even said that immigrants make the US "poor and dirtier and more divided."

Tucker Carlson failed to mention that Hitler and his henchmen cited American precedents to justify Nazi atrocities. Hitler praised America's racist Jim Crow laws and how enslavement of African-Americans was written into the US Constitution. Hitler used American race law to justify "the final solution," mass annihilation of Jews in death camps. Hitler pointed to Thomas Jefferson's statement of the need to "eliminate" Native Americans, and how a population of millions of Indigenous people had been systematically reduced to 200,000. California's forced sterilization laws (which began in 1909 to target Blacks, Hispanics, and the mentally ill) directly inspired the Nazi sterilization law of 1934. Zyklon-B was used to disinfect immigrants at the El Paso border, and was also used to kill a Chinese immigrant in the world's first gas chamber execution in Nevada in 1924. Zyklon-B's potency was modified by the Nazis for mass executions in the Auschwitz gas chambers. In *"Mein Kampf"* Hitler applauded America's practice of "excluding certain races from naturalization." A *"Vanity Fair"* report in 1990 revealed that Trump kept a book of Hitler's speeches at his bedside. When questioned about it, Trump was reported to have said, "If I had these speeches, and I am not saying that I do, I would never read them." Nevertheless, neo-Nazis were the first to compare Trump to Hitler.

Tucker Carlson also fueled the anti-vaccination and the anti-mask brigades: "If vaccines are effective, there's no reason for people who have received the vaccine to wear masks or avoid physical contact. So maybe it [the vaccine] doesn't work, and they are simply not telling you that." He called for his viewers to report parents for child abuse if they had their children wear COVID masks. He also called for his viewers to confront and harass mask wearers. Carlson described observing a mask wearer as "like watching a grown man expose himself in public. That's disgusting! Put that away please! We don't do that here." Evangelicals decried the vaccines as the biblical *"Mark of the Beast"* and a tool of the *"One World Government,"* falling in line with antisemitic *"Christian Identity"* terminology. These ideas motivated attacks against doctors who were fighting to stem the pandemic. All the doctors who served on Trump's COVID Task Force received death threats; some required full-time security squads to protect them and their families.

Identity

According to the *Institute for Research and Education on Human Rights*, once the *"Christian Identity"* prophecies failed to materialize in Trump's reelection, his followers immediately shifted their attention back to their favored conspiracy theories. *Facebook* alone had 3.2 million members dedicated to anti-mask and anti-vaccine groups. Another demographics study from the University of Chicago discovered the bulk of those involved in *Facebook* disinformation campaigns were educated middle class and upper-middle class women. Women carried signs to anti-vaccine rallies that read: *"Nurses Against Mandatory Vaccines,"* and *"This is America, Not Communist China."* More than 100 nurses and healthcare employees in Houston filed suit against one hospital in an attempt to avoid mandatory COVID vaccination. The nurses objected to being used as "guinea pigs" in a vaccination "experiment." The court dismissed the lawsuit, stating that the hospital was working in accord with public policy to save lives from COVID. The court noted that hospital staff were free to refuse the vaccine, but if they did, they would simply have to work elsewhere. As the pandemic progressed, employees working in government, healthcare, schools, and care facilities were mandated to get vaccinated or they would lose their jobs.

According to Samuel Perry, a sociology professor at the University of Oklahoma, "there is a tendency within White Christian Nationalism to want to believe those kinds of conspiracies, because I think it reinforces this idea of 'us versus them.' The problem is, the people who are feeding that fear [such as *Fox News*] have an incentive to keep stoking that fear because people keep clicking [on websites] and people keep listening." Fearmongering was an extremely lucrative business for right-wing outlets.

❖

I saw a woman in my styling chair only once before she moved out of my area with her husband. While I colored her hair, she described an incident at a local franchise barber shop that was witnessed by her husband as he was getting his haircut. A tense and angry White man walked into the barber shop without wearing a mask. His hand was on the grip of a gun that protruded from his waistband. The establishment was staffed entirely by women. The angry White man approached the front desk, where he demanded a haircut without being made to wear a mask. A terrified lady barber

The Climate of Truth

picked up the phone, dialed her corporate office, and handed the phone to the angry man. The corporate office explained to the angry man that mask wearing was required under state law for COVID safety, and then told him to vacate the premises immediately. Everyone in the room froze, wondering what would happen next. To everyone's great relief, the angry White man cursed a bit and then promptly exited the building. It was a situation that could easily have devolved into another tragedy that hit the national news.

Based on political identity, anti-vaccination and anti-mask sentiments were fed by distrust in government, ignorance about how the vaccines actually worked, and misinformation about the vectors of viral transmission. Sociologist Samuel Perry noted Evangelicals to be the group most likely to refuse vaccination and masks. For example, a pastor from Louisiana who declared himself to be a prophet, misrepresented the vaccines: "If you have a 99.6% survival rate, why do you want to contaminate your bloodstream with something that may or may not harm you?" The sentiment reflected the pastor's unfounded belief that the vaccines somehow altered human DNA upon injection. The pastor continued from his pulpit, "I'll tell you today, if being anti-mask and anti-vaccine is anti-government, then I'm proud to be anti-government!" That mindset proved to be a huge roadblock given that, according to the *Pew Research Center*, Evangelicals comprised 25% of the US population. At least 70% of the population needed to be vaccinated in order to achieve herd immunity against COVID, meaning Evangelicals could prevent the US from achieving that goal. Furthermore, distrust of the vaccine program was known to have been fueled by an aggressive disinformation campaign posted on social media platforms by Chinese and Russian cyber agents; the intent was to sow discord among factions in the US in order to destabilize the country, and it seemed to be working.

In March 2017, US House Republican Steve King wrote on *Twitter: "We can't restore our civilization with somebody else's babies."* In a January 2019 interview with the *"New York Times,"* King said, *"White nationalist, White supremacist, Western civilization — how did that language become offensive?"* Following the interview, King, a 16-year veteran of the House at the time, was stripped of his committee assignments, citing his incendiary supremacist remarks. He ran for reelection, but lost the 2020 Republican primary, and left office three days before the insurrection.

Identity

Only one month after the insurrection, lawmakers in the House stripped Georgia Republican Marjorie Taylor Greene of her committee assignments as well. Wearing a mask emblazoned with the words *"Free Speech,"* Greene held a press conference where she unabashedly proclaimed the Republican party "belonged to Trump and to no one else." An open *"QAnon"* conspiracist, Greene used her social media accounts to assert that a passenger plane never hit the Pentagon during the 9/11 terrorist attacks, and that the mass shootings at Parkland High School and Sandy Hook Elementary School were *"false flag"* events staged by Democrats. She also circulated statements that advocated for the murder of Democrat politicians, whom she targeted as *"Satan-worshiping pedophiles."* She often used anti-Semitic and Islamophobic rhetoric, including a claim that President Obama was a Muslim who *"opened up our borders to invasion by Muslims."* Greene did not apologize for her actions, but simply said her social media posts were "words of the past." Apparently, her shallow excuse was sufficient for the majority of House Republicans to vote in favor of keeping her in Congress. Minority Leader Kevin McCarthy declared that he had no plans to further discipline Greene, and that he had already given her a "firm talking-to."

Only three months after the insurrection, Congresswoman Greene continued with her antics by announcing her intent to form the *"America First Caucus,"* calling for "respect for uniquely Anglo-Saxon political traditions." The idea of the caucus, supported in advance by a handful of Greene's Republican colleagues, pushed the belief that "mass migration" posed a threat to "the long-term existential future of America as a unique country with a unique culture and a unique **identity**." Greene shelved her plans to form the caucus after a few days, having received public rebukes from other members of her party. However, several Congressional candidates popped up in campaigns across the country spouting the same *"QAnon,"* racist rhetoric, and many of those new candidates were leading in the polls. Furthermore, Marjorie Taylor Greene repeatedly denounced the effectiveness of the COVID vaccines and wearing masks to slow the spread of the virus. She went so far as to compare mask mandates to Jews being forced to wear the yellow star of David sewn onto their clothes as they were sent to their deaths at concentration camps during the Holocaust. On New Year's Day 2022, when only 62% of Americans were fully vaccinated, and when the US was soon to report more than 1,000,000 daily COVID cases (the

The Climate of Truth

highest numbers ever recorded anywhere on the planet during the pandemic at the peak surge of the Omicron variant), *Twitter* permanently banned Marjorie Taylor Greene for spreading COVID misinformation.

Simultaneously, Pennsylvania Republican Scott Perry used a House Foreign Affairs Committee meeting to sound off with White nationalism. In reference to the number of people attempting to enter the US from the southern border, Perry remarked for the record, "For many Americans, what seems to be happening, or what they believe right now is happening, is what appears to them, is we're **replacing** natural-born, native-born Americans to permanently transform the landscape of this very nation." The supremacist seed was not only planted, but it had also germinated and branched out in the hallowed halls of Congress.

In April 2021 the Anti-Defamation League called for Tucker Carlson to be fired for his "long record of race-baiting." The ADL wrote to the *Fox Corporation's* CEO, "*Last night, in a segment on his program dealing with voting rights and allegations of voter disenfranchisement, Tucker Carlson disgustingly gave an impassioned defense of the white supremacist 'great replacement theory,' the hateful notion that the white race is in danger of being 'replaced' by a rising tide of non-whites. While couching his argument in terms of what he described as the Democratic Party attempting to replace traditional voters with immigrants from third-world countries, Carlson's rhetoric was not just a dog whistle to racists – it was a bullhorn.*" The ADL went on to describe how Carlson's show earned praise from well-known White supremacists, David Duke and Richard Spencer. In a written response to the ADL, the *Fox Corporation's* CEO defended Carlson: "*A full review of the guest interview indicates that Mr. Carlson decried and rejected replacement theory.*" The CEO continued with the manipulation, "*As Mr. Carlson himself stated during the guest interview, 'White replacement theory? No, no, this is a voting rights question.'*"

Regardless of how any of the politicized rhetoric was couched, analyzed or defended, there were 693 mass shootings in America following the insurrection through December 31, 2021. There were more than 44,838 deaths attributed to gun violence during that same period. It was a 68% increase in gun violence in only two years. The numbers didn't lie like some politicians. Despite vehement objections from law enforcement, Texas lawmakers made provisions for anyone to purchase a gun without a license or a permit. A federal judge also

Identity

overturned California's ban on assault weapons that had been in place since 1989. The judge ruled the ban on assault weapons violated the Second Amendment and prevented Californians from owning weapons that were commonly allowed in other states. Comparing an AR-15 assault rifle to a *Swiss Army Knife*, the judge issued a permanent injunction so the assault weapons ban could not be enforced. The judge willfully issued his ruling on National Gun Violence Awareness Day, ignoring the fact that the AR-15 was the weapon of choice for mass shooters.

It was clear that identity politics had become entrenched in our constitutional system, and that political ideologies inflamed the "us versus them" dynamic. It was also clear that we were precariously close to destroying our Democracy because of those divides. The rise of militant thinking (when politics melds with religion) was the harbinger of decline. In June of 2021, 198 scholars of Democracy from colleges and universities across America issued a written *"Statement of Concern"* regarding the very real and active threats to American Democracy. The scholars noted and condemned many of the elements included in this chapter as the basis for their concern. The scholars wrote: *"When democracy breaks down, it typically takes many years, often decades, to reverse the downward spiral. In the process, violence and corruption typically flourish, and talent and wealth flee to more stable countries, undermining national prosperity. It is not just our venerated institutions and norms that are at risk – it is our future national standing, strength, and ability to compete globally."* They concluded, *"Our democracy is fundamentally at stake. History will judge what we do at this moment."*

❖

As usual, I was listening to the national news while preparing to open the shop for the day. It was a sunny morning in mid-August 2021, just eight months after the insurrection. I turned my head to face the television when I heard that another angry White man was threatening to detonate a bomb in front of the Library of Congress. He was in the driver's seat of a mud-stained, black, four-by-four pickup truck with a detonator in his hand, and a large metal drum at his side. He'd pulled the truck up onto the sidewalk. The Library of Congress was evacuated, as was the Supreme Court across the street and the US Capitol one block west. The streets were cordoned off by

The Climate of Truth

police. It took hours for emergency responders to negotiate the angry White man's surrender. All the while, he livestreamed his rants on *Facebook*. The suspect bomber demanded Joe Biden's resignation and Trump's reinstatement.

"We've got a few options here, Joe," the angry White man said. "You shoot me, two and a half blocks are going with me. And then you're talking about a **revolution**."

At that precise moment in time, the stereo began to play the angry White man's words, although delivered in a far different context. The song was from one of Tracy Chapman's greatest hits from her debut album in 1988.

"Don't you know
*They're talkin' bout a **revolution**?*
It sounds like a whisper
Poor people gonna rise up
And get their share
Poor people gonna rise up
And take what's theirs"

As an entirely unknown Black female vocalist in 1988, Tracy Chapman's debut album earned her three Grammys. The album remained one of the best-sellers of all time for a female artist and *"Talkin' Bout a Revolution"* went on to become one of the anthems of the *"Black Lives Matter"* movement.

On his *Facebook* livestream, the angry White man in the black, mud-stained pickup truck described himself as a "patriot." Looking into the camera during his standoff with police, he said, "The south is coming for you, Joe," referring to President Biden.

Police did not find a bomb in the black pickup truck. The whole event was a ruse, but it planted more violent ideas in the minds of those who agreed with the angry White man.

Anniversary

❧ ✦ ☙

My birthday was nine days after the insurrection. It was also the day the World COVID death toll surpassed two million souls and the US death toll reached 390,000. An American life was being lost every 28 seconds.

My birthday began with a text from a lady who was a special education teacher: *"Hi Mike, so my husband started to not feel well yesterday, and I encouraged him to get tested and he just now got a call from Dr that he is COVID positive. So, I will be in quarantine…after I have been cleared, can I contact you to reschedule? Thank you so much, and sorry for the late notice. This all just happened in the last 24 hours."*

She contracted COVID herself and suffered serious effects. She told me that she thought she was going to die. She also mentioned that her husband was an addict whose complete disregard for COVID safety caused her to become infected when he met his druggie friends without wearing a mask. "He had a cow just having to wear a mask when we went grocery shopping together!" she fumed. "I told him, 'You should try wearing a mask for eight hours while managing a room full of autistic children!'"

By early summer of 2021, her husband relapsed and disappeared for the fifth time. The special education teacher changed the locks to their apartment as she'd done every time he disappeared before. She divided the marital savings and stashed her half in a private account.

The Climate of Truth

For her safety, I urged her to alert her landlord to the situation, but she was too embarrassed to do it.

"When did this happen?" I asked her as I foiled her dishwater blonde in a tight weave with high-lift bleach mixed with protective buffers.

The special education teacher burst into tears. "Just last night," she cried.

"Why are you surprised? We've talked about the possibility this would happen for months," I said.

"I don't know," was all she could muster.

"You're really mad at him. I get it," I said.

"I told him if he did it again, I would divorce him." Her tears moistened the top edge of her mask and stained the fabric with mascara.

"And?"

"I guess now I have to make good on my threat," she said, barely able to breathe.

"You feel betrayed because he chose the drugs over you – but that's what addicts do," I said. "You already know this…His behavior is not your fault. You're not making threats. You're just protecting yourself, as you should. You would be harming yourself if you were to close your eyes and wish the problem away…As his wife, you are financially responsible for whatever he does. They will come after you if he causes harm to anyone else."

"I already took his name off the car insurance," she said, tracing her finger across a red and black tattoo of a mermaid that was wrapped around her forearm.

"That's wise," I said, gently touching her shoulder. "I know a very good attorney. Would you like her number?" I offered.

"I can't afford it," she said quickly.

"Just a consultation to figure out your options?"

"I'll think about it," she said, tugging at her bangs until several pieces snapped off in her fingers. She constantly pulled at her hair when she talked about her husband.

Anniversary

"OK then. It's really none of my business anyway," I said, "but I might also suggest the YWCA up the street here. They have a whole group of advocates who work on these kinds of cases for women. I'm pretty sure it's free."

"That sounds like a good idea," she said, her eyes fading further away from reality. "Right now, I just want to be very blonde. As blonde as I can be. Give me as much blonde as possible. I need you to make the highlights as close together as you can. Just give me a lot more blonde."

"When we met, your hair was breaking off in my fingers because it was overprocessed," I said. "We've spent almost a year healing your hair, and now we've got it in much better shape…I say this respectfully, so please receive it that way…I will not do anything to harm your hair. I'm not going to dump a whole bunch of bleach on your head, even if you push me to do it because you are in emotional turmoil."

She looked up at me with ice blue eyes that had swollen and turned bright red. "Thank you for saving me from myself," she said. "I'm just in a panic about my hair."

"Honey, you're in a panic about a whole lot of things. But you're safe here right now," I said. Satisfied that I did what I could for her, I withdrew from the discussion and let her rest with her thoughts while I finished my work. All her hair appointments went that way, drenched in her catharsis.

I sent the special education teacher a text to confirm her next appointment six weeks later. She texted me back: *"I won't be coming to this appointment. I need to cancel all of my upcoming appointments that I've made with you. Thank you."*

The lawyer I knew confirmed the special education teacher was an enabler who was unlikely to leave her husband, even though it was the healthy choice. The lawyer further explained that both parties in that dysfunctional marriage were locked in a vicious cycle of addictive codependency that was very common, and that both parties usually ended up destroying each other. I also knew the special education teacher would probably blame me for her problems if I continued to listen to them, so it was best that we parted company.

I responded to the special education teacher's text very briefly: *"I wish you well."* She swiftly replied, *"Thanks, you too,"* and that was the

The Climate of Truth

graceful end of it. One can only be of help to someone in crisis if and when that person truly wants to be helped. Dabblers never heal.

❖

A favorite client responded to a text I sent her to confirm her appointment: "*Beeeeooootttccchhhh! – wild rona couldn't keep me away! (Emoji: Red heart, Blonde woman waving.)*"

Confused, I texted back, *"What's a rona?"*

She shot back an eye roll emoji with the word "Corona!" I felt like a fool.

The doorbell rang, prompting Irma to bark her head off. Startled by the sudden outburst, another client nearly jumped out of the styling chair in fright.

"Sorry, darling," I said. "I wasn't expecting anyone to ring the bell." I unbolted the front door to find my legal assistant friend, Tiffy. She stood six feet away from the door in her mask. She'd placed a homemade birthday cake on my front doormat – Martha Stewart's devil's food German chocolate with roasted pecans and gobs of fresh shredded coconut. The cake was big enough for a party of 20, but no friends would be over to share it with me because it wasn't safe to celebrate together. Tiffy called it a "naked" cake, and it was wrapped in blue cellophane with stars and stripes poking out. A miniature balloon on a stick accompanied the display. Were it not for Tiffy's cake, I wouldn't have thought about my birthday at all. I didn't light the single candle imbedded in the top layer, and I felt guilty eating a small corner of the cake when so many people were dying.

"The feds have a lot of insurrection nutcases on a 'no-fly list,'" Tiffy said, excitedly as she kept her distance on the front porch. "Isn't that fun! Homeland Security is issuing a domestic terrorism alert. All the state Capitols are being boarded up. Russia is pushing the '*Antifa*' conspiracy, and Trump is eating it up. Radicalized right-wingers are beating up journalists in the name of freedom of speech. The '*Boogleoo Bois*' are at our state Capitol right now in their fatigues and helmets with Hawaiian shirts, carrying AR-15s, yelling that Democrats and Black people stole the election."

I realized that because of the *"Boogeloo Bois"* (a group of violent extremists), I would have to forgo wearing my signature Hawaiian shirts in the shop for a while because that was their uniform. The thought of it disgusted me.

"The terrorists say they are 'peacefully protesting' to defend the constitution," Tiffy continued. "Isn't that fresh! But hate speech is not free speech. How the heck do you cover this in the news without giving all the hatemongers a giant megaphone?"

"I don't have the answer. It's the Trump show all day, every day," I said. "That's some megaphone."

"What a relief they kicked Trump off *Facebook* and *Twitter*! It's almost like we can all relax a little! But dictators all around the world are still allowed to tweet! Happy Birthday!" Tiffy squealed "Weeeeee!" Then she ran off.

When I called her later to thank her for the cake, she told me that Trump wanted a 21-gun salute send-off on his last day of office. Tiffy said the Pentagon denied the request. She also mentioned the "*MyPillow* guy" (Mike Lindell, one of Trump's confidantes) was seen leaving the Oval Office with notes titled "TAKEN IMMEDIATELY TO SAVE THE CONSTITUTION." Captured by a photojournalist, Lindell's notes outlined the steps he thought Trump should take to overturn the election, including a declaration of martial law. It was bizarre to think that threats to national security had to be revealed through a reporter's telephoto lens.

Other news stories on my birthday detailed how the largest intercontinental ballistic missile in the world was engineered by North Korea to deliver multiple nuclear warheads to the US. Trump worked to execute more people on death row before he left office than had been done in the previous six decades. He would also issue another 100 pardons in his final days in office, but he did not offer any comment about the pandemic.

Conversely, Biden's incoming director of the CDC said the country should expect at least 500,000 COVID deaths by mid-February 2021. It was an accurate prediction. In one of his regularly televised news conferences as the President-Elect, Biden explained that the national COVID vaccine program was in shambles. Trump's Health Secretary, Alex Azar, lied about having vaccine stored in the national stockpile when none had been reserved or even ordered. Vowing to "manage the hell out of the vaccine program," Biden promised at least 100 million doses would be administered in his first 100 days in office. Critics said it was nowhere near the pace needed to

The Climate of Truth

bring the US to herd immunity. Biden's announcement was made at the same time a doctor died from an adverse reaction to the *Pfizer* vaccine. The doctor had no history of medical problems, but he died from a massive brain bleed following the injection. A few days later, after several other people had severe allergic reactions to a specific batch of the *Moderna* vaccine, a temporary pause in dosing was initiated when the vaccine rollout was already painfully slow. The adverse reactions to the vaccines fueled the ire of the anti-vaccine conspiracists and dramatically increased vaccination hesitancy across the nation.

❖

Crystal was the next appointment on my birthday. She had long, baby-fine hair and hadn't been to a salon in over a year. After spending eight months out of work, she finally got her first unemployment check from the state and decided to spend the money on a spiral perm and hair products to enhance the curl. She quit her last waitress job just before the pandemic hit, so she didn't qualify for regular unemployment benefits. However, she told me that she did qualify for COVID assistance.

"I'm rolling in the dough now, I tell ya! It's about time!" she said, sporting talons that were two inches long and painted bubble-gum pink. She worked previously at Bingo parlors, at the American Legion, at a nonprofit geared to assist at-risk youth, and even at construction sites. "I'm a worker bee!" she said proudly as she examined her enormous pink fingernails. "I'm fixing to get ready to go back to work now. So, I need new nails, new hair, new clothes, and the most important thing -- a new car! I'm hoping for a cashier's job at the *Winco.* They're employee owned, you know, and they have great bennies…I always wanted to own a grocery store!"

Crystal spent her unemployed days watching talk shows on television, and she took a fierce interest in the *Rue La La* shopping website where she bought some fancy facemask gizmo that was supposed to get rid of wrinkles. "It's usually pretty spendy," she said of the contraption. "But I got in for only $129.99! So I bought it because it's French. That means it must be good, right?"

Anniversary

"I have no idea, sorry," I said as I continued to wrap scores of perm rods in her long hair. "All I know is that I offer quality products made by dermatologists."

"Well," Crystal replied, "the lady sells it on TV, so it must be good, or else she wouldn't have a job."

"I can't speak to *Rue La La*," I said, "but I can tell you that you'll kill your spiral if you use crap shampoo. I won't be able to guarantee your perm."

Crystal was noticeably antsy, and barely able to sit still. Her legs bounced up and down rapidly. She had no eyelashes or eyebrows. Several of her teeth were missing; those still in her head were heavily stained. She had adult acne, and what appeared to be track marks up her arms. She had dark circles under her eyes, presumably from being deprived of sleep because she was so amped. I imagined that she tied rubber tubing around her bicep and held it in place with her teeth while she injected herself with narcotics. I wondered if someone in her family named her Crystal after their devotion to crystal meth.

Nazi troops were given meth so they would stay awake and alert for long periods of time. It made them far more aggressive, and they could march much further without stopping after being dosed. Nazi leaders used meth too because they believed it would help Germany win the war. So did Japanese Kamikaze pilots before they deliberately crashed their planes into enemy targets. Allied soldiers used meth to keep from getting drowsy during battle.

"My unemployment was extended until April. Isn't that sweet!" Crystal said. "I just might apply for a job before then, but there's no rush. Unemployment is a pretty good gig until then. I should just ride it out…I want to buy a tiny house. Or I can have one built for only $1500. That's all I need in the world. A small piece of land and a tiny house. That's my dream!"

It wasn't my place to judge her dream, but I felt incredibly guilty knowing (after the fact) that her spiral perm was being paid for with unemployment funds. I consoled myself by thinking she would have gotten the perm done somewhere anyway, and better that she got it done by me because I wouldn't wreck her hair.

"What do you think of Trump?" she asked, pointedly.

The question caught me by surprise. "Why do you want to know?"

The Climate of Truth

"Just curious," she said. "I think he's wonderful!"

I chose my words carefully. "I'm looking to the future. Biden's coming in with a very organized COVID vaccine program, and that's a huge priority for the country. Lives are at stake."

"Well…Everybody is welcome to their own opinion. I just think Trump was great because he helped a lot of people!"

I almost asked her to elaborate but thought better of inviting further discussion. In the end, she was delighted with her perm -- though I knew she wouldn't keep it up and that I would never see her again. Crystal was a one-perm wonder.

❖

The UK went into a month-long lockdown on November 4, 2020, because of the more infectious Alpha variant that originated there. On December 2, the UK rushed to be the first country in the world to approve the *Pfizer* vaccine as the local death toll surpassed 60,000. When two National Health Service workers had immediate allergic reactions to the first doses of the *Pfzier* vaccine, authorities urged those with a history of allergies to forgo vaccination. Also on December 2, Prime Minister Boris Johnson lifted the UK's COVID lockdown to begin the Christmas holiday season even though case counts were rapidly increasing. Scientists warned the UK was hurtling toward disaster, declaring the decision to open the country for Christmas a "mistake" and a "rash decision" that could "cost many lives." Scientists even warned the public not to gather with family and friends for the holiday. But just over two weeks later, the UK reported the most COVID infections since the start of the pandemic. The Prime Minister then pushed more than 44 million people back into lockdown to contain the "out of control" Alpha variant. More than 40 countries (including the US and Canada) suspended all travel to and from the UK just as a second COVID mutation emerged from South Africa known as the Beta variant. But it was too late; the Alpha variant was already confirmed in several European countries, all linked to UK travelers. While business revenues for the holiday season tanked, Queen Elizabeth tried to console her subjects in her annual Christmas message by telling them that they were "not alone."

Anniversary

Life in the UK was further complicated with organizational mishaps caused by *Brexit*, the UK's choice to leave the European Union. Supply chains were already falling apart because of COVID. Coupled with *Brexit* problems, supermarket shelves were increasingly empty and the supply chain was in danger of collapsing altogether. Lockdowns and increased COVID cases severely weakened the essential transportation workforce. Transport companies from the European Union began to avoid making deliveries to the UK because of bureaucratic red tape at UK ports. Deliveries of goods into the UK were cut in half, increasing fears of food shortages. Medical supplies were also becoming scarce and the cost of goods increased sharply because of those economic stressors. UK exports were also being held up at ports, causing boatloads of seafood to spoil. Fishermen threatened to dump mountains of rotted crustaceans on the steps of Parliament if the government failed to solve the export disaster.

Peggy was a petite UK citizen with a charming British accent. I'd known her for 24 years. She never gained an ounce in all the years I knew her. She was married to an American businessman. The day we met, she seemed so familiar to me that from then on I referred to her as "cousin Peg." She was disappointed with the haircuts she'd received before she met me because, as she explained, her ultra-fine hair always turned out flat and listless. She referred to her hair as "frog fur" and "wet seaweed on a rock." After her first appointment, she was so excited that I could make her hair look fluffy that she called her "Mum" in the outskirts of London to relay the news.

Over the years, Peggy's Mum came to my shop several times when she "popped over the pond to visit her fine, young American cousins." I did Mum's hair too on those occasions. Mum caressed my cheek adoringly as only a mother could do. "You remind me so much of my own dear, sweet Michael," she said, referring to her eldest son who died some years back. She offered to adopt me every time I saw her, and she even took to sending me Christmas cards each year from London. She wanted me to have as much Christmas as possible to make up for all the holidays I spent alone. It was odd that so many people wanted to shower Christmas upon me even though I was a Jew, but I didn't mind. I guess that made me an equal opportunity celebrator.

I watched Peggy's two young girls transform into married women with children and homes of their own. I was there when Peggy celebrated her American citizenship, and the few times she

The Climate of Truth

suffered broken bones. I applauded the opening of her café and was there when she decided to close it down years later. Through it all, the only sign of aging were the few additional silver strands that graced Peggy's head, and I always covered those up for her. I could have done her hair in my sleep. Like her mother, she always called me Michael instead of Mike, probably because the British preferred formality, no matter how many times you might insist otherwise.

Peggy was always cordial and appreciative. We never shared a terse word or disappointment, and there was never any angst between us. We were truly kindred spirits. Having lived in Italy for several years, Peggy helped me organize the trip of my lifetime to Rome, the Amalfi Coast, and the Adriatic Coast. She provided maps and travel guides, and helped me choose boutique hotels and sightseeing adventures. We would have made perfect travel buddies, and I often wondered if I could talk her into going with me to Florence, Venice and Milan because I didn't like having to travel alone. But I never asked, and I wouldn't consider traveling again until the pandemic was long past.

Peggy arrived for her usual hair appointment on my birthday, though I didn't inform her of the occasion. Our encounter began as it always did. "How's Mum?" I asked.

Peggy looked out at me from her mask with pain in her eyes. "It's not good, Michael."

"Did she fall again?"

"It's worse than that," she said.

"Let me mix your color, love, and then you can tell me everything."

In all the years I knew her, Peggy never raised her voice or got emotional. She was always very controlled with her choice of words, and she enunciated thoroughly and deliberately with delicate precision as if she was tasting each syllable. Nothing about Peggy was coincidental.

I returned with her color formulas, a cream base applied with a brush, and a liquid in a squeeze bottle to refresh the tone of her faded ends. I always counseled my clients that permanent color should not be applied over and over to the same length of hair, or it would cause damage and make the color look muddy. Good technique was all about color balancing -- making the hair color appear the same from

Anniversary

the scalp to the ends, even though different pigments were used in each section.

"So, what happened, my dear?" I asked as I began painting her roots.

"You remember when Mum had those terrible fainting spells a few years ago?"

"When your sister found her unconscious on the bathroom floor in a pool of blood?"

"Precisely," Peggy said.

"Because she fell and hit her head?"

A look of sadness filled Peggy's eyes. "We nearly lost her then."

"Yes, I remember."

"Well, it's happened again," she said. "What a saga."

"You're not going to tell me that she's…."

"No, but she's still quite ill," she said, adjusting her mask higher on her nose. "But I want you to know that she's doing better than she was."

"Fill me in," I said, working through the quadrants of her head with my color brush.

"The surgeries are all closed, you know, because of COVID," Peggy said. "It's nearly impossible to communicate with a doctor when there is a medical emergency. Mum was faint and lethargic, just like before, but no one would listen to us. I'm trying to call the doctors long distance on the telephone, and it's absolutely useless."

"If it's anything like here, the hospitals are all overwhelmed with COVID patients," I said. "The doctors and nurses are more than exhausted. They just can't keep up with all the cases."

"Mum waited her whole life to be taken care of by the National Health Service, and it's not even meeting her most basic needs. Not at all. I would venture that the National Health Service is actually killing her off, Michael."

"Malpractice?" I asked.

"It's worse than that. It's utter stupidity…We had to fight to get her in for a simple blood test to detect her sodium levels, because

The Climate of Truth

that's what had gone awry before. We had to take her to a car park of all places, in the cold of winter mind you, to get her blood drawn. And then they promptly lost her blood samples."

"As if an elderly woman in her condition has blood to spare," I said.

"My thoughts exactly," Peggy said with a stiff nod of her head. "The hospitals are barely functioning. There's COVID absolutely everywhere and it's now more contagious than ever. So I'm concerned, Michael, that if the sodium situation doesn't kill Mum off, COVID could take her instead."

"Did she have to go back for a second blood test because they lost the first one?"

"Yes, and as you can imagine, we were all terrified that they would lose the sample again," she said. "They called two days later to say that Mum's condition was quite serious."

"Duh!" I said.

"And they were sending an ambulance for her straight away," Peggy said. "They determined she had a blood clot."

"Oh no! How awful!"

"She's in hospital two days. We are not allowed to see her. It's impossible to get someone on the telephone to explain what's happening. Mum is delirious and can hardly speak. So my sister goes straightaway to the hospital and demands to speak to any doctor she could summon to the lobby. A doctor finally comes to her, and he insists Mum's suffering from a blood clot. But my sister explained to the doctor that it wasn't a blood clot, that it was more likely Mum's sodium was depleted like it was three years ago when she nearly died."

"I bet the doctor didn't like being told off by your sister. What did he say?" I asked.

"He said <u>prove</u> it!" There was an unprecedented flash of anger in Peggy's eyes.

"Get out of town!"

"My sister was told to hunt up all of Mum's medical records and thank goodness our family are excellent record keepers. My sister sent the pertinent information over for the doctor's 'consideration.'"

Anniversary

"When did this happen?" I asked.

"December 12th. They were treating Mum for a blood clot when all along she was actually suffering from depleted sodium again. She kept fainting because it got so bad."

"Did they get the sodium thing sorted out? Is she stable again?"

Peggy inhaled deeply. "On Christmas Eve they called and said for my sister to come get Mum immediately because they were closing the ward down due to COVID."

"Was she well enough to leave the hospital?"

"Not at all," Peggy said bluntly. "When they wheeled her out, my sister did not even recognize her. She looked like the victim of a concentration camp."

"Jeeze! Weren't they feeding her?" I said.

"It gets worse, Michael…We found out she was nearly in a coma in hospital. And we barely kept her out of a coma because my sister kept screaming at the doctor to give Mum the bloody sodium tablets!"

"Because they were still calling it a blood clot when it wasn't?"

"Thank goodness we got Mum out of there and my sister was able to take care of her and give her the sodium. It was a lot of work…And then my sister discovered they did not extend the prescription, and we couldn't get the doctor on the phone to get more sodium."

"Oh no. What happened?"

"Mum relapsed," Peggy said, trying very hard not to hyperventilate. "The regular pharmacist did not have more sodium tablets in stock. There wasn't any to be had anywhere. And Mum's regular physician was never informed about her condition. We couldn't get ahold of him either. So we did the only thing we could do. My sister sent her son to the hospital pharmacy wearing a visor, mask and goggles. Because no one else had a supply of sodium tablets. It took days for Mum to get well…We ran out of sodium tablets several more times, and it took days to get the prescription extended. The doctor said it wasn't safe to bring Mum back to hospital because of COVID and we were instructed to nurse her at

The Climate of Truth

home. This was three days ago, January 12, and the severity of Mum's condition required hospitalization, but she couldn't be admitted."

"I am so sorry to hear about this tragedy. What's happening now? Is she feeling better?"

"There's more," Peggy said defiantly.

"What else could they do to her?"

"The registrar called," Peggy said.

"Why?"

"To argue that Mum needed to be in hospital immediately to be treated for a blood clot and she was sending an ambulance because it was a life-threatening situation," Peggy said, making sure to sit perfectly still in her rage.

"Not again!"

"Thank God my sister is a fastidious notetaker. She relayed to the registrar how the doctor sent Mum home because of COVID, and that she was too weak and vulnerable to be carted back and forth like a sack of potatoes. I am quite proud of my sister. She got very firm."

"Good Lord."

Peggy cleared her throat with finesse. "She told the registrar off quite well. 'It would be prudent of you to think of Mum's future course of treatment, not what was done to her so shabbily over these past several weeks."

"Is Mum getting her sodium tablets now?"

"Thankfully, yes…I truly sympathize with the plight of doctors right now, but this was beyond ridiculous. They nearly killed Mum three to four times over the past month…My sister was a better doctor than they were…If it weren't for my sister, Mum wouldn't be with us anymore." Peggy looked down at her lap, desperately trying to contain herself.

I took her by the hand and held it to my chest. "And you can't get on a plane and fly over there to help."

"They won't let anyone in or out," Peggy said, stiffening her spine. "Dealing with life and death situations by text on a cellphone and using *What'sApp* -- that is what the world has come to."

Anniversary

The stereo began to play Michael Bublé's cover of the ballad "*Always on My Mind*," first recorded in 1972 by Gwen McRae, but made famous later that same year by Elvis Presley and then by Willie Nelson ten years later. As explained by one of the songwriters, the ballad "was one long apology. It's sort of like all guys who screw up and would love nothing better than to pick up the phone and call their wives and say, 'Listen, honey, I could have done better, but I want you to know that you were always on my mind.'"

> "*Little things I should have said and done*
> *I just never took the time*
> *You were always on my mind*
> *You were always on my mind*"

Peggy's eyes welled up with tears when she heard Michael Bublé's mellow voice sing those lyrics. "Before my father died," she said while wiping her eyes, "my husband used to sing this this song with him when they did Karaoke together. It was so beautiful. It always got me. Makes me cry every time." She made a point to look right at me. "I believe in signs, Michael. The fact that this song is playing at this moment while we've been talking about Mum -- it's telling me that my father is here listening to us. He's telling us that Mum is going to be alright."

When the Delta variant began to surge in our county over the following summer, I received a text from Peggy at the crack of dawn. She was scheduled for my first appointment that morning. "*Michael, I apologize sincerely, but I have to cancel my appointment this morning as I am not feeling well at all. I don't know what it is, perhaps a summer cold. I know this is difficult for you as a small business, so I am happy to pay the late cancellation fee. I would feel just terrible if I passed whatever this is on to you, so it's best to be cautious. I am so sorry this happened so last minute. Stay safe and well, and I will call you to reschedule when I'm feeling better next week.*"

Within days of Peggy's text, the Delta variant strangled her lungs with a thick carpet of green fungus. The Delta variant accounted for 98% of all COVID infections in the summer surge of 2021, and it was 60% more contagious than the original strain from Wuhan, China. Peggy died with a viral load 300 times higher in her nasal pharynx and lungs. She was infected along with her husband when they chose

The Climate of Truth

to fly to Michigan to visit her in-laws. Though they both wore masks the entire journey, they were crammed into crowded airport waiting areas for several hours because of travel delays. Her husband's symptoms were far worse at first, but his fever waned on the sixth day. Peggy's symptoms were initially mild, but on the seventh day she was unable to breathe. All of the local hospitals were over capacity and could not accept any more patients. She died sitting in her easy chair because the ambulance could not deliver her to the emergency room. There weren't enough doctors and nurses to offer treatment to everyone who needed it. People who were dying from heart attacks, strokes or car accidents could not be treated either because all of the hospital beds were filled with COVID patients.

Peggy cancelled her last hair appointment when her symptoms first began. She thought she had a mild cold until her husband tested positive for COVID. When I called to check on her, she sounded raspy, but not like someone who would die the following day. Her last words to me were, "You see, it was the right call that I cancelled my appointment with you when I was feeling a bit under the weather." Both Peggy and her husband were conservatives who refused to get vaccinated. More than 98% of new COVID infections at the time were among the unvaccinated, a situation that was entirely preventable.

❖

Because she was busy organizing her move out of the White House, First Lady Melania Trump had not been seen in public since New Year's Eve. She was exceptionally slow to condemn the mob violence during the insurrection on January 6. When asked to make a public statement, she simply said "No." She finally produced a written statement five days later after being called out for her silence. In the written statement posted to the White House website, Melania Trump listed the names of six people who died as a result of the insurrection. She then wrote: "*I am disappointed and disheartened with what happened last week. I find it shameful that surrounding these tragic events there has been salacious gossip, unwarranted personal attacks, and false misleading accusations on me – from people who are looking to be relevant and have an agenda.*" Rather than helping to guide the nation in a nurturing may, Melania Trump managed to cast herself as a victim

Anniversary

of the insurrection before she condemned the violence that overtook the Capitol.

During the hours-long insurrection, she was conducting a much-maligned photo shoot of rugs at the White House, possibly for a coffee-table book that she hoped to publish. She was described as being "checked out" and "not in a place mentally or emotionally" to address the nation about the riot. Finally, on January 18, two days before she moved out of the White House, Melania Trump released her official seven-minute farewell video on *Twitter*. In her recorded message, she said, *"violence is never the answer."* She urged Americans to *"rise above what divides us,"* despite being the only First Lady in modern US history to snub her successor by refusing the traditional White House handover tour.

The same day Melania Trump released her farewell video, an independent review panel issued a report that criticized both China and the *World Health Organization* for not acting forcefully and quickly to contain the original COVID outbreak in Wuhan. The international panel pointed to the month-long delay in the declaration of a public health emergency of international concern. The review panel also criticized the *World Health Organization* for waiting more than three months to declare COVID a pandemic after there were already 118,000 confirmed cases and 4,000 deaths worldwide; COVID was finally declared a global pandemic after other health experts had already done so in the media.

SARS (Severe Acute Respiratory Syndrome) was a novel coronavirus that first appeared in Guangdong Province, China, in the fall of 2002. It spread to 29 countries through air travel, and there were 8,422 documented cases and 916 fatalities. After an unprecedented global public health effort with international cooperation, the epidemic was fully controlled within seven months. Accurate media coverage around the world augmented scientific data on SARS. However, as later happened with COVID, widespread hysteria culminated in racist backlash against Asian communities in the US and Canada. Sensationalized headlines like *"the world war against SARS"* contributed to Asians being blamed for the epidemic, even when there were no cases reported in various Chinatowns.

China was considered a diseased threat to the rest of the world, particularly because the Chinese were known to eat exotic animals like civets and bats, both known to harbor the SARS virus. SARS

The Climate of Truth

became widely known as the "yellow peril," and the public wrongly believed that Asian businesses and neighborhoods were sources of contagion. Images in the news of Asians wearing facemasks resulted in the boycotting of Asian businesses that caused up to a 90% drop in their revenue. An Asian coughing in public would cause mass panic that could empty a bus or a train car. "Coughing while Asian" was the equivalent in racial profiling to "driving while Black."

The federal government was primarily responsible for controlling the transmission and spread of communicable diseases from abroad and from one state to another. Congress delegated the responsibility of designating specific communicable diseases that would be subject to federal quarantine measures to the executive branch. President George W. Bush added SARS to the list of communicable diseases that allowed for the "apprehension and detention" of individuals to prevent community spread. However, international containment efforts were so effective against SARS that quarantine measures were not implemented in the US. Quarantines of large groups were limited to countries with hot zones of infection, such as China, Singapore, Taiwan, and Canada. Travel restrictions were the primary tool used to prevent SARS from spreading in the US.

By the time COVID was declared a global pandemic, there were more than 13 times the number of cases than what occurred during the entire SARS outbreak. "We talked about quarantine," Trump said at the outset of the COVID pandemic. "And by the end of the evening, it was tough to enforce, and something we didn't want to do."

A few years after SARS was fully contained, President Bush was engrossed in a book about the Spanish Flu pandemic of 1918. The Spanish Flu was the most virulent pandemic of the modern era, and it was also an H1-N1 strain. When he finished reading, Bush decided it was imperative for the US to have a bold national strategy to deal with 100-year pandemics. The strategy would include a global early-warning system, funding to develop rapid vaccine technology, and a national stockpile of critical supplies such as face masks and ventilators.

"A pandemic is a lot like a forest fire," Bush said at the time. "If caught early, it might be extinguished with limited damage. If allowed to smolder, undetected, it can grow to an inferno that can spread quickly beyond our ability to control it. In a pandemic, everything from syringes to hospital beds, respirators masks and

Anniversary

protective equipment would be in short supply." Prophetically, Bush warned scientists that a vaccine would be needed in record time to immunize every American in a pandemic "surge capacity." He also said, "many lives could be needlessly lost because we failed to act today." However, Bush's national pandemic response strategy was shelved.

The first American case of H1-N1 swine flu was identified on April 15, 2009. Ten days later, only three months into Obama's Presidency, the *World Health Organization* declared a public health emergency of international concern. The next day Obama released supplies from the national stockpile, including antiviral drugs, respirators, and personal protective equipment for healthcare workers. At the time, Vice President Biden was criticized for saying (in a television interview) that it wasn't a good idea to get on an airplane or ride the subway with the highly contagious swine flu on the rise. The airline industry accused Biden of fearmongering, and White House officials tried to backtrack his comments.

Two-and-a-half months after the first cases of COVID were reported in the US, Trump falsely claimed the Obama administration had left the national stockpile as "an empty shelf." However, an *NPR* correspondent was allowed to visit one national stockpile warehouse just months before Trump took office. The correspondent wrote: *"The inventory includes millions of doses of vaccines against bioterrorism agents like smallpox, antivirals in case of a deadly flu pandemic, medicines used to treat radiation sickness and burns, chemical agent antidotes, wound care supplies, IV fluids and antibiotics."* There were six national warehouses stocked with $7 billion in emergency healthcare products and equipment. It was true that the Obama administration did not adequately restock the tens of millions of N-95 respirator masks that were depleted during the swine flu pandemic, but that was because Congress did not appropriate the funds to do so. Instead of masks, managers of the stockpile decided to use their limited budget to purchase vaccines, pharmaceuticals, and flu medications. The Obama administration's efforts to beef up the ventilator stockpile failed because of manufacturing delays.

Trump's senior advisor (and son-in-law), Jared Kushner, added more controversy when he made a rare appearance at a COVID task force public briefing three months into the COVID pandemic. Kushner declared the national stockpile was "supposed to be <u>our</u> stockpile. It's not supposed to be states' stockpiles that they then use."

The Climate of Truth

The next morning, the *Strategic National Stockpile* website was suddenly altered to downplay its main objective to help provide states with emergency supplies. This move forced states to compete with each other to purchase emergency medical supplies, which immediately caused prices to climb exponentially and left many states without access to reliable resources. It was unprecedented for the federal government to refuse to organize on behalf of all states in a strategic pandemic response.

The CDC reported the first death from the H1-N1 outbreak on April 29, 2009. The *World Health Organization* declared H1-N1 a pandemic on June 11. President Obama deferred to health experts (including Dr. Fauci) and allowed them to lead public messaging on television. Conversely, Trump muzzled health experts and refused to allow them to appear on television or even to speak at COVID task force briefings. Instead, the White House insisted on controlling the narrative of the pandemic response.

The first doses of the H1-N1 vaccine were given in the US less than six months after the first case was detected. This happened because Congress cooperated and approved $8 billion for emergency H1-N1 relief. President Obama declared a national health emergency on October 24, 2009, but the emergency authorization of new and experimental antiviral drugs did not blunt the surge of infection. While the Obama administration generally got high marks for a swift response to the H1-N1 pandemic, there were delays in the manufacturing of the vaccine. The delays prevented full vaccine efficacy when it was most needed. This caused a decline of confidence in the vaccine among half the US population. The government promised up to 160 million doses in time for the second wave of infection, but only 23 million were delivered. After a few more weeks, vaccine manufacturing had become far more efficient and plentiful, but by then the second wave had passed and the public lost interest. In general, Americans were an impatient breed who demanded the swine flu to be conquered instantly and without inconvenience; it was a terribly unrealistic expectation.

The H1-N1 pandemic lasted 19 months, during which time 60 million Americans were infected; global estimates ranged from 700 million to 1.4 billion infections, at least 200 million more than what occurred during the Spanish Flu. There were no mask mandates implemented in the US during the surge of H1-N1, and studies at the

Anniversary

time showed the public would not wear masks consistently or correctly.

Researchers determined H1-N1 most likely originated in a small region of central Mexico. Nationally syndicated radio talk show hosts and propagandists described Mexican immigrants as virus carriers who were spreading H1-N1 like venereal disease because of poor hygiene. Some conspiracists accused Obama of importing the virus with his open border policies, or that the virus was a bioterror weapon engineered by Islamists who intentionally infected Mexican immigrants, knowing they would cross the border into the US. American nationalists decried the "fajita flu" as a United Nations globalist scheme to launch a *"One World Government."* These same kinds of hyper-politicizations would arise again with COVID.

In April 2009, Trump, then a businessman and frequent critic of President Obama, appeared on *Fox News* to discuss how Obama was handling the H1-N1 pandemic. Trump's interview took place on the same day the first H1-N1 death was reported in the US. Trump said, "It's going to be handled. It's going to come. It's going to be bad. And maybe it will be worse than the normal flu seasons. And it's going to go away. I think it is being handled fine. I think the words are right." However, during his reelection campaign 11 years later, Trump deflected from his own failures in his handling of the COVID pandemic by attacking his predecessors. Trump tweeted, *"Biden/Obama were a disaster in handling the H1N1 Swine Flu. Polling at the time showed disastrous approval numbers. 17,000 people died unnecessarily and through incompetence!"* But only 12,469 Americans died from H1-N1 under Obama's watch, compared to more than 400,000 who died of COVID by the final day of Trump's Presidency. During the same *Fox News* interview in April 2009, Trump said, "I think the vaccines can be very dangerous…a lot of people feel that the vaccines are what causes autism in children." According to the CDC, there was no evidence that vaccines caused autism; it was an urban myth created by the anti-vaccination brigade. Trump incited vaccine hesitancy with misinformation even before he was President.

On January 19, 2021, the day before he left office, Trump released a 20-minute prerecorded video of his farewell address from the White House. The leader of the free world had been out of sight for more than a week because of the fallout from the insurrection and the impending second impeachment trial. He did not mention Biden's name even once in the video, but extended wishes of good luck to the

The Climate of Truth

new administration. He condemned the insurrection, saying *"All Americans were horrified by the assault on our Capitol"* and that *"political violence can never be tolerated."* Trump declared his administration *"restored the American dream"* and built the *"greatest economy in the history of the world."* There was only one short line acknowledging Americans who lost their lives in the pandemic. About the vaccines, he said *"Another administration would have taken three, four, five, maybe even up to ten years to develop a vaccine. We did it in nine months."* Once again, the Obama administration distributed the H1-N1 swine flu vaccine in under six months.

But to me, the strangest part of Trump's farewell speech was: *"We fought for the principle that everyone has a right to equal dignity, equal treatment, and equal rights,"* and that *"Everyone is entitled to be treated with respect, to have their voice heard and to have their government listen."* All I could think about was how Trump ignored the voices of millions who protested against systemic racism, how disenfranchised minorities were needlessly dying of COVID faster and in greater numbers than Whites, and how Trump urged his supporters to inflict violence against his opponents.

The following day, January 20, Trump got his wish after all. An Air Force band played *"Hail to the Chief,"* followed by a 21-gun salute as he walked along the red carpet to Air Force One for the last time at Joint Base Andrews. About 500 people turned out in the icy wind to wave flags and bid him farewell. It was the smallest crowd ever to attend a Trump event. They stood in a fenced-off area in front of the stage. They were asked to bring five friends each to bolster attendance, but half of the section remained glaringly empty. Many of those invited (including ex-officials who resigned or were fired) did not attend, claiming to have other commitments like Biden's Inauguration.

Trump's final speech as President was full of false claims and boasts as usual. He said he instituted the "largest tax cut and reform in the history of our country by far," despite his tax cut being ranked below several others. He boasted a "record setting" number of judges appointed to the federal bench as "almost 300" when the true number was 229, well below Presidents Obama (320), Clinton (322) and George W. Bush (322). He noted that he received 75 million votes in the 2020 election, a record for sitting Presidents. Yet Biden received 81 million votes, more than any other candidate in US history. Toward the very end of a long and rambling speech, Trump said, "The first

Anniversary

thing we have to do is pay our respects and our love to the incredible people and families who suffered so gravely from the China virus. It's a horrible thing that was put onto the world. We all know where it came from, but it's a horrible, horrible thing." The following day, headlines read: *"He's gone!"* But he wasn't. Trump's influence lingered as he continued to control the Republican party from his private golf resorts.

    At a time when 75% of Americans were the most pessimistic they'd been in decades about the direction of the country, Biden announced the four priorities of his incoming administration. He described multiple crises the country was facing as the "convergence of four storms," and that any one of the four could cripple a nation, let alone all four at once: the COVID pandemic, systemic racism, climate change, and an economy in tatters. Biden declared that all other priorities could not be addressed until COVID was under control. Biden's first official act was to hold a sunset ceremony at the Lincoln Memorial; 400 lanterns (representing the 400,000 Americans who had died to that point in the pandemic) were illuminated in the giant reflecting pool on the National Mall. Biden announced, "Between sundown and dusk, let us shine the lights into the darkness…and remember all who we lost." One month later, the death toll surpassed 500,000, and Biden commemorated the loss with 500 glass candles set upon the steps to the White House residence. The doors were festooned with the black fabric of mourning. More Americans died in the first year of the pandemic than in World War I, World War II, and the Vietnam War combined. When he first took office, Biden warned the US death toll would exceed 600,000; when that happened in mid-June 2021, there wasn't another ceremony to commemorate the loss. Biden attended a summit at that time where he warned President Putin not to continue Russian attacks against American Democracy. Days later, Putin answered Biden's warning by holding war games 35 miles off the coast of Hawaii where he sank a Russian aircraft carrier with bombings from his fighter jets and submarines. When the US death toll surpassed 700,000 and then 800,000 following the Delta and Omicron surges, there were no national ceremonies to commemorate the lives lost.

❖

The Climate of Truth

"The pundits are saying that Biden's Inauguration was incredibly boring," Bernice said with a chuckle.

"I'd rather have boring any day of the week over the hell we went through for the past four years," I replied.

"I don't think the Inauguration was boring at all," Bernice said. "I think it was appropriately solemn. It was traditional and respectful. It was wholesome. And it was sincere. You could feel it. It wasn't about flash and pizzazz and Biden saying, 'Look at me and how wonderful I am!' Isn't it a relief to see something 'normal' for a change!"

Bernice had broomstraw for hair. When I met her, it was bleached blonde on top with a chocolate brown wedge underneath that looked like shoe polish around her ears. She was unhappy with her hair, and it made her feel self-conscious. I highlighted the chocolate shadow away and changed the color base to a mellow, light ash brown. I redirected the cut so she could just use her fingers to push the style into place with the help of a little molding paste and argan oil. She was ecstatic when the finished look took years off her face.

Bernice was perpetually gregarious, and it always seemed like a party when she was around. Immediately upon meeting her, she told me that both she and her husband were alcoholic drug abusers, and they'd both been clean and sober for 17 years with the help of *Alcoholics Anonymous*. They'd recently moved up from California and were busy settling into their new home. She said she didn't know whose idea it was to get a pet, but their new puppy enjoyed shredding whole rolls of toilet paper at a time when it was a precious and scarce pandemic commodity.

"The prosecutors finally have Trump's tax returns," I said while painting the base color formula on Bernice's gray roots. "A lot of people think he's going to jail."

"I don't see it that way," Bernice said. "I just want there to be peace."

"How can there be peace when he's harmed so many lives?" I said.

"Shhhh…I'm still breathing in the calm of the moment," Bernice whispered. "Ahhhhhhhh. The pit of my stomach is relaxed, and I don't feel like I'm being gutted by a hunting knife. It's a very good thing when they say Biden's boring."

Anniversary

"May boring be the new normal," I said.

"No, no! Boring is the new thrill!" she said, sighing with delight. "Breathe in the calm of the moment...*'You reap what you sow.'*"

"Everyone has to make a choice," I said, reaching for another brushful of hair color to paint on her ultra-thick crop of bristles. "That's what COVID teaches us. The choice between compassion and selfishness...COVID forces you to declare which path you will take at this point in human evolution. You have to commit. One side or the other. Compassion or selfishness. Fence sitters are no longer allowed. It's the ultimate test of duality...We are going to see some very strange things go down, and in my opinion, kindness is the only answer. It's pretty clear that selfishness gave us the most COVID and the most death than anywhere else on the planet. So yeah, *'you reap what you sow.'* But it didn't have to be that way. People selfishly chose to suffer."

Bernice looked at me intently in the mirror before us. "Do people describe you as an honest person?"

"That's a very unusual question...Why do you ask?"

"I enjoy coming here because I find you to be very honest and straightforward," Bernice said. "Because you say it like it is without all the hoo-hah. That's a comfort to me...It's much more than just a color job and a haircut in here. I just wondered if other people feel the same way about you that I do."

"Well, I don't know. I just try to do my best."

"I respect what you are doing here in your little shop, and I think of you as a friend," Bernice said.

"I think the same of you," I said, feeling a little awkward with the compliment.

"Your adorable little Irma is everyone's friend too," she said.

Irma cocked her head sideways at the mention of her name and gave a little yip.

"That's right Irma! You say it like it is, just like your Daddy," Bernice said, clapping her hands. "Like my mother always said, 'you must stand porter at the door of thought.'"

"What do you mean?" I asked.

The Climate of Truth

"The train's in the station, and the porter reaches down to the platform to load the luggage into the vestibule. The luggage represents our thoughts. Luggage can be well-crafted and sturdy to last a lifetime, or it can be lumpy and haggard and fall apart at the seams, causing me to lose my belongings. I make the choice about which luggage the porter will load into my train of thought. It's all up to me, and no one can ever take that away from me."

"Cool analogy," I said.

"My mother had it going on upstairs," Bernice said. "I can only hope to live up to her magnificent example…I enjoyed the heck out of her. She helped me get through some pretty tough periods in my life. Like when I was so drunk, I was unconscious and woke up in a hospital. I nearly died from alcohol poisoning."

I worked silently for a few moments.

"This woman called for an appointment today," I said. " I don't know her, have never seen her before. Right over the phone, she said she got in a fight and someone took a knife to her hair and cut off a huge chunk right in the front. The way she described it, she was scalped. So she said she was in desperate need of a haircut and a perm, as if that was going to magically solve all her problems. They beat her up so she's missing a few teeth and has a black eye too. And a bloody scalp. You can't have a perm with a bloody scalp. All this violence is ridiculous. She never mentioned if the police caught whoever it was that did that to her."

"Stand porter at the door of thought," Bernice said.

"Right. Why would I reach for that ratty piece of baggage?"

"By Jove, I think you've got it!" Bernice said, whimsically.

"I try to help people whenever I can, but I don't think I could be of help in a situation that involved a bloody scalp. I prefer to think about making the world a better place, one hairdo at a time!...That's what I call living the beauteous maximus."

"All hail to the beauteous maximus!" Bernice shouted back. "Hey, I really do enjoy looking impressive! Thank you for that!"

"I should tell you about the *FedEx* man," I said. "He showed up at the front door without a mask. Everybody knows they're required to wear masks, but this one *FedEx* guy, he's a rebel. He's been coming to the door without a mask for weeks, and I never said anything. But

Anniversary

it finally got to me. So, I told him to put his freakin' mask on before he walked into my shop with a package, and he griped and cursed all the way back to his truck, shaking his head, waving his fist. What's the big deal with doing your part to protect other people?"

"Stand porter at the door of thought," Bernice said.

"It's harder than it sounds. A lot of people can't control their thoughts. They get combative and hysterical."

"When you get it, you can be impressive like me!" she said.

"Oh, so you've reached enlightenment already?" I said. "Do beams of light shoot out of your eyeballs?"

"Only when I lift my skirt!"

"Bernice!" The burst of my own hot air inside my mask made me cough in fits.

"Don't worry! I only do that for my husband," she said while fluttering her eyelashes.

I collected myself. "But I have to say, the *FedEx* man wears his mask all the time now when he comes to my door. He doesn't even fuss about it. So, I guess I got through to the young man…Even small ripples in a pond can make a change."

"Speaking of ripples, I saw this thing on the internet," Bernice said. "So many people are ordering stuff online, and then it gets stolen from their front porch when it's delivered. It's insane."

"Porch pirates! What a menace!"

"Happens every COVID day," Bernice continued. "But this one guy got sick of it, and he got even. He's some kind of engineer -- like for *NASA* or something. Anyway, he devised this contraption. He made it look like an authentic *I-phone* parcel. Porch pirates can't wait to kype an *I-phone*! So, one of the pirates steals this *NASA* guy's fake package. And the pirate takes the package to his car. And when he opens it up, it automatically explodes with a huge mess of glitter all over the inside of his car. A whole bucket of glitter that can never be completely vacuumed up, so the inside of his car will sparkle forever! And the porch pirate curses up a blue streak. It's hilarious. But that's not all. The gadget has an added attraction. When the glitter bomb goes off, so does a juicy fart bomb, and the smell is so horrendous that the thief tosses the package out the window and drives off gagging

The Climate of Truth

and holding his nose! And we know this because the gadget is equipped with a series of cameras that can record from every angle and upload everything to the internet. And then the porch pirate gets arrested because the cops can identify him from the video. Then the *NASA* guy can track the package with his GPS and do it all over again to the next porch pirate. Isn't that awesome!"

"Maybe somebody could send Trump a glitter-fart-bomb," I said. "I know! Stand porter at the door of thought! How did that nasty piece of luggage get into my mind? I shouldn't wish for bad things to happen to people…But…"

"You're catching on," Bernice said. "Besides, I doubt Trump opens his own mail."

"You're right," I said. "I shouldn't waste precious time thinking of revenge. I should be thinking about fun things, like this guy in San Antonio who said: '*My body has absorbed so much hand sanitizer during the pandemic that when I pee, it cleans the toilet!*' Hah!"

"Good one! Oh! And how about when you get to rip your mask off at the end of a very long day, it feels as good as when you rip of your bra!"

"I wouldn't know," I said.

"OK…It feels as good as when you rip off your jockstrap!"

"Does this body look like it exercises?" I said. "I don't even own a jockstrap. In fact, I don't think I've ever worn a jockstrap in my entire life."

"Not even for kink?"

"Moving on Bernice. Ew."

"Without kink, I got nothing," she said, wide eyed.

"Probably for the best," I said. "Hey, I heard Trump wanted to fly over the Capitol while Biden was being inaugurated. But it didn't happen. You know why?"

"Why?"

"Because he turned into a pumpkin at noon, pun intended."

"Huh?" Bernice said, looking confused.

"Air Force One had to land in Florida, and the motorcade had to drive Trump to *Mar-a-Lago* before all the Presidential toys

Anniversary

disappeared at high noon on his last day of office. So, he couldn't still be up in the air over Washington DC when he had to be in Florida by high noon. You know, the golden chariot turned into a pumpkin, not at midnight like *'Cinderella,'* but at high noon. Orange pumpkin. Orange Trump. Have I spelled it out enough for you?"

"I get it now. Thank you," she said.

"My pleasure…Trump left Biden a letter. On the 'resolute desk.' I wonder what it said?"

"It's a big secret," Bernice said with a snicker. "Biden won't spill the beans."

"I got it! Trump wrote, *'Dear Joe, you know I won!'*" I said, cackling.

"I love how you laugh at your own jokes!" Bernice said.

"Can't take the credit for that one. It's a meme."

"All the good ones are memes these days," she said. "It's not fair."

"Trump swore he wouldn't watch the Inauguration. But he saw it on the plane ride down to Florida. Couldn't help himself…I cried when I watched the ceremony," I said.

"You did?" Bernice asked.

"I was touched. I was relieved."

"Me too," she said.

"It wasn't exhausting for a change. There was decorum."

"And love," she said.

"You could really feel it."

"And no one shot Biden, thank goodness," Bernice said.

"My friend Tiffy kept sending me reports every five minutes when Biden walked from the Capitol to the White House. She texted me, 'He's still alive! He's still alive!' Everybody was worried about White supremacist snipers," I said.

"It's sad that poor Joe didn't get the inaugural ball, or a parade. He's been cheated by COVID as well as by mean and nasty people. As the saying goes from the *Grateful Dead*, "Mean People Suck."

The Climate of Truth

"True that," I said.

"I had that *Grateful Dead* bumper sticker on my *Lincoln Continental* way back in the 70's because I was a real-life hippie! Abraham Lincoln would have had the same bumper sticker, I'm sure. He would have been a "*Dead Head*…I loved singing along with '*J-Lo*' during the Inauguration." Bernice sang while tapping her foot and swaying her head, "'*This land is your land, this land is my land*'…How can 'J-Lo' make cheesy sound so wonderful?"

"Did you see Lady-Gaga's platinum blonde hair braided together with black hair extensions, black woven together with the white?" I said. "And the two red roses on the back of her head? Wasn't that a cool nod to George Floyd and '*Black Lives Matter?*'"

"And that huge gold dove thing on the front of her – was that a sculpture?" Bernice asked.

"I think it was hammered metal, covered in gold. A dove with an olive branch in its beak. An homage to world peace."

"It practically covered her whole chest. Must have been eight inches across," Bernice said. "That would be dove-e-ous maximus!"

"Good one!"

"Her '*Star Spangled Banner*' gave me the goosies," Bernice said.

"And Amanda Gorman's poem! '*The Hill We Climb.*'"

"Fabulous! With that red leather circlet in her hair and that powerful yellow jacket. What a gorgeous and talented young woman!"

"Can you believe she's only 22?" I said.

"'*Love becomes our legacy.*' Now that's a line to load into our train of thought forever! That beautiful young woman is just so incredible. Jill Biden discovered her; you know. The First Lady who is also the First Lady Doctor, the first National Youth Poet Laureate who also happens to be Black, the first Madame Vice President who is also the first Vice President of color. What a day for firsts!"

"There was this part in Amanda Gorman's poem," I said:

> "*Scripture tells us to envision*
> *that everyone shall sit under their own vine and fig tree*

Anniversary

And no one shall make them afraid"

"I swear," I said, "from now on, every time I eat a fig from the tree on my patio, my own little *Garden of Eden*, I will remember not to be afraid because Amanda Gorman said so!"

"What about *Fig Newtons*?" Bernice said excitedly.

"Especially *Fig Newtons,* and fig jam with Montrachet on crackers, and fig vinaigrette!"

"Just say everything fig, because it's all so good!" she said.

"Biden's ceremony was so peaceful," I said. "Remember Trump's inaugural speech -- how he used the phrase 'American carnage?'…What a difference a speech makes."

"Amanda Gorman said to be the light and climb the hill!" Bernice announced in a dramatic voice. "It's liberating, like ripping off your bra, baby!"

Finished with Bernice's color application, I wiped the pigment from her forehead with a wad of cotton. We both fell silent as our attention was drawn to the song playing on the stereo. The melody was instantly recognizable, but it was a revamped cover of a soaring *Rodgers & Hammerstein* Broadway show tune. Instead of being sung by the customary White woman in a nun's habit, it was performed by a young Black man sporting an afro in 2003. His name was Guy Sebastian, the season's winner of the televised singing competition, "*American Idol.*"

"Climb every mountain
Ford Every stream"
Follow every rainbow
'Till you find your dream"

"What strange timing with this song!" Bernice said. "We were just talking about climbing the hill!"

"I know. It happens all the time in here. The music Gods at *Pandora* are always listening. I've never heard this rendition from *"The Sound of Music"* before, but I really like it…It must be true that art imitates life, and life imitates art," I said.

I just got the goosies again!" Bernice said.

The Climate of Truth

"Me too," I replied. "You should know that I performed this very song in a professional production."

"You!" Bernice said, aghast.

"I made a very lovely Mother Superior!" I said, taking a bow.

"You've gotta be kidding me!" she howled.

"The Mule Barn Theatre in Tarkio, Missouri. It was a summerstock smash. I was fresh out of college and had one heck of a voice."

"I would pay to see that! Are there photos?" she asked with a chuckle.

"The evidence has all been burned," I said.

Together, we listened to Guy Sebastian and his orchestra for a few moments.

"It's all about breaking the mold, isn't it?" I said.

"It most certainly is!"

"Biden broke the mold too," I said. "He walked straight to the Oval Office after the Inauguration and got right to work to fight COVID...It's the one-year anniversary since COVID came to America."

Bernice sighed and cooed inside her mask. "Can you believe we've lived like this for a whole year already?"

"It's hard to fathom. And it doesn't look like COVID's going to be done with us any time soon," I said.

Bernice suddenly stood up and waved her hands in the air as if she were conducting an orchestra. She began to sing a different tune that mercilessly clashed with Guy Sebastian's buttery chord progressions. Her ditty sounded like a weird, discordant version of *"The Twelve Days of Christmas:"*

> *"On his first day in office*
> *President Biden said to me*
> *That Democracy didn't die*
> *And neither will we!"*

About the Author

D. Michael Bertish is an accomplished fine artist and a professional performance artist. A professional production of his play about survivors of the Holocaust, **Adroit Maneuvers**, touched audiences in 2018.

He lives in Washington State where he advocates for environmental protections and civil rights. He adores history, animals, and gardening.

CPSIA information can be obtained
at www.ICGtesting.com
Printed in the USA
BVHW040946070322
630815BV00011B/376